THE
Runaway
BRIDES
COLLECTION

7 Historical Brides Get Cold Feet at the Altar

THE
Runaway
BRIDES
COLLECTION

Vickie McDonough,
Rita Gerlach, Terri J. Haynes, Noelle Marchand,
Darlene Panzera, Jenness Walker, Renee Yancy

BARBOUR BOOKS
An Imprint of Barbour Publishing, Inc.

From This Day Forward ©2018 by Rita Gerlach
Legacy of Love ©2018 by Terri J. Haynes
The Elusive Heiress ©2018 by Noelle Marchand
A Day Late and a Dollar Short ©2018 by Vickie McDonough
The Groom She Thought She'd Left Behind ©2018 by Darlene Panzera
The Flyaway Bride ©2018 by Jenness Walker
The Irish Bride ©2018 by Renee Yancy

Print ISBN 978-1-68322-817-2

eBook Editions:
Adobe Digital Edition (.epub) 978-1-68322-819-6
Kindle and MobiPocket Edition (.prc) 978-1-68322-818-9

Published by Barbour Books, an imprint of Barbour Publishing, Inc., 1810 Barbour Drive, Uhrichsville, Ohio 44683, www.barbourbooks.com

Our mission is to inspire the world with the life-changing message of the Bible.

 Member of the
Evangelical Christian
Publishers Association

Printed in Canada.

Contents

From This Day Forward

by Rita Gerlach

In all thy ways acknowledge him,
and he shall direct thy paths.
PROVERBS 3:6

Chapter 1

Barely had the war touched her—at least that is what Amy Fairbourne wished to believe. She had an armoire stuffed with cotton dresses and one lemon-yellow ball gown. Her petticoats, stockings, and corsets were in good repair, all neatly arranged in her dresser drawers. She had little to complain about, even though she hadn't bought a new dress in four years. Papa refused to spend his money on frills during wartime, and she humbly agreed with him. Handy with a needle and thread, Amy could make a garment appear practically new. Her sister, Franny, on the other hand, had no patience to mend a frayed hem or stitch up a tiny tear.

Sitting on a bluff high above the Potomac River, Amy listened to the roar of the water. Spring had come and gone. General Lee had surrendered at Appomattox. Summer sounds echoed through the trees. The cicadas had returned.

The water rushed around boulders, and the cliffs were as high as the roofs of houses. The currents whirled, foamed, and plunged into deep pools. Across the river the budding woodlands of Virginia engaged her gaze. She recalled before the time of trouble how the family traveled downriver to placid waters and crossed on a ferry to the other side to visit people she no longer remembered.

She placed the tip of a pencil between her teeth and imagined a trip into George-town, where brick row houses lined cobblestone streets. Shops with broad windows displayed the latest fashions and housewares. Black fences of spiked wrought iron bordered yards.

Their horses had been confiscated during the war, leaving the family a gray donkey the Union men deemed useless. Ole Tim could pull a trap and carry them along the road that led into town or to church on Sundays. Amy wondered if things had changed much from the years of conflict and hardship. The trees were still tall and abundant—old trees that had been there a hundred years or more. She gazed up at the sky, the never-ending, eternal sky that no cannon or swing of a saber could change.

She opened her notebook and jotted down a list of items she and her sister desperately needed—along with what she could only dream of until her father improved his situation. They were not destitute, he told her. Just short on cash. But when she discovered he had pawned her mother's ivory brooch and gold wedding band, she knew that was a sign the cash had run out.

She turned at the sounds behind her. General, the family's bluetick hound, bounded toward her. Amy closed her notebook, stood, and grabbed hold of the dog and rubbed his black floppy ears. Franny stopped a yard away, breathing hard.

"What are you doing out here alone, Amy?" Franny held out her arms for balance and lightly stepped over the craggy bluff. "You should've brought General with you."

Amy smiled and raised the dog's head. "He's too friendly to be much of a protector."

"That may be, but he can sniff out copperheads." The linen slippers Franny wore, faded pink with ragged ribbons, were dusty. Amy reopened her book and jotted down that her sister needed a new pair of shoes.

"There are no copperheads here, Franny. Just harmless black snakes."

"Ew! They're mean and they bite." Franny looked fearfully at the piles of rocks and old branches.

"Do be careful, Sister," Amy said. "You're not as agile as I am."

"You do everything better. I wish you'd come away from the edge. It's dangerous."

To please her sister, Amy headed back to the grassy plain. She took Franny's hand, and they walked together to the towpath, across the bridge spanning the canal lock, and to the road. General chased a squirrel up a tree but gave up when Amy called him.

Wagon wheel grooves marred the surface of the narrow path. Cottonwood seeds lay dormant within the path, which had been hardened over cold winters and scorching summers. Summer brought warmth and beauty to the woods and fields again. Birds flitted and sang in the trees, and deer came through the forest to the water's edge to drink.

"Why do you come here?" Franny asked.

Amy's brows tensed. Why couldn't her sister see the beauty of God's creation? Why couldn't birdsongs be music to Franny's ears like they were to hers?

"Don't you know?"

Franny shrugged. "To waste time? To get away from Papa?"

"No, but if you stop and listen, if you look carefully, you'll understand."

Franny did as Amy suggested. But no enlightened expression rose in her face. Amy turned Franny toward the woods. A pair of doves cooed, invisible, somewhere in a tree. "Listen."

"Doves? So?"

"Look around you."

"I see trees. What's so special about them?"

"Do you hear soldiers marching, wagons and horses?"

"No, and there's no reason why I should."

"Didn't it make you sad whenever they came through?"

"Not sad. . .just scared."

"Me too. Now I sit by the falls and leave all that behind."

"I'm glad you can forget so easily, Amy."

"I won't forget. It's what keeps me thankful for this place."

Franny rolled her eyes. "Can't you do the same at home?"

Amy tugged on her sister's arm. "Ever hear the words 'It is easier to find God in a garden than anywhere on earth'?"

Franny stepped away and, swinging her skirts, headed toward home. She looked back over her shoulder. "Dear me, Amy. Mama always said you would grow up to be a poet."

"I lay no claim to the verse," said Amy.

"Still, you have a melancholy heart. That's usually a sign of a poet."

On they walked under shady elms. Franny plucked a dandelion and handed it to Amy. "Wildflowers make me think of weddings. You should get married before I do."

Amy ran her finger through the petals. "Don't wait on me. It may never happen."

"Pishposh. You're very pretty."

"Plain, you mean."

"I imagine with the gentlemen returning we'll have balls to attend. You're sure to have lots of beaus swarming around you like you did before the war."

Amy shook her head. "You're dreaming. I had no beaus."

Franny looped her arm through Amy's. "You know that isn't true. You had one admirer, as I recall. Whatever happened to him?"

"We lost touch. Besides, we didn't know each other but a few weeks, and then the war started. I imagine he went off to fight like the rest of the boys."

"Someday you'll have another. Maybe sooner than you think."

Amy smiled lightly, a smile that expressed regret. "You'll be the one to have beaus. You'll have your choice of any gentleman in the county."

Franny's eyes gleamed. Amy knew the look. Franny had a tendency to ignore most of what her older sister said, her mind filling with a distraction that interested her. "Oh I hope so." Franny sighed. "I refuse to be an old maid."

"You're decades away from being an old maid, and never will be one. As for me, I'm not sure I want to marry—not for a while anyway."

"That's foolish. Every girl should want to get married. We both need to in order to help Papa. He said so."

Amy tucked the dandelion through a ribbon on her bodice. "I know he hopes to have us set up, but when did he say that?"

"Before I left the house, Mr. Montague came to see Papa. He came in a brand-new carriage. And you should see his new horse, a stallion, I believe. I saw it the other day. It'll take your breath away."

"A new carriage. Hmm, he must have done all right during the war."

"Apparently so. The horses were new too, I believe, and decorated so prettily."

"What did he want?"

"I don't know. You know Papa. He talks privately with menfolk." Franny let out another long sigh. "Mr. Montague greeted me with that kind of southern grace that makes a girl blush, and he kissed my hand before he went in. I think he likes me. He has no wife, you know."

"Mr. Chester Montague. . ." Amy mocked their acquaintance's name, speaking as if he were royalty. In some ways, Montague held that degree of respect from Marylanders and Virginians alike. His wealth secured the good opinion of others. But how he had gained so much more during the war than his neighbors had yet to be revealed. It seemed no one cared. Money and a vast estate mattered to most people regardless of how it was earned.

Amy picked up a stick and tossed it. General bounded ahead with a howl, retrieved the stick, and pranced proudly back to her. She pulled it from him and threw it again. His tail swatted the air. Panting, his tongue hung from the side of his mouth. He retrieved the stick again and settled on his haunches to chew the end of it.

Franny strolled on. "Why do you mock Mr. Montague, Amy? He certainly has made a name for himself. Maybe he will choose me."

Stunned, Amy stopped. "You'd accept a proposal from the likes of him?"

"Sure, why not?"

"You don't love him."

"I could learn to love him. I do admit, Amy, I admire Mr. Montague for how he managed to hold on to his horses. Everyone we know lost theirs."

"Money and property aren't everything," Amy said.

Franny frowned. "You think being poor is better?"

"No need to get all riled up, Franny. You know being poor is the last thing I want for either of us. Just remember, if you do marry Mr. Montague, be generous to those who are poor, share your food with them, and be—"

"Stop preaching at me. I won't mind sharing a bit of bread or leftover pork parts, but don't ask me to share money with them. They're mostly lazy folks and should work for their food."

"If you do marry Montague, and I come across anyone that needs work, I'll be sure to send them to you, Franny, at Oak Hill."

"Oh, but you frustrate me, Amy. I can't tell if you're teasing or being serious."

"Serious, Sister."

Franny huffed. "Always with you it is being serious."

"You should be sometimes too."

"I am serious about marrying a well-to-do landowner. Papa's worries will be over."

"Money is tight, but Papa is little in debt."

"So he told us, but I'm afraid Papa's situation may be worse than we suspect."

"If what you say is true, he would have told us." Amy shook the dust off the hem of her dress.

"Not if he wanted to protect us."

"I don't need protection from the truth, nor do I wish to be used as a means of solving his money problems, which I doubt he has."

Franny sulked. "If he is in trouble, don't you want him to help him?"

"Of course I do."

"Then we should keep our eyes open for the best prospects. First on my list would be Chester."

" 'Chester' is it?" said Amy. "What about our third cousin, Landon? He's had a fondness for you since we were children."

"That's just the point. There would be no romance in him, since we've known each other so long."

"Landon is one of the kindest men I've ever known. If you let him, he'd romance you to his dying day."

"He's not as rich as Chester."

"That shouldn't matter. What's wrong with you, Franny? You know you shouldn't hope Mr. Montague starts courting you. Don't even consider him."

Franny looked at Amy, bewildered. "Why not?"

"He's too old for you, for a start."

"Papa was older than Mama, and they knew each other only a few months before they eloped. It must have been so romantic."

"That was different."

"How was it different?"

"They loved each other." Amy groaned. There was no convincing Franny to be patient—the virtue she lacked most. "You are not in love, are you?"

"No, at least not at the moment."

Amy pursed her lips. "Then be patient."

"Patient for what, Amy? This thing called *love* that you read about in novels?"

"If I had a beau who loved me," Amy said, "and I loved him, and we wanted to spend the rest of our lives together, then I'd be happy to marry. In the meantime, I'll be patient. I'll wait for the right man."

"Oh, dear Amy." Franny placed her arm through Amy's and sighed. "You *are* an old soul."

Chapter 2

Amy leaned against the wall beside the drawing room door, close enough for her to hear a bit of the conversation. She winced and placed her hand over her nose. Her father's cigar smoke crept out into the hallway and smelled like burnt coffee. When her mother was alive, smoking was not allowed in the house, not even if the visitors were high-ranking Marylanders who craved their homegrown tobacco. The smoke attached itself to everything, she said, from the drapes and wallpaper, rugs and furniture, to the hand-blown glass in the windows. Clothes would reek of it, and no gentle pecks on the cheek were permitted. Smoking was a grave affront to her mother's faith, and Amy grew up believing as she did.

The day of her mother's funeral, her father went into his study without speaking a word to anyone, not even his grieving daughters. He shut the door and turned the key. A moment later, a gray haze seeped out from beneath the door. She heard the red leather swivel chair behind his desk screech as he sat down. Silence followed that lasted until midnight when the old clock in the hallway chimed the hour.

Footsteps approached. Arrested from her memories, Amy drew back. Franny had put on her best dress and now hurried toward her, pinching her cheeks to bring out the color. She waited beside Amy. Then their father stepped out, followed by Chester Montague dressed in a black overcoat with wide lapels, a buff waistcoat, and striped trousers. When his eyes met Amy's, he lifted his brow. She hadn't seen him for the entire duration of the war, but judging by his clothes, he had not been made poor by it. The shoes he wore looked new, polished to a high sheen. A black necktie tied in a bow around a winged collar of white silk was no doubt the latest fashion. A diamond stickpin glinted through it. He bowed. "Miss Amy. Miss Franny."

Amy curtsied along with her sister. "Mr. Montague. What brings you all this way? It's a long carriage ride, isn't it?"

"Not at all, Miss Amy. It's well worth the journey just to see you—and your sister."

Amy glanced at Franny. A deep blush covered her cheeks. "You mean to flatter us, sir?"

He stepped up to her, lifted her hand, and kissed the top of it. His lips were moist against her skin. "Only in the sincerest way, Miss Amy."

"It's been ages since we last saw you."

"Indeed. I recall that it was at the spring ball before all the wretched fighting started. You were the prettiest girls in the room."

Franny let out a giggle. Amy grabbed her hand to quiet her. "Are you here for pleasure, Mr. Montague, or business?"

Her father cleared his throat. "Amy."

Montague turned to him. "It is all right, sir. Your daughter has an inquisitive mind—something I admire even in a woman." He looked back at Amy. "Your father tells me you finished your studies in French and Latin last year, Miss Amy. Quite an accomplishment for a young lady in wartime."

She smiled in order to be polite. "I had not much else to do, sir." Except keep her eyes out for raiders with a loaded pistol in her waistband. She knew how to shoot, but the fear of shooting a rebel or a wayward Union soldier rattled her to the core.

"With better days ahead, you and your sister will have many parties to attend."

Franny stepped forward. "Perhaps you could host one, Mr. Montague. I'm just dying for a dance."

Montague inclined his head. "I think that is a marvelous idea, Miss Franny."

"Then you will consider it?"

"For you, yes, at Christmastime perhaps." He took up his hat. "I bid you all a good day."

Montague sauntered out the front door. Amy looked at her father. She realized he disapproved of how openly she had conversed with a male visitor. She should have been shy, reserved, and kept her eyes down, only to lift them when spoken to.

"What's for supper?" To her surprise, her cousin Landon Fairbourne stepped through the front door. "I'm starved."

"Landon, what are you doing here?" Her father looked delighted and vigorously shook her cousin's hand.

"I thought it high time I pay you a visit, Uncle James."

"It has been a while, Landon."

Amy looked down at his boots and frowned. "There's a scrape outside the door, Landon. Mae will have your hide if you don't clean your boots."

He smirked. "The roads were rough on the way over. That gelding of mine stepped in a mud puddle. Splashed mud up to the stirrups."

Amy held up her hem and stepped over to the door. Montague's carriage rumbled down the lane and out of sight. She pointed to the boot scrape. A lock of

Landon's thick brown hair fell over his forehead, and he shoved it back. He tossed his riding crop down on the hall table, stepped out onto the porch, and cleared the muck off his boots. Amy looked out on the lawn to see the brown gelding munching on a patch of summer grass. He appeared well fed and his coat glossy.

"Poor beast."

"You're wrong, Cousin. Horses don't mind getting muddy. Keeps flies away."

"You didn't have him before you left. Where did you find him?" Amy asked.

"At an auction. That one is war hardened. Nothing frightens him, not even the blast of a cannon. . .so I was told."

Landon walked back into the foyer with Amy lagging behind him.

"Did you speak to Mr. Montague on his way out?" her father asked.

"A wave is all. He's looking rather prosperous."

"So he made it perfectly clear to me. He's fortunate."

"I'd prefer not to discuss him at the moment, Uncle. I don't want my stomach to grow sour."

"You don't like the man?"

"It's not that, sir. I just don't want to be reminded of my meager situation."

Amy pulled away from the staircase. "Papa, you never did say what Mr. Montague wanted."

Franny rose up on her toes, looking amused. "I think I know."

Amy spoke to her father softly, knowing how easily irritated he could become. He snapped his fingers at General, and the dog stood. "You must mind your own business, Amy. Now, I'm hungry and so is Landon. Aren't you, boy?"

"Famished, sir." Landon inclined his head.

"Do as you're told, Amy, and find out if Mae has supper ready. Tell her your cousin is here and we will need an extra seat at the table." Her father walked toward his study and waved Franny over. "Franny, come into the drawing room."

"Are you going to scold me too, Papa?"

"For what? You've done nothing wrong. You never do, Franny."

Amy wished she'd been given a name like her sister's. That way her papa would have called her by a nickname too. Franny was short for Francis. Nothing could be done with the name Amy. It seemed so uninspiring, so unromantic and ordinary.

"You want me to read to you, Papa?" Franny asked.

"The newspaper, Franny. You have the best voice for reading aloud."

"Papa?" Amy called to him, and he turned. "Can I join you all after I speak to Mae?"

"Later. I need to speak privately with you on a delicate matter."

Privately on a delicate matter? What could it be, other than marriage? Had he given permission to Montague to wed her. . .or her sister? Amy's stomach wrenched at the thought.

Landon gave Amy a shrug. "Don't be disappointed, Amy."

"I'm not. It's the way things are with Papa."

"He's always favored Franny." He leaned toward her. "I have too, but you are like a sister to me. I'll always be your friend."

She smiled. "You're a good man, Landon. I hope Franny sees that too."

"Oh, don't worry on that score. I'll win her eventually." He turned toward the door. "I have to go stable my horse."

"Come into the kitchen when you're done. I think Papa and Franny will be in the study the most of an hour."

She set her notebook on the hall table and looked at it. The list inside would be the topic of Franny's conversation—for a while. She heard her father plod across the hardwood floor. Franny rattled off something about the new dresses she needed. With a lift of her skirts, Amy slipped through the door and down the hall to the kitchen.

In the large room with an arched fireplace, Amy placed her hands on the table and took in scents of Mae's cooking. It seemed as if the years of bread and pies, savories and soups had forever lingered. Along the wall above a sideboard were bright copper pots. A teakettle hissed on an iron spit over glowing red coals.

Mae circled a wooden spoon through the contents of a cast-iron Dutch oven. "You want something, Miss Amy?"

"Papa asked about supper. Says he's hungry."

"Impatience won't help being hungry, Miss Amy."

"Landon is here. We will need an extra place at the table."

Mae turned with a proud smile. "I've got a pie. Just finished baking it."

"Apple? I smell cinnamon."

"You smell right, Miss Amy. As I recall, it's Mr. Landon's favorite. It's been a long time since he had some."

Amy put her arm around Mae's shoulders. "Your food is worth the wait, Mae."

"Ah, you're sweet, Miss Amy. I'll make sure he gets the biggest piece."

"You should give it to Papa," Amy said.

Mae laughed. "You're right, I should. He'd be sure to notice if I didn't."

"I don't know how you've managed to keep us all fed. There's been so little on the farms these past few years."

"If you got some root vegetables and flour, you can live through the worst of times, Miss Amy. Tell your papa I'll be setting out the stew shortly. Got no meat today, but it's got rich gravy."

Amy leaned over the pot. "It smells good. Can I help?"

Mae set her hands on her hips. "I don't need any help. Besides, it's not for you to be working in the kitchen. Your mama never did, and I'll be tossed in the river before I'll have one of her girls do any different."

Amy dipped her finger into the honeypot that sat on the worktable. "Mae?"

"Yes, miss?"

"Do you know why Mr. Montague was here?"

"Dear me, no. I let him in and that's all. I'm no eavesdropper."

"I know he owns a lot of land."

"Is that so?"

"And he's a widower."

"Hmm, more widows around these days than widowers."

"Franny told me Papa is in trouble and wants us to marry into money. You know anything about that?"

Mae narrowed her eyes. "Now you know he'd not tell me. He used to tell Cleveland everything before he was freed and left this place. But not me. It was your mama that did that."

Mae took out a handkerchief from her sleeve. She lifted it to her eye, and when Amy gave her a look of concern, she lowered it and blinked her watery brown eyes.

"This ain't for me. You got a smudge on your jaw." Mae dipped a corner of the handkerchief in water and proceeded to dab Amy's cheek. "That's what you get for all the trekking you do. Getting dirt on you, not to mention how you're ruining your hems."

"But I like trekking. A little dirt never hurt anyone."

"Is that so? Well, you tell that to gentlemen callers and see what they say."

Amy moved Mae's hand away gently. Mae was attentive, guiding, and apt to scold when a scolding was due. Amy loved her. She scooted up onto the table and placed her hands on her lap. "You'd tell me if Papa has plans for me, wouldn't you? I mean, you've got to if he has someone in mind and you know about it."

Mae picked up a knife and sliced corn bread into squares. "I can't think of anyone in these parts he'd consider, Miss Amy. Too many lawless men here about. Too many ungodly folk that don't care what the good Lord thinks."

"I'll not worry, Mae. Papa would never match me up with any of those sorts.

And believe you me, I'll have the final say about whom I spend the rest of my life with."

Mae paused. "Whatever happened to that nice young man you met at Mr. Lincoln's inauguration ball before the shooting started?"

Amy lost her smile. It had been a long time ago. Still, she had a lasting memory of the boy who had caused her heart to gallop. Over time, his young face had faded. She could remember his eyes though. He'd been well dressed and well mannered, and she never forgot how good a dance partner he'd been. Why, he swept her out onto the dance floor as if she were light as a feather, with a firm grip of her hand and a grasp at her waist that had no timidity in it.

"That was four years ago," she said.

Mae stood back. "Why, you were just a child."

"I was sixteen."

"And them beaus weren't much older. They probably all went off to fight. Could be none came back."

"It's sad to think of." Amy jumped down from the table. "Still, I suppose it doesn't matter. I wouldn't recognize any of them if they walked right up to me. They say the conflict changed men in bad ways, that it aged them."

Mae arranged the corn bread on a platter. "Well, don't worry. God will bring you a husband when He wills it, and a good one, one that will love and adore you. It's my prayer for you, child. And for Miss Franny too."

Chapter 3

Out in the yard, the Fairbournes' rooster crowed. Amy rose, put on a day dress, and headed downstairs. Mae would be in the kitchen brewing coffee and making buttermilk biscuits and eggs fried in bacon grease. Her stomach growled and she laid her hand across her belly. "Dear Lord, someday soon let Mae make us biscuits and gravy. We've not had sausage in ages. I know I should be thankful for whatever we have, but I could use some help on that score."

Franny and Landon had not yet risen. Her father, as was his habit, took coffee in his study. She poked her head around the door. "Papa, remember you wanted to talk to me privately?"

He looked up at her. "I'm not in the mood. Another time."

Perplexed, Amy left him and went into the dining room. The sun streamed through the windows and across the sideboard where Mae had set out breakfast in covered dishes. At the table alone, Amy moved the food around on her plate. Mae had stirred up her memory of that day in Washington. The city buzzed with celebrations. Red, white, and blue swags hung from windows and doorways. People picnicked on the White House lawn, and President Lincoln welcomed senators and dignitaries at the great door beyond the pillars of the people's house. All the while, Mrs. Lincoln hid her grief at the loss of her son Eddie and proudly celebrated her husband's election to the presidency.

Sixteen-year-old Amy never forgot the carriage ride past the White House. Her mother pointed out the upper room most likely to be the first lady's. Amy paid no mind to what Mary Lincoln suffered. All that mattered that day was the ball she was to attend at the Willard Hotel—the crown jewel of Pennsylvania Avenue. It was all too exciting.

At the ball, a pair of blue eyes caught hers as she stood beside her mother. They absorbed every part of her and caused her to look away. He approached. He held out his hand and took her out onto the dance floor. One dance and then another whisked her away.

I wonder what happened to him. Surely he fought for his state of Virginia. Did he live or die?

With breakfast over, Amy headed back upstairs. She sat on the side of the bed to lace up her leather boots. The springs squeaked and woke her sister.

"Up already, Amy?" Franny glanced at the window. "The sun isn't even up."

Amy smiled at her sister. "It's up. The sky is a glorious blue."

"What time is it?"

"Time for you to get out of bed."

Franny rubbed her sleepy eyes. "Where are you going?"

"Out for a walk, like I do every day."

"Every morning it's the same thing with you. I'm surprised you haven't worn out the soles of your shoes."

Amy leaned over her sister. "You should get up, Miss Lazy, and come with me."

Moaning, Franny flung the covers over her head. Amy picked up her shawl and pulled it over her shoulders. General looked at her as she tiptoed down the staircase.

"Good boy, General." He blinked and laid his head between his paws. "You want to stay in, don't you?" Again, he lifted his eyes to her, then rolled over on his back.

Amy opened the front door and welcomed the sun on her face. Hints of the earth warming drew her senses away from the still house. A blue haze spread over the land. Drawing in the balmy air, Amy's heart swelled. To be alone in such magnificence delighted her. No longer could the sounds of boots trudging over the road, the grind of wagon wheels, and the brays of weary horses be heard. At last a peaceful silence had returned to the land.

She regarded the hedgerows and the dew that dripped like raindrops from them. Wolf spiders had made overnight traps that held the dew like diamonds.

As she headed down the path, daylight brightened through the woods. A rustling movement caused the tree branches to crackle. Amy paused to listen. She watched as splashes of brown passed between the elms. A doe and two yearlings raised their heads and looked at her. Tawny tails twitched, and then the deer sprang away.

Near the lock bridge that crossed over the canal to the towpath, a keeper dozed on the porch of his house. Everyone seemed asleep—asleep to the glorious day.

She walked the towpath, picked up a stick, and swung it against the tall grass and blue chicory lining it. A noise came up behind her, and she glanced back. With a start, she stepped into the grass when she saw a great ox come lumbering around the bend. The beast's huge girth spanned half the road. Tall as her papa's open carriage, it cast a long shadow over the ground. The brass ring through its nose could have fitted around both her wrists together. Upon sight of her, the beast raised its head and snorted. She had never seen an ox this size before, and it frightened and fascinated her, so much so that she failed to see the man walking alongside it.

"Good morning." He tipped the brim of his hat, his eyes in shadow.

"Good morning," she replied, not looking at him. The ox moved slowly toward her.

"Don't be afraid. He's as gentle as a lamb."

"He looks terrifying. Keep him away." She stepped back. The man heeled the animal. Embarrassed to be out on her own without a male escort to protect her, Amy tightened the shawl over her shoulders. Her papa would greatly disapprove, insisting that ruffians and scalawags roamed. Unbeknownst to her father, she kept a lady's pistol hidden under her skirts, tucked safely in her ribboned garter.

"Bulldog didn't mean to scare you," the man said as he tightened the lead in his hand.

Amy looked at him. Finally, he caught her attention. My, oh my. Her eyes beheld the handsomest man she'd ever seen—since the war's end. His boots were set firm and his hand wrapped the lead about his arm to keep a hold on the beast. His clothes were clean, drab olive and brown. His hair touched the collar of his faded gray jacket, suspect of once being worn by a rebel. There were no signs of rank, no insignias for a battalion. Perhaps it was castoff, Amy thought.

"That's a strange name for an ox," she said, searching the man's face. He looked familiar, but many men from her past had sandy hair, blue eyes, and close-cut beards.

He ran his hand over Bulldog's snout. "He looks like one, doesn't he?"

"Yes, but much larger." She continued to watch as he pampered the beast. He stroked its head and spoke softly to it. "He is so calm," she said.

"Animals respond to kindness." The man smiled and patted Bulldog's neck. "Don't you ol' fellow?"

Amy liked his southern accent. Smooth yet robust, he spoke as an educated man and one accustomed to polite rules of conduct. Had he been a member of that old southern aristocracy? Surely not. His clothes were shabby, his hair longer than custom allowed.

Amy shifted her gaze to the docile beast. "May I ask why you are out on the towpath with your ox? Shouldn't he be in a field?"

The man patted the ox's neck. "I've fetched him from a farmer down the road. He'll be in the field soon." A silence fell between them as the man fixed his eyes on her. His brow furrowed.

"You look like a girl I once met before the war," he said.

"Oh, I doubt we have ever met." She realized, though he looked familiar, the streak of doubt in her came out of prejudice. He was, after all, a Confederate.

"Years change people," he said.

"Yes, and war does too. Every soldier I've met looks older than his years."

She walked on, swinging her stick beside her. The man pulled the ox's lead and followed her. "Looks like we're going in the same direction. Hope you don't mind if I walk alongside you."

"It's a public towpath."

"You live nearby?"

"Have you heard of Linden Grove?"

"Sounds old and British."

She regarded him, uncertain if he meant something by it. "My great-grandfather built the house." She stared at him a moment, for he gave no answer but kept his eyes fixed on hers. "I bet the next question you'll ask is which side my family was on."

"I hadn't planned to, but if you want to satisfy my curiosity, tell me."

"There's nothing much to tell except I sided with the Quakers." She spoke in a guarded tone and anticipated his reply.

"What about your brothers?"

"I had no brothers." She felt a lump form in her throat. Cousins she did have. There were six in all, two being a set of twins. They itched to get into uniform, believing the rebellion to be short lived. Yet it was their lives that were shortened, except for Landon's. The twins fell at Bull Run, the others at the Wilderness and Gettysburg.

"Were you in the fighting?" she diverted.

He kicked a stone. "I don't like to talk about it, especially to a lady."

Amy's mouth lifted into a slight smile. "Oh yes. I guess it would be considered improper if you did." *It was too horrible.* "I prefer to be spared the details."

He returned her smile. "Yet I can see in your eyes, you are curious."

"You read me wrong, sir."

"Pardon my mistake."

"You are. . . ."

"Confederate. The Twenty-Seventh Virginia."

Amy stared in rapt attention. She'd never spoken with a Confederate. He wasn't at all what her Papa described. Confederates were labeled as either gentlemanly southern aristocrats in shining gray uniforms, farm boys in their ordinary clothes, or poor backwoodsmen sporting rough beards and dirty hands.

This Confederate matched neither of the three. His manner was one of southern politeness, but his clothes were nothing to brag over. His eyes were kind, contrary to what some people said, that the rebels' eyes were filled with rebellion.

Although many a Marylander sided with the rebels, her papa remained faithful to the Union. She'd seen a few stragglers in blue, unbarbered and unwashed, heckling every female they walked by, or ravaged with hunger and ill from months of roughing it. The rebels were not much different, and often shoeless. On both sides the officers had it easy. They had good food, their cigars, women, and whiskey. Yet this man, with an uncanny familiarity, looked like the poorer of the troops. She could tell by the lines near his eyes that he had aged and been through things she could not imagine.

"I despised the fighting and rallied for abolitionist causes," she told him. The idea that she walked alongside a Confederate made her uneasy, but she had a strong urge to voice her beliefs. He had to have had views contrary to hers. They couldn't possibly find common ground. Their hearts could not have felt drawn to each other—not his—not with hers.

"You won't believe me, but I agree with you. The Constitution declares all men and women to be free." He then smiled with a look of contemplation. "The war. The emancipation of our fellow man. Those are subjects for another day."

Oh but she was itching to debate with him. This rebel let her down.

He pushed back the brim of his hat and looked at her. Her heart experienced a keen pang. Flushed, she looked away. "Have you a long way to go?" she asked.

Sadness rose in his eyes. "I'm not heading home. The war. . .well, you know how that went."

"Oh. . .I'm sorry."

"No reason to be." He moved ahead of her. "I'm rebuilding."

"If our house had been plundered, my father would do everything in his power to restore it. It shows you're not defeated." She plucked a leaf from an overhanging limb. "It's over now. I hope it never happens again. My mother used to say God wants us to look for the good that comes out of hard times."

"Can you name any?" he asked.

"Sure. There's plenty."

"For instance?"

"People were made free, and in the long run, our country will grow more unified."

He shook his head. "I sure hope you're right."

"Is it true what we read in the papers, that Sherman burned Atlanta. . .all of it?"

If she could be sure, a look of anger overcame the sadness. "You believe the

25

South should be punished?"

"I'm as southern as you."

"Barely. You're not from the Deep South, but then, neither am I."

She cocked her head to one side. "Then what are we?"

"Good question." He drew off his hat and paused alongside her. "What's your name?"

"Why? I shouldn't even be talking to you."

"Fine, don't tell me—neighbor."

"How's that?"

"We're neighbors. I'm the new farm manager at the Montague estate."

"Such charity that he would hire a rebel."

"I'll spare the details, but my family owed him money. My father was not wise when it came to whom he did business with."

"Like rebels? Did he do business for the Confederacy?"

He let out a slow whistle. "You're bold, Miss No Name."

Heat flamed in her cheeks. *Shame on you, Amy Fairbourne. You've no cause to judge this man—this man with familiar eyes.*

"That was unkind of me. I ask your pardon," she said. "I only meant, well—Chester Montague profited from the war."

"Say what you want. I suppose I deserve it."

"No, it was rude of me." She held out her hand to shake his. He looked down at it. A light sprang into his eyes, and he slowly brought his fingers tightly around hers. His touch made her feel something she had felt that night back in Washington many years ago. It felt electric yet soothing. Warm yet cool as a summer breeze.

She withdrew her hand. He gazed at her. "I still have the feeling we've met before."

Before she could answer, a howl echoed through the woods. Then the spring of black-and-white fur came bounding toward them. General skidded on his paws and carried on something fierce at the ox. Bulldog turned his massive head and blew out his nose.

Amy snatched General by the collar. "Dear me! I'm sorry. He's mine. Quiet, General! I hope he didn't frighten your ox."

One side of the rebel's mouth lifted. "He's a lot like me. Very little frightens him. Good day to you."

He pulled the beast on toward a path that led up a hill through the woods. Amy, left holding her dog, ordered him to stay, and when she reached the path where the man had gone, she called to him. "What is your name?"

He turned. "Rory Maguire." He tipped his hat to her and moved on.

Amy froze. Her mouth fell open. She stared. Speechless, her pulse beat in her temples. What had just happened? What were the chances that she and Rory would meet again on the Potomac towpath on a sultry August morning?

Shocked by this meeting, she turned. Finding her legs, she ran up the path after Rory. General galloped at her heels. Amy turned at a bend at the top of the hill and looked down a path deeply shadowed by ancient trees. Where had Rory gone? Baffled, she stopped. She stared at the ground. Then she looked ahead. She lifted her skirts and raised her eyes heavenward. Her heart beat against her breast and then stilled. The path twisted to the right. Stones slowed her, the soles of her shoes so thin she could feel their sharp edges beneath them. Then she saw him.

"Rory! Wait!"

He turned and pushed up the brim of his hat to see her. As she hurried to him, he looped Bulldog's lead around a low branch and headed back up the slope. When he reached her, Amy felt her legs freeze. Her chest heaved. She caught her breath. She gazed up into his eyes.

"Don't you remember me?" she asked.

Looking down at her, his eyes gleamed with knowing, slowly at first.

"It's me, Amy Fairbourne, the girl you danced with at the inaugural ball in Washington before the war." She swallowed as he stayed silent, beholding her face. "You probably danced with a lot of girls that night. But I was the one who. . ."

"Caught my. . .interest?"

"Did I?"

He swept off his hat. "Your eyes make me remember. I hadn't seen violet eyes before then and never have since."

"I look different—older." She lost her nerve and a cold flush rushed over her body. "Oh, but I'm being forward. I shouldn't expect you to remember me. Too much time has passed."

"Time wasted," he said. "Can I confess something to you, Miss Fairbourne?" He looked back at the ox and took a step forward. "I carried your image in my mind through the war. It kept me going. I had no idea where you were. I would have written, but I had no address. I only had your face."

"I only had yours as well."

"Do you recall meeting after that night?"

"I do indeed. We were always with others. We were only allowed to speak to one another discreetly."

"And sit next to each other on Sundays at the church."

"Until my mother decided we should return home. When Sumter happened."

"Yes. And I was called away. I went to find you, and they said you had returned home. The hotel wouldn't tell me where."

"I doubt they knew."

"We only had a few weeks together, yet it seemed we had known each other for years." Rory pushed back a lock of his hair as it fell over his forehead. "What should we do now?"

Amy pressed her lips together. "Can we be. . .friends?"

He moved closer. "Friends is a start. I want to see you again."

General howled and sprinted away. Amy turned. Off in the distance a voice called, "Amy! Amy Fairbourne, where are you?" She stepped away from Rory, and from the top of the incline, she saw Mae striding down the towpath toward them.

She looked back over her shoulder at Rory. She smiled. "I must go," she said. She could feel the glow in her eyes and the rapid gallop of a heart set free. She headed down the hillside, and he called out to her. "When can I see you again?"

"Tomorrow," she called. "On the towpath where we met."

As she skipped down the path under the shade of the giant elms, laughter fell from her lips—and joy filled her utterly.

Chapter 4

Early October

Amy blinked when her father tossed his newspaper onto the dining room table. "I declare, Amy. You worry me to death. You've been going out alone for far too long, and it has to stop."

Amy lingered in the doorway, her chest heaving. Her papa frowned. "Have you been running on the towpath?"

"No, Papa."

"Then why do you look as though you had?"

"I sprinted up the front porch steps."

"A young lady shouldn't behave that way." His brows creased and he looked her up and down. "You've been perspiring."

She pulled away from the door and slid into the chair opposite him. "No need to worry, Papa. It's hot today. That's all. You should see the falls. The water is so clear today. And the trees, they are glorious. The colors are changing."

"You look a mess. I don't like it." He snatched up his newspaper.

Amy lowered her eyes. "I'm sorry to have upset you."

"No you're not. If you were, you'd behave."

"There's nothing wrong with taking in the air and walking out of doors. It's healthy."

He frowned. "Healthy or not, you shouldn't be out there alone. Running around and traipsing about like a gypsy woman—what would your mother say?"

She looked at him. "The good Lord is with me wherever I go. Mama taught me that from the day I could walk."

"That's not all she taught you. Use your head, Amy."

No matter what she said, nothing seemed to disarm her father. The way he spoke to her hurt. She never could figure out why he was so abrupt with her. Had she done something terribly wrong in the past? "I take General with me most days, Papa. He's a good protector."

"I'd like to think General would defend you, but I'm uncertain."

Amy reached across the table and touched her father's hand. He pulled away.

"Papa, I'll do all I can to bring you peace of mind. But don't ask me to give up my walks."

Franny trudged into the room. She yawned and plopped down next to Amy. "Morning, Papa. Oh Amy, you're back."

"Morning, Franny. Did you know your sister was out again this morning?"

Franny picked up the coffeepot. "I have some recollection, Papa dear."

"You didn't bother to tell me?"

"She goes out every morning. We all know." She batted her lashes at him. "Do you really want me to tell you every morning when Amy goes out? Since she's in the habit of it, it's to be expected."

"I suppose you're right." Papa's tone changed. "You're certainly not your sister's keeper. Have a mess of eggs, Franny. Mae made them special this morning."

Franny lifted the lid to the serving dish and scooped out a bit of breakfast. "Yum, she cooked them in butter. Biscuits too." She broke a biscuit in two and put one of the halves on her plate.

"You barely eat, Franny. It can't be good for you," Amy said.

"I have to keep my waist tiny, Sister dear. A tightly bound corset helps, but not enough."

"Franny, why don't you come with me this Friday? We can watch the draymen lead the mules on the towpath. I heard there is a barge stopping that has goods we might look at."

Franny's brows shot up. "Me? It's too hot to go out of doors."

"You see, Amy. Franny knows better." Her father stirred his coffee. She held his eyes a moment and a deeper pang gripped her. What if he knew she met Rory on those early morning walks? What if he knew about the love letter tucked in her sleeve? Would he put her under house arrest—lock her in her room?

Franny bit into her biscuit. "Worrying will only give you gray hairs, Papa."

"I'm perfectly safe," Amy said.

"Can I be any clearer? You are not permitted to take walks anymore."

"Not at all? But you said. . ."

"I know what I said." He wagged his finger at her. "You'll have no allowances for clothes or those frivolous things women want if you don't listen. You'll not be allowed any visitors. Any invitations we receive will not include you."

She shut her eyes and forced back tears. "You can't prevent me from going to church."

"Of course not."

She shook her head. "I don't understand why you are so angry. I've done nothing wrong."

"Amy, don't you see?" Franny said. "There are people who would do you harm. The war is over, but there are still wanderers that would take advantage of you."

Amy reached under her skirts beneath the table. She laid her lady's pistol beside her plate. "I have this to protect me."

Her father's mouth curved. "That little thing. Why, it wouldn't wound a stray cat."

Amy straightened her back against the spindles of the chair. They were hard and cold, like the words she battled. She didn't want to argue or disobey him. He only wanted to ensure her safety and guard her reputation. She wondered. Could she reveal her secret? If she did, would he approve? After all, Rory was an honorable man, and no one would dare bother her if he were to escort her. Chester Montague would certainly vouch for him.

Her mind whirled with reasons why her father should approve of Rory. When her father cleared his throat and arrested her out of her wanderings, she realized he'd never allow a former Confederate in her presence, let alone let her take walks with him.

"Would you approve if Mae went with me?" A little lift of her brows and a coy look failed to change her father's stern expression.

"Mae, certainly, and your cousin while he is here."

She hadn't thought of speaking to Landon about her situation. Surely he'd understand and stand up for her. He'd keep her secret, and he'd be their chaperone from a distance.

"When you marry," said Franny, "you can take walks with your husband. But mind you, bring a parasol when you do to keep the sun off your face."

Such condescension could not be borne. "Thank you for reminding me, Franny."

Franny took another bite of biscuit. "Papa, Mr. Montague is looking for a wife, isn't he?"

He appeared not to hear her. He had gone back to reading his newspaper. When Franny repeated the question, he barely lifted his eyes from the page. "If you know he is."

Amy glanced at her sister. Franny's eyes were lit up. "Could I be considered?"

"It is possible."

"I hope so. I'd wed him in a blink of an eye."

"He's pretty well set up, that's for sure."

"Has he asked for my hand, Papa?"

He straightened his waistcoat, stood, and stepped away from the table. "Where on earth is Landon? He's not sleeping in too, I hope."

As he posed the question of Landon, Mae shouldered her way through the kitchen door into the dining room. She held a tray at her hip. "Mr. Landon went out riding, sir. He gulped down some coffee and went on his way an hour ago."

"Is he coming back?"

"He didn't say, sir, but I imagine he will. His belongings are in the guest room."

On that word, he walked out. Franny seemed unaffected by the conversation that had just occurred and spooned eggs into her mouth. She had delicate manners, and Amy wondered if they would make up for Franny's way of saying whatever came into her head. So much prettier than Amy, her green eyes were the shape of medallions, her lashes thick beneath slender brows, her complexion clear and bright.

Amy saw her own reflection in the silver bowl in front of her. Her hair hung in dark curls, her complexion was rosy, and her eyes large and violet.

Franny's blond curls quivered as she shook her head. "I know what you're thinking, Amy."

Amy looked up. "Do you?"

"You're upset because Papa wants one of us married to Chester. You won't accept him. You don't like him. You're afraid Papa will become furious. But don't worry. I'm sure Chester doesn't have his eye on *you*."

Amy set her napkin on the table. "Good. I want it that way."

She couldn't eat another bite. The mere mention of Chester Montague made her stomach turn sour. Her thoughts turned to Rory. His face caused her heart to flutter like the wings of a bird. She enjoyed the feeling, and she anticipated sunrise when she could meet him in secret. The days they had spent together were unlike any others. He shared the details of his life, and she taught him the names of the wildflowers. He showed her how to fish the river pools and how to feed chickadees out of her hand. One thing she knew for certain, meeting him again had not been by chance.

Franny huffed. "Oh, you do confuse me. Papa isn't going to live forever. We've got to marry and take care of him, and bury him next to Mama."

Amy found herself at a loss for words at the mention of her mother's grave. She wanted to debate but held her peace. She longed to tell her sister how she met Rory on the road. If she did tell, Franny would tell Papa. The only friend she had was Mae—Mae would understand.

"Is that what you really care about, Franny?"

"Of course."

"If we are dirt poor and have to leave Linden Grove, he'll still be beside Mama. You can't use that as an excuse for marrying where there is no love."

Franny stormed out of the room. Amy stood and started to clear the breakfast dishes. Her hand knocked over a cup, and the contents spilled onto the linen tablecloth. It gave her opportunity to vent her anger by blotting up the stain.

"I'll take care of that, Miss Amy." Mae moved her back gently. "You sit down."

"Oh, she rattles me, Mae. Now I've ruined one of Mama's best tablecloths."

"Nothing lemon juice won't mend."

Amy put her hand to her aching head.

"What's the matter with that child?" Mae went on. "Does she have a bee in her bonnet?"

"Some days I think she has a hive-full. We don't see eye to eye on the topic of marriage."

Mae set plates on her tray. "I'm not surprised. You're much wiser. Comes with a few more years you have ahead of her."

Amy stood and hurried over to Mae. She put her arms around her. "I'm worried."

Mae patted Amy's back. "Don't be troubled over your sister. She'll come to her senses. Let's talk of something else, like what you've been doing every morning. I think it's more than just walking. You meeting someone, Miss Amy?"

Amy moved back. "Nothing escapes you, Mae."

Mae lifted her brows. "Who is this person? You can tell me."

"Someone I knew before the war."

"Well, glory be. We talked about him before."

"Yes, and I never thought I'd see him again."

"What happened?"

"I was out walking the towpath, and there he was, coming up behind me leading the biggest ox I ever did see."

"An ox? Dear me, what for?"

"It doesn't matter. I didn't recognize him at all, but his eyes were like I remembered." She went on telling Mae what unfolded between them.

Mae's eyes widened. "A miracle. What were the chances of you two meeting up again after all this time, and on the towpath?"

"I never forgot him, and I prayed I'd at least know whether or not he survived the war."

"Well, I've lived long enough to tell you, when two people are meant to know each other, nothing can stop them coming together. I've seen it happen plenty of times, and in the most unusual ways. I remember how your papa and mama met. No one expected the two of them to match up. Miss Rachel was so pretty and came from an upper-class family, as you know. Her folks weren't too fond of him at first. But he proved himself."

"But surely I can't say this is what has happened with Rory and me." Then a thought occurred to her that made her trip over her words. "Oh my. Papa wants one of us to marry Chester Montague, and Rory works for him."

Mae squinted. "Oh my, indeed."

"Don't worry. We don't meet long. Rory usually hands me a letter, and we talk for a brief while."

"How long has this been going on?"

"Since August."

"And without anyone else knowing."

"It is all right though, isn't it? I mean, we aren't doing anything wrong, are we?"

"Just don't do anything you aren't supposed to."

"I won't." Amy wiped her eyes. "I'm sorry for the tears. I can't cry in front of Papa. It makes him mad. And Franny, she doesn't understand."

"I could be thrown out if your papa knew what I've been saying, but you hold your ground, Miss Amy. Dig in your heels like your mama did, and your papa will come around."

"Around to what?" Stunned, Amy turned with Mae. Her cousin leaned against the doorjamb, riding crop in hand. He had a mischievous grin on his face.

Mae walked up to him and looked down at his boots. "Glad to see you have clean boots, Mr. Landon. You know I don't like mud on my floors."

Landon nudged Mae's chin. "You ought to leave this place and be my house-keeper. I'd pay you well."

"I won't ever leave Miss Amy."

Landon looked over at Amy. "Maybe you won't have to if she agrees to be my wife. So, Cousin Amy, would you marry me?" He exaggerated a bow and laughed.

"Certainly not, Landon. You belong with Franny."

He picked up a biscuit and bit into it. "I declare! I'd marry Mae just to have her biscuits."

Mae uttered something under her breath and shook her head at him. "Eat them all, Mr. Landon. But I ain't gonna marry you. For one, I'm too old."

Amy smiled at her brash cousin. "You should hire a cook, Landon."

"You know I'm just joking. With my parents passed, I'm living hand over fist." He reached for another biscuit. "I have plans for restoring the old farm."

"Why aren't you living there now?"

"Are you getting tired of me, Cousin?"

"You know I'm not."

"The house is lonely. You know anyone who could help with repairs? I'm looking to hire some laborers."

"I might, but I'm not sure he'd do it."

"Well, let whoever it is know I've got work if he wants it. I'm heading over there today." He stopped Mae as she was about to go out the door into the kitchen. "Darlin' Mae, would you pack some of those biscuits for me to take along?"

Mae's face glowed with pride. "I sure will. I've got some ham too. We were going to have it for supper, but I'll tuck it in with the biscuits."

He tried to pinch her cheek, but she giggled and scooted away. Amy turned him to face her. "You've been here for more than a visit. When are you going to speak to Franny?"

"Soon as it's right."

"Don't wait too long."

"I asked Uncle if I could marry her, but he said unless I build my estate up suitably to take care of her, he'd not agree."

She gripped his sleeves. "If you love her, work hard, Landon. The other prospect for her is Chester Montague."

Landon's lip curled. "Him? I can't see Franny taking the likes of him for a husband. I'll win over Uncle James to my way of thinking. You'll see." He kissed her cheek. "What about you? You sure your papa has Chester in mind for Franny and not you?"

"I suspect he does."

"Haven't you had any offers?"

"Not proper ones. But there is someone."

He leaned forward, looking into Amy's face. "Who?"

"You don't know him."

"I might. Tell me."

"I can't."

"Why not? What's the big mystery? Afraid your father will find out?"

"You know I am."

He blew out a long whistle. "Amy Fairbourne. You've got a secret beau."

Never in her life had Amy been so happy. She had been meeting Rory along the river above the falls, where they listened to the water tumbling over the rocks. He said little about the war. She spoke of their time, their loss, and the hunger she felt not just for more food, but for the days past when life seemed a miracle.

He cautioned her to take care walking over the cliffs. They were rough and rugged—like him, she told him.

The day after speaking with her cousin about winning Franny, Amy waited by the tall sycamore waiting for Rory. A mockingbird sang in the tree. She spread out her arms and whirled as if dancing to his song.

"You're doing it wrong."

She stopped spinning and looked at Rory as he came up the path. She smiled at him. "What am I doing wrong?"

"You should never dance without a partner." Rory stepped up to her.

Tongue-tied, she stared at him.

"Here, allow me to show you." Slow and easy, he moved his arm around her waist and took up her hand. He pulled her closer, and then stepped—one, two, three.

"See what I mean?" he said.

She kept her eyes on his, warm eyes that made her skin prickle. "You shouldn't—"

He stopped. "You're right. Not without your permission. Do I have it?"

She gave him a coy look. "I suppose it would be all right. Besides, now that the war is over, there may be balls and country dances I'm invited to."

"You hope I'll be jealous."

"I hope you'll be there."

The mockingbird took up his song again. "Can you hear the music?"

She looked up as if bending her ear. "It's a waltz."

"That's right." He moved her back, to the side, and swung her round. Dollops of light danced with them through the trees. Birds flitted from limb to limb.

"It's like before," Rory said.

"As if it never stopped."

"Your hand is warm. Glad you aren't wearing gloves."

"I threw those old things out a long time ago." The way he made her feel caused her to shiver. "I should be going."

They looked into each other's eyes. She thought he was going to kiss her. Instead, he let go of her hand. Then, to her astonishment, his face grew taut with longing.

"Amy." He spoke her name like poetry. "You've taken me prisoner. You've bound me to a love I don't want to escape from. I'm not worthy of you, I know. I can't give you an easy life. But I cannot help how I feel." He lifted her trembling hand. "Don't try to free me by being cruel. Don't deny me how I feel about you. Reject me, but I'll still go on loving you."

"Are you in earnest?"

"Before God and all the angels, I am."

Amy swallowed down the lump in her throat. "Have you anything else to say?" she said in a lowered voice, soft and smooth as the breeze tousling her hair.

"Yes," Rory said, "at the risk of my heart, I do."

"There is no risk, Rory. You can tell me."

"Can you accept never to see me again?"

"Never?"

"Never."

"I cannot."

"Then can you see us together for the rest of our lives?"

"Only. . .only as man and wife I can."

His eyes glowed. "Would you. . .could you marry a man like me?"

Tears welled in her eyes and she longed to throw her arms around his neck and say *yes*. "It will depend on how determined you are." With a skip in her step, she whirled away from him.

"Won't you give me an answer now?" he said, sounding a bit frustrated.

"Not now," she told him. "Not today. Tomorrow, perhaps."

She lifted her skirts, smiled at him, and hurried on. Leaving him in this way, she gave him two choices. Forget her or pursue her. She knew it would be the latter.

Chapter 5

In her bedroom, Amy looked into the tall mirror next to the window. Her dress had lost its sheen over the years, and the flowers on it were faded, but it mattered not. Her heart soared after meeting with Rory. He didn't care if she wore worn-out homespun cottons. He liked her just as she was.

She kept her walking boots on, even though they were dusty from the road. She had to have some say concerning what she wore and when, and this did the job. She looked out the window in time to see a carriage drawn by two bay horses come swaying and bouncing up the path toward the house. Red-spoked wheels kicked up dirt and gravel. A driver pulled the reins and halted the horses out front. They were well fed and their coats were glossy, their manes and tails decorated with red, white, and blue streamers.

Franny rushed into the room and looked out the window with Amy. "Look at that. I've never seen horses so prettily dressed."

"Pretty, but a waste of money, don't you think?"

Amy kept her eyes on the carriage door. The driver leaped down and put down the step.

Franny dropped the side of the curtain she held. She raised her hems and darted out the door. Then she turned back, her blond ringlets bouncing about her shoulders. "Let's wait at the top of the stairs and listen."

Amy bit her lower lip and narrowed her eyes as she turned back to the window. The first thing to show from the carriage door was an ebony walking stick, then an ample leg with a shoe so highly polished it shown in the sunlight. Next, the man, his feet firm on the step. When he alighted, the carriage raised up, his bulk having weighted it down considerably.

With a swing of the stick, he headed to the front door. Amy snapped closed the curtains and plopped into a chair, picked up the book she'd been reading, and tried to distract her mind from the visitor. Not much good did it do, for when Franny came back into the room, her face lit with excitement, Amy shut the book and sighed.

"Come downstairs with me, Amy. He's bound to want to see us."

"You're welcome to him."

"You know who it is?"

"I do, and I don't care."

Franny headed over to the window and looked out. "It's Chester Montague."

Amy stood and set the book on her nightstand. She heard the front door open and close. Her sister sashayed over to the dressing mirror. "I think I look pretty enough in this old thing." She whirled back around and looked at Amy for approval. "Do I?"

"You could wear gray wool and look pretty."

"Good. I wish I had something new in pink. That shade always brings out the color in my cheeks. Chester will find this gown agreeable, I'm sure."

"And that gives you hope he'll court you?"

"For sure, Sister."

"He's twice your age."

"That doesn't matter."

"I doubt there's a streak of romance in him."

"There will be when I get ahold of him."

"What if he isn't interested in you, Franny? What will you do then?"

"Since you don't want him, he will be. You'll see," Franny said. "I sense these things."

"Landon loves you. Has he told you?"

Franny's mouth dropped open. "Not in those words. But until he does. . ."

She hurried from the room. Amy waited in the doorway. She heard her sister's flirtatious voice echo up the staircase. "Why, Mr. Montague, what brings you to Linden Grove on this fine day?"

Amy shut her eyes. She prayed the Lord would not allow her sister to give in so easily or end up embarrassing herself. *Landon better step up his game and quick, or he'll lose her.*

Heading down the stairs, Amy gripped the balustrade, knowing she'd never give in to anyone but Rory.

When Amy entered the drawing room, there was Franny, batting her eyes at Montague. Her father sat in his favorite chair across from his guest. For the next half hour, Amy endured Montague's boasts about how he had made a killing during the war selling his wheat to both sides. "Bread is the staff of life," he snorted. "Wheat is the only thing that can supply that staff."

Amy rallied. "Yet man shall not live by bread alone, Mr. Montague."

"Who says, Miss Amy?"

"I'm surprised you don't know our Lord said it. You should read the Gospels, sir."

Landon sat opposite Amy. Their eyes met, and he gave her a quick wink of approval. Franny gave Amy a scathing glance. Montague squirmed in his chair. "Oh, I forgot," he said. "Anyway, I'm richer than I was before the war."

"I'm surprised the soldiers didn't just take your wheat. How did you convince them to pay?"

"It was easily done. I signed my pledge to the Confederacy on the idea they would buy my wheat. A few officers were friends of mine. Southern gentlemen keep their word."

"What about the Union men—did they steal it?" To Amy's chagrin, Franny looked intrigued.

Montague stroked his closely cut beard. "I did the same with them, Miss Franny. One must be sly as a fox in times of war."

Amy wanted to shout him down. His greed disgusted her. As for Franny, she showed no sign of disapproval. Neither did her father. He looked at Amy and gave her a look that silenced her.

Montague stayed for supper. Conversation lost its appeal as he slurped his soup and shoveled chicken into his mouth. Gravy dripped from his beard, and Amy handed him a clean napkin. He nodded, swiped the gravy away, then returned to eating. Everyone else had finished by the time Mae brought in apple pie for dessert. Perturbed at Montague's lack of table manners, Amy watched him scoop two slices onto his plate and dig in.

"My, oh my, Mae. You sure are a good cook." Montague spoke with pie in his mouth. Amy looked away. "I've an exceptional cook myself. His specialty is beef dishes."

Mae said not a word. She stepped through the door back into the kitchen.

Montague dropped his soiled napkin on the table. "A fine meal, Mr. Fairbourne. I suppose you don't eat like this every day, seeing you're in dire straits."

"We do well enough, sir." Amy's father lit up the cigar Montague had gifted him.

Montague leaned back. "I'd like you all to come out and see my new carriage. Bought it at an auction in Richmond last week. It's a charm. My driver is cheap too."

His brows arched. He lit his cigar and put out the match. "I've a few workers that stayed on, and I pay them very well. They were happy with the quarters and food, and I promised them each a new suit of clothes every Christmas."

Franny's eyes widened. "You *are* prosperous. Now that the war is over, have you plans to travel? Most gentleman do."

Montague drew the cigar out from between his teeth and smiled. "You are knowledgeable of that custom, Miss Franny. I won't travel until I'm married. Then I'll take my bride on a European tour."

"How thrilling," Franny said. Amy looked away, wishing she could roll her eyes without anyone noticing.

Montague crushed his cigar into a tray. "I've a farm manager at present, but he's leaving me soon. I'll need to hire."

"How unfortunate to lose him," Amy said, knowing he was speaking of Rory.

"It is indeed. He's very good with thoroughbreds. I managed to keep my stallion during the war. He was too wild for the officers. I must say, my manager has a lot in common with old Piccolo." He looked over at Franny. "I hear you like horses, Miss Franny."

Franny lowered her eyes. "I do indeed, sir."

"Well, the next time I pay a call, I'll ride Piccolo over. Come outside and see my bays. They are excellent."

Franny cooed over the horses. Amy thought they were as beautiful as any she had seen. She stroked the velvety nose of the lead, and it made a low rumble of pleasure in its throat.

"Well, what do ya know," Montague said. "He likes you, Miss Amy."

"I like him too."

"Here, give him a sugar cube." Montague took one from his pocket and, drawing close to Amy, placed it in her hand. "He'll be yours forever."

She set it in her palm and held it out. The horse's lips flapped as he gobbled it up. "A treat indeed," Amy said. Then she caught the look of disappointment in Franny's eyes. "Perhaps my sister would like to try, Mr. Montague."

"Would you, Miss Franny?" Montague reached inside his pocket again.

Franny gripped her hands together. "He might bite."

"He's as gentle as a lamb, Franny." Amy took Franny's hands and moved her up to the horse. A whinny and a wide yellow eye frightened Franny, and she leaped back.

"I'd rather ride in the carriage." Again, she gripped her hands and shrugged away when one of the horses swung his head at her. "I had hoped you would ask me."

"Oh, did you? Well, I was going to ask Miss Amy if she'd accompany me on a little jaunt. But if you want to come along too, that would double the fun." Montague patted his waistcoat. Franny tossed back her head. Montague's smile fled, and a bewildered look crossed his face. With a swift turn, Franny stomped off.

Montague looked at Amy. "Did I say something to offend her?"

Amy let go of the bridle and stepped up to him. "My sister has taken interest in you. Do you understand my meaning?"

His brows pinched. "You mean she has hopes that I would. . ."

"Court her, yes."

"Oh, but she's too young for me. She hasn't the maturity and grace I seek in a wife." He picked up Amy's hand. "I've been meaning to speak to you about it. I was waiting for the right moment. I suppose this is as good as any."

"About Franny? But you've already said she isn't right for you."

"Yes, I know I did, but. . ."

"You want me to speak to her, to ease her disappointment?"

"You can if you like. I was hoping you'd give me the pleasure of courting you, Amy. I've already spoken to your father, and he approves."

With slow grace, Amy withdrew her hand. His eyes expressed such enthusiasm, warning bells went off in her head. She could not encourage him.

"An engagement would be wrong. We are not a good match, and you deserve so much better. You're entitled to a wife who will stand by your side in all circumstances."

It was the only thing she could think of that would put him off without hurting his pride. He pulled out a handkerchief and wiped his forehead.

"I don't know what to say, Miss Amy. Except—I will remain hopeful."

She almost felt sorry for him. "Remain hopeful for a loving wife, Mr. Montague. I'm sorry to say I do not love you."

"Such notions come from poets, Miss Amy. Marriage is not about love, you see. It is about companionship, two people combining whatever they may inherit in order to have a better life, which is far deeper than sentimental feelings."

"I disagree. A husband and wife should love one another."

He shook his head. "Well, perhaps you can persuade me to your way of thinking someday, but not today."

"It is up to me, sir. I'm inclined not to."

"You would be if you knew Linden Grove was safe, that your father will live out his life in comfort."

"Your meaning?" Amy frowned, anticipating his explanation.

"I can give your father cash in hand to save Linden Grove and make it prosperous, like days of old. It wouldn't be a loan. It would be a gift."

Shocked, Amy pressed her arms to her sides. "In exchange for me?"

"Well, not exactly as you put it. It's a kind of business arrangement to benefit both parties. These decisions are best left up to your father and me. He knows I can provide well for you, and I can ensure his well-being and save Linden Grove from ruin."

"That may be, Mr. Montague. But I do not love you. I never will."

"But you love your father and your sister, don't you? Think of them."

She narrowed her eyes. "All right, Mr. Montague. Lay out your terms."

"They are simple."

"I'm listening."

"Marry me, and your family is set up in perpetuity. Refuse, and Linden Grove will fall into decay. What support have you?"

"We'll survive."

"Wishful thinking, I'm sure."

"Not to me," said Amy.

"Oh come now, Miss Amy. I'd make you a good husband. Anything you want you'd have."

"What I want, I doubt you can give, Mr. Montague. Good day."

Upon the last word, Amy turned to leave him but stopped at the sound of a horse and rider beating down the road leading up to the house. The horse's hooves kicked up a haze of ochre dust. Once the rider reached the carriage, he reined in and the horse skidded to a halt.

"Maguire! What are you doing riding in here at that pace?" Montague shouted.

The horse veered. "Vagrants have stolen one of your mares and pistol-whipped one of the hands. He's badly injured. Joseph has gone for the doctor."

Montague turned red in the face. "Why didn't you stop them?"

"I and the other lads chased after them. Believe me, I got my fists in." Rory slid from the saddle. His boots pounded up dirt when he landed. "One got away, and we have the other under guard for the sheriff. William is holding him with a repeater."

Montague puffed out his cheeks and drew back his shoulders. "I'll come immediately." He turned to Amy. "The circumstances dictate that I do."

"I hope your men will be all right," she said. Amy looked at Rory, trying to hide the electric sensation he gave her. "You don't think they could come here, do you? Raiders are known to."

"They were headed south." Rory nodded to her. "No reason to fear, Miss Fairbourne."

Montague raised his chin. "You stay here, Maguire, and make sure there isn't. I'm sure my gracious hostess will provide you with a cool beverage."

Chapter 6

Rory pulled his horse into Linden Grove's barn. On each side, stables were empty and cleared of hay except one for the old gray donkey. It lifted its head and flared its nostrils as Rory passed by with his Regent, a tall, chestnut quarter horse. When the donkey brayed, Regent sidestepped and Rory soothed him with a touch of his hand and a quiet word.

Sunlight from a sliver in the roof fell over Rory's shoulders. He'd been handsome those youthful years ago, but now he looked more so, having aged deeper into his manhood. "There is a brush beside you if you want to brush him down," Amy told him.

He found it and gently rubbed the boar bristles over the horse's coat. It rippled with each stroke. The gelding lowered its head and shook it, causing the bridle to jingle.

Amy stayed back a few paces. "Is he always that skittish?"

"Only when he's in a strange place." Rory looped the reins around a post. "He's the best horse I've ever owned though."

"I wish we had our horses back."

He smiled at her. "A white mare should be your wedding present."

Amy placed her hand on a post. "Mr. Montague has asked me. I'm sure if I accepted he'd buy any horse I want—white, dapple, or chestnut, like yours there."

Rory looked away. A proposal from Montague obviously bothered him. "So, did you accept him?"

"I'd be a fool to." She traced her finger over the post. "I don't love him and he doesn't love me. It's just business to him."

"He loves his land and money," Rory said. "I've seen it firsthand. Nothing stands between him and his wealth."

"Yet you work for him."

"My family's debt is paid. He'll find a note on his desk when he returns home that I've left him for greener pastures."

Amy's heart went up into her throat. "He did say you were leaving. I didn't expect it so soon. Where will you be going?"

He didn't answer her but said, "Will you take seriously what I've said about Montague?"

"I'm not worried about him."

"He'll find a way to convince you that marrying him is the thing to do."

She gave him a sidelong glance. "How do you know this?"

"He's got a slick way of talking, if you haven't noticed."

"I appreciate the warning, Rory, but I can stand up to Chester Montague, no matter what he promises."

"Has he made promises?"

For a moment, she hesitated, but Rory's concern touched her. "He has. I can tell you're itching to know what. So I'll tell you. He wants to buy my father's estate. Things have been bad for us since the war, and Montague has enough money to fix it ten times over."

Rory set down the brush and went to her. "And you are to be the sacrifice."

Her eyes widened. "I'll find another way to help my father."

"What happens if Montague buys the estate? What will happen to your family?"

She lowered her head, not knowing what to say. Then she looked up at him. "You sure do have a lot to say to me, Rory Maguire. It's been two days since I last saw you. Has all this been building up to something?"

"I reckon it has, Amy Fairbourne." He leaned against the stall behind him. "You know, I'm sorry about not seeing you. I hope you weren't waiting. I would have sent word, but—"

"It's all right. You're probably getting tired of seeing me."

Rory groaned. "Not at all. You're the silver lining of a dark cloud." He pushed away from the stall. She gazed up at him, wanting him to put his arms around her, squeeze her close against him, and kiss her.

"I. . .I have never been complimented in that way before."

"It was time you were. Time you had many compliments. . .about your hair, your eyes, the way you stand in the light." He put his hand on her arm. "How long have we been seeing each other?"

"Months."

"And the time we had before the war."

"Yes, and we thought it would end in a few days. How wrong we were."

"It separated us."

"For too long, Rory."

45

He touched her cheek. She turned her face to his hand and sighed. Was he going away? Would he leave her behind and forget her? Tears touched the tips of her lashes, and she put her hand over them to wipe them dry.

"Why the tears?"

She pulled away and stomped her foot. "Mercy me, Rory Maguire! Don't you know? I asked you if you were going away, and you didn't answer me. I don't want you to go away. You're the only friend I have in this world and—"

He grabbed her hand and pulled her against him. "Yes, I'm going away."

"Then I'll never see you again," she said through her tears. "It's because of what I said the last time we met, isn't it? Remember?"

"I remember, and I believe you were testing me."

"You guessed right, Rory. I didn't mean to be unkind about it. I should have answered you then. I suppose I was thinking you really didn't mean it."

"I did mean it, and I'm going to ask you again. When I do, you don't have to answer me right away. Take your time. Be sure. But don't let me leave without knowing."

Amy swallowed. She knew how she'd answer, but what would her father say? Would he give his consent, allow her to wed a former rebel?

"I won't, Rory. I promise."

"All right. Here it is. I'm sure you know by now how I feel."

"Yes, but it would be nice to hear the words."

"That I love you and adore you?"

"Do you?"

"With everything in me." He held her hands and went down on one knee. A shiver passed over her. "I may not be rich, but I have a full heart and want you to be my wife. I told you about the land in Virginia. That's why I've been away. To settle things. The house has been fixed up and the stables look just the way they did before the war. I want you to share it with me. What do you say?"

Her breath caught and tears welled in her eyes. This is what she wanted. *Rory!* Rory to be her husband. Rory to love her. "I don't need to think very long," she told him. "The answer is, if you want me, you have me."

Standing, he picked her up and swung her around. "Wahoo!"

When he set her down, Amy patted her hair. Pins had come loose. "Mercy me. I look a mess."

"You look darn pretty to me." He planted a full kiss on her lips. It seemed as if she floated off the floor. His arms were strong and felt wonderful around her. Her heart pounded so fast she gasped.

With the tears dried, she smiled up at him. "What do we do now, Rory?"

"I need to speak to your father. Is he home?"

"He's probably in his study."

"I'll go speak to him now."

Rory grabbed her hand and headed for the barn doors. But they swung open, and in stepped Amy's father. "Amy! What's going on in here? Why is this man in here alone with you?"

At first her father's unexpected appearance startled Amy. Then she gathered her wits and stepped toward him, holding out her hand in Rory's direction. "Papa, this is Mr. Maguire. We were just—"

He frowned. "You, sir. I see your horse there. You're Montague's farm manager, aren't you?"

"Was, sir. I've resigned."

"Why've you come to Linden Grove?"

Rory untied his horse's reins from the post and went on to explain what had happened at Montague's estate. All the while, Amy's father's eyes were piercing and he had a look of distrust on his face. He looked at Amy. "You believe this man?"

"I do, Papa. I was with Mr. Montague when Mr. Maguire arrived. I heard everything."

"Well, I suppose I should prime my pistols in case these rebels show up."

Rory shook his head. "Not sure if they were former rebels, sir. Sure rough around the edges though."

"Criminals and traitors. I think you should be on your way, Mr. Maguire. My daughter is needed inside the house. And before you leave, if you should show up here again, make your presence known to me. Amy knows better than to be alone with a man, no matter who he may be." He raised his hand when Amy began to speak. "Don't argue with me, Amy. You know my meaning. Standing outside with your sister speaking with Mr. Montague was in the open."

Rory picked up his hat and approached Amy's father. "Sir, may I speak with you privately?"

Amy's father drew up his shoulders. "Go to the house, Amy. Mr. Maguire and I have something to discuss."

Chapter 7

Amy waited on the staircase for her father to return. She squeezed a banister spindle with her right hand, flexed her fingers, and squeezed again. Her eyes darted to the door, to the window, and back again. She heard a horse's neigh and hurried over to the door and opened it. Rory was mounting Regent. He pulled the reins to the right to turn him out onto the sandy path. The horse pranced as he tapped its ribs with his heels.

"Rory!" He turned the horse and looked at her. His face tense, she saw sorrow flood over him, disappointment mixed with longing. She rushed out onto the porch and watched him ride on past the two stone columns at the end of the drive, turn, and disappear.

If her father had approved of their desire to marry, they would have both come inside to tell her. But her father would be coming in alone. Her heart pounded and her palms were sweating. She leaned against a column, her pulse pounding in her temples. Around the corner walked her father. He glanced at her and headed inside, his boots tramping over the hardwood floor. Amy lifted her skirts and followed him.

"Papa?"

He looked at her over his shoulder. "There's nothing to say, Amy. I don't know what you were expecting."

She stood still, her hands clenched at her sides. "Why did Rory ride off like that?"

He shook his head. "I shouldn't have to answer that question. You should know the answer. Do you really think I would give consent to a rebel, a Virginian, to marry a daughter of mine?"

"He loves me, Papa, and I love him."

"You'll forget him soon enough." He moved on, and she hurried after him.

"The war is over, Papa. We need to put it behind us. Rory is a good man, and he will take good care of me. There's no reason why you should deny us our happiness. We knew each other before the war, and you did not disapprove of him when we spent time in the city."

Her father turned on his heel. "What I'm doing is for your own good."

Her eyes teared. "My good or yours, Papa?"

"You will not speak to me in that manner."

"I'm of age. I want to marry him." She spoke softly now, and for a moment, her manner seemed to cool his temper. Then he stormed to his desk and sat down. Ignoring her would not achieve anything, for Amy headed straight into the room, shut the door, and stood in front of him.

Shafts of light flowed through the tall mullioned window. Dust motes floated through them, alighting on the books on the shelves. Her father, however, remained in shadow. His desk and chair were opposite the window. The dark hues matched his mood, and Amy wished he'd move into the light. Perhaps it would somehow change him.

There were papers on the desk, and he began shuffling through them. "I've nothing more to say, Amy. Go find something to do. I'm busy."

She stepped closer. "I will always honor you, Papa, just as the commandment tells me, but I'm not obliged to do something that is wrong. Marrying Montague for his money would be a terrible mistake. I don't need your permission to marry the man I love."

He looked up from the papers and stared hard at her. Then he slammed his fist on the desk, and she flinched. "You'll do as I say!"

"Do you want me to be unhappy for the rest of my life?" She matched his anger.

"You're going to marry Chester Montague, and that's final."

"I'm sorry if it angers you, but I will not."

"You will, or I'll throw you out."

She drew in a breath. "You would do that, Papa? You'd disown your own daughter because she refuses to marry that man? You've forgotten how he was a profiteer during the war, how he has denounced God and the law. Rory fought bravely for Virginia, and he has a vast estate along the Shenandoah. He's not poor or destitute. He's not an unbeliever. He hasn't gained anything through the suffering of others. Yet you reject him because he was on the other side. It isn't right, Papa. You know it isn't."

"I will not be lectured to by you."

"Why do you want to tie me to Montague when you know it would make me unhappy?"

"Chester will make sure Linden Grove is safe, and you'll see how happy you'll be to have servants, pretty clothes, and anything your heart desires."

"My heart desires Rory."

Again, her father pounded his fist. Amy had never seen him behave this way, and it frightened her. She stood back and met his stern eyes.

"If you defy me, Amy, I'll see to it you never set foot on Linden Grove's soil again. I will forbid you from seeing your sister and cousin. You will be dead to me."

He might as well have stabbed her in the heart. Tears slipped from her eyes and down her cheeks. She opened her mouth to speak, but there were no words. Her hand covered her mouth to stifle a cry. He looked away, down at his papers. "I have nothing more to say—and neither do you."

Fleeing the room, Amy dashed upstairs to her bedroom and threw herself across the bed. She curled her arms under her head and wept. The tears were bitter, stinging—relentless. She brought her hands forward and clutched them. "Lord God, help me," she whispered. "I know I'm to honor my father. But must I obey him at the cost of my heart and happiness? Show me the way. . ."

A quiet knock fell on her door, and Mae slipped inside and closed it. "Dear girl. Are you all right?"

Amy sat up and reached out blindly for Mae. Mae went to her and cradled her. Wind blew against the windows as a gray sky formed outside. Where had that glorious silver light gone? Where had the soft whisper of a breeze passing through the trees fled to? Mae pulled a shawl over Amy's shoulders and stroked her hair.

"You don't need to say anything, child. I can tell your heart is breaking. You're surely in a mess, but God will take care of it. Don't you worry, 'cause I'll be praying for you to have your answer."

Footsteps echoed up the staircase and paused beyond the closed door. Without knocking, Amy's father opened it and stood on the threshold. "Dry your face," he said. "There's no use in crying."

She looked up at him, her face awash with tears.

"I've made a decision. In order to help you come to your senses and get over this infatuation, you'll stay in the house. No venturing out of doors unless you are with me. I don't want you tempted to see Maguire. Your wedding will take place here at Linden Grove a week from Monday. That will give you plenty of time to prepare. I'll speak to our pastor after church on Sunday."

He walked over to her and touched her shoulder. "Don't worry, Amy. Once you are married to Montague, you'll thank me."

She shrank from his touch. Then she drew out of Mae's arms and jerked her head up to him. "No, Papa."

Her father frowned. "What do you mean, 'no'?"

"There will be no need to thank you, because I'm not going to marry that man. Not on my life will I do it."

"You'll disobey me?"

"I have no other choice."

Franny came across the threshold and stood at the end of Amy's bed. "What's wrong? Why is Amy crying, Papa?"

"Franny, I want you to gather your things and move them into your mother's old room."

Franny looked at him, bewildered. "Why, Papa?"

"You don't need an explanation. Just do as you're told."

Quick to comply, Franny opened her top dresser drawer. "I can't do this by myself. Mae, you help me."

Mae stood, sighed, and proceeded to gather up an armful of petticoats, stockings, and laces. Franny handed Amy one of her handkerchiefs. "For your eyes, Amy." She leaned down. "You can tell me what's wrong. Why have you been crying? Did you and Papa have an argument?"

Amy sat silently still. Her father strode to the door and paused. "I've asked Montague back tonight. He replied to my invitation but will be late. Business, I presume. Be ready by nine. Wear something nice. We'll settle things with him then." He walked out without closing the door. Amy stood, balled her fists, and heaved a breath. She couldn't let this happen. No one could force her to marry, and she didn't want to see hide nor hair of Chester Montague.

Rory! Rory!

"Oh, my poor sister." Franny drew Amy down onto the bedside and sat next to her. "What will you do?"

"Not marry Chester Montague, that's what." Amy bowed her head. "The thought of him touching me makes my stomach turn. I can't do it. Did you hear Papa say he will disown me if I don't do what he says?"

Franny's eyes widened. "What? No, he can't. I won't let him."

"I don't know how you can stop him."

"I'll speak to him, Amy. It will be all right."

Amy looked at her sister. "You said you wanted him. Tell Papa."

"I don't care anymore about Chester Montague. You were right. I was foolish thinking I could ever marry him."

"What changed your mind, Franny?"

Franny smiled. "Landon did. He told me he wants to marry me—that he loves me. No one has ever said that to me, and my heart pounded so hard, I thought I'd faint right there in his arms."

Amy touched Franny's cheek. "I'm so glad you've come to your senses."

"If it weren't for you, I'd be in a mess."

"Try not to worry, Miss Amy," Mae said. "Your papa's eyes might yet open. I'll be sure to make food that man will hate. It'll put him in a bad mood, and then everyone will see how awful a person he really is."

Franny stood. "Good idea, Mae. And I'll do my best to make his time here miserable. I don't know how yet, but I'll do it. You can count on Landon too." She picked up her pile of clothes and left for her mother's room.

Amy wiped her eyes with Franny's handkerchief. "Mae, it isn't a sin to disobey my father's wishes if what he asks me to do is wrong, is it?"

Gingerly, Mae gathered the rest of Franny's nightgowns in her arms. "I believe the commandment is referring to children, Miss Amy. You've given honor to your papa all your life. God knows your heart. He's brought you to an age where you can decide for yourself."

"I'm struggling, Mae."

"All I know, Miss Amy, is you got to follow the higher authority."

A shadow crossed the threshold, and in stepped Landon. His cheeks were flushed and his boots dusty from a hard ride. He took off his hat, and when she stood, he took her hands.

"Cousin Amy, I've just come back after having a conversation with Rory Maguire. I know all about Uncle turning him down. He told me how he proposed to you, how you've known each other before the war and have been meeting in secret. I've got to say, you're braver than I thought."

"Don't tell my father," she said, her eyes wide.

"No worries on that score. I feel for you and Rory. You love him?"

"Yes, with all my heart."

"Then you've got to do the right thing. Don't marry that fool Montague. He's no good, and I don't care what he's promised. I've heard enough about him to know he won't follow through. If you marry him, he'll take your pa on a wild goose chase—he'll take everything he owns."

"Papa is facing ruin. What should I do?"

"Marry Rory. If Linden Grove falls, it's not your fault."

"Will you help us?"

"You know I will. Here, Rory gave me a note to give you. And don't you worry about your pa. I'm going to get proof so he'll regret ever considering Montague's offer."

She looked down at the note and back at Landon. "What about you and Franny?"

"Oh, Franny and I will be all right. I'm going to marry that girl when all this cools down. While you were seeing Rory, Franny and I were taking our own clandestine walks."

She leaned up and kissed his cheek. "Thank you." Then she opened the note.

Rory wanted her to wait for him. He'd be there at the stroke of eight when the house would be shrouded in misty darkness. He'd come to her window. He'd toss a pebble at the glass, signaling his arrival. He'd take her away—marry her—if she still wanted him. He understood the risk. He knew what she'd be giving up. Her family. Her home.

I cannot ask you to sacrifice so much. But I will still be there, waiting for an answer.
Landon touched her hand. "I know what he wrote."

"Montague is coming at nine." Rory's letter trembled in Amy's hand.

A sly smile crept over Landon's face. He picked up his hat and stepped to the door. "Don't worry, Amy. I'll go to Rory. Can I tell him you'll be waiting for him?"

"To elope. . ." Amy sighed. "Yes, tell him. And tell him Montague is coming."

"Rory can be here earlier."

"Not when it is still light out."

"That's true. It's a great risk of discovery. Nevertheless, he'll be here."

"I'll refuse to go downstairs. I'll say I have a headache."

"Even if your father insists you join us, I'll find a way of getting you out of the room."

Amy smiled. "I couldn't have asked for a better watchman than you, Landon."

"I know you'd do the same for Franny and me. For now, plan to be at the window at nightfall."

"Nothing would be more romantic than that!" said Franny coming into the room. "Do it, Amy. And here, take Mother's necklace, the one she wore the day she and Papa eloped."

She put it around Amy's neck, and Amy tucked it under her lace collar. She didn't dare let her father see it. He'd know what she was up to. She thought about her parents' elopement and wondered why he would think it any different from what she and Rory were about to do. No one had ever talked about it. All she knew was that her mother had also been a runaway bride.

Chapter 8

Secretly, Mae packed a basket of food and slipped it into Amy's room. "There, child. Do you have everything you need? You got enough clothes packed, and money?"

"I think so, Mae. I'm not worried. Rory will take care of me." She lit a candle and set it on the windowsill. The glass sparkled and reflected the flame for Rory to see. The moon had come out, full and bright, and the sky was spangled with stars.

Mae leaned over the sill and looked down. "How you gonna get down there?"

"The rose trellis."

Mae put her hand to her cheek. "It's a long way. Mr. Rory will catch you if you fall though."

"I've climbed down that trellis a dozen times." Amy pulled the curtains further back. "Where is Papa? Do you know?"

"He's in his study. I peeked in, and he was snoring in his chair."

Amy glanced at the clock on her mantel. "It will be a while yet before dinner. So he'll sleep before Mr. Montague comes as long as the house is quiet."

Mae nodded. "And if Mr. Montague arrives early, I'll distract them both."

"And Franny and Landon, where are they?"

"In the sitting room."

"You best go, Mae. If Papa does wake up and finds you here, he might think I'm planning something."

"Can I kiss you before I go?"

Amy hurried to Mae and placed her arms around her, and they kissed each other's cheek.

"Godspeed, Miss Amy."

"I will write as soon as I can. Now go ahead, and try not to worry."

Mae, looking reluctant, slipped out the door and quietly shut it. Amy returned to the window. The hour grew late. The moon higher. She bit her lower lip in woeful haste and impatient love, despairing that Rory might not come for her.

Out on the lawn, under the great oak tree that had been there a hundred years, a horse and rider rode beneath the lower branches. Amy's heart pounded as he drew near. She pushed the window open and leaned out. The rider brought the horse under the window, looked up, and in a low voice, called her name.

"No need to throw pebbles. I'm here," she said to him in a hush.

In the moonlight, Rory smiled and swept off his hat. "Amy, you wear white tonight."

"So you can see me in the moonlight."

"You look like a lady of King Arthur's day."

She leaned out a bit more. "How so?"

"Your hair over your shoulder, your face touched by the moon."

"You mean to woo me, Rory?"

"I do."

"But there is no need. I knew you'd come for me. I am ready to come down to you."

"And risk so much? I'm unworthy of you, Amy."

"I risk more if I do not come down."

He dismounted. "Down that rickety trellis?"

"I have your arms to catch me if I slip and fall, don't I?"

He held them up to her and motioned for her to come. She turned back and grabbed her bag and the basket, dropped them, and they landed beside him. She hiked up her skirts and swung her leg over the sill, then the other. She turned to face the window and slowly lowered herself down until her feet touched one of the rungs of the trellis. The ivy brushed against her as she scooted down. The trellis quivered but held tight against the bricks of the house. Her dress caught, tore, and she yanked it free.

"Be careful, my love," Rory whispered to her.

She looked down and saw his arms were still out to her. When she reached him, enough for him to touch her, she dropped down and Rory caught her. Setting her down, he took up her hands, warm and moist from the descent, and kissed each palm and her delicate wrists.

"You're not afraid of Regency, are you?"

"Put me on him, Rory, and I'll prove to you I'm not."

He lifted her into the saddle. Regency shifted, and a low grunt came from his throat.

Rory climbed up behind Amy, brought the reins over her head, and moved her close against his chest. He turned the horse and slowly walked him across the dewy grass, out to the pillars and the road beyond. The path glowed with moonlight. Spears of it shot through the trees. Amy looked back at the house and saw the candle in her window had been blown out.

Rory pulled Regency to the side of the road and turned the horse under the trees. "A horse is coming up behind us."

Anxious and afraid, Amy cried, "Hide us, Rory."

"And be a coward? No, my love. We'll face them together. I won't let them take you back."

She laid her head against his shoulder. "Hold me close."

A horse came charging around the corner, the rider's legs flying out from its sides. The horse skidded and reared, and when the rider drew off his floppy hat, Amy and Rory saw it was Landon.

"Glad I caught up. You need a witness."

"Landon!" Amy cried.

"I slipped out while your father was asleep. We best make haste to the minister before he finds you're gone and comes after you."

The minister's house was not but a mile from where they were. Rory pushed his horse into a gallop, and Landon rode alongside. They followed the road above the falls until they reached the parson's house that stood near the old stone church. Rory and Landon dismounted and secured their horses to the fence. Rory reached up and brought Amy down. He looked into her face and said, "I've never been surer of anything in my life. Are you?"

"Yes," she said. "Never surer."

With Landon and Amy beside him, Rory lifted the parson's doorknocker. Presently the door opened, and with candle in hand, the parson looked out. His fingers, so apparently aged and suffering from rheumatism, shoved his spectacles against his nose. "Is someone dying and in need of comfort?"

"Not dying, sir," Rory said. "We are in need of a parson to marry us. Will you give our hearts ease?"

The parson, dressed in rusty black, drew the door wider and motioned for them to come inside. He raised the candle higher. "Why, it is Amy Fairbourne, is it not?"

"Yes, sir." Amy felt her face turn scarlet.

"You are eloping with this man?"

"I am."

"Rory Maguire, sir." Rory held his hand out to the parson, who shook it. "And this is Mr. Landon Fairbourne. He is our witness."

The parson nodded to Landon, then looked at Rory with pinched eyebrows. "Maguire? You hail from the Maguires of Shenandoah?"

"I do, sir. You know our farm?"

"Indeed. A well-respected and wealthy family, the Maguires. Your father should be very pleased, Miss Amy. Does he know?"

"He knows we wish to marry, that is all," replied Amy.

Rory dug into his pocket. "I've the fee, sir."

The parson smiled and raised his hand. "A small one, so come into the next room, and I'll call my wife."

Amy could not keep her eyes lifted to the parson's. He'd known her since coming to their parish years ago, and here she was standing before him as a runaway bride. Rory asked that they lose no time, for no one knew how long before Montague and Amy's father would ride out after them.

The parson's wife came to his side. The parson opened his book of prayers and spoke softly to the couple of the importance of matrimony, how sacred it was, and how God the Father had declared it from the time in the garden. " 'For this cause shall a man leave his father and mother and cleave to his wife,' " he read.

And so, Amy and Rory were wed, there in the small parsonage along the Great Falls of the Potomac. Rory slipped a gold band over Amy's finger upon the parson's word. Then the good man raised his hand and blessed them.

Chapter 9

When Amy first glimpsed Shenandoah Oaks, it proved to be more than she had imagined. The house, painted a gleaming white, stood atop a slope of rich green grass beneath a full moon. Each mullioned window had black shutters. The front door was wider than Linden Grove's, with a beveled glass arch above it and brass figures gracing it. Oaks lined the long drive, and their shadows spread over the ochre drive from one side to the other. Moonlight glimmered through their branches.

As Amy and Rory rode in, the horse at a walk, birds fluttered from the trees. A Guernsey cow grazed nearby, and a foxhound loafed on the front porch. Rory whistled, and the dog lifted its head, pricked its ears, and then bounded down the steps. It raced up to them with its tail going a mile a minute as it leaped around Regency.

"Jack, you're glad to see your master?" Rory asked. "Wait until you meet your mistress."

Rory helped Amy down from his horse. The dog settled, and she bent down to him. He rubbed his nose across her hand.

"He likes you, Amy."

"He's wonderful. . .so much like General. How old is he?"

"I'm not sure. He was a stray I found after Gettysburg. He's been with me ever since."

"I adore him. May I have a cat of my own?"

"And a horse. We've a litter of kittens in the barn."

"I must see them!"

"Later." He grabbed her hand and led her up the steps. "You like the house?"

"It's not what I expected."

"You're disappointed."

She smiled and threw her arms around his neck. "No, it's beautiful, Rory, especially in the moonlight. Why didn't you tell me?"

"I tried, but I'm not so good at describing the place. It was a bit war-worn and needed fixing up. Come on. I'll take you inside, but I've got to carry you over the threshold."

Rory swept her up in his arms. "There are no servants to greet us."

"None? Not even a housekeeper?"

"It's just you and me. That is, until we hire a cook and housemaid. It'll be easily done. There are many folks who need work."

"Can we afford staff?"

"You really have no idea how well off I am, do you? I'll show you, but not today. There are other things more important than looking over account books and bank papers."

She smiled and ran her hand over his cheek. "Indeed, I would say so."

He reached the door and pushed it open. But just as he stepped over the threshold with Amy in his arms, a carriage rumbled over the drive toward them. He turned. "Who could that be?" he said. When it drew closer, they both knew.

"Dear me," Amy said. "It's Chester Montague." She looked at Rory's troubled face. "Maybe he means no harm. Maybe something is wrong at Linden Grove and he's come to tell us."

"If that were the case, it would be Landon coming on horseback."

"You best put me down."

And so Rory complied and waited at the edge of his porch. The carriage pulled to a stop, and immediately Montague stepped out. He looked up at Rory and Amy, tugged at his waistcoat, and set his lips.

"Mr. Montague. What a surprise. What brings you to Shenandoah Oaks?" Amy listened carefully to her husband's greeting with relief. He showed no anger, no willingness to throw the man off his property. He made her proud, and she drew up beside him.

Montague heaved a breath. "Don't you know, Maguire?"

Rory shook his head. "No, I really don't." He turned to Amy. "You know my wife, Amy. We are newly married."

"I know that!" spat Montague. "That's why I'm here. How could you do this, Miss Amy? You've let everyone down, including your poor father, who is at his wits' end."

"I know I've disappointed him, sir," she said. "But I don't see why it is any concern of yours, unless you've come to congratulate us."

Montague huffed. "I shall not. I offered you matrimony, and you ran away with this, this rebel. How could you choose him over me? I was about to secure your father's estate."

"Would you like to come inside and have some refreshment?" she said. "That is, if it is all right with you, Rory."

Rory smiled at her, but Montague frowned. "No," he snapped. "I'll be on my way, but not before I have satisfaction."

With his eyes fixed on Rory, Montague drew off his coat and threw it aside. He rolled up his sleeves. "Come on, Maguire." He circled his fists. "Get down here."

"You really don't want to fight me, Mr. Montague."

"Oh, I do, Maguire. I really do." Montague continued to circle his fists. He boxed the air and blew out between his ruddy lips. "Come on, let's do this like men."

"It's pointless," Rory said. "Amy and I are married. I'll not allow my wife to be subject to this." He turned to look at her. Amy shrugged.

Montague, growing enraged, bent down and picked up a clod of dirt. He threw it, and it smacked Rory in the chest. Jack barked, and Rory commanded him to stand down. The gauntlet was thrown. Rory bounded down the stairs. Montague swung his fists. Rory dodged each attempt to hit him.

Finally, Rory gave Montague a right hook across the jaw. Montague fell, dazed by the blow, and blinked up at him. He scrambled to his feet and charged Rory. Rory sidestepped and picked up the bucket of water he had left his dog and poured it over Montague's head. Doused, Montague sputtered and veered.

"Sorry, Chester. I had to do it to cool you off. You sure you don't want that drink my wife offered?"

Amy slapped her hand over her mouth and muffled a giggle. Rory picked up Montague's coat and handed it to him. "Now that that is settled, let's be neighbors at least. Let bygones be bygones."

Montague snatched back his coat and climbed into his creaky carriage, his lips moving with words Amy could not hear. The driver cracked his whip, and off the horses charged, the wheels spewing rusty dust into the air.

However, that was not the end of visitors arriving at Shenandoah Oaks. The moment Montague's carriage passed out of view, a trap pulled by a gray donkey and a man on horseback could be seen coming down the road. Amy set her hand above her eyes.

"Mercy me," she said to Rory. "It's my Papa and Franny, and Landon riding beside them." She lowered her hand and took Rory's arm. "Landon and Franny approve. But Papa?" She looked up into Rory's face. His eyes were fixed in a hopeful gaze.

He pulled her close. "If your sister and Landon are bringing him, then rest assured, they've changed his mind."

The foxhound cantered down the road and stopped. He stood with his legs wide apart and howled. Yet his tail wagged like a flag of greeting. As the trap rambled closer, he trotted alongside it.

Franny waved. "Amy!"

Amy lifted her hem and went down the steps to meet them. Franny jumped out and hugged her, then showed Amy an engagement bracelet. "Papa consented. We're engaged." Landon dismounted and held his horse's bridle. But Amy's father remained seated, his face drawn and pale.

Amy stood at the side of the trap. "Papa?"

He could not look at her.

"Do you forgive me for hurting you?" she asked.

He failed to speak.

"Have you come to tell me you've disowned me?"

He looked at her, and his eyes filled. "Disown you, child? I've been a foolish old man. I have asked God, but I need your forgiveness also. Will you give it?"

She held her arms out to him. He climbed down and embraced her. Then he drew from his coat a paper and unfolded it.

"You see this? Landon gave it to me." He looked up at Rory. "It is from you, sir, explaining the evils Montague has done. It was enough to persuade me that I was sorely in the wrong. I ask your pardon that I did not give you permission to wed my daughter. It was out of selfish reasons, and I was ignorant of Montague's ways. I believed I would lose Linden Grove and live the rest of my life in poverty. Montague is rich. He promised to not allow that to happen if he married one of my girls. It may not solve any ire you have toward me, but I give you and Amy my apology with a full heart."

"Oh Papa." Amy kissed his cheek.

He put his arms around her. "I was wrong, Amy. Forgive me for pressuring you the way I did."

"I do forgive you, Papa."

"All these years I put you last." He looked at her. It broke Amy's heart to see tears in his eyes. "I don't know why I have favored Franny."

"She is the baby, Papa."

"The youngest, yes, but a grown woman. I should have treated you equally. I spoiled Franny. I was angry when your mother left me with two girls to raise on my own, and you, being the spit and image of her, have been a constant reminder of her. Do I need to say more?"

Amy shook her head and could not reply. His words hurt her, but she finally knew why he had been so quick to be rid of her, to take a man's money to keep his home, and to give her sister anything she wished. Indeed, she looked like her mother. The same color hair. The same large bright eyes. She'd been told that her voice resembled her mother's. She was the firstborn but the last to be considered. She looked into her father's face and finally found the words to speak.

"What changed your mind, Papa? There is more to this than what you are telling us."

He picked up her hands. "When I realized you had gone, and how I had treated you, my transgression forced me to my knees. My heart was convicted by a higher authority. I am sorry."

Rory held out his hand to his father-in-law, and the two men shook. "Well, sir, Amy once told me your late wife said there is a silver lining to every cloud. Let us go into the house and celebrate."

Silver moonlight fanned through the oaks. As one family, they went through the broad door into the cool of the house that now belonged to Amy Maguire. Out in the field, the Guernsey lowed. The foxhound bayed somewhere he had run off to, and a mockingbird sang sweetly as Amy—the runaway bride—closed the door.

Rita Gerlach lives in central Maryland with her husband and two sons. She is a best-selling author of eight inspirational historical novels, including the Daughters of the Potomac series of which *RT Book Reviews* said, "Creating characters with intense realism and compassion is one of Gerlach's gifts."

Legacy of Love

by Terri J. Haynes

Chapter 1

Delia McClure strolled down Washington Street praying no one would ask where she was headed. If it were spring, the trees would be full of leaves, but in January they provided her no concealment. She carried her basket close to her body like a shield. In a way it was. No one would think it strange that she was out with a basket. As her father's assistant at McClure's General Store, she was doing what was normal, delivering her famous lotion to eager customers. But if someone watched her a little longer, saw her turn from the homes of Burtonsville's elite black residents, it would be clear that her trip took her away from that world. From a world of fine houses and well-turned-out citizens to a less fortunate neighborhood of Burtonsville. The needier one, the Farms.

The neighborhood had been given its name from the farmlands that were once located there. But after the war, many of the plantations had been abandoned, and newly freed blacks built shanties there. Her parents had once lived in the Farms. Her faded memories of that time were happy. She remembered summer days wandering the green fields around their home, amazed at her newfound freedom. It was like a dream, gaining a real childhood after slavery. A good dream before Mama died. The Farms was certainly not like it was then.

The houses lining the street took a sharp decline in quality as she turned the corner of Washington and Park. From brick homes to structures too battered to be called houses. The smell shifted from the hint of chimney smoke to the smell of rancid garbage. The noise changed too. From the calming clatter of coaches to shouts, cries, and demands. Delia kept her head high. Her gray work dress and her black cloak blended perfectly with the depressed mood of her destination. *Maybe I should have worn something brighter.* But if she had, the differences in her wealth and that of the residents of the Farms would be even more obvious.

She arrived at a two-story house with rotted window frames and rusted door hinges. She knocked. The sound echoed through the near-empty house. Two sets of footsteps approached the door. It opened, and two girls wearing faded yellow dresses smiled at her.

"Miss Delia!" The sunlight caught their smiles and warmed their skin to a glow. They bounced on their toes, bubbling with excitement.

"Hello, girls." Their joy lifted her mood. She touched the older girl's hair and then the younger girl as they moved aside to let her enter. "Is your mother sleeping?"

The older girl, Dot, nodded. "Yes, and the baby."

"Let's not wake them." Delia walked to the scuffed but clean table. "I brought the lotion she requested." She lifted two jars of lotion and a few sweets from the basket. "Tell her she can pay me when the baby is old enough to visit me at the shop."

"Yes, ma'am," the girls replied in unison. The younger, Annie, eyed the sweets.

Delia handed one to her. "You can have one now, but no more until after dinner."

"Tank you." Annie took the candy with a grin that revealed a missing tooth.

Dot looked up at her with a serious look. "Mama said to tell you about the stovepipe."

Annie nodded. "It's like this." The little girl leaned to one side, nearly toppling over. " 'Specially when the wind comes."

Delia laughed. "Let me look at it." At first glance, she saw the problem. The pipe had begun to separate from the wall. The screw in the bracket securing it to the wall had loosened. The wall it was attached to had crumbled. She frowned. To think that people had to pay to live in such conditions. She shook her head and focused on the repair. It was an easy fix, but she didn't have her tools with her. She hadn't brought them, because if she was spotted with them, they would broadcast what she was about.

I'll have to improvise. She turned to the girls. "Do you have an old knife?"

Dot nodded and fetched it for her. "Mama doesn't really use it."

Delia looked at the knife and made a funny face. "I see why. It's so dull it couldn't cut water." Both girls giggled.

Delia moved around the side of the pipe, holding her hand near it. Cold. Mrs. Thompson was probably saving her coal for colder days. Delia put on a bright face and beckoned to Dot. "How about you help me fix it?" The girl's eyes brightened. "Always check to see if it is hot first. You don't want to get burned."

Dot nodded. Delia helped Dot put the knife's dull point into the head of the screw. In two good turns, she had the pipe reconnected to the wall. Delia smiled at Dot, and the girl beamed, proud of her work. "If it loosens again, you can fix it yourself."

"You got your pretty dress dirty." Annie brushed Delia's dress.

She looked down and saw the black smudge down the length of the dress's skirt. "It's not too bad," Delia said. But the little girl's attempt had helped to blend the soot into the gray of the dress. "I must go. If your mother needs anything else, tell her to send you to the shop."

Another chorus of "Yes, ma'am."

Delia gave them each a brief hug. "Be well."

Delia stood outside the door for a moment eyeing the other houses and thought of all the other families like the Thompsons who could use some grace.

Mrs. Thompson had a hard time with her new baby. Little Mary Thompson had the worse dry skin. Sometimes it would crack and bleed. Delia had brought the lotion knowing the Thompsons couldn't pay for it. But they needed it, and one or two jars missing from the shop wouldn't hurt. It would hurt the Thompsons more not to have it. It would be one more care on their shoulders. She didn't expect them ever to pay her back, but the only way to get them to accept her help was to make them think they could pay off their debt at a later date.

Delia always set the terms so that no payments would be made for a year. Then she would close out the person's account before the year was over. So when they came to pay, she would tell them that the year's account was closed and offer to start them a new one. Several families had "accounts" with her. They never charged expensive items, making it easier for Delia to conceal the losses from her father.

It wasn't as if the families weren't trying to better their lives. Mr. Thompson had taken a job at the docks in Lexington to support his growing family. Most nights he couldn't come home because it would require him to travel in the middle of the night. The troops in Lexington had helped to decrease the number of attacks, but no black person wanted to risk meeting hooded men in the dark. Or the day. Now that the elections had passed, the attacks decreased, but the political uncertainty gave blacks pause. No one was exempt from the danger, rich or poor. Because of it, the air in Burtonsville always held a hint of watchfulness and worry.

Delia used the basket to hide the smudge on her dress. She would have to change into a nicer one when she got back to the shop. Daddy didn't like for her to wear her work dresses in view of customers. He said they didn't reflect the quality of service that McClure's General Store offered. He was right, of course. Their customers loved the goods they purchased, many of them things Delia had created in her backroom workshop out of odd, unsalable, and often broken items. But they didn't want to see the "ugly" side of her work. Her life would be so much easier if she could wear her work dress all day. But Daddy had his rules, and she followed them.

She greeted other pedestrians on the sidewalk as she made her way back to the shop. Several ladies she passed asked if she'd made another batch of lotion and inquired about other items. Delia was careful to answer each question and end the conversation with an invitation to come into the store. Daddy suggested the tactic, and it worked. Often people didn't think they needed something until they saw it on the shelf.

As she passed the storefront windows, she saw her little sister, Olive, and her father serving customers. Two ladies examined a bolt of silk and another eyed Delia's lotion. The lotion was an accidental creation. She had been making biscuits. The shortening coated her hands, and it took her several washes to get it all off. That's when inspiration hit. She mixed shortening with lanolin and lavender. Her first batch sold out immediately. Daddy allowed her a great deal of freedom with her creations because of it. He was waiting for the next great sales item.

And I may have it if I could only spend the rest of the day in my workshop. The project on her table, a drying wheel, had come to her when Daddy purchased a serving cart that had arrived broken. Delia had tried to fix it but couldn't. So she did the next best thing. She took it apart and worked to turn the pieces into something else. She imagined a vertical pulley system on the wheel that someone could hang small garments on and set in front of a fireplace. Once set in motion, the wheel would spin and the clothes would dry evenly.

She went through the back door of the shop that led to her workroom, sure no one would miss her. But as soon as she hung her cloak on the rack placed near the door, her father walked into the workroom.

"Where have you been?" His tone told her he already knew.

"Making a delivery to a customer."

"A paying customer?"

Delia looked down at the wheel in front of her. "Yes." But then in a lower tone, "Eventually."

Her father huffed. "How many times do I have to tell you that we are not a charity?"

"They will pay. They can't pay right now. And it was only two jars of lotion."

"You defied me and went into the Farms?" He pointed at her dress. "And you come out dirty like they are. You are not like them, Delia."

"I am like them. They have needs and hurts, the same as I do."

He dropped his shoulders. "I've been trying to be patient, but I will not let you run this store into the ground like your mother nearly did."

Delia sucked in a breath. "I won't. I promise. This store is our livelihood."

He eyed her. "No, you won't."

The bell over the door sounded. He looked over his shoulder and then back at her. "Get cleaned up and come help customers."

She dared not make eye contact with him. "Yes, Daddy."

Josiah Searcy smiled as he watched Mr. Abbott shake hands with Shadow's new owner. Another successful sale, which meant a little extra money for Josiah. He needed every cent he could get with the rent due today. Mr. Abbott wore a wide grin, his skin already pink from standing in the sun with the buyer, as he walked back into the stables. Josiah started to clean the stall that Shadow had occupied.

Mr. Abbott clapped him on the back. "Nice work, Josiah."

Josiah nodded. He would not show his pride in front of Mr. Abbott in case his employer would think that his black horseman was getting above himself, but inside he hummed. It had taken many hours to train Shadow and prepare him for sale. The horse's dark coat had shone like it was wet as Josiah had walked him out to the corral. And Shadow had walked out with his head held high—after a little coaching from Josiah.

"Stand proud. You are a fine animal," Josiah had whispered to the horse. That was all the encouragement Shadow needed.

"Mr. Downs said he's never seen a more majestic horse." Mr. Abbott reached into his pocket for the pouch of coins. "As promised, here is your bonus."

Josiah bounced the bag in his hand as he calculated how much he would have left over after paying the rent and buying a little food. He'd buy his sister, Grace, a new pair of shoes. She had started working at a fine house nearby. She was on her feet all day and needed better shoes. The remainder he'd save in the jar under his bed.

And for once, he had more than enough. *God, let Mr. Downs show Shadow off all over Burtonsville.* One look at Shadow and all the well-to-do men would want fine horses too. Especially ones like Mr. Downs. The man was one of the first black lawyers in Burtonsville and made a nice living. He was one of the richer members of higher black society, educated men and women with homes and jobs, not struggling from month to month like he was. Josiah didn't care for the elites, and they didn't care for him. Except one.

He smiled as he took his hat down off the rack. Delia McClure had been a friend for a long time. When he and his sister had arrived in Burtonsville, Delia was one of the first people to welcome them. In five minutes, she had extracted their family history from him. A history Josiah had to leave behind if he wanted to survive the heartbreak. Even more so, if he wanted his sister to survive. He had watched her slowly withdraw from the world in the months after their parents died and their situation grew more difficult. He had struggled to find work to support them both. Grace had stopped smiling and then stopped talking more than what was necessary.

His mother had made him promise that he would take care of his sister and himself. That was a promise he was determined to keep. After five years, it was clear that moving away from South Carolina was the best thing for his sister. With what little money they had, he got them to Burtonsville but no further. A good choice it turned out.

To Josiah's amazement, Delia had pulled his sister out of her quietness in that first meeting. Delia had recommended a place for them to stay and had escorted them to make a personal introduction to the owners of the boardinghouse. Before she departed, Delia had managed to make his sister smile, and Josiah had taken that as a sign that they were in the right place. As he got to know Delia better, he was sure he was in the right place. Delia was the smartest, most caring, and beautiful friend he'd ever had. Most men didn't have friends like Delia. *That's because they have wives like Delia.*

Josiah pushed that thought away as he walked down Main Street to McClure's General Store. He looked in the windows of each business he passed. The butcher held his attention the longest. He would check the cost of a cheap cut tomorrow after work. But now he needed to get to McClure's before they closed. As he passed the front window to enter, he saw Delia working alone on the sales floor. She wore a vibrant green dress with a wide cream belt. A dress his sister Grace would love to have. One that Delia could afford but Josiah couldn't. Not yet.

The bell over the door chimed as he opened it. Delia looked up and gave him the brightest smile. Oh to see that smile every day. "Good evening, Delia."

"Good evening, Josiah." She moved from behind the counter. "You look extra happy tonight."

"Shadow sold."

Delia clapped her hands. "Congratulations."

Josiah soaked in her happiness. Mr. Abbott's praise stemmed from the money he'd made. Delia's praise, that was sweeter. "Just in time too. Rent is due. But I need to get Grace some new work shoes. Hers are coming undone at the soles."

Delia motioned him to the other side of the store, although she didn't have to. Josiah had spent many evenings there and could find everything he needed himself. Delia moved gracefully to the stacks of boxes, lifted one, and opened it. "How about these?"

They were not the fancier shoes that Delia wore, but they looked comfortable and sensible. "How much?"

Delia tipped her head and gave him a sly grin. "How much do you have?"

He let out a chuckle. "Delia."

"One dollar and twenty-five cents."

He gave her a narrowed look. The shoes weren't pretty, but he was sure they cost more than that. "One dollar and twenty-five cents?"

"Yes."

He looked down at the shoes again. "How much do you normally sell them for?"

She shifted. "They are normally two seventy-five, but they are on sale for you."

"I can pay full price."

She placed the lid on the box. "Then pay me later."

He shook his head. "If you keep putting things on sale, the shop will go out of business."

Delia stiffened. "If you want to pay full price, fine." She turned in a huff and tromped to her workroom.

Josiah followed her, calling her name, but she kept walking. He caught up with her at the large table in the middle of the room. "I was only jesting," he said, trying to make eye contact. When he did, he saw tears shimmering in her eyes. "I'm sorry." His heart twisted in a painful knot, knowing he'd hurt her.

She brushed a falling tear from her cheek. "It's not you. Daddy said the same thing to me earlier." She sniffled. "Except he wasn't joking."

"I'm sure he doesn't mean it."

"I'm sure he does. He wants me to stop helping—" She shook her head and turned to the table. "Would you like to see my latest creation?"

He laughed at her. Nothing kept Delia down for long. "Yes."

She arranged the pieces on the table and explained how her drying wheel would work. As always, Josiah was amazed. How she could dream up these things, he could never imagine. He stayed and listened to her until every trace of her tears was gone.

Chapter 2

Almost every seat in Burtonsville Christian Church was filled. Delia scanned the crowd as she navigated down the aisle. She and Grace had gotten a late start with Daddy wanting them to prep the sales floor before they left for church. He only joined them at church when it would further his business. Money had been his idol since slavery ended, and in a way he gave thanks on Sunday by opening the shop.

Most shops closed on Sunday, but Daddy had taken up the practice of opening the shop on Sundays shortly after he'd launched the store. Mama had argued against it although there was an advantage to being the only shop open on Sunday. The residents of Burtonsville had frowned on it at first. Daddy's position was that he was free. Free to open his shop whenever he pleased. Eventually it became more acceptable. It had been a hard battle to get him to allow the girls to come to church and not work. Delia had finally won him over by mentioning that they could direct business to the shop while at church, although they never actually did.

Her eye caught movement near the left front of the church.

Olive tugged her arm. "Josiah and Grace have empty places next to them."

When Delia made eye contact with Josiah, he smiled and motioned to her. They had to squeeze down the row to get to him, but there was just enough space for her and Olive. Olive moved past Delia to sit next to Grace, leaving Delia to sit next to Josiah.

"Thank you," she said as she removed her bonnet.

"I thought you might be coming today, so I saved you a seat." He shifted in the seat to make room for her.

The first tones of the opening hymn sounded, and the congregation stood. Josiah had to turn slightly to face her. She tried to lean forward to give him more space but only succeeded in getting closer to him. His shirt smelled of outdoors, the way clothes smelled when they were dried on a clothesline. *For someone who works with horses, he sure doesn't smell like one. As a matter of fact, he never smells like one.*

She looked up at him. "Sorry."

He shrugged. "It's okay."

They sang through the hymn and then sat. Josiah sat first, bracing his arm on the back of the pew. She sat and found herself almost enveloped in his arms and close enough to feel the warmth from his chest. He shifted again but without much success for creating space between them. This is cozy, she thought, and suppressed a giggle.

Reverend Davenport climbed the stairs to the pulpit. "We have special guests visiting us today." He motioned to an older couple sitting in the first row. "Reverend and Mrs. Pell, my wife's family, are here from the West. I would like for them to give you their greeting."

The couple stood, Reverend Pell helping his wife to her feet. At the podium, he smiled wide, and the resemblance to Mrs. Davenport was clear. "I am very blessed to join you all today. We are visiting from Kansas where we have a small congregation."

Mrs. Pell smiled. "We would like to read a letter to you from one of our congregants." She unfolded a piece of paper and began to read. As she did, the congregation grew still. Every single person had heard about the land west and the promise of owning some of it. The promise seemed like a fanciful tale. But now they had the opportunity to hear from someone who had been there.

And the letter did not disappoint. The writer, a Mr. Cobb, gave a brief but detailed account of life in Kansas. He spoke of the hard work required to make a living there, but he also spoke of the beauty of the land. The wide open spaces. The freedom from segregation and oppression. An opportunity to make a life for oneself. The letter ended with an invitation to anyone who wanted to come.

Delia found herself holding her breath as Mrs. Pell read. A life of her own. An opportunity to be a part of founding a new state. Those who moved to Kansas were like firstfruits. She leaned forward so as not to miss a word and found Josiah also leaning forward. He glanced at her, a look of curiosity in his eyes. Could he be interested in Kansas too?

Reverend Pell scanned the crowd. "I can confirm that everything you just heard is true. There are several all-black towns in Kansas, and the government is truly giving away land. My wife and I will return home in several months and welcome anyone who is interested to talk to us."

As the Pells returned to their seats, a low rumble of many conversations filled the air.

Josiah sat back. "Free land. A chance to start over."

"It sounds too good to be true." Delia sat back too, nearly leaning against his chest.

"But I don't think Reverend Davenport would let them deceive us. They are his wife's parents, after all. Besides, they live in Kansas."

Delia nodded, her thoughts in a jumble.

Before they could continue their conversation, Reverend Davenport moved on to the next part of the service. But Delia didn't hear much of what he said or his sermon. She was sure Josiah didn't either. Living in Kentucky had not been as peaceful or easy as many former slaves expected. Yes, some like her father and his friend Mr. Hall did well in the years after slavery, but many found it hard to find jobs. They turned to sharecropping, which increased their poverty. Or they took low-paying jobs because that was all that was offered. Not to mention the restrictive rules imposed on blacks after the war. It was almost like slavery all over again.

But a chance to be free. It did sound like a dream. To be able to live without the Black Codes, midnight visits, and violence. And all-black towns. Delia smiled at the thought. There they could take care of the poor children better than they did in Burtonsville. The community would struggle together and not pick who would prosper and who wouldn't.

The closing hymn began, and Delia stood, surprised that she had missed the rest of the service while she was consumed by her thoughts. As soon as the song ended, half the congregation rushed to the Pells.

"I would love to talk to them," Josiah said.

"Me too, but I have to get back to the shop soon." Delia clutched her bonnet.

Josiah grabbed her hand. "I have an idea." He threaded his way through the row to the side aisle. Hurrying up it, they found themselves standing behind the Pells.

At the first break in the line in front of them, Josiah tapped Reverend Pell on the shoulder. "Reverend."

The man turned and gave them a wide smile. "Hello."

"That letter was truly fascinating," Delia said, and Josiah nodded. "Kansas sounds wonderful."

"It is like the land of milk and honey in the Bible. The promised land. Lots of open land with plenty of space for a nice homestead for a couple like you. Do you have little ones?"

Josiah sputtered. "Delia—" He coughed. "Miss Delia is my friend."

Reverend Pell raised one eyebrow. "Are you two planning to change that? I haven't performed a wedding in our new town yet. I would be honored to make you two the first."

Delia tried to laugh, but somehow it got stuck in her throat. She and Josiah. . . "We are not a couple. We are both interested in the land in Kansas."

Reverend Pell studied them a moment longer and then gave them a little more detail about the new towns forming. "All you need is a couple hundred dollars and you can own land."

Josiah frowned. "But I only make enough to support my younger sister and me."

"Where are your parents?" Reverend Pell's question was filled with compassion.

"They died shortly after the war ended. We moved from South Carolina for a better life, but we have struggled."

"The Freedman's Bureau has been giving out small sums for blacks to purchase land. I can help you apply." Reverend Pell turned to Delia, probably looking at the much finer quality of her clothing. "And what about you, young lady?"

She dipped her head. "My father owns a store here in town, and I doubt he would want to start over."

The reverend clasped her hands. "What about you?"

"Me?" she squeaked.

"What do you want, young lady?"

Delia opened her mouth and closed it again. "I—"

Mrs. Pell turned from the person she was speaking to and smiled at them. "More young people interested in moving west?"

Reverend Pell released Delia's hand. "One of them. I think the young lady needs more time to think."

Mrs. Pell patted her shoulder. "If you need to talk, please feel free to visit me. We are staying at the parsonage with my daughter."

Josiah thanked them, and as soon as they were far enough away, started talking nonstop about what a great opportunity Kansas was. Delia tried to listen, but all she heard was the reverend's question over and over in her mind. "What do you want, young lady?"

Josiah's stomach grumbled. He tried to ignore it, as usual. But hunger was his constant companion these days. Especially today, since he'd given most of his breakfast to Grace. He could stand to listen to his own stomach complain of its emptiness, but not hers. She was so young and already working. They couldn't survive if she didn't. But she wasn't used to being hungry like he was. He'd always made sure she had more than enough to eat, even if it meant he didn't have enough.

Harriet, one of his mares, ambled to the end of her stall, stretching her nose in his direction. "If I get really hungry, I'll have one of your carrots."

She nodded, as if she approved the idea. He patted her nose. "Thank you, Harriet. You've always been kind."

He prayed he wouldn't have to eat the horses' food, but there were some days that the fresh carrots and apples Mr. Abbott brought in for them tempted him sorely.

He grabbed a broom and set to work on the walkway between the stalls. The sounds of wagons clattering across the cobblestone outside Abbott's Livery and Stables echoed through the expanse of the barn. The sound of people coming and going. Of life arriving and leaving. Life beyond what he had now.

The broom felt like an iron bar. Exhaustion, hunger, and something else, something he hadn't been able to name of late, weighed his shoulders. The unidentifiable feeling had been growing strong lately and only stopped when he was around Delia.

Delia.

How nice would it be to talk to her right now. Maybe dream some more about living in Kansas, like they had on Sunday. Walk her home and listen to her chat the whole way and get lost in the sound of her voice. That was one of the things he liked about Delia. She didn't always need another person to have an interesting conversation. She never had.

He wiped his hands with a cloth and checked the street again. Delia had gotten him this job at Abbott's. Josiah still hadn't thanked her enough for that. But he tried, by listening to all her ideas, no matter how odd. And she had a lot of them. It wasn't long before he was convinced that Delia could be left in a room full of broken castoffs and she would emerge having created something new out of all of it.

He enjoyed going to McClure's—after hours, of course. He couldn't walk in the front door like he could afford to buy anything more than sweets. He would normally enter around the back of the building to get to Delia's workshop. And there she'd be, diligently putting together something she imagined. Sometimes she would be waiting for him to help her with something she wasn't strong enough to do. She made things to make others' lives better even though she had a good life herself.

He worked on cleaning the barn, his usual Thursday chore. Mr. Abbott normally gave him one day at the week's end off, but he had to finish all his work to take advantage of it. As he leaned the broom against the wall, the door squeaked behind him. He turned to find Delia stepping through the opening, carrying a basket over her arm.

She wore a blue dress trimmed in lace. Her hair was pulled up in a bun, highlighting her round face and wide eyes. His heart hitched and then pounded. He tried to smile, but the feeling in his chest confused his expression.

"Oh good. I caught you before you left." As she moved closer to him, the smell of food grew stronger. She uncovered the basket. In it was nested four pieces of chicken, two small loaves of bread, and a jar of corn. "Mrs. Morris's cook gave me food as a thank-you for an order I delivered for her." She held out the basket to him.

Food. Real food. "You're giving it to me?"

"Yes. Olive has already prepared our dinner for the night."

Josiah shook his head. "But it was for you."

"Think of it as a prize for selling Shadow."

"But this is a good bit of food."

She scowled at him. "Josiah—"

Before she could finish speaking, his stomach let out the most ferocious growl.

She cocked one eyebrow. "Your stomach is in agreement with me, so you are outnumbered. Josiah, please."

Her voice sounded like the softest breeze. He closed his eyes, his resistance to her and the food dwindling. "All right."

She grinned and handed him the basket. "Half is for you and half for Grace. But I think you should wash up and eat part of it now."

"I can wait."

"No," she said as stern as his mother would. "I know you, Josiah. You will give it all to Grace or someone else and go hungry. But you have to have some fuel to keep working. Who will take care of Grace if you can't?"

He chuckled. "You know me too well."

She took the basket. "I'll hold this while you clean up."

And as he did, she told him about her day, the customers at the shop, and the goings-on of the people in town. He listened in awe. They sat on a bench near the front of the barn. He thanked God for the food and began to eat with as much dignity as his hunger allowed him. The half-open door gave them a view of the street as a small group of soldiers passed.

Delia shook her head. "I don't think I'll ever get used to seeing that."

"Me either." He tore off another piece of bread. "But just think of what it would be like if they weren't here."

Delia hugged herself. "Things would be worse than they are." She turned to face him. "Did you hear that Mr. Coats had a late-night visit?"

The piece of bread wedged in Josiah's throat. "No. Is he—"

"He's alive, and his family, but they gave him a good beating for his trouble. I took some bandages over to them and some ointment."

They. She didn't have to name them for Josiah to know who they were. Hooded figures with torches, gliding through the shadows and arriving at someone's door in the dark of night. Even though the elections were over, the violence continued, especially against black men who had dared to vote. Josiah thought of voting day. With his heart pounding in his chest the whole way, he had cast his ballot. The troops were at his polling place, and their presence did more than provide safety. It gave him a sense of peace. "Thank God for the troops."

He closed the basket and stood. He had eaten only one piece of the chicken and half a loaf of bread. He would save the rest for their dinner if Grace hadn't managed to find something to cook. If she had, they would have it as a cold lunch tomorrow.

"Thank you for the food." Josiah set the basket beside him on the bench. "I'm sure Grace will be grateful."

She smiled. "You're welcome." She reached out and touched his hand.

His hunger was satisfied, but another kind of want played at the edge of his mind. He tamped it down. Delia was his friend. A good friend. Maybe even a friend too good for him.

He stood. "I should be going home. Grace will be waiting for me." He lifted his hat off the rack by the door. Another thing they had in common. They both loved their little sisters fiercely and would do anything for them. Josiah was committed to making sure Grace had everything she needed, and Delia was committed to making sure Olive grew up to be an intelligent woman.

As he donned his hat and coat, Harriett let out a whinny behind him. He turned to find her shaking her head and pushing against the stall door.

He walked over. "Hey, girl. It's not time to go out. I'm going home."

Harriet continued to push against the stall door. Delia joined him. "Why is she so restless?"

"She wasn't like this earlier." Josiah opened the stall and stepped inside. His presence calmed Harriet a little, but she pressed her muzzle into his shoulder.

He rubbed her mane. "What's wrong?" Harriet had been with him for over a year and hadn't had any trouble, not even when she was foaling. And even though he knew she couldn't answer with words, he quieted his own thoughts to pay attention to what she was doing. That was where the answers were. Harriet couldn't talk, but she could communicate. All it took was someone listening.

Delia reached out and rubbed Harriet's nose. "Did she eat today? Hunger makes man and beast restless."

Josiah nodded, warmed at the fact that Delia, always observing, had put her mind to figuring out what was wrong with Harriet. "She behaved fine when Mr. Abbot took her out today."

"Maybe she's tired." Delia tipped her head. "Or maybe she doesn't like the idea of leaving you."

That elicited a chuckle from Josiah. "I think she would be happy to go anywhere that treats her well."

"But no one can treat her better than you can." Delia was standing close, and the last light of the day filtered through the barn's high windows. Her big brown eyes were filled with both concern and admiration.

Josiah quickly turned his attention back to Harriet and pushed away the feeling of contentment of having Delia at his side.

Chapter 3

Conversation rumbled around Delia as she walked beside her father, surveying the room as she did. The Morrises stood off to her left talking to the Longs. Good. The two richest and most generous families in Burnsville. The Watts were already seated and waiting for the meeting to begin. She spotted the Halls, and as she did, Catherine Hall made eye contact. She pulled herself away from her father and quickly crossed the room to Delia.

Catherine greeted her with a kiss on both cheeks. "I had begun to think you weren't coming."

Delia took her friend by the hand. "I told you we would be here after we closed up the shop."

Catherine waved a hand, setting her lace embroidered sleeve swinging. "You probably did and I forgot."

Delia pulled her eyes away from the very expensive lace. "Shall we find some seats?"

As they moved near the middle of the seating area, other finery being worn stood out to Delia's eye. A string of pearls. A gold bracelet. A silk cravat. Tonight's meeting had been scheduled to discuss funding for Burtonsville's first school for colored children. If they took up a collection of all the expensive items and sold them, they would have all they needed and excess.

She took a deep breath as she lowered herself into a chair and shrugged out of her coat. *Buying expensive things isn't wrong, Delia.* She had nicer items than what she saw around her. All gifts from her father. But it felt wrong. She'd never fancied jewelry, clothes, and such. Most of her attire she purchased at Daddy's instruction. He had high standards for the McClure women's appearance. She and Olive complied even though they both preferred simpler dress.

Catherine leaned closer, smelling of rosewater. "I don't know if you've heard, but my brother has returned home."

Delia looked at her with shock. "I had not heard."

"I'm surprised my father didn't take out an ad in the papers." Her tone was sharp, not one of a woman excited about being reunited with her brother. "He should be here tonight."

"It's been some time since I've seen him."

"He's grown up and ready to assume his place by Father's side as heir apparent." She folded her hands in her lap. "Louis is all I've heard about since he graduated."

"You should be happy for him. He's accomplished a great feat. A black man with an education."

"Yes, I know. But Louis was barely tolerable when he left. He's already talking about how he's going to add class to Burtonsville. He'll be insufferable. And you should beware. He's looking for a wife, and you—"

Before she could finish, the meeting was called to order, leaving Delia wondering about Catherine's warning. There was certainly enough excitement about the school, and they had much to discuss. But the festive air cooled once the topic of funding was introduced.

Someone eased into the seat beside her. She turned to find Josiah carefully placing his hat in his lap. His hair shone, probably from him giving it a quick rinse after leaving the stables. Wet, the sun-kissed brown of his tight curls was more noticeable. There were times when Josiah was just her friend, but there were times, like this, when she was reminded that he was an attractive man. Why hasn't he married? Taking care of a wife along with his sister would be an expense, but surely some woman would take up that hardship for a gem like Josiah.

"How's Harriett?" she asked in a whisper.

"About the same. She keeps pacing the stall. I tried to take her for a walk today, but I couldn't coax her out."

"I'm sorry."

Josiah gave her a grim look, then looked forward. His jaw clenched, his habit when he was worried. She wanted to rub his jaw until the tension eased, but that would be improper. Delia forced her attention back to the meeting. The idea of an auction was proposed by Reverend Davenport and was given a good reception.

"Maybe Miss Delia can donate some of her lotion to be auctioned," Mrs. Davenport said. Several heads nodded in agreement.

"Or that shoe holder she designed," Mrs. Morris added.

Reverend Davenport eyed Delia with a smile. "Miss Delia, can we have a commitment from you?"

Delia squirmed. The lotion was no problem, but another shoe rack? She had built that from a broken wine rack that her father had gotten on the docks for pennies. She had split the rack in fours and then sold the pieces as shoe racks. She glanced around at her father, who smiled at her with pride. Another shoe rack meant constructing one from scratch.

Josiah spoke up. "I suppose that will depend on when the auction is. Everything Delia makes is done with her best craftsmanship. A process that cannot be rushed."

Delia let out a sigh. *What would I do without Josiah?* She reached over and squeezed his hand, hoping he felt her gratitude. Josiah squeezed her hand back.

"Of course, of course," Reverend Davenport said. "We will schedule the auction so she will have plenty of time."

"I would be honored to support the school," she said, regaining her voice. She took a deep breath for her next words. "I do have a question about who will attend the school."

The room stilled.

Reverend Davenport let out a nervous laugh. "Of course, the colored children of Burtonsville."

Delia gave him her brightest smile. "All the colored children in Burtonsville?" The silence around her told her that her point had been made. They had not intended for the children in the Farms to attend the school. But they must attend. Dot showed intelligence for a child with little schooling. Receiving regular instruction would help that intelligence grow even more, as it had done with Delia.

"Well. . ." Reverend Davenport started. He glanced at Mr. Pearson Hall, Louis and Catherine's father.

Mr. Pearson cleared his throat. "It is too early to know how many children the school will hold. Many of the poorer children in town work during the day. Coming to school may not be an option for them."

Delia considered what to say next. Mr. Hall was one of Daddy's oldest friends. Their closeness was formed in their drive to make something of themselves after slavery. To continue her point as she wanted would not go over well with her father.

"Is there a way to ensure a certain percentage of the students are from the Farms?" Josiah asked. A part of Delia's heart cheered but another part sank. The rich of Burtonsville would not appreciate being taken to task by a poor stable boy, even if he was right.

"As we said, we cannot make that determination right now, Mr. Searcy." Mr. Hall's sharp tone made Delia wince.

But not Josiah. He nodded like he agreed. "I think it would be wonderful if those children were to get opportunities some of us in this room never had. I sometimes imagine what my life would be like if I had been able to go to school. How much easier it would be."

If Delia's question made the room uncomfortable, Josiah using himself and his lesser state as an advocate for the poorer children made them squirm. No one dared disagree with him because they strongly disliked him for his poverty. At more than one dinner party, Delia had heard whispers about the shame of Josiah not having an education. But no one offered to sponsor him. If he could just better himself, they would say, knowing that he didn't have the means to do it.

And he hadn't done badly despite his history. He knew how to write and read. He was better at figures than Olive, who had the benefit of the tutor Daddy paid to come to the house. But what Josiah didn't have was money, and that strike against him overrode any good qualities he had.

Several people shifted in their seats, and Reverend Davenport mumbled something about giving all the children opportunities before moving to the next item on the agenda. Josiah didn't release her hand. It was as if he could feel that her heart was still racing from the tense moments. She tightened her fingers around his and balanced their interlocked fingers on his knee.

When the meeting ended, he slowly released her hand and stood. Delia did too. Soon they were surrounded by others, greeting her and asking questions about the inventory of the shop. Josiah stood just behind her, making Delia glad to have his support.

A tall, lean, handsome man soon joined the group. It took Delia a second to recognize that it was Louis Hall. It was the half-condescending look in his eye that gave him away. He had grown taller since she'd last seen him and was more attractive than before. She suspected that was going to make him even more popular than he was as a boy. If ever there was a child who was spoiled because of his looks, it was Louis.

It also didn't help that he was a charmer. Delia hadn't had a friendship with him like she had with Josiah, but when she and Louis were children playing together, she was sure to be filled with goodies the women of the town gave to him. He was kind enough to share most of the time. Other times he could be harsh and mean. He lashed out without warning and with little to no provocation. Delia, like Catherine, had been on the receiving end of Louis's sharpest jabs.

Then he had gone away to school, to Delia's relief. All the parents who were previously slaves worked hard at getting their children into a better situation than they had grown up in. Daddy had sent Delia to a woman's college near Lexington for a year. Louis, however, had gone to a four-year college and come back a degreed man. That, and his tall, handsome physical stature would gain him the attention of every single woman in town. Coupled with his father's prestige, Louis had come home a very eligible man.

"Good evening, Miss Delia." He tipped his head in a slight bow.

"Hello, Mr. Hall. So you have returned from school. You haven't come around to the store."

"I had intended to come for a visit, but I've been busy getting acquainted with my father's business." He grinned. "I shall have to remedy that soon. I hear McClure's is quite the place now."

Delia stood a little taller, his words setting her on edge. "It was quite the place before you left. You know that, Mr. Hall."

"I meant that the inventory has improved in quality since I left. And I think being my empty-headed sister's friend earns you the right to call me Louis."

Delia pursed her lips. She had heard Louis call Catherine empty-headed many times. He said it like it was a joke, and Catherine responded in kind. But it hurt Delia every time she heard it. Even if her friend didn't feel the insult in her brother's words, Delia did for her. Catherine was as smart as Louis was, and she would have done well if her father had allowed her to go away to school also.

Catherine swatted his arm. "So now you're concerned about what's going on in my head? I will inform Mother of your concerns."

"Compared to Miss Delia. . ."

Catherine arched her eyebrows. "Compared to Delia, you're empty-headed."

Delia heard Josiah stifle a guffaw behind her.

Louis turned serious, looking past Delia. "And who is this?"

Delia grinned. "This is my friend Josiah Searcy."

Josiah extended his hand. "Nice to meet you."

To Delia's horror, Louis delayed returning the handshake. "Right, you're the stable boy over at Abbott's." It wasn't a question. It was as if Louis already knew exactly who Josiah was.

"He's a horse breeder." Delia knew Josiah didn't care about the put-down, but she did.

"Hmm. Maybe I will go and visit him instead." Louis laughed. Delia didn't.

Josiah cleared his throat. "I'm heading out. Would you like me to see you home,

Delia?" He held her coat up for her.

"Yes, please." Delia slipped her arms into the sleeves and, after she'd fastened it, linked her arm with Josiah's. Daddy was engaged in conversation with Mr. Pearson and could find his way home quite well.

Louis reached out and touched her arm. "This would be a perfect time for us to catch up. I can take you home in our carriage. That way you won't have to suffer the cold." Louis gave Josiah a pointed stare.

Delia couldn't find words to say. But she didn't want to let go of Josiah's arm.

Josiah let out a forced laugh. "Oh no. Delia would much rather walk. She says the cold invigorates her mind." He gave Delia's arm the slightest tug.

That was true. She had said that to Josiah on many a winter's walk. Delia waved to Catherine. "I will try and stop by later this week."

Catherine lowered her voice. "I told you he was insufferable."

Delia reached out and squeezed her friend's hand, hoping to give her some hope but worried Catherine would need more than the brief act of comfort. "Good night."

Delia let Josiah lead her out the door. Outside the evening had cooled, but it was still pleasant. She loved the way the coolness made her cheeks tingle. "Thank you."

Josiah looked at her. "For what?"

"Speaking up for the less fortunate children."

He shrugged. "I hoped reminding them of how uneducated people turn out and what little opportunities they have for bettering their lives would sway their decision."

She pulled his arm closer. "That makes me sad, but you're correct."

He guided her around a broken cobblestone. "I know they don't want me around. I wonder who would be the focus of their dislike if I wasn't here."

She leaned her head back and laughed. "You'll always be here, Josiah. Where are you going?" When he didn't respond, she looked at him. A tendril of fear encircled her heart. "Are you going somewhere, Josiah?"

"I'm not going anywhere, Delia." He patted her hand. "Though I wish I could go to Kansas with the Pells. I don't like the struggle it is to live here. I need to support Grace, and Mr. Abbott doesn't pay enough. If I do get another job, I'll have to work long hours, and Grace would practically be raising herself. Like I did. She's barely fifteen."

"Things are going to get better." Delia infused her words with as much hope as she could. She couldn't deny the weight she'd seen on Josiah. The weight of being a provider so young. The weight of being alone.

"I'm sure they will. I just don't know if they will get better here." He sighed. "With the election still undeclared, I don't want to be here if Tilden loses."

Delia gasped. "That would be. . ." The next word escaped her. Horrible. Unbearable. The same party who kept them in slavery would succeed in regaining the power they had lost after the war.

"Dangerous," Josiah said, his tone flat. "That would be dangerous for every black person in the South."

They traveled to the shop in silence, both lost in their thoughts. He stopped at her front door. "Sorry to put such a damper on the walk."

She smiled at him, hoping it would lift his spirits a little. "I'm your friend, and I don't mind listening to your concerns."

"I don't want to burden you."

"You can't shoulder everything alone, Josiah. You have me, and I can help you." He stared at her, his expression unreadable in the dim light. "I have you?"

She grinned big. "Yes, you do."

He chuckled. "I guess you'll have to do."

Delia put her hands on her hips in mock outrage. "Keep talking like that and I'll withdraw my friendship."

Josiah bowed low, a smile playing on his lips. "Please forgive me, Miss Delia."

"Good night, Josiah," she said with a laugh.

"Good night, Delia."

She watched him disappear into the shadows, her heart stricken with the thought of him ever walking out of her life.

After Delia explained that she was working on something new for the auction, Daddy had allowed her to devote a whole day to her workroom. She had risen early and come down to work. The drying wheel was coming together. She just needed to find a way to add weight to the wheels so they would turn on their own.

A hand holding a plate came into her peripheral, and her stomach growled.

She looked to find Olive standing next to her. Four years younger, Olive looked more like their mother than Delia did. But she was just as bighearted. Olive often took care of Delia when she got lost in one of her creations, bringing her food and drink. "I thought food would get your attention."

Delia looked around at the dark windows. Had the sun set already? "Did I miss dinner?"

Olive handed her the plate. "Yes. I've already done the dishes."

Delia let out a sigh. "How many times have I told you to come and fetch me?"

"You were working."

"But it was time for dinner. We need to eat dinner together like a real family."

Olive shrugged. "It was fine. Besides, Daddy had a visitor."

Delia's shoulders sank. She had missed dinner and their dinner guest. "Who?"

Olive grinned. "Louis Hall."

Delia blinked. "Louis Hall came here? For dinner?"

"I don't know if he came for dinner, but he did eat." Olive took a seat in the chair on the other side of the table. "He said he had something to discuss with Daddy in private."

"Where are they now?"

"Daddy walked Louis out."

Before Delia could rise from her seat, the back door opened and Daddy stepped into her workroom. He looked at Delia first, then Olive, smiling. "There are my girls."

Delia's heart sank a little. He normally called them "his girls" when things were going well in his opinion. That normally meant bad news for her and Olive. "You had dinner with Louis. How did that go? He hasn't come to see me yet."

He looked at Delia again. "I think that will change."

"What did he want?" Olive asked before Delia could, which made Delia smile. Olive had the makings of a curious-minded woman. She wasn't afraid to ask questions, and lots of them, interested in how things worked. And how people worked.

"To ask me something serious." Daddy picked up a stool Delia kept in the corner and brought it to the table. "He wanted to ask me something. About Delia."

Delia frowned. "I saw him earlier this week at the school meeting. He could have asked me."

Her father shook his head. "That's not proper."

Confusion clouded Delia's thoughts, a feeling she didn't appreciate. "What could he have to ask you that would be improper to ask me?"

Her father took a deep breath and let the words come out on his exhale. "He wanted to ask me if he could court you. Court you to marry you."

Delia stood from the table so fast that she sent several tools crashing to the floor. "Me?"

Daddy smiled as he helped her pick them up. "Yes, you. He says he's been admirin' you for some time now."

Delia looked at Olive, whose expression was as confused as Delia felt. *Louis can't want to marry me. But then, didn't Catherine say I should beware?* "Are you sure, Daddy?"

"I think I would remember rightly when a man comes callin' on one of my daughters," he said with a chuckle.

Delia sank down to her stool. "And what did you say?"

Her father raised an eyebrow. "You have to ask? Louis is an eligible man whose family has been friends with us for many years. He's the right kind of man for you. He's got drive and ambition and will soon be the clerk for the top black law firm in town."

Delia focused on the wheels in front of her, the wheels in her mind turning at a breakneck pace. The Halls were friends of theirs. And she would gain another sister in Catherine. But marry Louis? Had she ever looked at him that way?

"I don't know," Delia managed to get out.

When she looked up, her father wore a curious look. "What is there to know?"

"I'd like to get to know him a little better. I'd like to think about it."

Daddy pursed his lips. "Always thinking."

"It's not a bad thing to think, Daddy." Delia picked up her fork and realized she wasn't hungry anymore.

"You don't think when it comes to love. You just feel." Olive stood and placed her hands over her heart, pretending to swoon.

Delia laughed, appreciative of Olive's attempts to lighten the mood. "This isn't only love. It's marriage. And people should think about marriage. Not just jump into it on emotions alone."

"Love is not a requirement for marriage. I expect you to give Louis your full attention when he comes calling." Daddy moved to the door. "He has plenty of other women he could court, so don't think too long. Men like Louis don't wait long for thinking women."

He left, leaving a chill in the air. Why hadn't he discussed this with her before granting permission to Louis? She stared at the plate in front of her.

Olive came and stood by her. "You could do worse."

Delia sighed. "It's not that I think Louis is bad. I just—"

"You don't love him."

"No. I don't, and I don't know that I ever will."

Olive grasped her hand. "Maybe spend some time with him. Get to know him better. Maybe he's different with you than with everyone else."

"You're right." She stood and embraced Olive. "You're pretty wise for someone so young."

"I got it from you." Olive gave her a squeeze. "I'm going to bed."

"Good night."

Alone, Delia looked at the wheels in front of her. Now she had another puzzle to solve.

Chapter 4

Josiah's trip from the tiny upstairs of a small house in the Farms to Abbott's stable on the other side of town took only fifteen minutes at a brisk walk. But he still needed to bundle up against the cold or he would fight off the chill all day. The barn was colder than his house but not by much. He would have to pitch hay to get himself warm. Or maybe take Harriet out for a walk. If she came out of her stall today.

He opened the stable door, grabbed the lantern he kept hanging there, and lit it with the matches he kept in his pocket. The instant the light flooded the stalls, he knew Harriet was dead. The knowledge hit him with such force that he almost dropped the lantern. Running toward the stalls, he gripped the lantern tight, praying he was wrong.

When he peered over the door of the stall, he saw her lying on the floor. Motionless.

"Oh no. Harriett. No." He swung the stall door open harder than he realized. It banged against the wall and roused the other horses, who were not asleep. They were all awake, quiet in their stalls. They knew too.

He touched Harriett's muzzle, the coolness of her skin shocking him. He pulled his hand back, the absence of the warmth he normally felt shaking him. "Oh Harriet." He sat on the floor next to her and gathered her head into his lap. He studied her lifeless stare and noted a white foam around her mouth.

Few things caused that. One of them, poison.

Harriett's behavior of the past few days flashed in his mind. Poison would have explained it all. But how—

The outing with Mr. Abbott. It was the only time she had been away from him. And she had returned acting strange. He carefully lowered her head back to the straw and stood. Mr. Abbott needed to know.

Abbott House stood on the other side of the corral. He went to the back of the house and rapped on the door. The housekeeper and cook would already be up preparing for the day. The door swung open, and Miss Bea gave him a warm smile.

"Good morning, Josiah."

"Not so good. I need you to wake Mr. Abbott."

His tone must have conveyed the seriousness of the moment because the older woman shuffled away from the door without asking him any questions. The sun had started to warm the horizon when Mr. Abbott came to the door, a sleeveless undershirt showing his pale arms and a dab of shaving cream on his chin. "What is it?"

Josiah swallowed. No sense drawing out the news. "Harriett is dead."

"Dead? How?"

"I believe poison."

Mr. Abbott rubbed his hand over his forehead. "She was fine a few days ago. And I've got a buyer lined up."

Josiah lowered his eyes. "She has been acting strange since you took her out—"

"Are you blaming me?"

Josiah's eyes snapped up. "No, sir. I was just saying she was fine until you took her to meet the buyer."

Mr. Abbott's eyes narrowed. "Sure sounds like you're blaming me."

Josiah held up his hands. "She could have eaten something while you weren't looking."

Mr. Abbott's anger hardened his posture and he stood up straight. "So now you're accusing me of not being able to take care of my own horse? How do I know you didn't poison her to stop her from being sold?"

"I would never do that. You know how much I love all the horses. I would never. She didn't die by my hand."

"Since you don't know how she died and I'm paying you to care for the horses, I believe that means you are negligent on your job." Mr. Abbott scowled. "And since you can't keep my horses alive, I don't think you should be in my employ anymore."

Josiah took a step back, almost falling off the step. "Mr. Abbott, I've done well by your horses."

"Leave now and I'll let you collect your last week's pay. If not, I'll call the police about the unemployed colored on my back step." He let out a low chuckle. "They'd work you twice as hard in the camps."

Josiah barely let him finish before he turned and left. The prison work camp was a harsh punishment for a dead horse. It was where all black men charged with loitering—being unemployed—were sent. Men died in those camps and left their families to fend for themselves.

The morning had dawned to a bright day. Josiah walked, not knowing or seeing where his feet led him. But when he looked up, he found himself standing in front of McClure's General Store. *Delia.* The front of the shop was still dark, but he knew the family had already started their day.

He walked to the back door of the shop and rapped on the window of Delia's workshop, a sound she would be likely to hear. He pressed himself against the wall, exposed to whoever passed by. A policeman. He may have to explain his unemployed state. *Calm down. No one knows by looking at me that I've been fired.*

The door clicked behind him, and Delia stared out from inside. "Josiah?" She reached for him, and he grasped her hand. "What's wrong?"

"Can I come in?"

"Of course." She stepped back and pulled him into her workroom.

He took off his hat and inhaled, already feeling the weight lifting just by standing near her. Delia clasped his other hand. "Josiah, what's wrong?"

"Mr. Abbott fired me."

Her eyes grew wide but filled with compassion. "Whatever for?"

"Harriett died last night. I believe she ate something she shouldn't have when Mr. Abbott took her out. When I tried to ask him what happened, he thought I was accusing him of killing her."

"Oh Josiah." She wrapped her arms around him, pulling him close. "I'm so sorry."

His heart hitched, her embrace soothing him in a way it shouldn't. Too much. The rightness of being in her arms. *Lord, help me. Delia is my friend.* But he let his arms slide around her waist anyway.

She continued to speak comforting words to him, and he continued to hold her close. But then she stopped speaking and pressed her cheek to his.

The moments dragged by, stretching into long ribbons of peace and something else. . .

Behind them footsteps sounded, and they quickly separated. Delia ducked her head, avoiding his eyes.

Her father stepped into the showroom. "Good morning, Josiah."

"Mr. McClure."

"You're here pretty early." Mr. McClure eyed him. "And looking out of sorts. Is everything all right?"

Delia spoke up quickly. "One of the horses died from something she ate, and Mr. Abbott fired him because of it."

Mr. McClure shook his head. "You can't take care of your sister without a job."

Josiah swallowed. Grace. He would have to tell her he got fired. Until he found more work, she would be their sole provider. Grace, not him. "I will need to find something quickly. Mr. Abbott threatened to call the police and tell them I was no longer in his employ."

Mr. McClure nodded. "You can come and work here. As a stock boy."

Beside him, Delia gasped, a thunderous expression on her face. He knew what she was thinking and feeling. Mr. McClure was having pity on him.

"I'll take it."

Mr. McClure shook Josiah's hand. "It will be nice to have a stronger, younger man around to help Delia with all her creations."

Josiah looked at Delia. "Yes, it would be my pleasure."

Over the weeks since her father told her that Louis wanted to court her, Delia had eaten more dinners at the Hall home than she had at her own. First there were Sunday dinners. Surprising, since her father had complained about her church attendance. Now it was completely fine for her to go off and eat whatever rich food was on the Hall table that day. Then Louis began coming to fetch her for a walk that ended up in his home. His mother would insist that Delia stay for dinner. Other nights she knew she would be having dinner with Louis because her father would say, "Delia, go on upstairs and change into something nice." And she did, although she didn't like not knowing what her plans would be from one moment to the next.

All that courting, and she still felt exactly the same about Louis. His attitude had gotten a little better, but not much. He'd only added education to his arrogance. His temper was the same too. They had had several conversations that ended with Louis fuming at her for simply stating an opinion different than his. Delia had quickly learned to choose her words carefully.

She bent down to pick up a box of smelling salts to stock the shelves behind the counter. A pair of hands reached into her view.

"Let me get that."

She looked up to find herself face-to-face with Josiah. "I can get it."

He shook his head. "I'm not going to have your father find you lifting a box with me nearby."

She giggled and let go of the box. "He would not be happy."

He lifted the box with ease. More than once since he'd started at the shop she'd caught herself or Olive admiring how strong he was. He had spent several years lifting bales of hay in the stables. *He could probably lift me with no problem.* Face heating, she cleared her throat. "Thank you."

Josiah set the box on the counter and glanced over his shoulder. "I saw Mrs. Thompson today on the way here."

Delia stepped close beside him. "Is she well?"

"No." Josiah reached in the box and pulled out one of the small jars of salts. "All the children have colds."

"Oh no." Delia reached for a bottle and placed it on the shelf. "One sick child is enough to deal with."

"I helped restring her laundry line and helped carry some of the laundry out to the yard."

Delia looked at him. "I'm sure she appreciated that."

Josiah shrugged. "Well, I figured that was what you would do, and if I did it, you wouldn't have to sneak over there."

She ducked her head to hide her smile. "Since you're in such a caring mood, would you take some soup over to her? There is more than enough left over from our dinner."

"Of course."

He reached into the box at the same time as she did, and their fingers brushed. And again, heat flushed her face. Josiah looked at their hands, both still sitting atop the bottles, close to touching. How many times had he held her hand, in church or in the school meeting, and she didn't notice? But now something hummed between them.

Josiah looked up from their hands to her eyes. "Delia—"

The back storeroom door opened, and her father stepped in. Josiah grabbed a bottle and pressed it into her hand. She lifted it in a flash and set it on the shelf.

Her father walked across the room to the front door and looked out. "I think Josiah can finish this up by himself. Delia, go upstairs and get ready for dinner with Louis."

She stifled a groan. But she could not argue with her father. "Yes, Daddy."

Josiah traded places with her and in a low voice said, "I'll get Olive to get the soup for me."

She gave him a small smile. "Thank you."

As she headed to the staircase, her father said, "Wear your purple dress with the lace."

She paused. Her fanciest frock. "Yes, Daddy." She climbed the stairs, her mind racing. By the time she finished dressing, the sun had begun to set, the store was long closed, and Josiah had already gone home. She stood by the front door and watched for Louis to walk down the street. But a carriage pulled up instead. The footman hopped down and walked briskly over to the door.

She opened it before he could reach the stairs. "Miss Delia?"

"Yes?"

"Mr. Hall is waiting." The man motioned for her to come to the carriage.

Her stomach did a sour little twist. "Thank you."

The footman opened the door for her, and she climbed inside. Hiring a coach to carry her a distance she could walk was a great expense. She watched as they passed the street to the Thompsons' house. And Josiah's house. *I wonder if he's left the Thompsons' yet.* She sat back in the seat. *I wonder what he would think of this carriage.*

The lights in the Hall house shone out into the growing darkness. The coach stopped directly in front of the door, and she placed her hands in her lap to keep from fidgeting while the driver came around. As she stepped out of the carriage, the front door opened and Louis stood in the doorway.

He watched her ascend the stairs. "Delia, you look beautiful tonight."

She tried to hide it, but a growing sense of dread weighted every step she took toward him. "Thank you."

He took her hand. His fingers were cold, missing the hum she felt when she even got near Josiah's hand. She blinked and shook her head. *Stop thinking about Josiah.*

Louis looked at her. "Is everything all right?"

She nodded and gave a nervous laugh. "Yes. I was only thinking about something that happened earlier at the store."

Delia peered ahead of them, expecting to see Catherine or his parents, but they appeared to be alone. They walked to the dining room, not talking. The house felt colder than usual. Maybe because it was quieter than usual. When she stepped into the dining room, it was clear why.

The room was adorned with several candelabras, their flickering creating intermittent glimmers on the two place settings on the table, but no one else was there save one servant.

"Where is everyone?"

Louis escorted her to her seat. "It's only us tonight."

Her stomach sank. A private dinner and her best dress. Something serious was planned. But was it what she suspected? He wouldn't be planning to propose tonight?

They were served. The dinner was as excellent as ever. Chicken roasted to perfection and potatoes. The Thompsons flashed in her mind. A meal like this could do them great good.

They engaged in small talk, and when the plates were cleared, Louis turned to her. "Did you enjoy dinner?"

She nodded and gripped her hands in her lap. "Yes, I did."

He smiled. "I wanted it to be special. Something you would remember fondly for the rest of your life." He reached over and took her hands in his. "I want us to look back on this night and see it as a milestone. The beginning of something great."

Her heart sank, and she fought to keep the pleasant look on her face. "I will remember it."

He slipped out of his chair and down on one knee. "I hope so. Delia, will you marry me?"

Thankful for the chair, she felt the room swim. "I—" But her father's voice filled her mind. *A man like Louis isn't going to wait for a thinking woman.* She knew that it was her father's wish to make a stronger connection with the Hall family. Louis was as good a man as any. Well, not as good as Josiah.

She swallowed, the weight of the moment, this proposal without love a heavy drape around her shoulders. "Yes," she said, because she knew she couldn't return home and face her father after saying no.

Chapter 5

Everything looked the same. Same bedroom and same cream curtains in front of the same windows. Windows that held the same view. Same sounds from downstairs. Probably Josiah getting the shop ready to open.

Being engaged to Louis Hall hadn't changed her life at all.

She did her morning routine as fast as she could, noting her eyes looked the same and that not even her expression had changed. No rosy glow of happiness under the rich brown of her cheeks. She picked a blue day dress with a small flower pattern. A part of her wanted to wear black.

She went into the kitchen, ate a quick breakfast of an apple and a piece of bread, and headed straight to her workroom. Surely there was something to make her forget about her yes to Louis last night. Her mouth was still sour from saying it. His reaction also haunted her. They had spent the rest of their time together with him bragging about capturing the most eligible woman in Burtonsville. Like she was a prize.

Sunlight warmed the workroom, and a calm settled over her. She sighed. Things weren't so bad, were they? Josiah sat at the small counter space they used to write out invoices.

He turned, his expression trying to be happy, but his eyes were puffy. "Good morning." His voice came out in a grumble.

"Are you all right?"

He turned back to the invoices. "I didn't sleep much last night."

"Me either." She walked to her worktable and eyed the base of a lamp she had been trying to repair. The shade was made of painted silk, and Delia hated for something so pretty to be wasted. As she turned the lamp over to inspect it again, she thought of all the candles from last night. Candles that were supposed to be romantic. She nearly groaned. She would have to play the happy, doting fiancée, staring into Louis's eyes and kissing—

She set the lamp down with a thump and braced herself on the table. She would eventually have to kiss Louis. But how? She'd never kissed a man before. Maybe she could figure it out before it came time for her to kiss him at their wedding. She tipped the lamp to its side and picked up a screwdriver. Well, she would have to figure it out. But how fast could she learn to pretend to like Louis's kisses? Somehow she knew she wouldn't. She dropped the screwdriver.

"Are you all right?" Josiah's voice broke the silence.

"Oh." She shook her head. "I'm just trying figure something out."

Josiah turned. "Maybe I can help you so you can stop interrupting me with loud noises."

"I'm sorry. I need to figure out a kiss."

A slight eyebrow raise. "You need to figure out a kiss?"

"Yes." She turned and leaned back against the edge of the table. "Like, how do you do it? How long should it last?"

Josiah let out a low chuckle and turned back to his invoices. "It doesn't work that way, Delia."

"What way? How does it work?"

"You don't figure kisses out like how you took apart that lamp. You feel them."

She swallowed. "Feel? There has to be more to it."

"Not really."

"I—" she started. *I have feelings about being kissed by Louis, but I'm sure that's not what I'm supposed to feel.* "No. There have to be some rules."

"No rules. Just feel." Josiah didn't turn, but his words sounded tight, like he was clenching his teeth.

She let out a frustrated huff. "Josiah, you're the only man I can ask about this. I need more information than that. I mean, I've seen people kiss before, but always a kiss on the cheek. I want to know how to kiss someone you're in love with. How—"

Before she could finish, Josiah stood, scraping his stool across the floor. He turned, his expression piercing. He crossed the room with two long strides till he was in front of her. He slipped one arm around her waist and braced his hand on the table behind her.

And he kissed her.

Shock froze her as their lips met, but she didn't remain frozen. The softness of his lips sent warmth flooding through her. He withdrew a hair's width and then brought his lips to hers again, tenderly. Her heart pounded as she tipped her face up to his. His grasp on her waist tightened, bringing her closer.

He broke their connection, his eyes closed. Only the sound of their breathing could be heard in the room. Her emotions tumbled over one another. She didn't, however, have time to sort them out, because Josiah leaned in again and gave her another dizzying kiss. But this time, there was a little more longing to it. Like it would be his whole world if she returned his kiss. And with awkward movements, she came to her tiptoes and tried to return his kiss. He took a deep inhale through his nose, his other hand coming up to cup her face. They fell into a rhythm, him capturing her mouth, pulling slightly away and her coming up to her toes, stretching till their lips met. She struggled to remember to breathe, not wanting to break the spell.

The longer he kissed her, the more she forgot about all her questions. About Louis. About everything. There was only him and the warmth of his mouth. The smell of his soap. The coarseness of his fingertips on her cheek. She slid her arms around his shoulders and forgot that she was kissing her friend.

Before she could close the circle of her arms around his neck, he jerked and pulled away. The look of half confusion and half pleasure on his face made her heart thunder even harder in her chest.

He looked down at her mouth and moistened his lips. She held her breath. But he didn't move.

"Did you feel that?" he asked, his voice low.

She parted her lips to say. . .to say. . .what, she didn't know, but Olive's footsteps tromped down the stairs. Josiah picked up his hat from the rack in the corner and was out the back door by the time her sister entered the workroom.

Olive watched him go out the door, then turned and stared at Delia. "Where is he off to in such a hurry?"

"I'm not sure." Delia wanted to race out the door to tell Josiah that, yes, she had felt it.

Josiah rushed down the street in no particular direction. His lips still hummed from the feel of Delia's lips against his. And so did his anger at himself. He had already pushed the boundaries by holding her hand or letting her take his arm when they walked, but this. . . He had kept his feelings for Delia at bay for years. Contenting himself with being her friend so he could continue to be near her. Not even letting himself imagine anything more.

But working at the store with her had undone him. Brushing against her in close quarters. Eating lunch at her worktable. Watching her do ordinary things like yawn and then gracefully press her fingers to cover her mouth. He was grateful for the job, but it was harder than working at the stables. It had closed the safe gap between him and Delia, making her a part of his daily life. And now he'd crossed a line he shouldn't have.

He looked up to find himself standing across the street from the church. He headed to the small garden planted at the side of the building. There was a bench there. He would sit and sort himself out. And repent. The bench had been dedicated to the church in honor of their first reverend. It sat in the shade, surrounded by fragrant flowers. He sat and breathed deeply. He would have to have a good explanation for the kisses when he faced Delia again. The look of shock on her face. . .

"She wanted a kiss," he grumbled to no one. But that didn't mean he had to give it to her. He leaned back against the cool stones of the building. He would love to head home after this, but he would eventually have to go back to the shop and face her. Voices caught his attention. He scooted deeper into the shadow of the tree. He wasn't fit to talk to anyone right now.

"It's been some time since we've had a society wedding in Burtonsville," Reverend Davenport's unmistakable voice said.

"Yes, it has. We've been lacking eligible young men, which is why I was relieved when Louis returned from school," Mr. McClure replied.

"I must admit that I didn't think Delia had eyes for Louis," Reverend Davenport said as the pair continued down the stone steps.

"Delia spends so much time in her workshop that she hasn't got eyes for anything but her tools and the poor people in the Farms."

"I thought she might have fancied Josiah Searcy."

At the sound of his name, Josiah sat forward but then remembered he was trying not to be seen. He rose from the bench and stood on the opposite side of the tree where only someone coming from the back of the church could see him. But he could still hear.

Mr. McClure laughed. "There was no way my daughter was going to marry that boy. He doesn't have a penny to his name and has no ambition. I thought he might get some fight to him when Abbott fired him. That's why I hired him. But he's still a sad sap. He worked for Abbott for years and never tried to better himself. It's like he's proud to be poor."

"He's a good lad and a hard worker," Reverend Davenport said, his words soothing Josiah's emotions. "My father always said a hard worker will never be poor."

"Well, he hadn't met Josiah Searcy yet." Mr. McClure laughed again, and Josiah's stomach turned. "Delia and Louis will be the premier couple of Burtonsville. Maybe I could even convince my future son-in-law to run for office. Make some real change here."

Soon the two men were beyond hearing, but Josiah remained in his hiding place. *Is that what people think of me? That I'm proud to be poor?* He hated being poor.

Waking up every day with less than he had the day before. Hated figuring out how to get food for himself and Grace without relying on Delia. How could anyone be proud of that?

But they were right. There was no way a poor boy like him was going to win Delia. Ever. The kisses they shared was no more than a wisp of a dream that would never be. She was engaged to Louis now if he understood her father correctly.

Leaves crunched behind him, and he found himself facing Reverend Pell. He wasn't dressed in his collar but wore a shirt that matched the white strands of hair on his head.

He smiled at Josiah. "Hello, young man. I see I'm not the only one enjoying the garden today."

"Reverend Pell." Josiah took a step back.

"Don't leave on my account. I don't get to talk to many people in town. My son-in-law keeps me busy visiting all his friends." The older man motioned to the bench where Josiah had sat minutes before. "Why don't we sit down?"

Josiah took a seat and watched Reverend Pell slowly lower himself. "Enjoy youth while you have it." He let out a loud exhale. "So, tell me more about yourself."

"Not much more to tell." Josiah looked down at his hands. "I used to work at the livery, but now I work at McClure's General Store."

Reverend Pell looked up into the trees. "He was just here. Mr. McClure. Planning a wedding for one of his daughters. My son-in-law says I've met her."

"You did. She was with me the Sunday you talked about people going to Kansas."

"Ah, the young lady." He studied Josiah. "And she is not marrying you."

"No."

"That's unfortunate. I thought you two would run off and make a life on the prairie."

Delia couldn't be further from that. She was marrying one of the richest men in town. That didn't change the fact that she probably would have been perfect in a homestead. "Not the two of us, but I may."

"To get away from her?"

Josiah shook his head. "I need a fresh start, Reverend. To have a fighting chance. I don't have that here. With the Black Codes and the violence, it's impossible to get ahead."

"But you have some very rich friends here. It shouldn't be hard to get one of them to be your patron until you get on your feet."

"Friends." Josiah let out a huff. "Delia is my only friend, and her father is not."

Reverend Pell leaned forward. "Well, young man, I will be your friend. Although

I don't have as much as some of the people here, I will do all I can to help you. If you do decide to go to Kansas, I will make sure you and your sister have a place in my party."

Josiah gaped at the man. Only Delia had been that generous to him. "Thank you."

Reverend Pell patted him on the leg. "Consider it my Christian service. Someone helped me out long ago. I want to sow that blessing into you."

"I'll need to think about it. And talk to my sister."

"Of course." Reverend Pell rose as slowly as he had sat, and shuffled toward the back door of the church. "And talk to Miss Delia too."

Josiah swallowed. That would not be an easy talk.

Chapter 6

Delia's strength almost failed her as she climbed the stairs to the Hall home. She had been there many times in the past days planning her and Louis's engagement party, but tonight was harder. Especially after the kisses with Josiah and having to tell him that she and Louis were engaged. He had not reacted when she told him, and she knew their friendship had been broken beyond repair.

Louis met her at the front door. "Good evening, my dear." He leaned in and kissed her on the cheek. She forced herself not to flinch or draw back.

Louis reached over and shook her father's hand. "Mr. McClure. What a happy night."

Daddy beamed, and Delia's heart sank lower. "Indeed it is."

Louis took her arm, and they walked to the dining room, her father and sister behind her. All of Burtonsville's elite black community was there. And somehow, having them all in one room made her feel more out of place. This wasn't the life she'd imagined having. Yes, she wanted to be taken care of. Nobody wanted to be poor. But being wealthy wasn't something she had ever dreamed of.

Louis's family waited for her in the dining room. Catherine wore a pretty pale pink dress with lace at the throat. Mrs. Hall was more plainly attired, but her dress was made of silk.

Catherine came to her and gave her a light hug, different from her normal hugs, careful not to wrinkle either of their dresses. "Congratulations."

"Thank you." Delia hugged her back.

Catherine's voice dropped to a whisper with a hint of sarcasm. "Don't be so happy about it."

Delia straightened her posture and put on a happy face. She was at her engagement party, after all. They were soon joined by other well-wishers, and she stood between Catherine and Louis as a line formed.

Reverend and Mrs. Pell stepped in front of them. "Miss Delia. Congratulations."

Their words sounded as hollow as her happiness felt.

"Thank you."

"I guess you won't be joining us on our trek back to Kansas." Reverend Pell took her hand.

She let out a nervous laugh. "No, I'm afraid not."

Louis gave Reverend Pell a stern look. "Delia in Kansas? Oh no. Too much work. She'll be here living the finest life I can give her."

Delia swallowed. "The Pells spoke about Kansas a few weeks ago at church."

Delia didn't clearly hear Louis's response, but it sounded like he said, "And she won't be going there anymore either." She suppressed a shocked look. He wouldn't restrict her from church, would he? Come to think of it, she never saw Catherine or Mrs. Hall at church. They donated to the church's fund-raisers, and she was sure they had dedicated a bench in the sanctuary, but no more than that.

The line continued to flow, and Delia longed to sit down. Although many of the guests knew her, they talked to Louis the longest. And none of them were her real friends. She stifled a sigh.

She looked down at her gloves and felt Louis stiffen beside her. She looked up to find Josiah and Grace standing in front of her. She grinned wide. "Josiah. Grace." She longed to hug them, and as if he could sense that, Louis tightened his hold on her arm.

Josiah struggled to make eye contact. "Hi, Miss Delia." Grace didn't make eye contact. Her reason for avoidance wasn't the same as Josiah's. Grace was shy. Josiah had kissed her.

Delia pressed her hands together. "Thank you both for coming."

"Thank you for inviting us," Grace said quietly.

They stood awkwardly, and Delia sensed that they were waiting for Louis to acknowledge them. Which he hadn't done. "Louis, you remember my friends Josiah and Grace."

Louis gave them a once-over before smiling. "Mr. Searcy."

"Mr. Hall." Josiah had no problem meeting Louis's eye. The tension in their little circle increased, and Grace shifted to stand behind Josiah. "You are a blessed man."

"I am," Louis said with a laugh. "The luckiest man in Burtonsville. I am certain every single man here is jealous of me."

Delia tugged on his arm. "Jealousy is such a negative thing to talk about tonight."

Louis slowly looked away from Josiah to Delia. "I suppose so."

She looked back at Josiah and smiled at him, but she could see his mood sinking.

"Be sure to get something to eat. As much as you like. I want you to fully enjoy all that I have at my table." Louis tipped his head toward the dining room. The implications of his words hit Delia full force. Grace and Josiah too. The muscles in Josiah's jaw worked, and Grace slid further into his shadow.

But neither of them said a word. They simply turned and walked away. The next guest stepped up to greet Delia, and from the corner of her eye she watched Josiah disappear into the crowd.

Once they had properly received all the guests, they moved to the dining room for dinner. She and Louis took their places at the top of the table. Her father and Olive sat across from them. Delia noticed immediately that Josiah and Grace were gone, their two empty seats standing out at the crowded table. She sank into her chair as her heart sank in her chest.

Louis looked in the direction of the empty seats. "Your friend and his sister must have left."

"Josiah and Grace."

"Yes, of course." Louis sat down beside her. "I guess some people aren't comfortable with nice things."

She swallowed, choosing her words carefully. "I don't think nice things were the problem."

"Then what was?"

Louis's father interrupted them before she could answer. "Very true, Miss Delia. Nice things are never the problem." He laughed.

Delia tried to smile. "I would have to kindly disagree with you, Mr. Hall." She hoped to keep him from asking her what they were discussing.

"I'm sure they're not the problem," he continued, lifting his fluted, crystal champagne glass from the table. "I think money can fix any problem. Enough of it, anyway."

Delia thought about the Thompsons. "I know people who, if they had a little more money, their lives would be better. Particularly the people in the Farms."

"Yes, they could do with more money, but they need to be willing to work for it." Mr. Hall turned serious. "Look at your father and me. We were once slaves, and the only time we got to touch something this nice"—he motioned to his glass—"was to clean it."

Several men, all ex-slaves, chuckled, adding their agreement to the statement.

Mr. Hall grinned. "But after slavery we made something of ourselves. We worked hard and built wealth. We didn't go begging to our old masters for jobs. We made our own way."

Another round of agreement.

"Not only did we make a better life for ourselves, we worked hard to make our children's lives better."

Delia mustered her courage. "Some were not as fortunate as you and my father, who found employers who would pay you a living wage. What about those who, through no fault of their own, worked just as hard as you but illness or misfortune struck their households? Don't we who have done well have a higher responsibility to help those less fortunate?"

At that, Louis laughed beside her. "The Bible says that we'll have the poor with us always. If we give all our money away, we'll be as poor as they are."

Mr. Hall laughed. "You have a very generous soul on your hands, Louis."

"That I do." Louis smiled at her.

Mr. Hall tipped his head in Daddy's direction, a grin on his face. "You'll have to watch her like McClure had to watch her mother. She would have given away everything they owned and happily lived in the Farms with the rest of the lazy lot."

Delia's head snapped up to look at her father, but he wasn't looking at her. He was glaring at Mr. Hall. Mr. Hall, however, didn't see it because he was still laughing at his own joke.

Louis lifted his fork. "I don't mind her being generous as long as she does it with someone else's money."

Delia's stomach turned. Her eyes went to Catherine, who wore a sad look. It turned even sadder when their eyes met.

What kind of family am I marrying into?

The shop had a slow stream of customers for the morning, which was fine with Delia. She had been overrun the past few days with well-wishes on her engagement. Even at church, people kept coming to congratulate her. None of their words improved her feelings about it.

Worst of all, Josiah hadn't saved a seat for her at church. It hurt, but she understood why. It wouldn't look right for her to be sitting with a man who wasn't her fiancé, but it still stung, and she missed him dearly. And he had given her the cold shoulder every day at work. She longed to talk to him beyond the one-word answers he was giving her. But after Louis's treatment of him, she didn't expect he would talk to her.

Delia had busied herself with sweeping the floor when the door opened and Mrs. Davenport stepped in. She crossed the room quickly to Delia. "Miss Delia, have you recovered from your festivities this weekend?"

Delia set the broom aside. "Almost."

Josiah stood and left the sales floor.

"I wanted to pick up a few things." She lowered her voice. "I'm taking food to some of the families in the Farms."

Delia smiled at the woman, envy hidden. "That's kind of you."

"Apparently some of the landowners have decided that they no longer want people living on their land. They have started evicting people."

Delia gasped. "But where are they supposed to go?"

"I'm not sure, but there was talk that once the land was cleared, more homes, and possibly the new school, would be built there."

Tears swam in Delia's eyes. What cruelty this was. "I can't believe it."

"I'm surprised you didn't know. Louis Hall was the main spearhead of the decision."

Her eyes snapped up to Mrs. Davenport's face. "He was?"

"Yes, his father owns part of the land, and he convinced the other landowners that the Farms could be of better use to the town without the current residents living on it."

Delia looked down at her hands as if they held the reason why Louis had withheld that information from her. Even though she wasn't his wife yet, he could have mentioned it. But then she knew why he hadn't. He knew how she felt about the poor there. "How many families have been evicted?"

"Only a few, but the Halls want to move forward quickly."

Delia's outrage grew. "How quickly?"

"The senior Mr. Hall wants the land cleared by summer." She shook her head, her expression sad. "At least they will have time to find somewhere to live while it's still warm. Imagine if this had happened four months ago before the snow melted." She pulled a slip of paper from her bag. "I have a list of things I want to buy for the poor evicted souls, but I must hurry. My husband would not be pleased to know I've been to the Farms alone."

Suddenly Josiah appeared at her side. "I will go with you."

Mrs. Davenport gave him a wide smile. "Will you? That's very sweet."

Josiah took her list. "It would be my pleasure. I live in the Farms, and this eviction is going to hurt all of us."

The three of them collected the goods on Mrs. Davenport's list, and Josiah loaded up a wheelbarrow to help her deliver them. Delia watched the two leave with a pang in her heart. There was a time when she would have made that delivery. Not only that, she wanted to discover if the Thompsons had been affected by the evictions. She tried to focus on the customers that came in, but her thoughts were with the people in the Farms. With Josiah.

He returned an hour before the store closed, and at first glance, he appeared tired. But once he turned from hanging his hat on the rack, she could see that he was angry.

"Josiah, how bad was it?"

He took in a deep breath. "Chaotic. Depressing."

"How many families have been evicted?"

"About ten." He dragged himself over to sit on a stool. "All their belongings, what little they have, are piled in the streets."

Delia clasped her hand to her mouth and came to stand next to him. "Are the Thompsons all right?" she asked when she had composed herself.

"Yes. That's why I went. I knew you would worry, not knowing what had become of them." He sighed. "I also went to see if Grace and I had been evicted. We haven't, thank God."

He sounded so much like he used to, when they were friends, that Delia forgot herself and touched him on the shoulder. "Thank God."

"I cannot understand how a person can do this to their own people. We expect this kind of treatment from the whites, but—" He rubbed his hand over his face. "Doesn't Mr. Hall know that if the police are called on the evicted residents, the people in the Farms could find themselves in the work camps? The other residents of the Farms are banding together to help the families with small children, but how sad that they have to."

She rubbed his shoulder. "I am sure there are more people like Mrs. Davenport who will step in to help."

"I'm not sure." He stood, and her hand dropped off his shoulder. "The Farms has lost some of the friends it had." He left her and went into the stockroom.

She stood next to the stool where he'd sat for several minutes, heart seared, knowing that his words were directed at her.

Chapter 7

Mr. McClure entered the stock room smiling. "Good morning."

Josiah glanced over his shoulder at his employer. "Good morning."

Mr. McClure picked up a list of delivery slips from the counter. "I will take care of these today. I have a special task for you."

Josiah hoisted the bag of rice and poured it into the bins they used to sell it from. "I'm finished here."

"Delia's wedding dress is ready. I want you to take her to Lexington to pick it up."

Josiah fought the urge to squirm. "Yes, sir."

"I've rented a horse and wagon for the trip." He flipped through the slips, not looking up at Josiah. "You can handle a horse and wagon, right?"

"Yes, sir." *Of course I can—I worked at a stable.*

"Good."

Delia and Olive came down the stairs dressed in bonnets and gloves, and Josiah almost laughed. The McClure women were not happy about this trip. They greeted their father with cordiality but not warmth.

"We are all ready, Josiah."

They walked from the shop to Moore's Stables, where the wagon and horse were waiting. Josiah breathed in relief that Mr. McClure hadn't rented a horse from Abbott's. He helped the ladies aboard. He petted the horse's nose as he passed in front of the wagon. "I know this is a long ride, but you'll be fine. We'll stop and take a few breaks, all right?" The horse neighed and pressed its nose against his shoulder like Harriet used to do. "Let's go then."

He climbed into the driver's seat and set off in the direction of Lexington. As they passed out of town, he was aware that Delia, who had taken the seat next to him, was watching him.

He stole a glance at her. "What?"

"Do you miss working with horses?"

He chuckled. "Very much."

"You're still good at it."

He let the compliment hang. He was. Better at it than any other job he'd ever worked. His conversation with Reverend Pell floated to his mind. He did not have much, but with the right help, he could have his own breeding farm in Kansas. Grace could help him with the bookkeeping and housekeeping. They would finally have a better life. He was so lost in his thoughts that he didn't speak for much of the ride. Delia had abandoned trying to have a conversation with him and had started talking to Olive. A few months ago, he and Delia would have talked the whole ride. He sighed and kept his eyes focused in front of him.

Lexington was much busier than Burtonsville could ever be. Of course, part of the reason was because there were so many more people in Lexington. Josiah navigated the buggy to the shop where Delia was to pick up her dress. He slowed to a stop and hopped down. He came around and handed the women down. "I'll be right here waiting."

Olive gave him a sly look. "Oh, you're not coming inside?"

He gave her a mock scowl, and she giggled and followed Delia into the shop.

People bustled all around him, and Josiah felt like he stuck out. There were people from all levels of income, but he felt plainer than everyone else. There were also groups of soldiers standing on several corners. Some of them were black. Josiah stared. He'd heard about black troops, but the ones who occasionally patrolled Burtonsville were white. *Now you really look like you don't belong.* He led the horse and wagon into a cross street alley where other wagons lined the curb. He walked back down the street to the shop and waited.

Josiah had found himself a seat on a bench in front of the shop, and a half hour passed. He soon learned that the seat was a stop for a horse-drawn trolley. Amazingly, it carried at least ten people and ran along rails like the train but was pulled by horses. He picked up a newspaper discarded by one of the passengers. It was several days old. Not that he minded. He only needed to occupy his thoughts and not think about the reality that Delia was inside picking up her wedding dress.

From down the street, someone let out a cry, and Josiah looked up. A group of white men came pouring out of one of the buildings. They let out whoops and cries. But when one of them fired a shot in the air, the sound set off another kind of moment on the street. Some paused and some ran. Another whoop and a shot.

Two black men rushed up the street toward Josiah. He moved to intercept them. "What's going on?"

One man continued, but one slowed enough to say to Josiah. "A telegram just arrived. Hayes has been declared president, and he's pulling the troops out."

The man didn't stick around to see the horror on Josiah's face. Tilden had lost. Josiah stumbled backward and groped for the bench he had been sitting on. The men continued to whoop as more white men joined them. Josiah looked back at the door of the shop. Delia and Olive hadn't appeared yet. He'd turned to mount the stairs when the air on the street shifted. He didn't even have to turn to know it had gone from bad to worse. It was almost the same feeling he had when he walked into the stable after Harriet died.

He turned, and to his horror, the mob of white men surged forward toward the soldiers on the corner across from them. The black soldiers. With speed, weapons were drawn on both sides. Josiah dove inside the door just as the first shot was fired.

Delia and Olive looked up at both the sound of the shot and Josiah's entrance. He didn't have time to explain, but by the looks on their faces, he didn't need to. "We need to go now." He extended his hands to both women, and Delia took one hand and Olive the other.

The shop's clerk, a black woman a few years older than Josiah, glanced toward the windows. "What's happening?"

Josiah moved to the door, using the windows to survey the street. "Tilden lost."

He heard the shop woman gasp behind him. Delia tightened her grip on his hand. "Where is the wagon?"

"I moved it into an alley down the street."

The shop woman came to block the door. "No, go out the back."

With quick steps, they followed her through the shop to the back door. She pointed down the alley. "Take this way to get to the alley." Her expression was grave, and they were off, calling their thanks to her as they ran.

The alley was empty. Josiah gripped Delia and Olive's hands even tighter and raced forward, glad they could keep up. The alley dropped them off a short distance from the wagon. They climbed in, neither woman waiting for Josiah to hand them up. He grabbed the reins and spoke to the horse. "I need you to be calm and help us get out of here." The horse shook his mane nervously, spooked by the shots going off behind them. Unfortunately, the only way out of the alley was in the direction of melee.

Josiah took a deep breath, turned the wagon in the direction of the street, and slapped the reins. Delia and Olive held on to each other tightly to keep from falling out. The wheels clattered on the cobblestones as they reached the mouth of the alley. Josiah stood in the seat to search for a way around the madness. But what he saw caused him to sit again.

Several bodies lay in the street, both white and black. A brawl covered the entire intersection. They watched as the black soldiers fell, quickly outnumbered by the armed whites. Josiah steered the wagon sharply to the left, almost setting it on two wheels. Although the fighting had been concentrated in the intersection, small skirmishes had broken out up and down the street. In front of him, two men struggled, one a black soldier and one a white man. The white man obviously had the advantage on the soldier. He shoved the soldier backward and pulled a weapon.

Beside him Delia cried out. Josiah steered the horse right toward the men. The white man fired just as they drove between them. The horse reared on his hind legs, tossing the cart sideways. For a moment, Josiah felt weightless, but then the wagon came crashing to ground. It fell sideways, untethering the horse. Josiah, Delia, and Olive were thrown from the wagon and landed just feet from the spinning wheels. Pain jolted through Josiah's shoulder and elbow.

Josiah clambered up to his hands and knees, looking for the women first. Delia was helping Olive. They were covered in dust but alive. He checked for the soldier. He was lying a few feet from the front the wagon, coming to his feet too. He looked over at Josiah, a look of gratitude on his face. Josiah didn't want to see if the white man had managed to get out of the way of the horse. He suspected that his intervention probably saved the soldier's life by the fact that the white man hadn't come around the wagon to get to them.

Josiah crawled to Delia. "Are you two all right?"

"I scraped my elbow, but I'm okay," Olive said, her eyes wide and tears streaming down her cheeks.

Delia was crying too. "I'm okay. We need to go."

Josiah looked at the horseless wagon. "We'll have to walk."

The three rose, and the soldier made it over to them. He reached for and shook Josiah's hand. "Thank you."

"You're welcome."

"You folks should head out. Stay away from main streets."

They started out, darting to the shops lining the streets. Josiah's heart pounded, and all he could think of was getting the women home safe and alive.

The trip out of town was slow, and more than once Josiah had to defend them from an angry white man. He fought, took a few licks himself, but he led them beyond the city with only a few more scratches than he had gotten from the wagon overturning.

As they made the trek from Lexington to Burtonsville, he went through a cycle of emotions. First anger, then sadness, then shock, and back to anger. This was the scenario none of them wanted. He was so lost in his thoughts that he didn't realize he was moving faster than the women could keep up.

Delia tugged on his arm. "We need to rest."

He slowed and turned to them. Both of them wore looks of fright. Olive had stopped crying, but her cheeks were still wet. He surveyed their surroundings. They were near a patch of trees just starting to bloom. They sat in the grass, Delia looking to get a better assessment of their injuries. Josiah let her tend to him in silence, knowing that their world had shifted, and not for the better.

Once the news got out that Delia, Olive, and Josiah had been caught in the riot in Lexington, the shop had a constant stream of visitors. The residents of Burtonsville came to express their outrage, hear the details, and share new developments. Delia accepted their comfort even though she wanted to do nothing more than forget what had happened. But she couldn't. It was burned in her thoughts. She had never experienced fear like that and hoped never to experience it again.

It did, however, do her heart good to see people taking to Josiah. Many of them hailed him as a hero for getting Delia and Olive home safely and for saving the black soldier's life. That she could hear over and over. It was like the town was just discovering how wonderful Josiah was. She had known all along. He shrugged off most of the praise, but she knew every word was well deserved.

Her father's praise was the most effusive. He thanked Josiah over and over for saving his daughters' lives. Josiah assured him that he would have done it for anyone. Daddy didn't care about that. Josiah's heroism had increased his standing in Daddy's eyes. And in the eyes of many others. She nearly cried when several of them pressed coins into his hands. He tried to refuse, but Delia wouldn't have it. She made it so he couldn't decline by setting up a thank-you jar on the counter.

Even Louis put something in the jar. It wouldn't be right if he didn't thank the man who saved his fiancée. Which set Delia's thoughts off in a depressing direction. *Would Louis have gotten us out safely?* That was a question she already knew the answer to. Josiah's hard life had prepared him to think on the run. To be ready to fight when he needed to. To get them home safely. Louis was too soft for that. His book smarts would help in some situations, but not one like this. Of course Louis would never find himself in a situation like Josiah was in yesterday. He had the protection of money and education to keep him from it.

The shop closed, and Daddy gave Josiah a firm handshake and the tip jar. "Young man, I thank you."

Josiah accepted the jar, head lowered. "You don't have to thank me."

"I do." Daddy pulled out several gold coins and dropped them in the jar.

Josiah's jaw dropped, and tears sprang to Delia's eyes. Daddy gave him a solid pat on the arm and went to balance the day's sales. Delia moved over to Josiah, who stood staring into the jar.

"You deserve every cent of it."

He took a deep breath. "I just don't like the idea of being rewarded for doing what was right."

"All the more reason for the reward."

She took the jar to the counter and dumped out the contents. Josiah watched the coins fall, a look of shock on his face. Delia counted it out for him. She gave him a bright grin. "Almost one hundred and fifty dollars."

Josiah staggered backward. "I have never had this much money in my life."

"Then you should do something special with it."

He looked up at her with a frown creasing his forehead. "I am. I was going to tell you this later but. . ." He took a deep breath. "I'm leaving."

"Leaving?" Delia struggled to understand what he was saying. "Leaving where?"

"I'm leaving Burtonsville. Leaving Kentucky. I'm going with Reverend Pell to Kansas, and this money will help me go."

Delia gripped the counter. "You—you—"

"Grace and I have already decided. She's excited about it. And so am I."

"But—" Struggle as she might, she couldn't come up with one reason why he shouldn't go. "I'm happy for you."

He took half a step closer. "Are you truly?"

"Yes." That was not a lie. But she was not happy about losing her friend. Their relationship hadn't been great since her engagement party, but she had hoped it would get better. If he wasn't in Burtonsville, that would be impossible.

"I can't stay here, Delia. I'm probably about to be evicted by the Halls. Grace is working hard but not making much for it. And I can't stand the violence." His shoulders drooped. "What would have happened if I had been standing in front of that man instead of the soldier? Grace would be alone in the world. There's nothing left here for me. I may as well strike out for Kansas. I may even own land and horses."

Tears filled her eyes. *There is nothing here for him anymore, not even our friendship.* "I wish you the best."

He wiped a tear from her cheek. "I promise to write. Maybe one day you'll be in Kansas—maybe."

His touch seared the agony she felt. She knew she wouldn't ever be in Kansas. Louis would be too busy building his kingdom here. She would never see Josiah again. She reached out to hug him, but he had already turned to put the coins back in the jar.

She helped him and watched him leave. And then she let the tears fall freely.

Chapter 8

Delia rose and counted off another day. Josiah would be leaving soon. He'd been spending a lot of time with Reverend Pell, leaving as soon as his shift ended. Watching him leave with nothing more than a short, "Good night," was a knife to her heart. After spending nearly six months in Burtonsville, the group of Exodusters, which included many of the evicted tenants from the Farms, were eager to be off. Josiah's excitement was high. Although he hadn't given her any details, she could tell the plans were progressing to his satisfaction. They were due to leave on the twentieth of July.

The day of her wedding.

She rose and dressed, off-kilter at the thought that Josiah's departure meant more to her than her own wedding day. Oh, if she could only tell Daddy no. She paused, looking at herself in the mirror. Could she really go through with this? She definitely wouldn't be poor. She would certainly have a name marrying a Hall. They were definitely an upwardly moving family in Burtonsville, and would soon be one in Lexington also. She had heard Mr. Hall mention more than once that he planned to open an office in Lexington. And once they sold off the land in the Farms, they would be rich indeed.

Even as she thought about her life with Louis, her mind drifted to Kansas. Land. Almost free land. New all-black towns. That would be a legacy, for sure. She would be the first McClure in the West and have that name remembered down through history. More than that, she could open a workshop there. Surely a new town would need someone to fix their things. She could fix just about anything. And with Josiah's help. . .

She stopped. She was marrying Louis, and Josiah would be going to Kansas alone. Alone. . .for now. She had little doubt that some woman would see what a wonderful man he was and hitch her wagon to his. He would be happy with his wife, his sister, and a few horses. And she was certain she would not be happy with Louis.

But I can do great good with the family's money. That will have to be my legacy. That and a broken heart.

As she descended the steps, she heard voices in the showroom. She quickly picked up Louis's raised tone.

"There are over fifty going now, almost all of them from the working population of Burtonsville."

Her father huffed. "I'm already feeling the loss. One of my workers is going. He hasn't been with me for long, but he's become invaluable."

"Searcy?"

"Yes. He has been the real muscle in the shop."

She heard footsteps like Louis was pacing the floor. "Something needs to be done. Who will work in the houses? My scullery maid is leaving too. And it's all Searcy's fault. After he came back from the riot in Lexington, he's been a hero in everyone's eyes. It didn't help having him tell everyone he was leaving."

Delia gripped the stair railing. How could Louis even think that? The real reason people were leaving was his evictions.

"I can't find too much fault with the boy right now. He did save my daughters."

"I can find plenty of fault in him. He's forgotten his place. Why was he even allowed to escort Delia to Lexington in the first place? You were putting false hope in his mind. He'll never be more than he is."

"I sent him because I trusted him and I wasn't about to send the girls alone. And you were unavailable." Her father's voice was tight as he answered.

She had listened as long as she could. She continued down the stairs louder than she needed.

Both men stopped talking when she walked into the showroom. "Good morning, Daddy. Louis."

"Good morning." Louis stepped close and planted a kiss on her cheek. Unfortunately, it took her mind straight to the kisses she'd shared with Josiah. Those wonderful, sweet, amazing kisses.

She moved away from Louis and began arranging the wares behind the counter even though they didn't need it. Her father and Louis changed the subject, but her mind remained on Josiah's kisses. His words echoed in her head. *"Did you feel that?"*

She tipped over a bottle of lotion. It rolled, but she caught it before it hit the floor.

"Are you all right, Delia?" her father asked.

She nodded but didn't turn to face him. She had felt it. There was love in that kiss. And that's what she had asked. What it felt like to kiss someone she loved. Josiah had showed her.

She gripped the counter. He loved her. She knew it. Could feel it thrumming through her veins. How silly that it took him leaving to show her what was right in front of her face. She closed her eyes and thought of his hand at her waist. Silly, silly girl. For all her smarts, she had been rather slow in noticing his evident love.

"Delia?" Louis's voice broke through her thoughts. "Are you well?"

She knew her attempt to lighten her expression failed. "Yes. I'm fine."

"You don't look it." Louis studied her face.

"She's been down in the dumps since Josiah announced he was leaving." Her father folded his arms. "Like she's in love with him or something."

She held her face neutral, but she felt her world swoon. Yes, she loved him, had for a long time, but now she was in love with him. She swallowed, unable to deny the claim. Louis studied her, his eyes narrowing. Then he laughed, a little too loudly. "She couldn't possibly be in love with a poor, lowly boy like that. Land sakes, she would be living right in the Farms with him, surrounded by the dregs of society."

"We once lived in the Farms." Her father folded his arms.

Louis laughed. "What a humiliation it would be for your daughter to go back there after you worked so hard to get her out."

Heat flared in her chest. So this was what Louis really thought of the less fortunate. "Louis, I do not think it is a dishonor or humiliation for a woman to marry a man she loves, no matter how much money he has."

"Love grows faster with money." Louis laughed, but his words seared her heart.

She turned to go into her workshop and saw Josiah standing in the doorway. He glared at Louis. Her father shifted uncomfortably. How much had Josiah heard? And did he know she was talking about him?

Josiah looked around the ragged house he'd shared with Grace for the past five years. The broken window that he and Delia had patched up with some heavy leftover curtains from the shop. Of course, the fabric had to be aired out after each rain. The chimney that they used only on the coldest nights because it needed cleaning and would fill the house with heavy smoke. The table and two chairs, both looking as bare as the rest of the room. The small straw pallet he slept on and the rickety bed Grace slept on behind a sheet they'd hung to give her some privacy.

Hard to believe they were about to leave this place. The winter had turned to spring and spring to summer since he'd heard Reverend Pell talk about Kansas back in January. Since he first heard of the open lands. Now he heard and thought about it every day. He spent a lot of time with the reverend and enjoyed the older man's company. The Pells were different from their daughter and son-in-law. Refreshing. Like they weren't caught in the trap of trying to impress society. More than once they'd pointed out how the Davenports were showing favoritism and how the Bible spoke against it. Josiah had tried not to chuckle at the older reverend taking the younger to task.

Evening had fallen and the song of crickets filled the air. Today had been his last day at work. An odd day it was. Surprising, so many people coming to say goodbye. Delia, on the other hand, had remained silent and distant all day. He wanted to go, but not like this. He'd imagined they would spend their last day together remembering their happy times. Not estranged from one another. No matter how excited he was about the trip, he couldn't shake the sadness in his heart.

But in a way, he was glad. He wouldn't have to face Louis or Mr. McClure again. Their words had hurt him because they had hurt Delia. The image of her wounded expression filled his heart. Oh, if only he hadn't waited to express his feelings to her. Now he knew that she might have been willing to marry him even though he was poor. But it was too late. Her wedding was taking place very soon.

He would leave during her wedding and follow the rest of the crowd to the train station for the first leg of the journey. One he could now pay for. He'd used his money from the thank-you jar to pay for his and Grace's tickets. He'd reserved another fifty dollars from the jar for whatever else he needed. The reverend told him that because of the length of the journey, they would make several stops in cities and towns along the route.

"The docks are always in need of good strong hands," the older man had assured him. "You can join crews as a daily worker to make more money. Most pay well." His future was in front of him.

His heart, however, was another matter.

It was fixed on Delia. He'd always loved her but thought she was above his class. She was too good for him, no matter how much money he had. Her grace with people. Her caring heart. But no matter how much he tried, he couldn't get her out of his mind.

Maybe the fact that we will be separated by several states and the Mississippi River might help. He wished that were true, but he knew it wouldn't matter. She would always be in his heart, and no distance could change that.

"Josiah!" Grace's voice broke through his thoughts. He turned to find her standing in the middle of the floor holding two pots. "I was asking if you thought the Thompsons could use these."

He shook his head. "I'm sorry. I was lost in my thoughts."

She put her hand on her hip. "I see that."

"I think we should keep them. Reverend Pell said when we get west of the Mississippi, we might have to set up camp. We may need them to cook over an open fire."

"I'll find a place for them in our sacks." She continued to stare at him. "What were you thinking about? Have we forgotten something?"

"No. I think everything is ready."

She walked over to him, looking very much like their father. "Did you say goodbye to Delia?"

Josiah turned before she could see his expression. "I did. Before I left work."

"Did you beg her to come with us?"

He turned and folded his arms. "She's getting married the day we leave."

Grace shrugged. "So?"

Josiah threw up his hands. "What else do we need to do?"

"Oh no. You can't change the subject."

"I can." He went over to the bags. "Delia has committed to marry Louis."

"But she doesn't love him. You can just look in her eyes and see. She doesn't look happy."

Even though he had his back turned, he could feel her glaring at him. "Do you think she would leave all she has to run away with me?"

"You don't know if she would or not, since you've never asked her."

"Leave it. If she wanted to go, she would have said something by now."

Grace huffed from behind him. "Men are impossible."

Facing her, he scowled. "What is that supposed to mean?"

"What if she is waiting for you to ask her? What if she realizes how much she will risk by running away and wants to know if you love her? And not just as a friend."

Grace's words hit their mark, and he dropped his shoulders. She might go with him. She might want to live on the homestead with him. But Delia would be risking everything, including her father's wrath, to go with him. He loved her, but he couldn't ask her to sacrifice all that for him. She may not be completely happy in Burtonsville, but she would have a decent life. Or maybe she wouldn't. Was she unhappy enough here to want to tough it out in Kansas? That he wasn't sure of.

What if he asked her?

Chapter 9

Delia paced the floor again, stirring Olive from her seat. "Please, Delia. You should relax."

"I can't." She rubbed her hands together. The situation mirrored the turmoil she felt. Even though the sun shone brightly through her windows, Delia felt like it was the dark of night.

Her wedding dress had not arrived from Lexington.

She hadn't been back to the shop since the day of the riot. Some businesses were burned and looted. The dress shop could have been one of them. The information coming out of Lexington was sparse. She prayed no one in the shop had been harmed. Her father kept reassuring her that the dress was on its way. He had talked to the shop owner a week ago but not since.

She started to pace again.

Olive came to her and held her hands. "Don't worry. You have plenty of dresses you can wear instead."

"It's not about the dress."

Olive looked at her with curiosity. "Then what is it?"

"I—" Could she say it? "I don't want to marry Louis."

Olive didn't even appear shocked. "I know."

Delia pulled her hands away. "How do you know?"

"'Cause I saw you and Josiah kissing in your workroom."

Delia groaned. "Why didn't you say anything?"

She gave Delia a shy smile. "I didn't want to interrupt. I always thought Josiah was sweet on you. But when I saw you two kissing, I thought maybe he had told you."

Delia took a deep breath. "I didn't see it. I thought he was being a good friend. Now I'm afraid it's too late."

She donned a plain work dress and went down the stairs. At the bottom, she heard raised voices. She stepped into the showroom and found Daddy and Louis, who was dressed in his wedding suit. Beside him stood his father and Reverend Davenport.

Louis's face shifted into a sneer. "What are you wearing?"

His words were so sharp that Delia took a step back. "My dress isn't here."

Her father reached out for Louis. "Everything is going to be okay. I'm sure there's an explanation for the delay."

Louis whipped around to her father. "I know what the delay is. She's dragging her feet. This wedding has been planned for months. I can't believe the dress isn't here."

Reverend Davenport patted Louis's arm. "Why would Delia lie about the dress?"

"Because she wants to run off with that boy." He stepped closer to her. "Don't think I didn't see you making eyes at him. Pouting before he left." He grabbed her arm. "I will not be humiliated by someone who couldn't even get himself out of the Farms."

And in a flash, Delia saw what her life would be like with Louis. He would control her. He increased her social standing, but woe to her if she ever did something he didn't agree with.

She tried to pull away, but he increased his grip.

"I think you should unhand my daughter." Daddy's voice sounded from behind her.

Louis looked past her, shock on his face. He let Delia go. "You can't allow her to continue to pine after—"

Her father's demeanor changed as he turned to her. "Go upstairs."

"Yes, Daddy." Delia hurried. She knew that tone of voice. It normally meant she was in trouble.

Olive gave her a puzzled look when she returned to their room. "What happened?" she whispered, as if Daddy and Louis could hear her.

Footsteps sounded on the stairs a few minutes later. The door opened, and Daddy walked in. "Olive, can I talk to Delia alone?"

Olive scooted out of the room without answering, surely as terrified by her father's expression as Delia was.

Her father crossed the room and sat next to her. Then, after a moment, he took her hand. "Delia, I believe I owe you an apology."

She stared at him. "Daddy—"

He patted her hand, interrupting her. "I thought I could give you a better life than your mother and I had. And I also thought you were becoming too much like her. That's why I agreed to your marriage to Louis. I thought he would be strong enough to keep you under control."

She turned to her father. "Daddy, do I have to marry him?"

Her father studied her for a moment, his eyes filled with what looked like sadness. "I want the best for you."

She touched her father's arm. "He's not the best. Money doesn't change the fact that I'd be unhappy."

Her father didn't speak for the longest time. Delia held her breath. Finally, he stood, not releasing her hand. "Come." They descended the stairs together.

Louis and Reverend Davenport still stood in the showroom. Her father cleared his throat. "It appears my daughter doesn't want to marry you."

Louis's face blackened with anger. "Then I will make sure no one ever shops in this store again." He spun around and stormed out the door.

When he left, the tension in the room deflated. More than that, a flicker of joy flashed in Delia's heart. She was free. She didn't have to marry Louis. But. . .

She hugged her father. "Thank you, Daddy."

And for the first time in a long time, her father pulled her into a tight embrace. "I thought he would be a good match for you." He took a deep breath. "Your mother and I invested too much in you to have you mistreated."

Delia looked up at him. "Daddy, I—"

"You want to go to Kansas with Josiah."

"Yes," she said, and held her breath.

"You have to marry before you go."

Please let Josiah still love me. "I think Josiah would be willing to marry me before he leaves for Kansas."

"We better hurry to catch him."

She let out a sob and squeezed her father tighter. "Thank you."

"Go and pack before I change my mind."

Delia rushed to the bottom of the stairs, and the front door opened. In stepped the woman from the dress shop in Lexington holding a long box. "I'm sorry I'm late, but here is your dress."

Delia laughed. Now she would actually be happy about wearing it. If she could only catch Josiah in time.

The caravan to Kansas started in the Farms. There were lots of tears and hugs. The residents had bonded together since the evictions started. They had pooled together and supported each other. As a matter of fact, over half of the Farms was going with Reverend Pell. Josiah hugged each person who came to wish him well. His eye kept checking the crowd for Delia, and he had to remind himself that she probably wouldn't be here to see him off.

An uneasiness kept him from being truly happy about leaving. The slight possibility that Delia might have come with him if he had asked. And now, saying his goodbyes to his neighbors, he couldn't come up with one good reason why he hadn't asked. All his excuses paled in light of leaving her forever.

But what if I don't have to? The thought stilled him. Could he still ask? It wouldn't hurt to ask. He was prepared to go to Kansas without her. If she said no, his plans would remain the same. But if she said yes. . .

He looked at Grace talking to Mrs. Pell. Grace was right. He should ask.

Mind made up, he started walking.

But Mrs. Thompson blocked his path, the baby in her arms. "Thank you for all you've done."

He shifted, wanting to step around her before he lost his nerve. "You're welcome. I hope you'll do well."

She smiled at him. "You may see me sooner than you think."

"What do you mean?"

"My husband and I are considering coming to Kansas." She glanced down at the baby. "She's too young right now. Reverend Pell promised to come back and help us make the journey."

Josiah grinned. "I hope to see you before the winter."

She nodded. "Too bad Miss Delia isn't going. If anyone could make homesteading work, she could. She could make anything work."

She could. He could already imagine her in the house, building something while he worked with the horses in the yard. He could see their home filled with all the gadgets she created. He could see it, and he could have it.

"Excuse me, Mrs. Thompson. I need to get to Delia."

Mrs. Thompson gave him a surprised look but stepped aside.

Someone called his name. It sounded like it came from the back of the crowd. He squinted, not seeing the source. The call came again, and his mind put a face to the voice. Delia. But she wouldn't be here.

Mrs. Thompson looked over her shoulder. "That sounded like Miss Delia."

"I thought so too." Josiah stood on his toes, eyeing the crowd. The people shifted, giving him a clear view to the back, and he saw her.

Delia was running toward him. "Josiah!" she cried out again.

He surged forward to meet her. Why was she here and not at the church? Could she be coming for him? He continued to move toward her, his heart lightening with every step. He would ask her. He would ask her to go and ask her to be his wife.

She closed the distance much faster than he did. When she reached him, she stopped two steps from him. "I—" she huffed.

He grasped her by the shoulders. "Is everything all right?"

"Yes," she managed to say, but leaned forward in an effort to catch her breath.

Josiah looked her over. *She's not wearing her wedding dress.* Not unusual, since she wouldn't have worn it to the Farms. But she was here and not wearing the dress and actually not getting married.

She took a big gulp of air and said words that shook him even though he already anticipated what she would say. "My father called off the wedding."

His heart stopped. This was it. His chance to ask. "Delia—"

"I'm not marrying Louis."

Josiah took one step closer to her. "Delia, I have something to ask you."

"Daddy saw the truth about Louis's character. He told me I didn't have to marry him." It was clear she thought his question was about the broken marriage.

"I was—I wanted—"

"I want to come with you."

Josiah staggered backwards. "What?"

Delia dropped her gaze. "I mean, I want to come with you, but Daddy says he will only allow it if we're married."

Her words made his mind muddy. *If we're married.* . . "Are you saying your father is allowing you to marry me and go to Kansas?"

Delia didn't look up but nodded slowly.

His heart leaped in his chest. He didn't even notice that a crowd had gathered around them, including Reverend Pell. "I'm not sure, but I think the young lady wants you to ask her to marry you," the reverend said.

Delia didn't look up, but she tensed. Like she was expecting him—

He dropped to one knee. "Delia, I may be the poorest man in Burtonsville, and I can't promise all the fine things you would have gotten if you had married Louis, but I promise to do everything in my power to make you the happiest woman in the world." He took her hand. "I've loved you ever since I met you. Will you marry me?"

Her head lifted, and she wore the brightest smile. "Yes!" She threw herself into his arms.

He caught her, laughing. His friend and soon to be his wife. She placed her cheek against his. "I'm sorry it took me so long to see. I love you so much," she whispered in his ear. He didn't think he could be happier than hearing her say yes to his proposal. But he could. He could be happier to know she loved him.

The crowd erupted in cheers and applause. Josiah stood and pulled Delia into his arms, and she came freely.

Josiah turned to Reverend Pell. "We would be honored if you married us." Delia nodded, tears in her eyes.

"It would be my pleasure." Reverend Pell smiled and raised his voice above the din. "It looks like we'll be having a wedding before we set off."

Another cheer. Soon Delia was pulled out of Josiah's arms by Mrs. Thompson. "Let's get her ready." Delia let them lead her off, giggling and looking back at Josiah.

A small clearing near the middle of the Farms was soon designated as the place where the wedding would take place. The Thompson girls and a few other children were tasked with picking whatever flowers they could find. People brought out chairs and blankets from their houses for seating. Reverend Pell and Josiah had found a place under the shade of a large tree as an altar of sorts.

Josiah's heart twisted in his chest. He was marrying Delia. When he looked up, Delia and her father stood at the end of the makeshift aisle. Delia wore a lovely wedding dress and wildflowers in her hair. Olive stood behind her, holding the train of her dress. Josiah was suddenly self-conscious about his worn, tattered clothing.

Reverend Pell leaned near him and in a low voice said, "I wouldn't worry about that, son."

He didn't have time to. With each step toward him, Delia grew lovelier, overshadowing all other thoughts. When she stood next to him, he felt as rich as all the elite in Burtonsville. And he was, since he had the greatest treasure he could ever want.

Terri J. Haynes, a native Baltimorean, is a homeschool mom, writer, prolific knitter, freelance graphic artist, and former army wife (left the army, not the husband). She loves to read, so much that when she was in elementary school she masterminded a plan to be locked in a public library armed with only a flashlight, to read all the books, and a peanut butter and jelly sandwich. As she grew, her love for writing grew as she tried her hand at poetry, articles, speeches, and fiction. She is a storyteller at heart. Her passion is to draw readers into the story world she has created and to bring laughter and joy to their lives.

Terri is a 2010 American Christian Fiction Writers Genesis contest finalist and a 2012 semifinalist. She is also a 2013 Amazon Breakthrough Novel Award Quarterfinalist. Her publishing credits include *Cup of Comfort for Military Families*, Crosswalk.com, the *Secret Place Devotional*, Urbanfaith.com, *Vista Devotional*, and *Publisher's Weekly*.

Terri holds a bachelor's degree in theology, a master's degree in theological studies, and a certificate in creative writing and graphic design, meeting the minimal requirements of being a geek. She and her husband pastor a church where she serves as executive pastor and worship leader. Terri lives in Maryland with her three wonderful children and her husband, who often beg her not to kill off their favorite characters.

Follow Terri at www.terrijhaynes.com and www.inotherwords.terrijhaynes.com.

The Elusive Heiress

by Noelle Marchand

Prologue

New York, New York
April 1898

I wouldn't do that if I were you."

The gentle warning made Georgiana Price gasp. Fighting to maintain her balance, she hugged the column tighter and dug her dancing slipper into the outer ledge of the stone verandah. Wisteria vines cut into the delicate silk of her dress as she peered through the purple flowers at the man impeding her escape. Henry Chadwick. He was her father's right-hand man as the president of the Pinnacle Hotel and Spa, one of her father's biggest investments.

Once a month, Henry had dinner with her and her parents, boring her to no end with his talk of dividends and strategies. The consummate yes-man, he never heard an idea from her father that he didn't like and would never even think of doing anything Maxwell Price might find objectional. That made one of them.

Holding Henry's gaze, she loosened her grasp on the column in order to take hold of the railing. He relaxed slightly. She turned to face the garden. His warning was low and exasperated. "Georgiana."

She leaped. Air rushed through her skirts, making them flare out around her until they obscured the ground. She hit the grass with a rather impressive thud, but her hands and knees took the worst of it. With a huff of frustration, she stood and brushed the grass from her hands. If Henry hadn't distracted her, she would have remembered to hold on to her skirts. As it was, her gown was likely grass-stained. Yet another reason for her mother to be displeased by Georgiana's behavior tonight. Oh well. In for a penny, in for a pound.

A softer thud set her whirling on her heel in time to watch Henry absorb his landing with a surprising amount of grace. She stared in confusion as he stood. Her softly spoken, "What are you doing?" collided with his, "Where do you think you're going?"

"Georgiana," a strident voice called from nearby.

Her eyes widened. Catching Henry off guard, she pushed him around the corner of the house until they were both concealed in the shadows of night. She put a silencing hand over his mouth just as the voice called again. "Georgiana?"

Biting her lip, she dared not peer around the corner at her fiancé—Baron Robert Granville, the Earl of Stamford. She heard his footsteps approach the porch railing and could easily imagine his hawkish features twisting in annoyance. "Where the devil did she go?"

She rolled her eyes even as she held her breath and leaned closer to the wall. Or rather, closer to Henry, since he stood between her and the wall. Only when he tensed did she realize just how improper a situation she'd placed them in. For Pete's sake, she'd never even shared a dance with Henry before, and now she was practically. . .well, accosting him, for lack of a better term.

Lost between amusement and the fear that Henry's puritanical nature would prompt him to give her away, she met his narrowed gaze. She couldn't seem to stop the corner of her mouth from hitching upward, but the pleading look she sent him seemed to do the trick well enough. He relaxed slightly, though he did not spare her a responding look filled with frustration.

She bit her lip to keep from laughing, then watched as Henry's gaze traced her features searchingly. No doubt trying to figure out why she felt it necessary to hide from her fiancé. Why should Henry care? No one else seemed to. They were all too busy telling her how lucky she was to be marrying Stamford. She would be a baroness. Apparently nothing else mattered.

Stamford's voice made her tense. Why hadn't he moved on? He seemed to have paused only feet away from where she'd jumped. "Whitcomb, have you seen my fiancé?"

A chuckle sounded, growing nearer. Finally, a posh but teasing British accent labeled the newcomer one of her fiancé's compatriots. "Misplaced your millions, did you?"

Stamford snorted with laughter. "I'll have them stashed away at Stamford Abbey soon enough. If she runs off there, she'll trouble nothing but cobwebs and old Stamford ghosts."

A shudder rushed down her spine. That was exactly what she was afraid of. Not old ghost stories, but the dilapidated condition of the estate that was to be her home. Flush toilets had yet to cross the Atlantic, apparently, let alone adequate heating. Why, she'd heard some of those old country estates hadn't been substantially updated since medieval times.

The lack of creature comforts wasn't the only thing that concerned her. She'd be a stranger in a strange land with the only familiar faces being those of a few friends scattered hither and yon at lonely country estates. They would be living at the beck and call of titled husbands of their own, so who knew when or if she'd ever see them.

Beneath her hand, Henry's mouth slid into a frown, making her refocus on her fiancé's conversation. "No, my mother will have naught to do with her, nor will the rest of the family, I'm afraid. Grateful lot, aren't they? While they run up accounts in town and burn through coal like there's no tomorrow, I'm here in barbarous America, selling myself to the highest bidder."

Her chin lifted in indignation. She'd suspected he felt that way, but to hear him say it so brazenly. . . Henry's hand tightened around her wrist. A squeeze indicating solidarity? No. A request for her to remove her hand. She did so, cautiously. He wouldn't give her away. Surely he wouldn't.

He made not a sound. In fact, he barely moved other than to rest his hand—the one still holding her wrist—on his chest. Perhaps he wasn't quite as awful as she'd assumed.

In fact, there seemed to be a small amount of sympathy, kindness, and understanding in his intelligent brown eyes. Actually, through the frames of his glasses, they seemed almost amber. She'd never noticed that before. Or perhaps she'd never seen them in the moonlight. They were quite. . .nice. The rest of his classical features were rather pleasing as well. Not that it mattered.

"Are there really no other options?" Whitcomb asked. Georgiana pulled her gaze slowly from Henry's to glance toward the porch. Tufts of white cigar smoke drifted in the candlelight, lending a sickly sweet scent to the breeze. Awful stuff. It always gave her a headache. Did Stamford care? Certainly not. Odious man.

"Of course there are, though none nearly as lucrative," he grumbled. "Once I renovate the abbey, all I'll need is my heir and a spare, and then I'll be done with her."

Her mouth fell open even as she flinched in disgust. A broodmare. Was that all she was? Millions and a broodmare. Denial rose within her—and anger. So much anger. She'd tell him exactly who was done with whom. Not to mention a few other choice words too.

Henry's hands clamped onto her arms. Before she could blink, she was the one with her back pressed against the wall and a hand over her mouth. She stared at him in shock, then speared him with a look of betrayal. How could he stop her from telling Stamford what she thought of him? Did he agree with the man?

Henry shook his head, then leaned in until his whisper filled her ear. "I'm sorry. Just wait."

Wait? She calmed slightly. Right. Her reputation. And his. It wouldn't do either of them any favors to be discovered in what would surely appear to be a liaison. It would be utterly inappropriate for several reasons, not the least of which that Henry was married. Or was he? She hadn't been entirely sure of late. He wore a wedding band, but she'd never met his wife. He never talked about her or brought her to parties. It was all very odd. To be honest, Georgiana had never given it much thought until now.

He must have seen her temper fading because he removed his hand from her mouth. She let her head fall back to gently rest on the stone wall and closed her eyes, trying to block out whatever else Stamford might be saying. She'd heard enough. There was no way she could marry that man, which is exactly what she'd been telling her father from the beginning. Surely now he'd have to listen. If he didn't. . .

"Georgiana," Henry murmured. Her eyes flew open, and she met his gaze, suddenly aware that the voices on the porch had faded away. Brow furrowed, Henry watched her with a mix of concern and unease. "I know that didn't sound good, but. . .don't do anything impetuous."

"Impetuous?" She gave him a wan smile. "I would never."

If her parents didn't listen to her concerns and call off the wedding, she wouldn't do anything rash. No, she'd plan it out well. Very well.

Chapter 1

Denver, Colorado
Six months later

E xtra! Extra! Police closing in on the madcap runaway heiress!"

Lies. Neither the police nor her father nor any of his private investigators could possibly have any idea where she was. Half the time she didn't even know where she was. Shivering and damp from a persistent drizzle, Georgiana huddled in the entrance of the train station and tried to get her bearings. Denver's huge gray sky hovered over the impressive backdrop of mountains already covered in snow.

A little more than four weeks. That's how much time stood between her and her twenty-first birthday, when she would receive the inheritance her grandmother had left her and the complete independence that went along with it. Until then she'd be known only as Gigi Smith. Hardly inventive, but it had allowed her to get by these past six months with hardly a raised eyebrow among the middle class. The dowdy dresses she'd bought from a pawn shop outside of New Jersey had helped, as had the spectacles and several wigs.

"Can I help you, miss?"

Startled, Georgiana glanced up to find a porter eyeing her curiously. She smiled. "No. I'm waiting for someone."

He nodded. "Let me know if you need anything."

"I'll do that." She let out a breath of relief as he walked away. That was the third porter who'd offered his assistance in the last hour. It wouldn't be long before they figured out she was little more than a vagabond and sent her on her way. She really did need to find someplace to go.

Discreetly reaching into her pockets, she rubbed the few coins she had left. If only she'd been more frugal when she'd first run away. She'd felt like a princess on holiday back then. Smug with the idea that she had so cleverly slipped through everyone's fingers, she'd stayed on the move. She'd ridden the rails from Newport to the Carolinas on to Florida and then to Texas. She'd lost track after that. Not only of her location, but of her suitcase—the one containing much of the pin money she'd saved for her escape and all of the dresses she'd purchased at the pawnbroker except the one she'd been wearing.

All she had left were the frivolous gowns she hadn't wanted to leave behind at home. She'd considered giving them away a hundred times since simply to rid herself of the inconvenience of having another suitcase. But by then she'd been too afraid the distinctive designer gowns would draw undue attention. Perhaps. . . perhaps she ought to brave it. Sell them, then take the next train out of Denver. It truly was her only option at this point.

"Miss?" The porter was back again, this time a frown furrowing his brow. "Are you sure there is nothing I can do to assist you?"

Swallowing her pride, she smiled. "Actually, I was wondering if you knew where I could find the nearest pawnbroker."

When he hesitated, she added, "Please."

A few moments later, she hopped over a puddle, her worn boots nearly slipping as they searched for purchase on the wet street. A wagon rushed past her close enough for the wind to stir her mussed hair. She paused to catch her breath. A few blocks. Just a few more blocks, then she'd have funds again.

The weight of someone's gaze made her glance across the street. A group of four rangy-looking men watched her with unabashed interest. Breath catching in her throat, she suddenly became aware of just how deserted this street was. She grasped her suitcase tighter and walked purposefully in the direction she was supposed to go. At the next block, she paused to look around. This was the right direction, wasn't it?

The group of men crossed to her side of the street. She picked up her pace. So did they. One of them called out something to her—something so foul she dared not even acknowledge it. Panic rose in her throat. A cab turned the corner. She stepped to the edge of the sidewalk and lifted a shaky hand to hail it.

It careened to a stop. She hopped inside, calling, "The train station, please, and hurry!"

Sinking into the cab bench, she let out a breath of relief as it left the men far behind her. She removed the coins from her pocket and tried to calculate how much the fare would cost. At least half of her meager savings. Her stomach rumbled, filling her with dread. It was time to face reality.

Her plan had failed. She had no choice but to go crawling back to her father. Yet she wasn't even sure that was an option. He'd made it perfectly clear that if she refused to marry Stamford, he'd wash his hands of her. She didn't want to believe he meant that, but he'd seemed serious—and livid. She had nowhere to turn.

The cab rolled to a stop at an intersection. Bright lights filled the carriage. Blinking, she glanced out the window to see an electric sign that announced in elegantly scrolling letters THE PINNACLE OF DENVER HOTEL & SPA. She stilled, then leaned across the cab to stare at it. One of Henry Chadwick's hotels. Members of the board and their families could stay there free of charge, and her father was the chairman.

She could hardly walk in and announce herself as Georgiana Price, but. . . By the time she arrived back at the train station, an entirely new plan had formed in her mind. It wasn't entirely honest, and it might get her thrown out on her ear. But if it worked, it would solve her problems—at least for now.

She hurried to the ladies' restroom, changed her wig, and dressed in a House of Worth traveling gown. A few minutes later, she exited a cab outside the Pinnacle of Denver and stepped into the lobby. Oh, what heavenly warmth and luxury!

White Italian marble stretched out before her like a gleaming moonlit lake. Its shores were walls painted in cream and pearl. Gold brocade chairs lined the walls and were gathered in seating arrangements with rich, dark wooden tables here and there. Crystal chandeliers gleamed with candlelight as they hung from the ceiling. Refusing to gawk despite an appreciation created by months without access to the finer things in life, she glided toward the front desk.

The man, whose golden nameplate declared him the hotel manager, greeted her with a smile. "Good evening, madam. Checking in?"

"Yes," she confirmed confidently. "For an extended stay."

"Excellent. And what name shall I use for the reservation?"

Heart pounding in her chest, she smiled and answered with the utmost poise. "Mrs. Henry Chadwick."

Ensconced in the study of his mother's house, Henry Chadwick studied a set of ledgers, willing them to make sense. "You're absolutely correct. Something isn't right."

Concern and exasperation filled her voice. "I knew it. Things aren't adding up. I can't make heads or tails of it anymore."

"I know, Ma. That's why I'm here. I'm going to help you sort this out. I promise." He set the ledger he'd been perusing onto the desk with the others. "Is this everything?"

She pressed a finger to the spine of each ledger as she spoke. "These two are for the soup kitchen. These three are for the women and children's home. This one is for the evangelism team. Yes, that's everything."

Seeing all the account books piled together in one place made him realize exactly how much he'd been asking of his mother for the past three years. "You need an assistant."

"I know I do. I've been telling you that for two years. It's too much for one person."

He frowned. "I thought you said hiring the departmental directors helped."

"It did, but now I spend just as much time overseeing them, developing new initiatives within each organization, making sure they stay in compliance with our standards and bylaws—all while safeguarding your anonymity, which is work in itself." She sighed. "I still don't understand why you don't reveal yourself as the benefactor behind Mercy Ministries."

"Because I'm not doing it for me. I'm doing it for the Lord. 'Let not thy left hand know what thy right hand doeth' and all that."

His mother lifted an eyebrow. "What about 'Let your light so shine before men, that they may see your good works, and glorify your Father which is in heaven'?"

He pulled in a deep breath. "Fine. I'll think about it."

"Well, hallelujah! That's progress. Truly, this isn't about seeking recognition for good works. It would simply be to make things easier on us, especially when it comes to overseeing the organization. Do you think anyone in their right mind would cheat Mercy Ministries if they knew the powerful Henry Chadwick was the one behind it? Not likely."

"We don't know that anyone is cheating us. It's possible someone is simply confused or their numbers got crossed. I don't know yet, and I don't want to assume wrongdoing." He sighed and checked the clock. "I need to head over to the Pinnacle to prepare for my meeting with the governor's staff tomorrow."

She patted his shoulder. "All right, son. I'll be praying things work out with that. Hosting the inaugural ball would be such an honor."

"It certainly would." He gathered the pile of books. "I'll see you tomorrow for luncheon."

"Tell Linus and the rest of the staff I said hello and I'll visit soon. Goodness knows Mercy Ministries has kept me far too busy as of late."

"Yes, ma'am." He kissed his mother on the cheek and waved a quick goodbye. Fifteen minutes later, he crossed the Pinnacle's gleaming white marble floor toward the front desk. The hotel manager, Linus Middlebrook, glanced up from his work, then did a double take and stood up straighter. "Mr. Chadwick, welcome! I apologize. We weren't expecting you until next month, sir."

Henry gave the man an understanding nod. "No need to apologize. I will return next month as usual. However, I received a call from the governor's staff. The venue they were going to use for the inaugural ball fell through. They are considering this hotel as a substitute."

Linus set the ledger aside and pulled out the registration book. "You don't say, sir."

"Yes, it's all quite sudden, I know. The meeting is scheduled for tomorrow. I'd like to meet with you, our event manager, and the caterer later this afternoon if you would arrange that for me."

"Certainly, sir." The man jotted a quick note on a notepad. "How long will you be staying with us?"

"Only three days. You haven't rented out the penthouse, have you?"

"Yes, sir, but I believe you'll find the company agreeable." At Henry's blank look, Linus grinned. "Your wife, sir."

Henry stilled. "I'm sorry. What did you say?"

"Your wife."

"My wife?" A vision of Amelia filled his mind—so full of life despite her delicate health. He frowned. "What about her?"

"She's rented out the penthouse, of course."

He stared at the man before him, wondering at just what point this man had lost his mind. "My wife rented out the penthouse?"

Linus nodded. "Why, yes. She's been staying with us for the past ten days. It's been a pleasure to have her, I assure you."

Henry held up a silencing hand. "Linus, you know very well that my wife died three years ago. You were at her funeral."

"I mean your new wife." Linus hesitated. "You. . .don't have a new wife?"

Henry shook his head.

"But she said—"

"She *lied*." Watching the color drain from his manager's face, Henry continued. "I assume this woman has been given free room and board, the finest of everything."

"Of course." The slight man shifted from one foot to the other, twisting the pinkie ring commemorating his five years of service at the Pinnacle of Denver Hotel and Spa. Linus swallowed hard. "Shall I call the authorities and have her removed?"

"No." Henry drummed his fingers on the counter as he considered the situation. "Not until I've had a chance to sort this out privately. Besides, I think it's only fair I have the chance to meet the little charlatan claiming to be my wife. Have you the penthouse key?"

"Yes, sir." Linus began to hand it over, then hesitated. "Perhaps I ought to go with you, sir."

Henry gestured to the gold-plated elevator doors. "Lead the way."

Possibly thinking this might very well be his last duty as manager, Linus gave a resigned nod and led the way to the elevator. Henry shook his head as he followed. This situation was entirely untenable.

The utter gall of someone to claim to be his wife and presume to live upon the largess of the business he'd built from the ground up. The complete lack of regard it showed for the woman who had once rightfully owned the title of being his wife was like a kick in the teeth. What had Amelia ever done besides be kind and caring, looking out for those less fortunate? To have this charlatan attempt to take her place—

"Penthouse suite," announced the elevator operator.

Henry led the way across the hall to the private entrance of the penthouse suite. He rapped on the door. Not wanting to frighten the perpetrator into hiding, he called through the door, "Housekeeping. Anyone there?"

Another knock went unanswered. Henry stepped aside and nodded to the door. "Open it, Linus."

Linus unlocked the door, then stepped inside. "Mrs. Chadwick?"

Henry sent the man a cutting look. There was no Mrs. Chadwick here, whether or not the woman in question was present. "Does the woman step out often?"

"Yes, sir. She's usually gone for most of the day."

Racking up more bills for him to pay? Eyes narrowing, Henry surveyed the suite. Obviously the woman had not intended to give up residence anytime in the near future. Several gowns lay strewn across the room. Two on the gilt settee. Another on the bed. A pair of worn black boots tipped precariously on the floor near the coffee table as though they'd been kicked off and abandoned. A comb, brush, and a few hairpins cluttered the vanity table. Henry couldn't help but frown at the condition of the place. "Has she not allowed housekeeping in?"

"Once every two days, sir. She prefers her privacy."

"Hardly surprising." He moved toward the luxurious bench at the end of the bed to peer into the vestiges of the dilapidated suitcase resting on it. "Most criminals prefer to do their deeds in the darkness. Linus, pull back the curtains."

A few seconds later, light filled the room, revealing the worn clothes inside the suitcase. This woman apparently lived two different lives. One of wealth and privilege, the other of want and need. Not surprising, considering her line of work.

Henry strode to the wardrobe and pulled back the door. More gowns—and two wig stands, with one wig missing. He frowned as he eyed the auburn hair she'd left behind. "What does this woman look like?"

"Green eyes, dark hair, about five feet four inches tall, pleasant figure. Overall, a pretty sort."

Henry held up the reddish-brown wig. "Well, she is certainly trying to disguise herself. If she is wearing a dark wig now and this one is red, I'd say our perpetrator is likely a blond."

Linus's brow furrowed. "I can't understand it. She seems so kind and genuine. Quite personable. Not at all the type to do something like this."

"We are obviously dealing with a professional here." Setting down the wig, Henry searched through the remaining dresses, then paused to check one of the labels. House of Worth? Someone had paid a hefty sum for these. Hopefully it wasn't him. "Perhaps I should call the authorities, after all."

When Linus failed to respond, Henry turned to find the man staring at the gown on the bed. Linus blinked, then glanced back at Henry. "Quite a dress, isn't it?"

Henry took a step closer. Clearly intended to reveal as much of the wearer's shoulders as possible while still hanging on to a vestige of decency, the concoction of violet tulle was softened with a periwinkle overlay. It looked like something out of a ballet. It looked. . .like something he'd seen before. Cautiously, he edged closer, drawn by an odd sense of familiarity.

His gaze caught on the pink ribbon and the delicate leaves of sage-colored silk that rested about the waist of the dress. He'd felt the silken texture of those leaves beneath his palms before. His fingers had touched that satin ribbon. They reached for it again as his mind traveled back to a darkened garden and that unexpected meeting with Georgiana Price.

How often had he blamed himself for her disappearance? It wasn't his fault. He knew that. Yet he couldn't help wondering how things might have happened differently if he'd done more to help the troubled woman. She'd obviously been searching for a way out of her impending marriage. If he'd spoken to Maxwell Price about what he'd heard Robert Granville say, maybe Maxwell would have seen the benefits of calling off Georgiana's doomed engagement.

Instead, Henry had been too afraid of reaping the displeasure of the man who was not only the Pinnacle's largest investor, but also the chairman of the board. He'd told himself to mind his own business and let Georgiana handle her own affairs. Then she'd run away. . .or was abducted. . .or murdered, depending on who was speculating. If this was really her. . .

"Mr. Chadwick? Are you all right, sir?"

Henry let the dress float back to the bed. "I'm fine. I just realized I know who this is. Someone is playing a joke on me, that's all. There's no need to call the authorities."

"Oh." Surprise filled Linus's voice. "Are you sure?"

"Almost entirely." He forced himself to turn and offer a smile.

Frowning, Linus shook his head. "Well, it isn't a very amusing joke, is it?"

"Not in the least. Someone will pay dearly, I assure you. But you needn't worry. In fact, take the rest of the day off. I don't want you to see the woman and accidentally tip her off. I have a joke of my own to play."

Linus tensed. "Just the rest of today off? I mean, I'm not—"

"You aren't fired." Henry frowned. "I'm not sure what I'll tell the rest of the staff. I'll need some time to decide."

"Of course, sir." Linus took a hesitant step toward the door. "I suppose I'll go then."

"Leave the key and close the door behind you."

"Yes, sir." Linus handed him the key, then hurried out the door.

Shaking his head, Henry surveyed the woman's belongings with new eyes. "Georgiana Price, where in the world have you been?"

Bells chimed from the cable car as it approached the next intersection in downtown Denver, and Georgiana couldn't help but smile. She ridden on New York City's "El," the London underground, and the Paris Metro. Yet nothing compared to the feeling of complete freedom that filled her every time she hopped onto a Denver cable car. Her friend of nine days, Margaret Moore, nudged her arm and grinned. "It never gets old, does it, Gigi?"

Georgiana shook her head. How could it get old when everything was so new—including her. God had seen to that by arresting her attention the first morning after she'd arrived in Denver. She'd been wandering, looking for something to fill her time as she waited for the days to slip by so that she could reach her majority. Knowing, if only briefly, what it was like to have no idea where her next meal would come from, she'd found herself at a soup kitchen run by Walter and Margaret Moore. The couple had eagerly accepted her offer to help.

The joy and purpose with which they lived had piqued Georgiana's curiosity. She'd wanted to know more, and they'd gladly shared the Gospel with her. Georgiana had attended church her entire life, but faith and God's love had never been as real to her as it had in that moment.

She'd chosen then and there to stop living for herself, to start living a life in pursuit of God's purposes—a life that helped others. For nine days she'd worked twelve-hour shifts at the Moores' soup kitchen. It was hard, hot, and tiring work, but she didn't regret a moment of it.

The cable car slowed as it neared her street. She hopped off and turned to wave at the couple. "See you tomorrow."

"Have a good night!" Walter called as the cable car began moving again.

It had taken quite a bit of effort to convince Walter that he and Margaret didn't need to escort her all the way home every day. Knowing he was watching, Georgiana strolled toward a nearby boardinghouse until the cable car turned the corner. She stopped on the boardinghouse's doorstep to pull out a great coat from the small traveling bag she carried.

She slid her arm through the lavish fur-trimmed coat and tied the belt around her waist to completely conceal the modest working clothes she wore beneath it. She hated deceiving her new friends at the soup kitchen and the staff at the Pinnacle, but she couldn't afford to have anyone asking any inconvenient questions. So far she'd been careful to reveal only generalities about her past.

The Moores hadn't pressed for more, though they had hinted that she should feel free to tell them about her past whenever she felt ready. She wasn't ready. With a sigh, she set off down the street with a haughty pep in her step. She smiled at the friendly doorman as she entered the Pinnacle of Denver Hotel and Spa, then headed directly for the elevator. The elevator operator snapped to attention. "Good evening, Mrs. Chadwick. How are you this fine day?"

The door closed on the lobby, and the elevator began its journey to the penthouse. "Very well, Thomas, and you?"

"Quite well indeed, ma'am." The tawny-haired youth seemed ready to say more, then clamped his mouth shut and smiled.

She narrowed her eyes at him even as an amused smile tilted her lips. "What else were you going to say?"

He shook his head. "Nothing at all, ma'am."

"Hmm." The elevator smoothly came to a stop. With one last suspicious look at Thomas, she stepped onto her floor. She dug into her satchel for the room key, then unlocked the door and pushed it open with her shoulder. As usual, room service had left a tray for her just inside the door. Her stomach rumbled in appreciation.

She hadn't eaten since breakfast. It didn't seem right to take food from those who needed it at the soup kitchen, so she usually skipped luncheon and had a late dinner. Today was no exception. Dropping her satchel, she kicked off her shoes and used one of the napkins to grab a buttered roll.

She'd just sunk her teeth into its soft warmth when a throat cleared across the room. Her gaze shot toward the sound. Expecting to see a member of the hotel staff, she froze at the sight before her. Henry Chadwick.

"Oh," she said on a breath. Realizing she'd dropped the roll, she picked it up and set it on the cart, then stared at the man across the room.

He sat at the mahogany secretary desk and had apparently been there for some time taking care of hotel business of some sort. He peered at her over his glasses as though he was inspecting a new real estate investment. Finally, he removed his spectacles and leaned back in his chair. "Good evening, *wife*."

She grimaced, then tried to control the ridiculous urge to smile by biting her lip. "Henry. . ."

He lifted an eyebrow. She pressed her lips together, realizing the gravity of the situation. She swallowed hard. "Listen, I. . .I don't know what to say."

He set his pen down and stood. Looking tall, intimidating, and, oddly enough, concerned. "You are well?"

"Yes." She crossed her arms over her waist.

He shook his head in disbelief. "Six months. The whole nation has been trying to find you for six months. And you're here. Posing as my wife. Why?"

She lifted one shoulder in a gentle shrug. "I was desperate. I ran out of money. I needed a safe place to sleep. My family is allowed to stay at the Pinnacle for free, so I told myself it wasn't exactly stealing. However, I couldn't stay under my own name—"

"So you chose mine. Or rather, my wife's."

Her gaze faltered for a moment before she forced herself to meet his gaze once again. "I am sorry for that. I apologize to you, and I'll apologize to her too."

He frowned. "My wife died three years ago."

"Oh." She glanced at the wedding band still on his finger. "I didn't realize. . . I wouldn't have. . ." She shook her head. "I'm so sorry."

He gave a short nod that seemed to acknowledge both her apology and her sympathy. "Exactly how long were you planning to keep this charade going?"

"Until I reach my majority." She paused. "Henry, what are you going to do with me?"

"I don't know." He let out a troubled breath, then sat down in the desk chair again. "Why did you run away?"

"You were with me in the garden at my engagement party. You know exactly why."

"But your father, surely you could have reasoned with him."

She offered a sad smile and sat on the bench near the edge of the bed. "I tried. He refused to listen. Ultimately he threatened to throw me out and disinherit me if I didn't go through with the wedding. I decided there was no point in having his money if I had to be miserable for the rest of my life to get it. Besides, I knew I would inherit a modest sum from my grandmother's estate upon my twenty-first birthday. I didn't trust myself not to cave to his pressure to marry Baron Granville.

Since it was only getting worse, I ran."

His brow furrowed. "Georgiana, people think you've been kidnapped or worse—murdered, either by your father or your fiancé."

"Granville is not my fiancé anymore, and I know." She shrugged. "I've read the headlines. I've heard the gossip."

He leaned forward, searching her face. "And you still didn't come forward?"

"For what purpose? All the rumors will be dispelled when I reveal myself after my twenty-first birthday. It would do me no good to come forward before then."

He frowned. "So that is your plan? Hide out until you reach your independence?"

"Yes. It seemed reasonable enough at the time." It still did, despite all the difficulties she'd faced. More important, it was so close to becoming a reality. "I suppose you have a different plan?"

He seemed to know exactly what she was truly asking and immediately shook his head. "I can't possibly conceal your presence here, Georgiana."

"You could if you wanted to, if you dared." It was hardly in her best interest to issue the man a challenge. Yet it was out before she could stop it.

"Your father is the chairman of the board, my biggest investor. Betraying him by withholding the whereabouts of his missing daughter would likely cause irreparable damage to my relationship with him. I have plans to open three more resorts in the next five years." An apology filled his voice. "I can't afford to risk my life's work like that."

She nodded even as disappointment and dread knotted in her stomach. Ignoring the tears that burned her eyes, she offered a resigned smile. "I understand. I just. . . I don't know. Somehow I thought you might be different."

Curiosity filled his voice. "Different? Than what?"

"The other men I know. The ones who weigh the worth of a woman against that of real estate, stock options, and inheritances, then find her wanting—find *me* wanting."

He was quiet for a moment before his low, steady voice filled the room. "That is not my intention. Nor do I think it's a fair assessment. I am merely pointing out the enormity of your request. You're asking me to risk everything I've built and my entire future just so you don't have to face your father and tell him you don't want to marry someone."

"I have already told my father I won't marry Granville. That didn't stop him from trying to coerce me into it anyway. However, I realize that it is not your responsibility to help me." She pulled a deep breath and sent a silent prayer heavenward. "Will you at least give me one last night without the newspaper frenzy and the turmoil with my father? Let me decide how I want to handle this since I have yet to reach my majority."

She could see him mentally calculating and recalculating. Finally, he nodded. "It might be best for me to have time to decide how to approach this as well."

"For the hotel's reputation," she added softly.

His gaze met hers without equivocation. "Yes, and out of concern for yours and mine. You were staying here *as my wife* for ten days."

"I was *claiming* to be your wife. There is a difference. Besides, you only arrived today."

"And I will not be staying here tonight."

"Of course not." She stood. "Now, if you don't mind, I've had a long day. I would like some time to rest and think."

"Fair enough." He slid his papers into a portfolio and started toward the door. He paused halfway and turned to meet her gaze. "Georgiana. . .I'm glad you're all right."

"Thank you." She offered a gentle smile that turned slightly rueful. "I do appreciate the hospitality your staff gave me, though perhaps it was wrongfully taken."

"It was your due as Georgiana Price, so we'll call it even."

She gave a nod of thanks before he offered a slight smile and left. Walking to the door, she waited until she heard the elevator come and go before she locked it. She turned to survey the room that had been such a haven to her. She couldn't stay. That much was clear, but in no way was she ready to go back home. Not yet.

Three more weeks. That was all she needed. Yet she couldn't ask that of Henry. Not again. It wouldn't do any good, and as much as she hated to admit it, he had a point. This problem didn't involve him. If he put a horse in this race, he was sure to lose one way or another. She needed to absolve him of responsibility entirely. There was only one way to do that.

It was time to run again.

Chapter 2

Georgiana was gone. Again.

For three days, Henry had searched for any sign of her. He'd questioned his employees, coming clean about the fact that the woman had been a charlatan. He'd also questioned the railroad employees to see if she'd bought a train ticket. He'd searched the streets in the direction that the Pinnacle's doorman had said she'd headed the last time he'd seen her.

There had been no sign of her.

The one saving grace had been that he hadn't had time to inform Maxwell Price about his daughter's whereabouts before she'd disappeared again. Perhaps Henry should have done so anyway. This was the first lead the authorities would have had about Georgiana's location in months. Yet he'd hesitated.

He wasn't sure why other than the memory of how happy she'd looked before she'd seen him in the penthouse. She'd look healthier too. Much better than the drawn, pale version of her he'd seen at her engagement party. Still, she wasn't his concern. That's what he kept telling himself with every step he took around the city, searching for her knowing she was likely long gone. He hadn't managed to absolve himself yet.

With a sigh, he sat on a park bench to think. He had to tell her father. What other option was there? Unless he trusted that she would take care of herself and emerge unscathed into the public eye after her birthday.

He shook his head. He should have been more understanding. He should have listened more, been less concerned with himself. Isn't that what he'd said the last time she'd disappeared? Maybe she'd been right. Maybe he was putting himself and his business above someone who needed his help. How long had it been since he'd personally stopped to help someone even if it would provide no personal profit to him or his interest?

Too long. Yet it hadn't been that long since he'd been in need of help himself as a desperate youth growing up working at whatever job he could find to help his mother keep food on the table after his father died. Eventually he had found a way out of poverty through a church internship program. His rise to riches had been hard-fought, though meteoric. Putting that at risk, for any reason, seemed foolish.

However, maybe he could have found another way to help Georgiana. One that didn't involve sending her back into the situation she'd fled from or exposing her to public scrutiny. He rubbed his jaw and frowned. Well, it was too late to consider that now, wasn't it? He'd lost another chance to help her.

Standing, he shoved his hands into his pockets and set off through the park toward the hotel as the jaunty sound of a mission band filtered through the trees. As he neared, a female evangelist's silvery speaking voice grew louder, carrying out over the small crowd that had gathered and making Henry stop in his tracks. "I realized that even if no one else cared about me, God did. He cares about you too. Do you feel lost today? Do you feel as if the world has turned its back on you? Come to the Father who will never forsake you. . ."

"It can't be," Henry whispered as he eased his way to the front of the crowd. There stood Georgiana Price, proclaiming the Gospel in a city park. He shook his head to clear his vision, but he wasn't imagining it. Dressed in a somber dark blue uniform that identified her as a volunteer of Mercy's Proclaimers, she faced the crowd without an ounce of timidity. Her blond hair was pulled back and all but hidden beneath a wide-brimmed bonnet. The subtle sheen of tears in her green eyes and the heightened color on her cheeks revealed her sincerity and passion. The soft smile on her lips hinted at an internal sense of peace.

Her gaze scanned the crowd as though meeting and reaching into every soul with a measure of the love she spoke of—until her gaze found his. Her eyes widened, but she didn't panic or try to run. Instead, she tilted her head and didn't look away. "Build your life on His love for you. That is the only true, unshakable foundation we have in this world. Not money or influence or anything else the world says matters. As our Savior said, 'For what is a man profited, if he shall gain the whole world, and lose his own soul?' "

Henry shook his head, unable to stop his reluctant smile. She returned it with a warm one of her own before looking to one of the missionaries for guidance. The missionary stepped forward to lead a prayer of salvation. After inviting everyone to Mercy's Kitchen for a free supper, the missionaries dismissed the impromptu service.

Georgiana paused to speak to the head missionary, then made her way over to Henry. She tilted her head toward a nearby bench beneath a large pine. "Shall we?"

He followed her to the bench, then angled toward her to search her face. "I didn't know you were a Christian."

She shrugged. "I always have been *nominally*. It wasn't much different than pretending to be Mrs. Henry Chadwick, in many respects. I went through the motions of going to church, but it wasn't real. It didn't affect my heart."

"And now it does."

"Yes." She glanced around the park. "There's something about this city right now. It's. . .electric. The faith here. The way it shapes so much of what the people do. It's inspiring."

"True. There's another side of the city, though," he cautioned. "A much darker side."

"I know. I've seen it. Perhaps that is what makes the light shine so brightly." Her brow furrowed. "What about you, Henry?"

He let out a quiet laugh. "Are you asking after the state of my soul, Miss Price?"

She hushed him, glancing around surreptitiously before sending him a chiding look. "Call me Gigi, please."

"Gigi?"

"Gigi Smith."

His eyebrows rose, and he tilted his head toward the missionaries who had lingered to speak with new believers. "They bought that?"

"They respected the fact that I didn't want to tell them more."

"Nice of them."

"Indeed. Are you avoiding my question?"

"Not at all." He paused, trying to condense his history of faith into a few sentences. "I became a Christian when I was in my teen years. It was a life-changing decision that truly meant something. It still does. I do my best to let it govern how I live my life."

She smiled. "Well, since you have a reputation for being a man of integrity, it seems to be having some effect."

"Speaking of that. . ." He hesitated, feeling almost loathe to bring it up. "What are we going to do about this, Georg—Gigi?"

She sobered. "It should be my decision to go home, Henry. No one else's. I am not asking you to lie for me. I'm simply asking you to let me choose."

He considered her request for a moment, then asked, "Are you safe? Wherever it is you're staying?"

Her nod was a bit too hesitant for his liking. The only thing that could make this situation worse was Georgiana ending up in some kind of trouble or hurt. He didn't want that on his conscience. He was struggling enough as it was. Finally, she admitted, "I'm staying at a home for women and children. It's safe, but it isn't the easiest place to live."

Georgiana Price was staying in a shelter for women and children. The notion was inconceivable. He shook his head. "You can stay with my mother."

"Your mother?"

"She lives here in Denver. She's always glad to take in friends who need a place to stay."

Georgiana lifted a brow, looking pleasantly surprised. "Am I your friend?"

He chuckled. "Would you like to be?"

She tilted her head as though considering it, then offered a gently teasing smile. "I believe I would. However, that doesn't mean you have to let me stay with your mother. I'm fine where I am. Truly. I don't want to impose."

"Where do we pick up your things?"

She hesitated. Finally, with a shrug, she gave in. "I've been staying at Mercy House."

His eyebrows rose. "Mercy House?"

"Yes, it's a charity home for women and children."

"I've heard of it." He glanced away, trying to come to terms with the fact that the woman he'd spent three days searching for had been staying at his own charity house. Maybe his mother was right. Perhaps he needed to start taking a more hands-on approach to Mercy Ministries. He frowned, recalling her comments about the shelter. "What did you mean when you said it isn't the easiest place to live?"

"It's just so sad there. Everyone has a story. Most don't want to share theirs, but even if they don't, there's still so much hurt there. It's almost tangible. The mood can be a little disheartening at times." She shook her head as though to free herself from morose thoughts. "I suppose we could go there now to pick up my things if it's convenient for you. I have a bit of a break before I need to report to Mercy's Kitchen."

Biting back his frustration, he simply asked, "Oh? You're involved with that too?"

"Yes, I have been since the second day of my stay in Denver. Margaret and Walter run the kitchen. They are wonderful people. In fact, they're the ones who helped me find a place to stay when I left the Pinnacle." A new idea lighting her eye, she laid a hand on his arm. "You should go with me this evening."

"To serve at the soup kitchen? I'm not sure that's a good idea." The staff, including the Moores, wouldn't recognize him as their benefactor, but someone might recognize him as Henry Chadwick and put two and two together. Besides, he'd promised his mother he would go over the ministry's books. Between looking for

Georgiana and his meeting with the governor's staff, he hadn't had a chance to do more than that first cursory scan. "I have a lot of work to do this evening."

That light in her green eyes faded into disappointment. She gave a light shrug. "I understand. I'm sure you're very busy."

He nodded, trying not to let her disappointment bother him. After all, it couldn't be helped. "Let's go gather your things from Mercy House."

Georgiana said a quick goodbye to the Proclaimers of Mercy and led the way to the nearby cable car. A few minutes later, they arrived at the doorstep of the charity house Henry had established years ago. Pausing as they entered the foyer, Georgiana told him, "You'll have to wait here. Men aren't allowed past this point. I'll be back momentarily."

The stern-faced woman at the front desk eyed him suspiciously as Georgiana explained her impending departure in low tones. Mrs. Higgins, wasn't it? She was a housekeeper who'd been set upon by hard times. Her history of mission work and the essay portion of the application she'd submitted had confirmed her heart was in the right place. However, she seemed to be advising Georgiana against leaving with him.

Henry shifted uncomfortably under her threatening stare. Georgiana offered him a reassuring smile, then headed up the stairs. He wasn't aware that his gaze had followed her until Mrs. Higgins cleared her throat. He met the woman's threatening look with a respectful nod. She wasn't satisfied. "Mr. Chadwick, you have a reputation of being a man of honor. I would hate for that to change."

His eyebrows lifted. "As would I, madam. I assure you my mother will take good care of—Geor—Gigi until she is ready to move on. My travels will soon take me back to New York City."

"Very well." With one final suspicious look, she began to make notations in the visitors' ledger.

Threatened by his own staff. He turned away to hide his amusement and found himself staring at a painting that seemed to have been done by one of the residents. It was a rather ominous scene that showed a shadow chasing a startled woman down an alleyway. He couldn't help muttering, "My goodness."

A parlor door opened, emitting a little girl who looked to be about six years old. Her eyes widened as she caught sight of Henry. Keeping her back to the wall and her eyes on him, she stayed as far away from him as possible as she skirted her way past. Finally, she called out, "Mama?"

"I'm here," a woman called back as she exited the parlor with a few small dresses laid across her arm. The small, dark-haired woman caught sight of Henry. She grabbed her daughter's hand and ushered the girl up the stairs. "It's all right, sweetheart. We don't have to worry. . . ."

He couldn't hear the rest, no matter how much he strained. Finally, they turned the corner and went out of sight. Mrs. Higgins spoke up. "Poor little thing. It's not right for her to be so afraid of men. She and her mother got caught up with a bad sort, that's for sure. Don't take it personally."

Concern filled him. "Is there anything being done to help the child?"

"Well, she's got a roof over her head, a safe place to stay, and warm food every day. That's more than most."

Perhaps, but obviously it wasn't enough. How would the child overcome her fear of men if no one helped her? And what about the rest of the women and children? Who was helping them heal from the scars that went deeper than mere physical wounds?

The questions continued to bother him as Georgiana returned to say her goodbyes to Mrs. Higgins, and he hailed a hansom cab that brought them to his mother's home. A moment later, he let himself in, calling, "Mother, are you here?"

"In the parlor," she called back. He led the way through the foyer as she continued, "The cook is down with a nasty cold, poor thing, so I picked up lunch from the Pinnacle. Did you know there is a rumor among the staff that you're—"

He stepped inside the parlor with Georgiana. His mother's eyes widened as she stumbled over her next word. "Married?"

He followed his mother's gaze from Georgiana to the satchel he carried for her, then back again. He cleared his throat. "Yes, well, obviously that isn't true. Mother, this is Georgiana Price."

For a stunned moment, neither woman made a sound, though both their mouths fell open. His mother recovered first, if he could call it that. Her brow furrowed. "Did you just say Georgiana Price? *The* Georgiana Price?"

Before he could respond, Georgiana hit him on the arm and speared him with a glare. "I did *not* say you could tell anyone who I was."

"You don't know my mother. She would have figured it out anyway."

Georgiana shook her head, then took a step back. "I should leave."

He took her arm in a gentle but firm grasp. "Don't you dare. I'm not chasing you all over kingdom come again."

"Again? When have you ever chased me anywhere? Besides the night of my engagement party, I mean, and even then I told you not to follow me."

"I've been looking all over Denver for you for three days," he insisted. "I think that qualifies as chasing."

"Well, you shouldn't have."

"But I did, and I found you right as I was giving up hope. Surely that means something. You should stay. It's only for two weeks."

She held his gaze for a long moment. He could see her resolve wavering. "I don't know, Henry. Perhaps it would be best if I went back to Mercy House."

His mother's surprised echo filled the air. "Mercy House?"

He dragged his gaze from Georgiana to give his mother a meaningful look. "She's been staying at Mercy House, but she says the morale there is abominable."

A mix of concern and alarm filled Abigail's voice as she stood. "Is it?"

Georgiana released an exasperated sigh. "I didn't say it that harshly, Henry."

"Well, it's true," he said gravely. Almost certain she wouldn't bolt, Henry released her arm. "Whether you said it nicely or not, the fact remains."

His mother's concern only seemed to increase. "Well, then, my dear, you absolutely must stay here."

"Oh, but—" Georgiana bit her lip. "Do you. . .do you think it's safe? I don't want to get anyone in trouble. I've caused too much already by staying at the Pinnacle."

It was his turn to send Georgiana a silencing look, but it was too late. Henry's mother lifted a knowing eyebrow. "I see. So you are Henry's new bride."

"Yes. I mean, no," Georgiana said quickly. "I was desperate and—"

An amused smile crossed his mother's lips as she waved away Georgiana's concern. "That's quite all right. We're just solving one mystery after another today, aren't we?"

Henry rubbed his forehead. "So it would seem."

His mother reached out a hand. "We didn't finish the introductions earlier. I am Henry's mother. You may call me Abigail. Let me show you to the guest room. You can tell me all about what you've been doing since you arrived in Denver. You said you've been staying at Mercy House?"

Georgiana sent him a helpless look as his mother ushered her out of the parlor. He gave her a reassuring nod, then released a relieved breath. His mother would take care of everything. Likely, she and Georgiana would become fast friends. He could get back to the business of running his business and auditing Mercy Ministries' books.

He lingered for a few moments longer, intending to make sure Georgiana settled in. However, realizing he might be waiting a good long while if his mother and Georgiana were having a heart-to-heart, he decided he may as well return to the Pinnacle. His mother would send for him if she needed anything. Grabbing his hat, he made his way toward the front door.

His mother's voice stopped him in his tracks. "Where do you think you're going, Henry Ezekiel Chadwick?"

He turned on his heel to see his mother standing at the bottom of the stairs with her arms crossed in front of her. He lifted his eyebrows hopefully. "The Pinnacle?"

"The parlor. We need to talk." She barely waited until he closed the door behind him to begin whispering, "What in the world were you thinking, bringing that young woman here? The entire country is looking for her. Am I going to have police show up at my door? What if they think we kidnapped her?"

"Georgiana is not a child. It is not a crime to run away from a wedding. As for our role, I'm sure she would explain the situation to the authorities. Besides, if anyone did show up, it would likely be a private investigator, not the police. It will be fine. . .probably."

"Oh well, as long as it will 'probably' be fine, we needn't worry." His mother shook her head at him, then glanced upward toward the guest room. "She's been through a lot, that much I can tell. I would never turn her away. You know that, but I still feel like I'm harboring a load of dynamite. However, it might be a good thing. Did you know that besides staying at Mercy House she's involved in the Proclaimers of Mercy and Mercy's Kitchen? She could give us so much insight into how things are being run."

He tilted his head. Surely he was mishearing her. "Are you saying you want us to use Georgiana to get information?"

"No, I want to let her continue doing what she's doing and. . .*gain* information." His mother rolled her eyes. "Oh, why do you have to make it sound so sinister? She could be our eyes and ears within these organizations. Or. . .you could. As her friend, you'll be a nonthreatening presence. You can learn firsthand what's actually happening with Mercy Ministries."

"Ma, I don't know if that is a good idea."

She crossed her arms. "Well, I don't know if harboring Georgiana Price is a good idea either, but I'm doing it anyway because you asked me to. It seems only fair for you to trust me when I say this is a good idea, doesn't it?"

He groaned. "How can a son say no to that?"

She gave him a cheeky grin and winked. "You couldn't, which is why I asked."

He sighed. "It looks like Mercy Ministries just gained another volunteer."

Chapter 3

Abigail Chadwick was a force to be reckoned with. Far from being intimidated, Georgiana couldn't help but admire the woman's drive and independence. A mining accident had made Abigail a widow when Henry was only eight years old. She'd raised her son while working to keep the rent paid and food in their stomachs. Some times had been leaner than others, which was why Abigail had taken such an interest in Georgiana's recent charity work.

Georgiana had half expected the woman to accompany her to Mercy's Kitchen to assist with dinner preparations, but Abigail had a previous engagement scheduled for this evening. However, the woman had succeeded where Georgiana had failed in convincing Henry to take an interest in Mercy Ministry's work. He'd accompanied Georgiana today with only a small amount of reluctance.

She couldn't help but smile as she watched him tote a crate of frozen chicken into the large freezer. It was nice to see a man as busy and powerful as Henry Chadwick take the time to give back to the community in a hands-on way. Not many of their class seemed interested in doing anything more than writing out a check to whatever charity happened to be most fashionable at the time. This would be a good experience for him.

"He's a hard worker, that one," Margaret commented over the sound of the carrots she was chopping. "How long have you known him?"

Georgiana refocused on the peas she was supposed to be shelling. "Oh, about five years now, I suppose."

"It's fortunate you ran into him then."

"Yes, he's a good man." She met his gaze as he passed through on his way back to the alley where the supply wagon was parked. "Trustworthy."

Margaret made a noncommittal sound. "And what about his wife? What is she like?"

Georgiana's gaze shot to Margaret, but her friend didn't glance up from the food preparation. "I have no idea what she was like. She passed away several years ago."

"Oh, thank goodness." Margaret sagged in relief.

"Margaret! How is that good?"

"No, I didn't mean good in that way. I just meant—I'm glad he's not married, that's all."

Georgiana shook her head in confusion. "Why?"

Margaret set the knife on the cutting board, then leaned across the island to confide, "Gigi, that man can't keep his eyes off you."

Surprised, she stared at Margaret. Henry couldn't take his eyes off of her? Well, of course he couldn't. He was probably afraid she'd run off if he so much as blinked. Honestly, she might. Her scheme to stay in hiding seemed to be slowly unraveling. The secret of her identity seemed more precarious than ever—especially now that the folks at Mercy Ministries knew she was connected to Henry Chadwick. Why, it might only be a matter of time before someone started putting the pieces of this puzzle together.

Realizing Margaret was still waiting for her response, Georgiana shrugged. "I'm sure he's only trying to make sure I'm safe."

Margaret considered that for a moment before nodding slowly. "I see. In that case, it seems you're every bit as concerned with his safety as he is with yours."

Her mouth fell open. Pressing her lips together, she ignored the warmth rising in her cheeks. "I have no idea what you mean."

"You won't do yourself any favors by ignoring it, you know. Especially not if he's half as good a man as you seem to think he is. He still wears his wedding band though. That could present a challenge—if he isn't ready to move on, I mean."

"Oh stop." Georgiana shook her head and trained her gaze on the snap peas. Even so, she was increasingly aware of each time Henry entered the room. Perhaps it was the power of Margaret's suggestion, but she could feel his gaze on her every time. So what if he was watching her? That didn't mean he thought of her as anything more than Maxwell Price's daughter. A liability, and a load of trouble at that.

However, what if he did see her as more than that? What if he could? A warm hand touched her back, and she jumped. Somehow realizing it was Henry only made her heart gallop harder in her chest. He winced in empathy. "Sorry, Gigi, I didn't mean to startle you. Walter suggested you might need some help with the peas."

"That's fine," she said quickly. She positioned the bowls in the middle of the kitchen island. Moving to the far end, she pointed Henry to the other side. "This way we can both help."

A soft snort of laughter sent Georgiana's gaze careening toward Margaret.

Georgiana sent her a warning look. It was the wrong thing to do. They both struggled to hold in their laughter. Finally, another soft laugh escaped despite Margaret's valiant attempts otherwise. The woman rather unsuccessfully turned it into coughs. Henry was not fooled. He glanced back and forth between the two of them. "What is so funny?"

Georgiana tried to wave away his concern but only succeeded in accidentally knocking a pea shell on the floor. "Nothing."

Henry picked it up and set it in the discard pile. "Seems like something."

Margaret took that as her cue to be far too forthcoming. "I was just asking Gigi if your relationship was romantic in nature."

"Honestly, Margaret," Georgiana chided as Henry stilled.

His gaze caught hers. "Not as of yet. Why? What did Geor—Gigi say?"

"She said you simply wanted to keep her safe."

He smiled and lifted one shoulder in a shrug. "True enough."

"There you go," Margaret said as she scraped the carrot pieces into a bowl. "It's all out in the open. Nothing to worry about now."

"I wasn't worried," Georgiana interjected.

"Well then, I'll leave you to it." Margaret winked at them both before toting the large bowl of carrots across the kitchen to wash them in the sink.

Not entirely sure what to say, Georgiana slowly glanced up to meet Henry's gaze. He stepped around the kitchen island to stand on the side nearest to her. "Did you know this place used to be one of the best restaurants in town?"

She immediately relaxed at the change in subject. "No. What happened to it? How did it become Mercy's Kitchen?"

"It went out of business when the recession hit. Since then things in Denver have been pretty desperate." He glanced around the kitchen at the five other volunteers who worked tirelessly to prepare dinner. "Many of these mission organizations were created as a response to that."

"Mercy Ministries have been around longer than that, though, haven't they?"

"Eight years," he said confidently, then added, "I think. Did you do any volunteer work in New York?"

"No. I was more than a little preoccupied with myself." She couldn't help glancing at his wedding band. "Apparently I didn't take much time get to know anyone who didn't serve my purposes."

He captured her gaze again. "I think you're being a little hard on yourself."

"Am I?"

"You really are. Besides, it's never too late to start over. You've shown me that.

The zeal you have for your faith and for serving others has helped me realize that mine is not what it once was. I want that hunger for the Lord and for His purposes again. For me it's a challenge to slow down long enough to do those things."

"Slow down," she echoed softly. "That's hard to do when you're on the run."

He smiled. "Well, the great thing about God is, no matter where you run to, He's already there waiting to take you in."

She tilted her head. "Hmm. He's starting to sound a bit like someone else I know."

He paused in surprise. "You don't mean me, do you?"

"I certainly do. Of course, you haven't always had a choice in the matter, but you've been. . ." She cast about for the right words, then held his gaze to make sure he knew she was being genuine. "You've been very kind and fair about the whole situation—even when you didn't have to be. I do appreciate it."

He seemed a bit unsure of how to respond and eventually acknowledged her statement with a nod. "I just want you to be all right."

"I will be. Soon. It will all work out. I'm certain of it. Well, almost certain." She gave him a rueful smile before realizing she had somehow gotten around to talking about herself again. She shook her head. "Since we're clearing the air about a few things, I need to apologize for never expressing my condolences to you about your wife's passing until recently. I'm not sure why I didn't know about it."

"You and your mother were in Europe at the time, I believe, on your grand tour. By the time you returned, I'd stopped speaking about it."

Concern filled her. "Was it too painful?"

"I don't know. Maybe. It simply seemed easier not to." He lowered his voice. "We were a love match—a convenient one, but a love match all the same. Amelia was a shining light. She helped keep me grounded. I knew she didn't have a strong constitution when I began courting her. She'd been getting progressively better, though, until she started volunteering at a hospital. She caught an infection and. . . She just wasn't strong enough to fight it off."

"I'm so sorry that happened."

His gaze clouded as though he was seeing into a memory. "When the time came, she had such courage and peace. She tried to comfort me, of all things. She made me promise that I wouldn't stop living, that I—"

"How are those peas coming?" Walter asked as he stopped to eye the bowl.

Georgiana blinked. "What? Oh. Fine."

"Well, we need better than fine. We're opening our doors in thirty minutes. Can you speed it up?"

"Of course," she said, even as she realized she'd stopped shelling peas altogether. "I'm sorry. I didn't mean to slow down."

"Henry, will you help me move the tables and chairs out front?"

"Certainly." He left, following Walter out of the kitchen.

Margaret returned to the kitchen island. "I told Walter not to interrupt, but he's right. We do have a meal to put on. Perhaps you and Henry can finish your conversation later."

"It's fine." She went back to shelling peas, even though it didn't really feel fine to be interrupted. She wanted to sit down with Henry and hear the rest of his story, offer him the comfort of being listened to and understood. Not that she could understand. Not really. She'd never been married. She'd never lost anyone that close to her. Perhaps she should be more appreciative of that fact.

She frowned. How much of her life had she taken for granted before? She didn't want to live that way anymore—oblivious to the needs and concerns of those around her. She didn't want to go back to being too caught up in herself to make a positive difference in the world, even if that difference was simply spending time with the people who mattered. Of course, that was assuming the people who mattered to her would actually want to spend time with her.

Her parents were often too busy. Her mother always had some society event to attend. Her father was usually caught up in business. Her friends. . . Well, she hadn't talked to them in months. She'd been too busy trying to survive to miss them much. And not one of them had been someone she could confidently say would help her in a time of need. Especially not if it meant putting their own interests at risk. Perhaps she had been running with the wrong crowd and ignoring the right one.

No more. From now on she'd associate herself with people of good character, people who would challenge her in the right ways, people she could encourage. People like. . . Well, people like Henry Chadwick. Getting to known him more would be a good thing purely from the standpoint of becoming a better person. That was her end goal now, wasn't it? To improve herself and. . .

All right, and maybe Margaret was right. Maybe it wouldn't hurt to see if something deeper could come of their relationship. At the very least, she would make a new friend. There was absolutely nothing wrong with that.

What was wrong with him? To stand there and glibly flirt with Georgiana Price was tantamount to insanity, wasn't it? Yet somehow he couldn't quite regret the look on her face when he'd responded to Margaret's inquiry about whether his relationship with Georgiana was romantic in nature. *Not as of yet.* That's what he'd said, as if there was the possibility of something occurring. As if he wasn't still wearing a wedding band on the third finger of his left hand.

He lifted his hand, letting the ring gleam in the moonlight that shone through the window of his mother's study. Three years. How had it been three years since Amelia's death? Some days it seemed like yesterday. Other times it felt like an eternity. He'd kept his promise to his wife. He'd gone on living as best he could. As far as the other part of his promise, he hadn't even considered marrying anyone else. No woman since Amelia had inspired so much as a thought of romance. No one until Georgiana.

He'd known that she was unaware of his wife's passing. Despite Georgiana's harsh critique of herself, she'd never been so self-absorbed as not to offer sympathy to someone in pain. For years it hadn't mattered that she didn't know. It had been rather nice, actually, to know that in someone's reality Amelia was still alive. Lately things had changed.

He'd felt an attraction to Georgiana for a while now, though he hadn't admitted it to anyone. Perhaps not even to himself. Besides, they wouldn't have been equally yoked, because she hadn't shared his faith—until now.

Was that why he'd continued to wear the wedding band? To ward off the possibility of something happening with Georgiana, or anyone else for that matter? Perhaps he was simply trying to avoid the pain of losing someone all over again. But it had been worth it the first time, hadn't it? Surely it would be again. *If* he allowed himself that possibility.

He stared down at the ring, spun it around his finger one last time, and then slid it off. He'd just clutched it in his fist when a light knock sounded on the door. Sliding the ring into his pocket, he called out, "Come in."

His mother stepped inside, offering a sympathetic smile. "Tired?"

He released a quiet laugh. "Worn out. Walter runs a tight ship, I'll give him that."

"Well, that's good to hear." She closed the door behind her and took a seat in the armchair nearest the rolltop desk where he sat. "I believe Georgiana has settled in for the evening, so please tell me everything. Did you discover anything at Mercy's Kitchen to explain the missing money?"

He nodded. "They serve second and third portions to the hungry even though our written policy is to provide one portion per person in order to feed as many people as possible. They tried that at first but discovered that many people eat at Mercy's Kitchen as a last resort. In other words, they are already starving. Serving one portion means they come hungry and leave still hungry."

His mother put her hand over her heart. "Oh my. Well, that does explain the discrepancies."

"Walter and Margaret had been taking the funds for the extra food out of their own paychecks. However, after their child got sick, they couldn't afford that anymore. So they've been borrowing from Peter to pay Paul from the funds they are allotted for supplies and deliveries."

His mother shook her head in what seemed to be a mix of confusion and concern. "I don't understand. I mean, I certainly applaud their dedication and their heart for people, but why didn't they request more funds?"

He rubbed his hand over his chin, then reluctantly admitted, "According to Walter, it's incredibly hard to contact the higher levels of ministry. They're never sure a message has gotten through to us. Plus, they weren't sure the ministry could afford it."

A knowing light filled his mother's eyes. "Secrecy strikes again. So what are you going to do?"

"Send them more money and supplies. Figure out better lines of communication." He picked up the ledger for Proclaimers of Mercy. "Unlike Mercy's Kitchen, our evangelists have a surplus. It makes me wonder how much proclaiming they're doing versus how much they're soliciting for money. Georgiana invited me to go along with her to volunteer with Mercy's Proclaimers tomorrow."

"You're going, aren't you?"

"I suppose I must."

"Good. Speaking of. . ." She nodded toward the window. He turned to see Georgiana wandering aimlessly through the lantern-lit garden behind the house. His mother's voice filled with compassion as she walked over to the window. "It seems Georgiana couldn't sleep, after all. I do wonder about everything she must have been through these past few months. It couldn't have been easy—all that traveling and hiding, always fearing discovery, running out of food and money, feeling alone in the world. She must have been pretty desperate to get away from the situation she was in. What was her fiancé like?"

"Awful." Henry grimaced. "Oh, he put on a nice enough show when he felt like it, but he didn't care one whit about Georgiana other than the money she brought to the table."

"And her father?"

"Ruthless. That's what makes him a good businessman. As far as I can tell, he never seemed to take much of an interest in Georgiana. She was closer to her mother, I believe. Clarise Price is. . . Well, from what I've seen, she loves her daughter, but she'd no sooner stand up to her husband for Georgiana's sake than she would jump off a bridge."

"That is incredibly sad." His mother shook her head. "It just goes to show you can have all the money and influence in the world and still lack the things that truly matter. Georgiana needs someone to fight for her. She needs to know that someone really cares. You should go down there and talk to her. I would, but she knows you better than she knows me."

"But I'm not. . ." He pulled in a deep breath, then admitted the one thing that had bothered him about all of this from the beginning. "I'm not sure that I'm willing to fight for her."

She frowned. "What do you mean? You're already fighting for her. You brought her here, didn't you?"

"To save my own skin. I was afraid she would get hurt in some way and Maxwell would find out that not only did I harbor her in my hotel, but I let her go and let something happen to her. I didn't want that to be on my head." He pulled in a heavy breath and ran his fingers through his hair. "This is awful. I don't know when I stopped caring about others, when I started putting my interests and only my interests first. All I know is this situation terrifies me."

"Why would you be terrified?"

He leaned forward. "Ma, what is going to happen when Maxwell finds out about this? I mean, he will eventually, right? It could ruin my business relationship with him. How could it not?"

Patience filled his mother's voice as she shook her head. "Henry Ezekiel, you and the Lord are what made the Pinnacle successful. Not Maxwell Price. If looking out for Georgiana in her time of need puts you out of favor with her father, then maybe he isn't someone you should be currying favor from anymore."

"But my plans—"

"Exactly. *Your* plans. But what about the Lord's plans? I'm sure He has one for this situation, so stop worrying and let Him work."

He gave her a weary look. "You make it sound so easy."

"Son, maybe you're making it too hard." She reached out to place a hand on his shoulder and gave it a gentle squeeze. Her head tilted toward the window. "Now, please go talk to Georgiana before she thinks of a reason to run away again."

He let out a short laugh. Yet his mother's words were enough to send him down the stairs and out the back door in search of Georgiana. He found her sitting on the bench next to the fountain. She set a faded rose blossom in the center of the water and watched it drift to the outer edge. He cleared his throat softly to announce his approach, then gently asked, "Are you all right?"

She blinked a few times before glancing up with a soft smile. "I'm fine. I just needed some air, that's all."

The unshed tears in her eyes belied her statement. He claimed the seat next to her. "Somehow, I don't think that's entirely true. Why are you upset?"

She hesitated, then admitted, "Being around your mother has made me think about mine. They're very different."

He smiled. "That's true."

"I miss her. Even though she didn't stand up for me or help when I asked. . .I miss being home. It's been so long now—almost seven months. After everything that's happened, I wonder if it will still feel like home when I go back." She paused, frowning at the tottering rose blossom. "Will I go back? I suppose I could find a place of my own, turn into the eccentric heiress that the newspapers say I am. Perhaps I'll go back to Europe. It's quite beautiful there and—"

She let out a soft laugh that turned into a sob. Pressing her fingers to her lips, she turned her face away. "I'm sorry. I don't know what's gotten into me tonight. I think I'm only now realizing that I really don't have much to go back to when this is over. My family has all but disowned me. I'm sorry. I don't need to tell you all of this. It doesn't concern you, and—"

"Hey," he interrupted, gently catching hold of her hand. "Look at me."

Rather reluctantly she lifted her gaze to meet his. He gave her hand a squeeze. "You concern me. Greatly. Especially right now."

She released a quiet, watery laugh. "I'm sorry. I don't mean to—"

He stood and drew her to her feet and into a hug. She stilled in surprise, then melted into his embrace. Another sob shook her body as she grasped the fabric of his coat and held on as if he were the only solid thing in her life. Maybe he was.

A huge sense of responsibility settled upon his shoulders. He would fight for her. He knew it then and there. That didn't make it any less terrifying. Even so, he couldn't help but comfort her. "You aren't alone, Georgiana. You don't have to face it alone."

"I can't ask you to risk everything for me," she said between hiccups. "That isn't fair to you."

"It's already done. In for a penny, in for a pound, I say." He shifted her to one arm and fished a handkerchief out of his coat pocket to offer her.

Taking the handkerchief, she shook her head. "I'm so sorry. I never should have involved you in this. There may have been another way, if I had taken more time to think. Everything is such a mess."

"You don't need another way. Stop worrying about me. Everything will work out as it's meant to. God has a plan in all of this. Be patient. Trust Him. And me."

"Trusting you is easy. You're tangible, and I know you mean well. I know God means well too, but. . ." She offered a helpless shrug. "I'm still new at this. Having faith in Someone unseen is hard sometimes."

"Then we'll pray God reveals Himself to you in an undeniable way. Don't give up hope. Maybe God is up to something you aren't aware of. Something good. In the meantime, try not to worry so much and to find ways to enjoy the process."

"I can do that." She pulled in a deep breath and nodded resolutely before she smiled. "I suspect you're going to help me with it too. We're volunteering with the Proclaimers of Mercy tomorrow. Are you ready for that?"

He gave her a reassuring smile. "Absolutely."

Chapter 4

Henry was most certainly *not* ready. Georgiana did her best to stifle a laugh as he stared at the Proclaimers of Mercy uniform he'd been assigned to wear. He looked thoroughly disgusted and more than a little disturbed. His gaze met hers, revealing what seemed to be alarm. With a sidelong glance at the distracted volunteer supervisor, Henry gently caught her arm and eased closer to whisper, "This uniform is practically falling apart."

"I've been informed that once it does, a new one will be ordered. Until then. . ." She handed him the navy coat. With a grimace, he shrugged it on, then began fastening the few golden buttons still clinging to the fabric. She blinked and leaned closer for a better look. "Oh no. Henry, you've lost your ring."

He glanced down at his hand, then met her gaze again. "I didn't lose it. I decided to stop wearing it."

"You did?" She asked as if her heart hadn't suddenly started racing in her chest.

He nodded and seemed ready to say something else about it before frowning again. "Why is this uniform damp? That is what I want to know. Or maybe it's better that I don't."

Giving him an impatient look, she helped him put on the drum set. "We don't serve for our comfort, Henry. We serve the Lord."

He let out a strangled laugh. "I think it is possible to be comfortable while serving the Lord."

"Stop complaining. They'll hear you. Besides, it's somehow making the uniform feel worse." Having resisted the temptation as long as possible, she gave in and scratched an itchy spot on her neck.

Henry frowned. He slid the collar of her coat out of the way to peer at the spot. "You're getting a rash. This is ridiculous."

She caught his wrist and removed his hand. "It's fine."

"No, it isn't. This makes no sense," he muttered while he strapped on the drum and picked up the drumsticks. "They have more than enough funds to provide suitable uniforms for their volunteers."

"How would you know?"

He hesitated, then admitted, "Because I gave it to them."

"What?" she asked as the lead proclaimer announced the first hymn.

He grinned at her, lifted a shoulder in a shrug, then began banging on the drum in time to "At the Cross." She reached out to stop him, but he dodged her. She followed after him, calling over the music. "Henry, what do you mean?"

Someone shushed her. Another volunteer all but shoved a tambourine in her hand. The lead proclaimer sent her a censoring look. She had little choice but to file into the spot next to Henry in the processional. For the next four hours, they marched through the downtown streets, stopping to share testimonies every thirty minutes. It was hot, exhausting work—not to mention itchy.

She was more than happy to turn in her uniform. Not that she'd ever admit it to Henry. She didn't have to. He took one look at the rash on her neck on their way out the door and shook his head. "I'm going to tell them to burn those things."

"And they'll listen to you because of all the money you donate?"

"Not exactly."

"Henry." She sent him an impatient look. "Would you please stop being mysterious and tell me what this is all about?"

"Not here." He glanced back at the Proclaimers of Mercy office, then caught her hand and set off down the street. "Come on. I know where we can go."

A few minutes later, she couldn't help laughing as Henry paddled their canoe toward the center of the big lake in City Park. The cloudy blue sky reflected across the rippling surface of the lake that abutted the red-roofed boathouse. Mountains stood in the distance, their craggy blue and purple silhouettes just visible over the tops of the young trees lining the shore. Shaking her head in awe, she met his intense gaze. "Not that I'm complaining about the view, but is all of this secrecy really necessary?"

His brow furrowed as he let out a quiet laugh. "You sound like my mother. She thinks I should do away with the secrecy, forget protecting my anonymity, and confess to being the founder and benefactor of Mercy Ministries."

Georgiana's head reared back in shock. She froze, then blinked. "What did you say? You *founded* Mercy Ministries? *You're* the mysterious benefactor everyone keeps talking about? How? When? Henry, are you serious?"

He smiled at her shock. "Yes, I'm serious. I founded it eight years ago when I—"

"Oh my," she said on a breath, then rushed out of her seat to hug him.

"Whoa." He caught her to him, desperately trying to stabilize the rocking canoe as he warned, "Sweetheart, the boat."

Heart melting even more at the endearment, she hugged him tighter before finally releasing him and carefully returning to her seat. She captured his gaze. "Thank you."

Smiling, he lifted his broad shoulders in a shrug. "For what?"

"You don't know?" She reached out to touch his arm. "Henry, I became a Christian through my work with Mercy Ministries, the ministry that you founded. Isn't that amazing?"

He paused in surprise. "Gigi, that's incredible."

And uncanny. She would have been content to sit there basking in the glow of their shared faith and connection, but movement to her right caught her eyes. It was the brown paddle of their canoe drifting ever so steadily out of reach. Her eyes widened. "Henry, the paddle!"

They both reached for it at the same time. The canoe tipped over, and they plunged into the lake. Her skirts dragged her downward until Henry caught her waist and pulled her upward with him. They emerged in the cool shade under the capsized canoe. She gasped for a breath, which quickly turned into a laugh. Henry laughed too as he swept the curtain of her sodden hair aside. He searched her face in concern. "Are you all right?"

Between gasps and laughs, she nodded. "I'm fine. I just need to stop laughing long enough to catch my breath."

He grinned as he slid his glasses back into place. "Breathe, please."

She pulled in a deep breath, then wrinkled her nose when the air smelled decidedly like fish and feathers. Water lapped beneath the boat, casting glimmers of light among the shadows that hovered on the bottom—now the ceiling—of the canoe. Henry's arm tightened around her waist. Her gaze met his. Somehow, she drifted even closer. His head lowered as her hand tightened on his shoulder.

His kiss was like a gentle question. She answered with a soft smile. He kissed her again, deepening the kiss. Her fingers slid up the nape of his neck and into his hair. He paused long enough to murmur, "Georgiana—"

A sudden onslaught of bright sunlight sent them recoiling apart as the canoe was lifted and set upright. She blinked up at the amused stranger who had apparently come to their rescue. The man grinned. "Sorry, folks, didn't mean to interrupt anything. Just wanted to make sure no one was drowning."

Warmth rushed over her cheeks. "No. No one is drowning."

"Thank you for checking, though," Henry added. "Would you be so kind as to help stabilize our canoe as we climb back in?"

"I'd be happy to." The man swerved his boat around to get into a position to help.

Henry formed a stirrup with his hands to help boost Georgiana back into the boat. Soon they were both safely ensconced inside the canoe with their newly recovered paddle and waving goodbye to their would-be rescuer. With a chuckle, Henry shook his head. "Well, that was unexpected."

"The plunge or the kiss?" she asked as she braced her shivering arms around her waist against the wind.

"The plunge. The kiss was overdue." As though to prove it, he leaned forward to steal another quick kiss.

She couldn't argue with that, although she did lift her chin and announce, "For the record, I did not have designs on you when I thought you were married."

"I know. That's why I kept wearing the ring." He grinned when her mouth fell open. "I had a feeling something like this might happen."

"And you kept the ring on to avoid it?" She chided, "Henry, that's hardly fair."

He shrugged. "The timing wasn't right."

True. But was the timing right now? She was still technically on the run from her father and his detectives. Henry still had so much to lose by aiding and abetting her elusive ways. This would not help him where her father was concerned. Of that much she was certain. Yet she couldn't find it within herself to warn him. He knew what he was getting into by consorting with her.

Perhaps she ought to be concerned for herself. After all, what were the chances that Henry was trying to create this new connection as a way to gain leverage for his business?

She shook her head, unable even to finish that thought. Henry wasn't like that. He was genuine. A man of standards. A man of faith. He was a safe place. Her heart knew that.

She sighed. Too bad her head wasn't quite ready to be convinced. This wouldn't be the first time she'd thought a man cared for her only to find out that his true interest was in gaining access to her father's influence or pocketbook. Until she was certain—completely certain—that Henry didn't have some other endgame in mind, she'd keep her wits about her and proceed with caution. A lot of caution.

This was a bad idea.

He never should have agreed to it. Yet here he was, crawling into the recesses of Mercy House's dusty porch. Spotting a baseball in the far corner, he headed that direction and snatched it from the jaws of a large spiderweb before crawling out again. He wiped it off on his work pants, then handed it to six-year-old Joanna Carney. Her brown eyes filled with delight as she took the baseball from him and clutched it protectively to her chest. She offered a shy smile and whispered with a slight lisp, "Thank you, Mr. Henry. It's been under there so long. I thought I might never get it back. Um, do you think maybe you could play catch with us kids sometime?"

"I'd love to," he said without a moment of hesitation. She ducked her head and hurried back into the house, her shyness taking over once again. However, the invitation proved just how far Joanna had come since she'd all but panicked at the sight of him eight days ago. His continued presence at Mercy House as a frequent volunteer had helped. So had the couple he'd hired to minister to the residents.

Under Georgiana's directions, they'd made a few cosmetic changes to the interior and exterior of the mansion to make the atmosphere fresher and brighter. Already the overall mood had improved substantially. Even Mrs. Higgins offered an almost friendly smile whenever he arrived, since he'd received special permission to serve as a volunteer at Mercy House.

His mother was as pleased as she could be by his more hands-on approach to running Mercy Ministries, despite his refusal thus far to reveal his true identity as its founder. To be honest, he wasn't sure how much longer he would be able to maintain this level of involvement. While he had the ability to run the Pinnacle from any of its three locations, most of the operations staff was based in New York. Business would call him back there, and soon. However, he wasn't ready to leave yet. Not until the Mercy House improvement projects were complete.

Beyond that, Georgiana was still here. She couldn't return to New York for another week. And then he'd have to face her father and let him know that not only had he harbored Georgiana for part of the time she'd been missing, but he'd also fallen in love with her. How could he not have?

The past week since their kiss had only made their relationship deepen. They'd talked for hours about everything from their childhoods to their hopes for the future. Georgiana's enthusiasm and hunger for the Lord had reawakened his own. They shared a devotional every evening, often including his mother, who had said very little when it came to the obvious change in his relationship with Georgiana. Every now and then he caught a look of relief in his mother's eyes when she watched them together. A subtle smile hinted at her approval of his choice. No doubt she knew it had not been made lightly. He could see a future with Georgiana, and the more time he spent with her, the more he wanted to spend with her.

Hammering the last few slats into place on the newly repaired porch, he set his toolbox in the storage room and went in search of the subject of his thoughts. He found her in the dining room at a painting party that had apparently turned into a prayer meeting. With paintbrushes and rollers coated in a cheery yellow hue, the five women in the room seemed to be taking turns praying for each other.

He was about to step away from the doorway and leave them to it when Georgiana's voice stopped him. "Finally, Lord, we thank You for the changes you have brought to Mercy House, and for the benefactor who has made those changes possible. May this be a place of healing and hope. As soon as someone walks in the door, may they feel Your love and compassion for them in a tangible way. Help each of us live our lives as an expression of that love. Increase our desire for You, and take us deeper in our knowledge of You. Let us always be an encouragement to each other, filled with grace, and spreading hope as You redeem the messes that were our lives and make us into masterpieces that showcase Your glory. In Jesus' name we pray, Amen."

"Amen," they all said.

Henry couldn't help watching in admiration as Georgiana reached out to hug Samantha, one of the younger ladies, who seemed to have been crying. By the time Georgiana finished whispering something into her ear, Samantha laughed. Another quick hug, and the women separated. Georgiana caught sight of him, and her eyes lit up. She lifted her eyebrows inquiringly, silently asking if it was time to leave. He nodded. She turned to hug the rest of the ladies goodbye and met him at the door. "How did the repairs to the porch go?"

"I finished it today," he said as he placed a hand on the small of her back to guide her toward the front door.

"Wonderful! I know the ladies will be excited to hear that. Now we just need to put a table and a few chairs out there." She paused as they stepped outside and lifted her face toward the warm caress of the sun. "Can you feel that? It's pure hope. They'll feel it too when they sit in the sunshine to work on the sewing and mending they take in."

"I feel it." He grinned. Catching her hand, he tugged slightly to get her moving again. He really did need to get back to his office at the Pinnacle, but he wanted to see Georgiana safely to his mother's house first. He set off down the street toward where the cable car would stop in a few minutes. "You'll never guess what else happened today. Joanna asked me to play catch with her sometime."

Her breath caught in her throat. "Really? Oh Henry, I wish I'd been there to see that. You said you would, didn't you?"

"Of course."

With a soft smile, she shook her head in awe. "God is doing amazing things at Mercy House, isn't He? Through you, I mean. Don't you think it's time to tell them who you are?"

He groaned. "Oh no. Not you too."

"Well, why hold back? You've improved their morale considerably just by show-ing them how much you care about them. Can you imagine how much safer they would feel, knowing the great Henry Chadwick is not only a volunteer at Mercy House but their very own benefactor? They're already starting to love you. This would simply cinch the deal."

He laughed. "You think they're starting to love me?"

"Of course. Just look at little Joanna. They all look up to you and—"

He stepped in front of her, wrapping an arm around her waist while her forward momentum brought her into his embrace. Her eyes widened, but she didn't step away. Instead, her gaze locked with his. He tilted his head. "What about you?"

"Me?"

"You said they're starting to love me. So. . .?"

"So what about me?" A smile tugged at her lips. Her eyes narrowed thoughtfully. "Well, I must say, I've grown quite fond of you."

" 'Quite fond'?" he echoed, matching the playful formality of her tone. At her affirming nod, he frowned, then wiped a stray mark of paint from her chin. "I see. I suppose I'll have to work on that."

She caught hold of his lapel. He lowered his head. The cable car chimed its arrival in the distance. They shared a wide-eyed look, then took off running toward the corner. They managed to reach it just in time for him to lift her onto the cable car and hop up beside her. As they neared the stop closest to his mother's house, she leaned closer to him. "You don't have to walk me home, Henry. I can get there safely. It's only a block away from your mother's house, and you'll already be getting back to your office later than you hoped."

"Are you sure? I don't mind. It won't take that long," he said as the car began to stop.

"I'll be fine." She held on to his arm as a few others disembarked. He was just about to warn her that she was about to miss her stop, when she leaned in even closer to whisper, "In case you're truly wondering. . .I love you, Henry Chadwick."

It took an instant for her whispered words to process through the noise and his thoughts. By the time he realized what she'd said, she'd hopped down from the cable car all on her own. He tried to dash after her, but other passengers blocked his way. He finally made it to the end of the car as it rushed away from the corner. Georgiana stood there waiting for the traffic to clear. Catching him watching, she smiled. He mouthed, *I love you!*

Her smile spread, and she threw him a kiss before heading in the direction of his mother's house. Feeling relieved and on top of the world, he couldn't stop grinning on his way to work. He detoured to the penthouse for a quick change of clothes, then headed to his office. He'd barely sat down to read his most recent correspondence when a knock sounded on the door.

"Come in," he called, not glancing up until a familiar, deep voice filled the silence. "Henry Chadwick."

He froze. Dread filled his stomach. Even so, he stood to face the imposing figure and met the man's piercing green eyes. "Maxwell Price, what brings you to Denver?"

"As you know, my daughter." Eyes narrowing, Maxwell tilted his head. "You and I? We need to talk."

Chapter 5

Georgiana stirred a huge pot of stew in Mercy's Kitchen. She paused while Walter dipped a small spoon into the pot and tasted it. After a moment of consideration, he said, "A little more pepper, I think."

She added a few more shakes of pepper. "When did you say the new chef would start?"

"Early next week is what I heard."

Margaret called softly, "You have a visitor. He wouldn't wait out front."

Georgiana turned to see her father step into the kitchen. She stared at him in shock. He looked even taller and more imposing than she remembered, with his stern features and silver hair. Gathering herself to her full height, she lifted her chin. Tense silence stretched between them, but she wouldn't be the one to break it. She had nothing to say to him.

He seemed almost nervous as he slid his hands into his pockets. "May we talk?"

"If you wish."

"Out front," Walter ordered, having no idea he was speaking to *the* Maxwell Price. Although somehow she didn't think it would have mattered to Walter one bit had he known. He confirmed that with the suspicion in his voice as he said, "Where I can keep an eye on you."

Her fathered bristled slightly at the man's impertinence but complied by turning on his heel and walking back through the door that led to the dining hall. She hesitated. Oh, how easy it would be to walk out the back door and run away yet again. But knowing he'd only keep pursuing her, she followed him into the dining hall. It was nearly empty except for a few volunteers who were setting up for dinner—and Walter, who joined in the volunteers' efforts but kept an eye on her.

She sat at the humble wooden table across from her father and lifted her brows inquiringly. He leaned forward in his chair to speak in low tones. "How are you?"

"Better than I have been in a long time."

His brow furrowed. "You haven't been hurt or injured in any way, have you? If anyone has so much as laid a finger on my daughter—"

"I'm fine," she said firmly. "Why are you here?"

"To ask you to come home."

She gave him a disbelieving look. "You want me to go home with you after you threatened to put me out on the street if I didn't marry the man you chose for me?"

Impatience filled his voice. "You know I didn't mean that, Georgiana. Is that why you left? Because you thought I was upset with you?"

"I left because you were forcing me to marry someone who valued me even less than you do."

"I value you, Georgiana. How can you say I don't? I'm your father. I want what's best for you."

"No. You want what's best for you."

"I am trying to protect you." He paused to pull in a breath. "Don't you understand? People like us can't trust anyone. We can't let them into our hearts until we've settled the terms of the relationship to our benefit. Otherwise they'll take advantage of us. It happens all the time. I don't want it to happen to you. Trust me, Georgiana. I only have your best interests in mind."

She shook her head. "How can you possibly know what my best interests are when you've barely taken the time to get to know me?"

"I've done my best. I. . ." He swallowed hard, then shook his head as if warding off emotion. "I know that I haven't always been the best father. Business has consumed much of my attention, much of my life, but that doesn't mean I don't love you. I wanted to give you the world on a silver platter. I wanted you to be happy."

"I didn't need the world. I needed a father—parents who were willing to spend time with me, love me for who I was, listen to me, and—" She rubbed her temples. "It doesn't matter now. The fact is, you have no idea who I am or what will make me happy. I may go back to New York eventually, but not now. Not until I finish the work I'm doing here. Not until I receive Grandmother's inheritance."

"Your grandmother's inheritance." Maxwell's eyes narrowed before a hint of amusement curved his mouth. "Is that what you've been banking on? Georgiana, I'm the executor of your grandmother's will. You won't get a cent without my approval."

She stilled even as her heart sank in her chest. He was right. She remembered that now. He'd been a key player at the reading of her grandmother's will. She'd only been eight years old when her grandmother died. In the years that followed, she'd never considered the implications of his role as executor. "That inheritance is mine. You can't keep it from me."

"I could."

She squared her shoulders. "If you do, I'll sue you."

"And get tied up in a messy legal battle for years?" He gave her a chiding look. "That seems unnecessary when you could receive your inheritance next week by simply yielding to my wisdom. Marry the Earl of Stamford."

She let out a laugh. "You must be joking. I'd just as soon stay right here in Denver without a cent to my name."

"Without a cent is right, I'm sure. How would you provide for yourself?"

Her mind scrambled for an answer. Henry. He wouldn't let her down. "I could find a position with Mercy Ministries. With all the volunteering I've done for them, I'm sure they'd be happy to hire me on full-time."

"Mercy Ministries?" He scoffed. "Do you have any idea who runs this organization?"

She tried not to tense. "Why? Do you?"

He grimaced. "No, and that is exactly my point. This whole organization is cloaked in secrecy. Innocent people are giving money to a cause they know nothing about. It could be a front for money laundering or prostitution, for all the public knows. Why, I should have the whole thing shut down."

"No. You can't. The community needs this organization." She bit her lip, trying to stem the flow of desperate words issuing forth. She'd said too much and revealed a weakness. Her father knew it too.

His visage turned calculating. "I would never leave it alone—not as long as my daughter was innocently involving herself in a fraud. Come home with me instead. We'll forget about all of this and work through the issue of your inheritance."

Her nails dug into her palms. "I have other obligations."

"You refer to your relationship with Henry Chadwick, I suppose," her father said as though he was perfectly bored by the entire situation. "He told me that you have feelings for him. He tried to use that as leverage to get me to fund his expansion. I saw right through him, of course. I agreed to fund his expansion as long as he left you alone. He took the deal."

"I. . .I don't believe you."

Something akin to pity filled his eyes. "Georgiana, how do you think I found you here in Denver? He told me exactly where you were. His mother packed your belongings. They're in my carriage. When it came down to a choice between you and my funding of the Pinnacle's expansion, he chose the funding."

As loathe as she was to believe him, he seemed to be telling the truth. One thing would prove it. A challenge rang in her voice. "Show me the suitcase."

Her father motioned to a man standing beside the door. The carriage driver? He must be, for the man returned a few moments later with her suitcase in tow. Heart aching, she watched him set it on the table between her and her father. She stared at it until her father urged, "Check inside. Make sure it's all there."

She unsnapped the buckles and peered inside. Clothes that she'd placed in the wardrobe, stockings she'd left draped on the foot of the bed, the Bible she'd bought at a nearby bookstore—it was all there, neatly packed. She closed the suitcase with a loud snap.

Feeling numb, she considered her options. If she stayed in Denver, she might never receive her inheritance. Her father would dismantle Mercy Ministries to break her will. And Henry. . . She couldn't even think about him right now. The betrayal. . . How could he?

"Well, Georgiana, are you ready to go back to New York?"

She met her father's gaze and gave a slow nod of acquiescence. "I'm ready."

"Shall I assume your melancholy mood means Georgiana still hasn't contacted you?" Henry's mother asked as she took the seat across from him at the patio table of his New York estate.

Abandoning any pretense of an appetite, Henry pushed his dinner plate away and buried his hands in his hair. "I feel as though I'm losing my mind. It's been a month since I saw her last. Every day I think, 'This is it. She'll reach out to me today.' Every day all I hear is silence. It's torture. I never should have agreed to Maxwell's terms."

"He's a shrewd one. That much is true, but I honestly don't understand why you aren't supposed to contact her first."

He released a deep breath and leaned back in his chair. "Everything between Georgiana and me happened so quickly. I'm supposed to give her time to sort through her emotions. I just never thought it would take her this long. I thought for certain she would say something or send something when I went public about being the founder and benefactor of Mercy Ministries. And yet nothing."

She sighed. "Well, you aren't the only one who is hearing silence. She hasn't kept in contact with me or anyone from Mercy Ministries either. Then there's the way Maxwell's maid just happened to arrive to pack her things while I wasn't home. I still say the whole thing was planned too well. Within an hour of arriving in Denver, he'd whisked her and everything she owned onto a train back to New York."

He hesitated. "I'd hate to think my biggest investor and the chairman of the Pinnacle's board of directors is that devious."

"Not necessarily devious, but. . . What did you call him? Ruthless? What would a ruthless man do to get what he wants?"

"Whatever it took." He frowned. "But what does he want? Besides my silence where Georgiana is concerned."

His mother bit her lip. "Perhaps time."

"Time?"

"To convince her to marry someone else."

Alarm filled him. "What are you talking about?"

"This morning's gossip column." She handed him the newspaper. "It looks like this Stamford fellow is still in the running after all."

" 'Wedding bells may yet chime for New York's most elusive heiress. . .' " The article went on to speculate that Stamford and Georgiana would soon make amends. Reportedly, his family was traveling to America to meet her, and a wedding would take place soon after. Henry shook his head. "This can't be. Georgiana would never agree to this. Unless. . . If Maxwell lied to me, he could be lying to her as well. I have to speak with her."

Caution filled his mother's voice. "Henry, are you prepared for the consequences of that? You might lose your biggest investor and maybe even your company if you pick a fight with the chairman of the board."

He frowned. "You're right. Maxwell was pretty forgiving the first time because I was able to say I'd kept Georgiana safe. This time I'll be wrecking whatever plans he's made—with relish. I have no doubt he'll come after me with everything he has."

A soft smile played at his mother's lips. "Are you still going to do it? Do you love her that much?"

"I do." He paused. "And I trust God that much. You were right all those weeks ago. God gave me this business. He'll enable me to keep it. If He doesn't, then He has another plan for me."

His mother reached over to squeeze his hand. "I don't think I've ever been prouder of you, Henry Chadwick. Now go get our girl."

One month.

It had been one month without as much as a word from Henry. Her father continued to hold her inheritance hostage. Meanwhile, to pacify her father, she'd cut off all contact with anyone related to Mercy Ministries. Not out of concern for the man who had betrayed her, but for the many people his ministry touched. She had never felt more alone in her life.

"Almost ready, my pet?"

She startled as her mother swept into her bedroom. Gathering herself enough to offer a wan smile, Georgiana asked, "How many people are we dining with tonight?"

"Twelve, including Stamford's mother and sisters all the way from England. Surely you haven't forgotten that."

"No, I didn't forget." Eyeing herself in the mirror, she straightened the rosebud sash on her gown. "I simply didn't think they could afford it."

Her mother laughed, though her tone held the slightest edge of warning. "How clever you are, but do remember, your father has gone through a lot of trouble to arrange all of this for you so that you could become more comfortable with Stamford's family. Please make sure they feel welcome."

"Of course."

Her mother gave her a comforting pat on the back. "Stamford is doing his best to make amends. I hope you recognize that. He sincerely regrets the words you overheard all those months ago. They were said in a moment of frustration and nervousness. He meant nothing by them."

"So he has said."

Her mother smiled and squeezed Georgiana's hand. "That is the way of great men, I'm afraid. They're rash, and sometimes it may seem as if. . .well, as if they don't care, but they truly do, Georgiana. It's only that they carry such tremendous responsibility. It wears on them. We must do what we can to make this world easier for them. That is our tremendous responsibility."

Oh, but there was another way. Georgiana had seen it with her own eyes in Abigail, a woman who ran a large charity organization with oversight from her son. She'd seen it in Margaret, who'd worked side by side with her husband as colaborers for Christ. She'd even seen it in Mrs. Higgins, who carried enough authority to oversee and protect an entire household of women. Unfortunately, the longer Georgiana stayed with her parents, the less such a life seemed possible for her.

Perhaps her lot in life truly was simply to be a pawn for one powerful man or another. The prospect wouldn't hurt so much if it wasn't for Henry. She'd given him something she'd never given anyone else—her heart. In return he'd used it for his personal gain and then abandoned her. She shouldn't have been surprised. He told her from the start that he'd worked too hard to risk everything for her. Apparently whatever else they may have shared ultimately couldn't outweigh his ambitions.

She blinked her tears away and turned from the vanity to smile at her mother. "I'm ready. Let's go greet our guests."

Dinner was a strained affair. Though Stamford's family tried to be friendly, there was an undercurrent of desperation they couldn't quite hide. Eight months without an influx of wealth must truly have left them struggling. Stamford, however, seemed at ease, attentive, even kind.

Perhaps her mother was right. He might not be so bad, after all. Besides, to whose standard was she comparing him? Henry's? At least with Stamford she knew where she stood. They'd had numerous talks over the past month about what their future together might be like.

After they fulfilled their marital obligations of producing children, she would be free to travel or focus on whatever charities she found most worthy in England. His estate would be equipped with modern plumbing and heating as soon as possible. It was all quite agreeable.

Swallowing against the lump in her throat, she glanced up as her father suggested she and Stamford take a turn about the garden. Dread filled her. So this was it then—Stamford's proposal. He hadn't bothered to issue one in person last time, which made this an improvement.

He ushered her out to the verandah, not knowing she'd once hidden from him there. She'd been so desperate, so willing to do anything it took to ensure she didn't end up married to the man who now took her hands in his and stared into her eyes. His tone was humble and sincere. "Georgiana, there's no denying we got off on the wrong foot. That was entirely my fault. I should have taken the time to get to know you. Now that you have given me that chance, I am much more aware of the honor you would pay me by bestowing upon me your hand in marriage."

She pulled in a deep breath. Could she do this? Could she let this happen? Was the life Stamford offered, the one her mother had chosen, the one her father thought safest, truly the most she could expect from this life? To be wanted for her money and her social standing and not for who she truly was? Yet what was the alternative? To be poor and broke and alone?

Hadn't she already faced that moment, though? And through it, she'd found out the truth. She was never alone. God was always on her side. He loved her for who she was. He would look out for her. He would fight for her—even if no one else would.

A contented smile curved her lips, apparently sending errant encouragement to Stamford. He smiled back and gave her hands a gentle squeeze. "Georgiana Price—"

"Wait!" A voice called from the shadows of the garden.

She froze as recognition shot through her. She turned toward the sound just as a familiar form stepped into a pool of golden lantern light. Her breath caught in her throat, then released in one disbelieving word. "Henry?"

Weeks of waiting, praying, hoping, and agonizing all culminated in that single, precious word from Georgiana's lips. Finally, she'd broken the silence between them. Heart thundering in his chest, he watched as she pulled her hands from Stamford's grasp and braced them on the verandah railing. "What in the world are you doing here?"

"They wouldn't let me in through the front door. Besides, I couldn't wait any longer." He eyed the man behind her. "Apparently it's a good thing I didn't."

"Maxwell," Stamford bellowed with uncertainty in his voice.

Henry ignored the man to focus on Georgiana. Approaching the verandah railing, he captured her gaze. "Georgiana, I love you."

"What?" she asked breathlessly.

Maxwell skidded onto the verandah, took one look at Henry, and growled, "Chadwick. Don't say another word. Leave my property at once."

Henry squared his shoulders and met Maxwell's gaze in defiance. "Why? Are you afraid I'll tell Georgiana the truth? That you told me to give her time and wait for her to contact me? Meanwhile, you told her what, Maxwell? That I didn't love her? That I betrayed her?"

Georgiana turned to her father. "What does he mean, Father?"

Maxwell's face tightened. "It was for your own good."

"My own good?" she asked. "Then who packed my suitcase?"

After a moment, Maxwell grumbled out, "Your maid."

"Lucy. Of course. She was waiting for us at the train station. To see to my comfort, you said." She let out a disgusted scoff. "I should have known better. I was devastated and shocked, and I trusted you. How could you do this to me? What else have you lied about?"

"I haven't lied about wanting what's best for you."

Seeking her father's gaze, she took a step closer. "You need to let me decide what that is."

Maxwell reluctantly gestured to Henry. "You think it's him?"

Georgiana met his gaze. He saw the hurt she'd thought he'd caused begin to change to understanding and pure vulnerability. "Yes. As a matter of fact, I do."

Relief filled Henry. He took another step toward her, then stopped when Stamford cleared his throat. "This is all well and good, but where does it leave me?"

Maxwell sighed. "Come to my office, Stamford. We have some legalities to discuss."

"Indeed we do," Stamford said.

Steel filled Georgiana's voice. "While you're in there, go ahead and sign my inheritance over to me, Father."

Maxwell stilled. Finally, he nodded, then turned away. A moment later, the men's voices faded into the house.

Alone with Georgiana at last, Henry stared at her for a moment, soaking in the feeling of being together again. Finally, he grinned and reached for the railing, intending to climb over it to reach her, but she was already sitting on the railing and swinging her legs over it. She reached for his shoulders at the same time he grabbed for her waist. He lowered her down in front of him. Suddenly, every word that had been missed between them seemed to burst forth at once. She shook her head. "Oh Henry, it was horrible."

"I'm so sorry, sweetheart. It was only this morning that I began to realize what was happening. I saw that article—"

"What article?"

He grimaced. "The gossip about you and Stamford marrying again."

"Oh." Dismay filled her voice. "I didn't know. I don't read the papers."

"That's why you didn't see me go public about Mercy Ministry."

Tears of joy filled her eyes. "Did you? That's wonderful! How is your mother?"

He grinned. "Angry and missing you."

She laughed. "I've missed her too. And you. So much!"

"I missed you too." He gave her a helpless look. "It was agony. Pure agony. I thought I'd lost you."

Her arms wrapped tighter around his shoulders. "Only because I thought you'd betrayed me."

"Never."

Her brow furrowed. "I still don't understand. How did Father find me in Denver if you didn't tell him?"

"One of the private detectives he hired caught up with you. The man who tried to save us after the canoe tipped over."

"Oh yes. The canoe." Her gaze fell to his lips.

He eased her closer. "You will marry me, won't you?"

She laughed. "As soon as you ask."

He searched her gaze. "Do you need more time?"

"I've had plenty."

"In that case. . ." Catching her hands in his, he knelt. "Will you marry me, Georgiana, as soon as possible?"

"Of course, my love." She tugged at his hands until he stood, then stepped into his embrace again. "May we move to Denver? And may I help your mother run Mercy Ministries? And—"

"Whatever you want, it's yours." He claimed her with a kiss. When they were both good and breathless, he pulled back to capture her gaze. "No more running, my elusive heiress?"

She laughed. "Only to you, Henry. Only to you."

Noelle Marchand is an award-winning author who graduated summa cum laude from Houston Baptist University with a BA in Mass Communication and Speech Communication. Her love of literature began as a child when she would spend hours reading under the covers long after she was supposed to be asleep. At fifteen, she completed her first novel. Since then, she has continued to pursue her writing dreams. She enjoys spending time with family, learning about history, and watching classic cinema.

A Day Late and a Dollar Short

by Vickie McDonough

Chapter 1

Callie Webster stood at her bedroom window looking at the choppy waters of Lake Erie. The gray skies mirrored her mood. She glanced down at the letter in her hand. Never had she thought she'd choose to become a mail-order bride, but Uncle Roger had forced her hand.

"Oh Mama, you'd be so disappointed with how things have turned out."

She returned to her bed and folded her skirt and blouse, then placed them in her satchel. Next she took the picture of her parents, with Callie and her sister when they were young, from her chest of drawers and laid it on top of her skirt. She folded her dark blue dress and put it on top of the picture, hoping to protect it during her travels.

She glanced around her bedroom, once a place of joy and comfort. But no more. She'd buried her loving parents just two months ago, and coldhearted Uncle Roger had taken their place. And he had changed everything.

Closing her eyes, she relived her conversation with Uncle Roger at last night's supper.

"I gave you a month to find a husband on your own, but since you've dragged your feet and chosen not to find one, I have arranged for you to marry my good friend Otto Krenz. Because of your comely looks, he's willing to overlook the fact that you are destitute."

Callie had been stunned, unable to respond to his surprising news. Gathering her composure, she'd glanced around the opulent dining room. A beautiful Louis XVI table and chairs that seated twelve and two matching sideboards with lovely marquetry of walnut and kingwood filled the large room. Her European ancestors had brought the furniture with them when they emigrated to America. Expensive indigo-colored damask wallpaper she and her mother had selected adorned the walls.

Callie caught Evelyn's eye as the servant quietly exited. The woman's expression remained still, but Callie could read the disgust in her gaze. Evelyn despised Uncle

Roger. Where her parents had been kind and generous, her uncle was a cruel, stingy ogre.

Callie was only destitute because Uncle Roger had taken everything her father had owned and claimed it as his. If only Father had felt she could run his business and care for their lavish home on her own. Instead, she was being ordered to marry or leave with nothing. Either way, her uncle was dictating her future. Fortunately, she had seen the writing on the wall and had made her own plans. She'd kept them a secret from him for fear he would intervene.

She folded the letter from her future husband and placed it in her handbag. She gazed out the window one more time. No matter where she ended up, she would always treasure her view of the lovely lake, even on a cloudy day.

A knock sounded at the door. "Come in."

Evelyn stepped back into the room, her eyes red and a handkerchief in her hand. "Jasper has the carriage out front, Miss Callie."

"I'm as ready as I ever will be." Tears blurred her vision. She rushed forward and hugged the woman who'd been a part of her family as far back as she could remember. "If only I could take you with me. I will miss you so much."

"We'll all miss you terribly." Evelyn dabbed her eyes. "Please write and let us know you arrived safely."

Callie stepped back. "I will. Uncle Roger hasn't returned, has he?"

"No, missy." Evelyn took Callie's satchel off the bed.

"I left an envelope for him on my chest of drawers. Perhaps you could put it on his dinner plate this evening?"

"It will be my pleasure." The gleam in Evelyn's dark eyes almost made Callie smile.

She breathed in a resolute breath, took one final look around her room, then followed Evelyn down the stairs for the last time.

Outside she entered the carriage and stared at the only home she'd ever known. Tears blurred her final view as the carriage turned the corner. She would always remember the life she had enjoyed so much when her parents and sister were still alive.

Uncle Roger may have taken her home and everything she held dear, but he wouldn't steal her future.

Northwest of Dallas, Texas
May 23, 1882

The closer the stagecoach drew to Sowers, Texas, the harder Callie's heart pounded.

She was doing the right thing, wasn't she? But then, what other choice did she have?

"We're almost there, dearie." Miss Elliot, the elderly spinster seated across from Callie, clapped her hands. "It's all so exciting. I only wish there was such a thing as mail-order brides when I was young. Perhaps I wouldn't have had to endure so many years alone."

Callie smiled at the kind woman, but she knew there were things far worse than living alone—like being forced to marry a man you despised. If only Uncle Roger hadn't insisted she marry Otto Krenz. Oh, the man had treated her well enough when Uncle Roger was in the room, but the second they were alone, he'd turned into a predator, just like the wolves she'd seen running across the prairie as she rode the train west. She shuddered at the thought of being his wife. She might have been able to overlook their age difference had the man been kind, but she'd seen enough of his character to know what would become of her if she married him.

The stage hit a rut, and she grabbed hold of the window frame. The hot breeze blowing in did nothing to relieve the stifling heat of the coach. It would have been better if she could have waited until fall to travel, but Uncle Roger had forced her hand. Saying no to him would have meant being tossed out onto the street.

She longed for the comfort of her parents' arms. Things would have been much different had her parents lived. Not only had she lost them, but she'd also lost all the heirlooms her mother wanted her to have—her family heritage. All she managed to take were the two necklaces she'd kept hidden from her uncle. He'd sold the rest of her mother's and grandmother's jewelry to fund his taste for fancy liquor and who knew what else. But she couldn't allow her mind to travel down that dark alley. Tears burned her eyes at the thought of never seeing her home again.

They hit another bump, and the elderly woman across from her opened her eyes. Miss Elliot cleared her throat and wiped the dampness from her face with a lacy handkerchief. "Tell me about the wonderful man you'll be marrying again."

She repeated her story of writing to Mr. Butler and how he wrote back with a request to marry her. *But was he wonderful?*

She knew so little about Harvey Butler. "Did I mention that Mr. Butler owns a store—a mercantile, I believe. He is in need of a wife to help him run it. He mentioned in his letter that he is a godly man who attends services regularly."

She swallowed the lump in her throat. Attending church didn't guarantee a good character. Would Mr. Butler be a kind man or one like her uncle? Had she jumped out of one frying pan into another? What if he was cruel and beat her?

She blew out a sigh. Worrying wouldn't change anything. Leaning her head back against the seat, she stared at the passing scenery. Where tall, stately trees neatly lined the organized streets of Sandusky, short squatty ones dotted the Texas landscape with bushes that actually rolled in the brisk wind. Miss Elliot called them tumbleweeds.

Callie was also surprised at how little water she'd seen. She would miss the cooler temperatures of the North and strolling along the shores of Lake Erie in the summer with her friends. Texas certainly wasn't her first choice of places to live, but at least Harvey Butler was her pick for a husband and not the one being forced on her. *Please, heavenly Father, let him be a kind man who'll be patient with me. And help me to love him, even if he never loves me.*

"I can see that you're worried, dear. This might sound a bit harsh, but you told me you prayed about coming to Sowers, so now you need to trust God. He won't fail you. If I've learned nothing else in my sixty-eight years, it's that. We fail God all the time, but He never fails us, even on our darkest day."

"Thank you, Miss Elliot. That does encourage me. I do believe coming to Texas and marrying is an answer to my prayers. I believe God will give me the courage to wed, even though I haven't yet met my future husband."

"I think that might be easier than leaving your home and traveling so far to a strange land. I remember how hard it was when I first came here, but now I can't imagine living anywhere else."

"Maybe I'll feel that way one day." But she couldn't fathom ever coming to love such a hot, dry place. If it was so hot now, how would she endure the heat of summer?

"Oh look! There's the windmill at the Southern Star Ranch. It's the biggest in the area. You know you're getting close to Sowers when you see that."

Callie looked out once more, then sat up and studied her clothing. Wrinkled and dusty. What would Mr. Butler think? She swiped at the dust, but it only stirred up a cloud that made her cough.

"You best wait until you're off the stage to tidy up." Miss Elliot waved her handkerchief in front of her face. "Your man won't even notice the dust once his eyes land on that pretty face of yours."

Callie felt her cheeks heat. No one since her mother had said she was pretty. "Thank you. I wish you lived in Sowers."

Miss Elliot smiled. "Well, I'm not sure that I wish I lived there. I'm quite content with my little house in Fort Worth. I tried for a final time to get my sister to move in with me, but she doesn't want to leave her grandbabies. I can't say I blame her, but I told her that I might not ever see her again. I'm getting too old to travel in these shaky contraptions."

If only Christina had lived, perhaps her sister would have been married by now and Callie could have lived with her. Or at the least, she might have had a traveling companion. But a sickness had taken Christina when she was only seven. With stinging eyes, Callie stared at the vast barren landscape. She was alone in this world, with not a soul who cared for her.

Well. . .not totally alone. She had her heavenly Father, and He was a big source of encouragement. But she did get lonely at times. Perhaps having a husband would solve that problem.

"Sowers!" the stage driver hollered.

Excitement overpowered her concerns. Callie scooted closer to the window to get a peek at her new home—and her mouth dropped open. Was this the whole town? She glanced out the window across the seat and saw nothing but grassy land, then looked back at the tiny town. There were only a handful of buildings—no more than two dozen at the most. What had she gotten herself into?

"Now don't start fretting. You can't judge a town by its size. There are mighty good people in Sowers. You'll find that out soon enough."

"I sure hope so." Callie lifted her satchel off the floor, gripping the handle until her fingers turned white.

The stage rolled to a stop. Miss Elliot reached over and laid her hand on Callie's. "Look at me, dear."

She lifted her gaze to meet the kind woman's.

"If things don't go as planned, you come to Fort Worth and stay with me. I have an extra bedroom and would love the company."

Blinking back tears, Callie gently squeezed Miss Elliot's hand. "That is so kind of you. I can't tell you how much it relieves me to know I have an option if things here don't work out. You're a godsend, Miss Elliot."

The elderly woman leaned back and waved her fan. "I don't know about that, but I can say that I thoroughly enjoyed your company. It's a long trip on a good day, but it was much more pleasant with you along."

Callie rose and hugged her new friend, then helped her to the door, where the shotgun rider assisted her down. Then Callie followed, taking her first steps in her new town—where no one was waiting to meet her.

Miss Elliot touched Callie's arm. "Would you mind helping me inside? I'd like to get out of this heat while the men change the horses. They usually have some sort of refreshment, and I need to sit on something that isn't moving for a bit."

Callie smiled in spite of her discomfort that Mr. Butler wasn't there to meet her. Perhaps he had a customer in his store and couldn't leave. She helped Miss Elliot into the slightly cooler depot and to one of the chairs lining the wall.

The clerk, a middle-aged man with a furry moustache, nodded at them. "There's coffee in the pot, or water, if you prefer. Pastor Sanders's wife brought over a fresh batch of cookies. If you want any, you'd best grab 'em afore the driver and shotgun get in here." He shook his head. "There won't be none left, for sure." Then he grinned—she thought—but she wasn't sure because his whole mouth was hidden behind that moustache. He pulled open a drawer, revealing a napkin with half a dozen cookies on it. "Got my own collection right here. Name's Dave Westfall, by the way."

"Callie Webster, and this is Miss Elliot."

The man nodded. "Seen Miss Elliot afore."

"Yes, you have, young man. Thank you for saving us some of the refreshments."

After Miss Elliot was seated with a cup of water and two cookies, Callie walked to the window and studied the town. Across the street was a doctor's office with an apothecary next door. She could hear the sound of a blacksmith's hammer but couldn't see his place of business from where she stood. No one walked the streets, although a horse was tied in front of the doctor's office. Far down the dirt street was a church and some kind of large business with steam rising from the top.

"That big place is the cotton gin. Kind of hard to miss it," Mr. Westfall said.

Callie didn't realize people raised cotton in Texas. She crossed back to the refreshments and poured a glass of water and took two cookies. She'd had precious little to eat since boarding the stage two days ago. Her stomach had been upset from the jostling and her worry over her future. She sat beside Miss Elliot just as the door burst open and the driver and shotgun rider charged in, making a beeline for the cookies. After a few minutes of shoving and then chewing, all the cookies were gone.

"Told you so." Mr. Westfall shook his head. "Them two's as rowdy as a stampede."

The driver shuffled over to Miss Elliot and held out his hand. "Time to go, ma'am."

Callie rose as her friend did, dreading to see her leave. "I'll miss you."

"Oh, me too, dear. Write to me if you wish."

"I will. Have a safe journey home."

"Thank you, and try not to worry. Things will work out as God has planned."

As the stage drove away, Callie realized that Miss Elliot had forgotten to give her an address. With a sigh, she turned to face Mr. Westfall. If Harvey Butler wasn't going to come meet her, she'd go find him. "Could you please direct me to Harvey Butler's store?"

"Sure can, but it won't do you no good. He ain't there."

Callie's heart tripped. "What do you mean?"

"He's gone. Got married up yesterday and left town. Went off somewhere with his new bride to celebrate."

She dropped onto a chair as she felt the blood drain from her face. Harvey Butler was married? But how could that be? He told her to come—even sent her the money for the travel costs.

"Hey! You're that mail-order bride, ain'tcha?" He shook his head. "Just ain't right to order up a bride, then marry someone else afore she comes. That Alma May's been chasin' after Harvey for a long while. Guess he figgered a bird in the store was better than one on the stage."

Callie couldn't look at the man. Harvey Butler had played her for a fool.

Mr. Westfall shuffled toward her. "Now, I know things seem bad, but I wouldn't worry none. There's plenty o' men in town that'll be happy to marry up with a purty gal like you."

Marriage was the last thing she wanted now. If only the stage hadn't left already. She opened her bag and pulled out her few remaining coins. God knew ahead of time about Mr. Butler's desertion, and He had provided a place for her with Miss Elliot. Now she just had to get to Fort Worth and find her. "How much is a ticket to Fort Worth?"

"A dollar twenty-five."

Callie stared at the piddling amount of coins in her hand. She was a whole dollar short. Her stomach clenched. What in the world was she going to do? "Umm. . .never mind."

She picked up her satchel, walked out of the stage office, and dropped onto one of the hard benches outside. She was alone in Texas, and the only person who could help her just rode out of town.

Why, Lord? Why did this happen? Why did you have Miss Elliot offer me a place to stay but didn't provide a way for me to get there?

She couldn't help feeling betrayed once again as she stared at the tiny town. What was to become of her?

And how had she ended up a day late and a dollar short?

Erik Kessler waved goodbye to his daughter as he walked away from the parsonage.

He appreciated Mrs. Sanders's willingness to watch Anika while he attended to his business in town. It gave his sister some time to herself back at the ranch after caring for his five-year-old all week. He tried not to think about what he would do when Janna left in two weeks, but God would provide someone to help him. As he stopped in front of Butler's Mercantile, he stared at the sign on the door. "Closed. Got Married."

Erik rubbed the back of his neck. With the mercantile closed, he would have to make another trip into town to get supplies. Not that it was all that far, but it was an inconvenience. He had known this was the day Butler's bride was supposed to arrive—everyone in and around Sowers knew—but he had not thought they would marry right away and then leave town. It would have been the decent thing for Harvey to let his customers know when he would return, but there was nothing posted about that. He blew out a sigh. At least he could get his shovel repaired at the blacksmith's shop. As he gazed down the street, his eyes paused on a woman sitting outside the stage office.

"Sad thing, ain't it?"

Erik glanced over his shoulder to see the town's postmaster and barber, Hank Stephens, walking down the boardwalk. Come to think of it, he probably should get a haircut. Janna had been badgering him to let her trim it, but he was not about to allow his sister to get near him with scissors. "You are open for business, *ja?*"

"Yup. I was just stretchin' my legs and eyein' that purty gal."

Erik walked alongside Hank. "What did you mean when you said something was sad?"

Hank pulled up short. "You mean you ain't heard yet?"

Erik shook his head. "Heard what?"

Hank yanked his hat off and slapped it against his leg. "That gal sittin' over there is Harvey Butler's mail-order bride."

"What is so sad about that?" He gazed across the road at the woman on the bench. She looked young. Now that he thought about it, if he were a woman, he might be sad at the thought of marrying Harvey. "Wait just a minute. The sign on the mercantile says Harvey has married and left town."

"Yup, he did." Hank grinned. "Married up Alma May yesterday and went somewhere's to celebrate. The big yella belly. After gettin' a look at the purty gal over there, I'm thinkin' about askin' her to marry up with me."

Erik finally grasped the seriousness of what Hank said. "Alma May finally managed to lasso Harvey?" Imagine that. The woman had been after the storekeeper to wed her for two years. He glanced over at the stage office again. But what a cruel thing to do to an unsuspecting woman. He could not help feeling bad for her. What would happen to her now?

While Hank wielded his clippers, Erik could not keep his eyes off the woman at the stage office. So far she had not left the bench. Was she so distraught at learning her intended was already married that she was left unable to move? What would happen to her? Sowers did not have a hotel or even a boardinghouse.

He could not help feeling that he should do something, but what? He supposed Pastor and Mrs. Sanders would take her in until the next stage arrived. The least he could do was escort her there so she would not continue to be the town spectacle. When he had first arrived in Sowers half an hour ago, there had not been a soul on the streets. Now several groups of men watched the woman. How long before some yahoo asked her to marry him?

"All done." Hank clapped him on the shoulder. He'd been so lost in thought, he had not heard a thing the chatty man had said. Erik paid him, then walked out of the barbershop. Two men approached the woman. Dave Westfall rushed out the door of the stage office brandishing his rifle and shooed them away. They crossed the dirt road but did not go far, reminding him of vultures. Dave bent and said something to the woman, but she shook her head.

Erik crossed the street to get a better look at her. He still had not decided if he should offer to help. As he approached the woman, she glanced up at him. His heart lurched at her sad expression. Her pretty brown eyes were rimmed with red. Had she been crying? He tipped his hat and forced himself to break her gaze and keep walking. His chest pounded as if he had raced across the pasture after a cantankerous horse.

He reached his wagon, grabbed his shovel, and headed to the blacksmith's shop. He had enough things to worry about without thinking of the jilted bride. But as he stood there, half listening to Smitty, all he could see were those sad eyes. He had to do something.

"Smitty, I will be back in a few minutes. Got something to do."

The big man nodded. "Give me fifteen to twenty minutes, and I'll have your shovel ready to go."

"Thank you." Erik's feet pushed into motion, almost as if they had a mind of their own. A sudden thought nearly made him halt. He needed someone to watch Anika when Janna returned home in two weeks. Was this stranger the answer to his prayers?

He stared at her as he walked toward her. More men had gathered across the street. He was surprised she had not gone inside the stage office. Most women would be antsy with so many men watching.

He slowed his paced. Was he loco to ask a stranger to care for his precious daughter? But what else could he do? He had asked most of the women at church, but they were too busy to take on a troubled five-year-old. The closer he got, the better the idea seemed. But would the woman turn him down flat?

Chapter 2

Callie clutched her damp handkerchief in her fist. She'd been praying, asking God to help her, but she still was at a loss as to what she should do next. She wished she could leave town and not have to face Mr. Butler, but she feared she was stuck here for a while.

She glanced over her shoulder and into the stage office. Perhaps Mr. Westfall would know of a family who needed help in exchange for room and board. She didn't need much. Even though her family was wealthy, her mama had taught her how to cook, clean, and sew—all useful skills. Perhaps one of the businesses in town needed help.

She longed to walk the streets and see what the town had to offer, but she was afraid to move away from the stage depot. The men across the dirt road had become peskier than the flies buzzing around her. Thankfully Mr. Westfall had chased the men who'd approached her away. Just imagine—three marriage proposals—and she'd only been in town two hours.

Her stomach grumbled, making her wish she'd eaten a few more cookies when she first arrived, but she'd been too nervous at the time. From what she could see, there wasn't a café in town, and she certainly hadn't smelled anything as pleasant as the cookies she'd eaten earlier.

The nice-looking man who'd tipped his hat to her walked toward her again. Perhaps he was returning to his place of business. He'd been the first man other than Mr. Westfall who hadn't gawked at her. His eyes had been curious but kind. She ducked her head, waiting for him to pass by again—but he stopped.

Oh no. Not another proposal.

Perhaps she should just accept one and get it over with. At least she would have a place to stay and food to eat.

He cleared his throat, and she saw him holding his hat.

Oh, where was Mr. Westfall?

"Excuse me, ma'am. I. . .uh. . .need to talk to you about something important."

Although instantly intrigued by his accent, she couldn't look him in the eye. "I can't marry you."

He shuffled his boots. "I did not ask you to."

She gasped and shot up. "I'll have you know that I am a decent woman. I am only here now because I was deceived."

He had the audacity to grin, and that made him look oh so handsome. His clean-cut blond hair glistened in the sun, and she'd never seen eyes quite so blue. His twin dimples gave him a roguish air. She edged toward the door, fearing if he actually asked her to marry that she would agree for the wrong reason.

"I am glad to hear you are a decent woman. I could not ask you to care for my daughter if you were not."

She paused, her heart pounding. "Your daughter?"

"Ja." A muscle in his jaw clenched, and he looked away. "Anika is five. Her mother was killed nearly two years ago, and Anika witnessed the murder. She has not spoken since."

He faced her again, and she saw genuine pain in his eyes. "My sister has been staying with us, but she is returning home in two weeks. I own a ranch, and I need someone to care for Anika and the house and to prepare meals. I wonder if you would be interested? I cannot pay much, but you would have your own room and all the food you are willing to prepare. Anika is not much trouble. She is such a quiet little girl."

All manner of thoughts raced through Callie's mind as she tried not to think about the man's faint but intriguing accent—an interesting cross between something like German and western lingo. Was this the answer to her prayers? But how could she live with a man and not be married? It wasn't proper. And now she had to tell him.

"I appreciate your kind offer, but I wouldn't be able to stay with you after your sister leaves. It"—she cleared her throat—"isn't proper." Her cheeks heated, and she looked away, mortally embarrassed.

He stood there, not saying a thing. Finally, he sighed and slapped on his hat. "All right then, if you will agree to come home with me today, I will make you a promise. In two weeks, if things are going well, when I come back to town to bring my sister to the stage depot, I will marry you—if we both agree that is what we feel we should do. Until then my sister will be in the home, so everything will be proper."

Mr. Westfall pushed out the door. "This fella botherin' you, ma'am?"

She glanced at the stranger. "Um, no. Thank you. We're talking over a business arrangement."

Mr. Westfall nodded. "I can tell you that Kessler is a decent sort. Not like those others I chased off."

Callie smiled, glad to know the stranger's name and that Mr. Westfall had spoken up for him. "Thank you for that valuable bit of information."

He nodded and disappeared into his office again.

"So, what do you think? Have we got a deal?"

Callie took in the man's clothing. The denim pants and blue shirt were in good condition, unlike the ragged overalls of some of the men across the street. And he didn't smell of rotten onions like the others. He wore a gun, but then every man she'd seen in this town did. Callie tensed. Three of those men were walking her way.

"Hey, Kessler! I asked the lady to marry me first. So you just mosey along." The tallest of the ruffians shook his fist at Mr. Kessler.

Instead of running off, Mr. Kessler turned, hand on his gun. "I have my own business with the lady, so *you* should turn around and walk away."

"You gonna take on all three of us?"

Mr. Kessler spoke over his shoulder to Callie. "You should go back inside."

The door opened, and Mr. Westfall exited again, rifle in hand.

Callie hurried toward the door, then paused. "I accept your offer, Mr. Kessler."

Erik's relief at finally finding a woman to help him battled the tension he felt at promising to marry her. Inge had filled his whole heart. After her death, he never planned to marry again, but he realized now that Anika needed a mother's love. Janna had helped fill the gap, but she was returning to her husband, who had been more than generous in allowing her to stay so long. In a few months, Janna would have her own child, and she needed to be home.

Marrying would ensure that he would always have someone to care for Anika, but there was no guarantee that a new wife would love his daughter and help her overcome the frightening experience of seeing her mother shot and killed during a stagecoach robbery. His heart still ached at what Anika had suffered. If only he knew what to do to help her.

The woman trotted alongside him, her breathing labored. He slowed his pace so she did not have to hurry. What had she said her name was? He swatted a fly away from his face as he pondered that thought. Had she ever stated her name? For that matter, had he?

Erik stopped suddenly in the middle of the street. He yanked off his hat.

The woman also halted, looking around with a worried expression. "What's wrong?" She gazed up at him. Her eyes widened, then she nibbled her lip. She cleared her throat. "You've changed your mind, haven't you?"

He shook his head. "No, I have not. I just realized that I was so nervous about approaching you with my offer that I never told you my name, and I don't believe you mentioned yours."

"Oh."

The relief on her face made him feel guilty for scaring her. Had she put all her eggs in one basket? Had Harvey Butler's desertion left her destitute? That would explain why she had sat outside the stage office for so long.

His attitude softened toward her. He had always had a nice home, albeit a small one when he still lived with his *fader* and *moder*. Their farm had always yielded a bountiful harvest, and his moder was a wonderful cook. He missed her delicious meals. But he'd had a desire to raise cattle not crops, so he had moved to Texas, leaving his parents and siblings behind in Kansas.

"Callie Webster," the woman said softly.

Pulled from his woolgathering, Erik nodded. "I am Erik Kessler. A pleasure to make your acquaintance."

Miss Webster smiled. 'What's your daughter's name again?"

"Anika." He started walking again.

"Where is she now?"

"Mrs. Sanders, the pastor's wife, sometimes keeps her for me when I come to town. Anika does not like shopping."

"That's nice. I'm glad there is a pastor here."

"Ja, Pastor Sanders is a good man." But he had been to services only a few times since Inge's death, and that was at Janna's insistence. "That is the parsonage—the white house next to the church."

Main Street at this end of town was quiet, with no one other than himself and Miss Webster out on the hot afternoon. The crowd watching her had quickly scattered as she had walked down the street with him. His new employee fanned her face with her handkerchief. The tiny hat she wore would do nothing to block the sun from her pale skin. Without a head covering, she would be sunburned before they reached the ranch. Perhaps Mrs. Sanders would have a bonnet she could borrow.

As they neared the house, Miss Webster's steps slowed. She twisted her hankie in her hands. "I should tell you, Mr. Kessler, that I can cook, clean, and sew, but I have never supervised a child before."

His heart bucked. Why had he assumed Miss Webster knew how to care for a child? But then, he realized that Janna, as the youngest of his five siblings, had not overseen a youngster all that much either, and she had done a good job caring for Anika. Sure, she had helped with the neighbors' children a few times when the parents had been ill, but watching a child all the time was different.

"I can promise that I will be kind to Anika and take good care of her if you could just give me some instruction."

That sounded reasonable. "I can do that, and I am sure Janna, my sister, can help too."

The door to the parsonage opened, and Anika stepped onto the porch. She waved and smiled, but she did not shout a greeting. He missed hearing her call him Papa—the name she had adopted after hearing the neighbor children call their fathers that. He missed her sweet chatter and childish voice. Would God ever heal his daughter and restore her fully to him? Was taking Inge not enough?

The delicious aroma of baking biscuits drew Erik from the barn. He paused at the pump and washed his face and hands, then started for the house again. His stomach rumbled, urging his feet to move quicker. Janna had stew simmering when they returned from town yesterday afternoon, but Miss Webster had jumped in and mixed up a batch of biscuits that had nearly melted in his mouth. His sister was a passable cook, but she had never been much of a baker. Her corn bread and biscuits were best used to throw at the crows sneaking around the garden.

He was eager to see if Miss Webster had made breakfast or if Janna had. He pushed open the door and was greeted with tantalizing scents and a little barefoot angel trotting toward him, still in her nightgown. He lifted Anika up and kissed her cheek. Her blue eyes twinkled, and her wispy hair, not yet in its braid, tickled his chin. Love for this child swelled his heart. "Where are your clothes, *Schätzli*?"

Anika motioned in the direction of her room.

"Did you forget to put them on?" He grinned, letting her know he was teasing. She shook her head. He glanced into the kitchen at the back of the house and saw Miss Webster bustling about. "And where is your aunt?"

Anika folded her hands together as if she were praying, then laid her cheek against them and closed her eyes. Erik's heart leaped. Was his sister sick? Surely her baby was not coming already. No, if that were the case, Janna would have sent Miss Webster to get him.

"Anika?" Miss Webster turned, and her eyes widened to see him. She held a steaming bowl of something he was sure would taste delicious. "I'm sorry. She was just here a moment ago."

"It is all right. She saw me and came running." He crossed the parlor toward his new employee. "This girl may be tiny, but she is speedy."

"I'll do better about watching her."

"It might help to give her a chore. She can set the table and do simple tasks. Ja, Schätzli?"

Anika nodded. Erik caressed his daughter's soft cheek, enjoying the moment. Soon enough he would be back at work. "Janna is still in bed?"

Callie grabbed a towel, then bent and removed the biscuits from the oven, filling the house with a delicious aroma. She set the hot pan on top of the stove. "I suggested she sleep late today. She seemed quite tired when she awoke this morning."

"She is not sick?"

Miss Webster shook her head. "I don't believe so."

"I hope caring for a youngster while in her condition has not been too hard on her."

"I wouldn't think so. Women have been bearing babies while tending their older children for many centuries. But it doesn't hurt to allow a mother-to-be to get some extra rest."

Her compassion for his sister touched his heart. He watched her bustle about, glad he had asked her to work for him. She put the biscuits in a bowl and set it, along with a platter of fried ham, on the table. The scrambled eggs steamed. Miss Webster untied her apron and hung it on the hook beside the back door. "Please, have a seat, and I'll see if Janna is ready to eat."

Erik placed Anika in her chair, then sat down and buttered a biscuit for her. He glanced at the door, then sneaked a bite. His eyes closed as he enjoyed the pleasant flavors. A tug on his sleeve drew him from his savoring, and he looked down at his daughter. She pushed her plate toward him, obviously not pleased that he had stolen a bite of her food and not given her some. He chuckled at her cute pout. Since she quit talking, her facial features had become far more expressive. "How about I just keep this one and fix you a new one?"

Anika smiled and nodded.

Footsteps came their way, and Erik shoved the last of his biscuit in and washed it down with hot coffee. Normally he would not eat anything until everyone was seated and the prayer had been said, but today he could not wait to try Miss Webster's baking again. He had to be sure he had not imagined the biscuits had tasted so good.

Janna strolled in looking more refreshed than he had seen her in weeks. She hugged his shoulders. "Hiring Callie is the best thing you have done in ages, Brother."

"I am happy you feel that way. Perhaps you will not worry about us so much when you go home." He glanced at Miss Webster as she took her seat and bowed her head.

If she cared for Anika as well as she cooked, Erik would be very pleased that he hired her.

Chapter 3

After cooking in the heat of the kitchen, Callie enjoyed the cooler temperature of the porch while she stitched up a tear in one of Anika's dresses. She peeked at the sweet little girl. She sat on the steps playing with a doll while Janna sat in the porch swing, gently swaying.

"I've been meaning to ask you something. What does *Schätzli* mean?"

Janna smiled. "It is Swiss German for 'little treasure.' Our parents originally came from Switzerland."

"I've heard that is a lovely country."

Janna nodded. "I have heard that too, but I have never been there. Although you might not know it when you hear us talk, Erik and I were born in Kansas. We grew up in a town with quite a few Swiss immigrants who still spoke their native tongue."

She sighed. "I am going to miss Erik and Anika so much when I return home, but I can hardly wait to see my Ben again. We've only been married a little over two years. Moder and I came out to help Erik right after Inge was killed. We've taken turns coming back to help him. I have been here for nearly three months this time."

"You must miss your husband terribly."

Janna nodded. "I do, but carrying his child has helped me to feel closer to him."

"He must be a compassionate man to allow you to be gone for so long."

"Ja. God blessed me with a good husband." She glanced at Callie, her blue eyes twinkling. "Perhaps God will also bless you in such a way."

Callie's heart leaped. She looked across the sunny yard to where Erik worked with a horse in the corral. One of his workers stood outside the fence watching him. Her cheeks warmed as she listened to Janna's chuckle.

"I came here to take care of Anika," Callie whispered, then glanced at the girl, who was walking toward the corral. "Is she allowed to go out there?"

"Not alone, but that doesn't keep her from trying." She raised her voice. "Anika, come back here."

The girl stopped, but she still faced her father.

"She loves the horses."

Callie folded up her sewing. "Why don't I walk her out there?"

"If you would like, but I would make her obey first. You do not want her to think she can outsmart you."

Standing, Callie called out, "Anika, please come back. I have a surprise for you." The girl slowly turned, obviously curious.

Callie walked down the steps and motioned for the little girl to return to the porch. When Anika did so, Callie felt a small victory. She bent down and smiled. "Thank you for obeying. Now, would you like me to walk you out to watch your father?"

Anika tucked her lips in and glanced at Janna, then pointed to her aunt. Callie's heart twisted. Of course she'd prefer her aunt.

"I'm resting, sweetheart. Callie can take you."

After a moment, Anika nodded. Callie held out her hand. When Anika placed her tiny hand in hers, Callie gazed up at Janna and smiled.

As they walked toward the corral, Callie studied the ranch. The red barn was a bit bigger than the two-story house. She longed to peek inside. As a child, she'd loved the carriage house and watching the big horses, but as Callie grew older, her mother told her it wasn't a place for a lady. Was it the same with a barn?

Anika skipped, pulling on Callie's arm. At the corral, Callie glanced down. "Could I hold you so you can see over the railing?"

The girl seemed to consider her offer, then nodded. Callie hoisted her up, surprised at how light she was. She prayed that God would heal Anika, restore her voice, and help her to forget the horror of seeing her mother die. A child should be able to talk and sing and express herself.

One of the workers peered over his shoulder, then straightened and lifted his hat. "Mornin', Miss Anika." His gaze shot to Callie's, then dropped down. She wasn't certain if his tanned cheeks were reddened from the sun or a blush. "Ma'am."

Anika waved at him, then reached for the top of the fence and climbed out of Callie's arms in spite of her tight grip. With no other choice, she stood beside the girl, keeping her arm around her legs.

Callie watched Erik ride the big brown horse in a circle. Then he suddenly turned it back the other way. After riding in several circles, he once again made a quick turn, then rode back and stopped next to them. Anika clapped her hands.

Erik looked every bit the cowboy, from his Western hat down to his boots. Only his faint accent hinted that his heritage wasn't native Texan—that and Janna's explanation of how their parents had first come to Kansas after leaving Switzerland.

"Would you like a ride, Schätzli?"

Anika nodded and shinnied over the fence, making Callie's heart race. "Hold on, sweetie."

Erik rode closer and reached out, taking his daughter. He smiled at Callie, and her racing heart took off once again. My, but he was a handsome man, especially when he relaxed. She couldn't imagine the burden he must carry after losing his wife in such a dreadful manner and then having his daughter stop talking.

She thought about her own loss and unfortunate situation. Had all that had happened to her been part of God's plan? Perhaps He brought her here to help this hurting family instead of to marry Harvey Butler.

In just eight days, Janna would be gone. Callie stirred the clothing in the washtub, trying to remember all that her new friend had taught her about doing laundry.

Make sure Anika stays away from the fire.

Keep your skirts clear of the flames.

Use multiple tubs of water and scrubbing boards.

Blue dye for the white clothes, salt for the colored.

If that wasn't enough, she had to make the soap too. All the wash had to be done on Monday here in Texas. Monday was always wash day, Janna had adamantly stated, but she never explained why. Callie didn't mind doing the work; she just prayed she could remember each step correctly.

She pushed down one of Erik's shirts that had floated to the top, forcing it underwater again. Back in Sandusky, she'd had a servant take the laundry out on Tuesday, and it was returned, washed and ironed, on Thursday. Almost as if it were magic, her clothes reappeared in her wardrobe. But not here. She looked up to check on Anika. The girl was running toward her father, who was almost to the house.

Janna suddenly squealed. Callie searched for her, then saw Erik running toward *her*, not Janna. At his fierce expression, she dropped the stir stick and backed away from the fire. Had she done something wrong?

He paused at the rinse tub, grabbed a bucket off the ground, and shoved it in the water.

Callie searched the area, trying to understand what was wrong. Janna and Anika stood beside one another, looking fine but alarmed. Callie glanced at the fire, and everything looked fine. Then she smelled smoke. And suddenly Erik tossed the whole bucket of water on her skirts. She sucked in a sharp breath as she realized that the hem of her skirt had been smoldering. How had she not felt the heat?

He knelt beside her, flipping over the hem of her skirt and petticoats. "Good.

No more fire. God was watching over you."

Mortified, Callie backed up again. "It all happened so fast. I had just checked my skirt to make sure it wasn't near the fire."

Janna hurried to her side as fast as she was able. "You are not burned?"

Callie shook her head, thankful God had put Erik there just when she needed him.

"Thanks be to God." Janna glanced heavenward, then back at Callie. "It was most likely a spark the wind stirred up. I actually wore some of Erik's old trousers to do laundry before this babe grew so big. It made things much easier—and safer. You should try it."

Callie lifted her hands to her cheeks, sure they were ruby red. She could hardly imagine what her mother would say about women wearing men's pants. She glanced at Erik.

His eyes sparkled, and he looked as if he were holding back a grin. "I still have the pair of britches Janna wore if you would like to borrow them."

Anika lifted her hand to her mouth and leaned against her papa's leg. By the expression on her darling face, she must have thought Callie would look funny in pants.

Callie lifted her chin. "I will simply have to be more careful, because I can promise you that I will never wear trousers." She turned away and hurried to the basket of clothes that had already been rinsed, hoisted it up on her hip, and marched toward the clothesline.

Chuckles echoed behind her, but she found herself smiling. Imagine—trousers. She shook her head. No, that would never happen.

The sheets snapped in the breeze as Callie hung one of Erik's work shirts. Anika raced past her, followed by her father. The girl dashed between the sheets, then hunkered down. Erik stalked around the double line of clothes and sheets hanging from two large T-shaped structures. "Where is my little girl? I know she is around her somewhere."

Anika shook as if giggling. Callie longed to hear the sweet sound of her laughter. *Please, Lord, heal Anika.*

Erik roared like a beast, causing Callie to jump. She bent down to pick up the sock she dropped.

"Watch out, little Anika. There is a bear nearby." He growled again.

The girl jumped to her feet and took off running. The sheets flapped up in the wind, and Anika ran smack into her father. He grabbed her, tossed her in the air, and Anika squealed in delight.

Callie's hand froze on the line. Erik's flabbergasted gaze shot to hers, then he smiled. He tickled his daughter as if nothing had happened, but the happy look on his face told her all. He cherished any sound that came from his little girl.

Twenty minutes later, Callie sat next to Janna on the porch, swinging and fanning her face with a wooden-handled advertisement for Butler's Mercantile. She smiled at the irony of it. "I never realized so much was involved in doing laundry."

"It is a big task to be sure, but it is even more difficult in the winter."

"How did you manage?"

"Fortunately, the winters here are not all that cold. But there were times I did the washing in a tub on the stove. It took all day, and you tend not to wash things as often. Since it is not as hot outside, Erik doesn't sweat as much, so he often wears his shirt several days."

Callie pondered that. She'd never worn a dress more than once before it was cleaned, at least until her uncle forced her hand and she'd left home. Life when her parents were still alive had been wonderful. She had taken so many things for granted. Her friends had teased her about learning to cook, but she was thankful now that her mother had insisted on it, even though they'd had kitchen staff. Her mother's family had been hardworking farmers, and Mama had made her own clothes, so she had taught Callie to sew dresses, petticoats, and unmentionables, not merely pretty samplers or pictures. At least she wouldn't have to struggle to learn those things now.

Janna glanced sideways at her. "Could I ask you something?"

"Of course."

Twisting her hands, Janna stared into the yard. "It is a bit intrusive."

Callie touched her friend's hands. "Ask anything you'd like."

"Well, I have read about mail-order brides before but never met one. I cannot imagine leaving home to go to a foreign place to marry a stranger. What if he was cruel or. . .old and toothless? What made you decide to do that?"

Callie glanced at Harvey Butler's name on the fan, then laid it in her lap. "How long do you think Anika will be out with your brother?"

"They never ride very long. I imagine he will check on the cattle in the south pasture, then return."

"I just wondered. My story is a bit of a long one, so I'd hate to be in the middle when he comes back." She drew in a deep breath. "I grew up in a wealthy family in Sandusky, Ohio. Our house was only one block away from the shores of Lake Erie. I had a lovely view of the water from my room. I thought I had the perfect family until my little sister died. That shook my world when I was young. Years later I faced another similar nightmare when my parents fell ill with influenza and died within a week of one another. Mama was actually on the mend, but when she learned Papa was gone, I think she lost the will to go on."

Callie took a calming breath. Why hadn't Mama wanted to live for her?

Things might have been much different if she had. Uncle Roger never would have staked his claim on her family estate, for one. "A month after they died, my uncle moved in. Said the house and everything in it belonged to him now since he was Papa's only male heir."

"No!" Janna squeezed Callie's arm. "That is so unfair."

Callie shrugged although she agreed. "It wouldn't have been so bad except that Uncle Roger changed. He had always been cordial to me whenever he visited us in the past, but after Mama and Papa died, he became mean. He said I needed to marry fast and get out from under *his* roof."

"I am so sorry, Callie. Families should take care of one another."

Like Janna had been doing for Erik and Anika. Callie's heart ached for things to be as they once were. But Papa, Mama, and Christina were all in heaven now. Why hadn't she been taken with them? She sniffed. "Uncle Roger informed me one day that if I didn't marry soon, he'd find a man for me. I was afraid he would do that very thing, so I immediately started looking at newspaper advertisements for mail-order bride requests."

"There was not a young man in Sandusky who caught your eye?"

"No." Callie watched a rabbit hop out of the open barn door—a sign the men were all gone. The darling creature hopped a few feet, then stopped to nibble on something. She couldn't remember ever seeing one in Ohio. There were always too many people about.

"I had found Harvey Butler's advertisement and had written him when Uncle Roger informed me he'd found someone willing to marry me."

"Oh dear."

"The man was named Otto Krenz. He was my uncle's age or older." She glanced at Janna with tears burning her eyes. "I just couldn't marry him. I was more than a little thankful when Harvey wired me the money to come."

Janna's blue eyes sparkled. "And did you sneak out in the middle of the night?"

Callie smiled. "Nothing quite so dramatic. I packed a satchel and slipped out while my uncle was gone. Two of the dear servants who'd worked for my parents for as long as I've been alive helped me get away. I left a note for Uncle Roger telling him that I couldn't marry Mr. Krenz and I wouldn't be back."

"Do you think your uncle will come looking for you?"

Callie shook her head. "No. I'm sure he was upset that I disappointed his friend, but he got everything he wanted." Everything that should have been hers. She didn't care about the money, other than she could have used her resources to help others less fortunate, but she'd love to have some of the furniture that had been passed down in her father's family. But they were only things, and she had to forget about them. God had given her the chance to make a new life here in Texas, and that was what she was determined to do.

Chapter 4

Something was bothering Janna. Erik glanced at his sister, then back at the boots he was polishing. She walked to the parlor window, lifted the curtain, and stared out for a moment. She suddenly spun around. "You had better be nice to Callie and keep your promise."

"I am always nice to Callie." Erik looked up again to meet his sister's intense gaze. "What has you all rankled?"

Janna lowered herself onto the couch, caressing her baby bump with one hand. Erik removed his gaze from his sister's swelling belly and focused on his boots, rubbing the oil in a bit harder than normal. He and Inge had wanted more children, but God had only blessed them with one sweet daughter. Although he was extremely grateful for Janna's help, being near her sometimes made his loss harder to bear.

She picked up the baby gown she had been stitching. "It is just that she has been through some difficult hardships since her parents died."

Was that why she had answered Harvey Butler's advertisement for a wife? He had wondered what would drive a woman to do such a thing. "What kind of hardships?"

Janna nibbled her lip. "She shared with me in confidence, so I do not feel comfortable talking about it any more than I have. I am simply asking you to be kind to her."

He felt a stab of insult. "I told you that I am always kind, except on the rare occasion when I am angered. Where is Callie?"

"She went to bed early. Doing the laundry wore her out. Of course, if she had let me help more, she would not have been so tired."

"Has she not done it before?"

Janna shook her head. "She grew up in a wealthy family that had servants, but even they did not do the wash. They sent it out somewhere to have it done. Imagine that." Her eyes widened. "Oh dear, I should not have said that."

"I will keep your confidence until Callie feels comfortable talking to me about such things." He considered all he had to do on the ranch, but his conscience ate at him. "I will help her with the laundry until she feels comfortable doing it alone."

Janna stared at him like he was a stranger, then her lips tipped into a smile.

"Do not laugh." He would get enough teasing from his workers. "I sometimes helped Inge, especially when she was carrying Anika."

"I know. It is just that I think you like Callie."

He shrugged and poured some more oil on his rag, not taking the bait. "She seems to be a kind woman, and she works hard. I think she will do well here."

"And you are willing to marry her?"

Erik thought of his life with Inge. Was he ready to start over with a new wife he did not love? Callie was nice and pretty, and she treated Anika well. She was also a wonderful cook, but were those qualities enough to base a marriage on? She had been willing to marry Harvey, so maybe marrying *him* would not be too difficult a choice for her. What if she did not like him?

"You are scowling. What are you thinking about?"

"Different things."

Janna ran her needle through the hem of the baby gown. "Do you want to know what I think?"

He was not sure he did, but she would tell him anyway. He set down the finished boot and picked up the other.

"I believe God brought Callie here for you and Anika."

His hand paused, and his heart thumped at the thought. He had prayed long and hard for a woman to help care for Anika and the house and was beginning to think God had chosen not to answer. Had God actually brought him a woman from so far away? That meant she was already on her way to Texas while he was still praying for God to send him someone. The idea that God had answered his prayer in such a way sent a shiver of excitement through him.

"I never liked that Harvey Butler." Janna slapped a hand against the settee. "What kind of man orders a bride and then marries another woman before his bride even arrives? A man of good character would never do such a thing."

"I will admit that I have also thought Harvey's behavior was wrong, but then, Alma May has been after him to marry her for years."

"That is true. Perhaps Mr. Butler realized he loved Alma May and that it was a mistake to marry another woman."

"I can understand that, but he should have been a gentleman and had the decency to face Callie and tell her—and to provide for her to get home to her family."

"Callie cannot go home." Janna gasped and slapped her hand over her mouth.

"Why not?"

His sister rose and placed her stitching in her basket. "I do believe it is time for me to retire." She crossed the room, bent down, and kissed Erik's cheek. "Good night, Brother."

"Sleep well." He chuckled as she hurried away. He could press her, and she would tell him everything Callie had told her, but he would rather respect Callie's privacy. In time she would tell him whatever she wanted him to know.

He leaned back and stared at the ceiling. Above him Callie slept in her room. What would force a woman from a wealthy family to do something as drastic as becoming a mail-order bride? Had something befallen her family, causing them to lose all they had? It was not an uncommon thing to happen. That would explain Callie's choice to come to Texas. Did she miss her family as he missed Inge—and his parents who stayed in Kansas when he moved south?

His thoughts circled back to what Janna had said. Had God truly sent Callie here as an answer to his prayers? His chest warmed at the thought, and the longer he pondered the idea, the more he believed it to be true.

Erik heaved a loud sigh. God had sent him a woman—maybe even a bride— and now he had to do his part.

First he had to say a final goodbye to Inge. He would always love her and could never forget her, but he could not treat Callie like Harvey had. She deserved more. She deserved a man's love.

He set aside his boots and wiped his hands on a clean cloth, then leaned over, elbows on his knees. He had a lot to think and pray about. "Heavenly Father, I thank You for answering my prayer for help and for blessing me with a fine woman and cook—one who treats Anika well. Show me how to let Inge go, and fill my heart with love for Callie."

Callie snipped off the thread she'd just knotted and held up the lightweight blanket she was making for Janna's baby. She was over halfway done and hoped to get it finished before Janna went home. At the sound of the door opening and shuffling coming from the downstairs room Janna shared with Anika, Callie quickly folded the blanket and shoved it into her sewing bag. She yanked out one of Erik's socks that needed darning and glanced up to see Anika slip into the parlor.

The girl rubbed her eyes and yawned, then crawled up onto the couch and sat down beside her. After a moment, Anika laid her head against Callie's arm.

Callie's breath caught as love for the sweet child poured through her. "Did you have a good nap?"

Anika nodded.

"Is Aunt Janna still sleeping?"

Another nod. Anika sat up and looked around, then at Callie. She held open her hands, palms up, then lifted one hand up high, palm facing down—her sign for her tall father.

"Are you asking where your papa is?"

Anika grinned and nodded.

Callie smoothed down a wisp of the girl's pale hair. "He rode into town to get some horseshoe nails and several other things."

She stuck out her lower lip.

"Are you sad he is gone, or that you didn't get to go with him?"

The girl pushed against Callie and scooted to the edge of the couch. Then she held out her hands as if she were holding a pair of reins and bounced.

"Ah, so you wish you could have gone. I'm sorry he wasn't able to take you this time, but there will be plenty of other trips. Would you like to do something with me?"

Anika glanced toward the rear of the house where her room was, then at Callie again. Finally, she nodded.

Callie would give anything to know what she was thinking. "I thought we might go outside and have a little picnic where we could eat our afternoon snack. And then maybe we could pick a pretty bouquet of flowers for the supper table. How does that sound?"

Anika slid off the couch, trotted over and picked up her shoes near the front door, then carried them back and handed them to Callie.

Warmth flooded Callie's heart. She opened a shoe and pulled it onto Anika's foot. The girl had mostly been reserved around her the first few days after her arrival, but things had taken a turn for the better. She had been friendlier all day, and oddly enough, so had her father. Callie didn't know if Janna had talked to Anika or if the child was getting used to her being around all the time. Whichever it was, Callie was thankful.

With both shoes on, Anika jumped down and hurried to the kitchen. Callie put away the rest of her sewing supplies, then followed. "I packed some cookies and a jar of water to take with us. Just let me retrieve the water from the cellar, and we can go. Could you please get a small basket for us to carry?"

Smiling, Anika hurried out the kitchen door to the back porch where the baskets were stored. Callie made her way down into the cellar, got the jar of water she'd prepared earlier, then returned to the kitchen, squinting from the bright light of the open back door. Anika held two baskets.

"Why two?" Callie set the water on the table and fetched the cookies.

Anika pointed at Callie and then herself.

"Oh, I see. You want to carry something. How about the water?" Callie bit back a grin, knowing how the imp would respond.

The girl shook her head and pointed at the cookies.

"So you want the cookies." She tapped her lip and pretended to be thinking. "That's a big responsibility for a little girl. Do you think you can manage it?"

Anika puffed up her chest and nodded again.

"Very well." She took the cookies, wrapped them in a towel, and placed them in Anika's basket, pleased with the girl's wide smile.

With her borrowed bonnet on and the water in her basket, Callie shepherded Anika out the door. She aimed for a place she had spotted while on a walk with Janna one evening. It wasn't far from the house and had several trees and a field of wildflowers.

A warm, gentle breeze tugged at her skirts, and a bird overhead screeched. She'd been surprised at how much she enjoyed the warmer weather of Texas. Back home the days would be warming but the nights were still chilly. She wasn't sure how she would tolerate the heat of July and August that Janna and Erik had talked about over dinner, but she hoped being here now would help her acclimate somewhat.

Anika skipped over to a tree, then looked up at her, the wide-brimmed sunbonnet blocking much of her face. Callie nodded and joined the girl. She spread out her skirts and sat, smiling as Anika did the same. Without waiting for permission, the girl pulled out the cookies. She handed two to Callie and kept a pair for herself. Callie opened the jar and set it between them. "Would you like to pray?"

The cherub's eyes widened. She folded her hands and bowed her head. After a short moment, she looked up, smiling.

"Amen. Let's eat." Callie couldn't help wondering what the little girl had prayed.

They ate in silence, but several thoughts kept running through Callie's mind. The one that kept returning was to tell Anika about her own parents. Janna had encouraged her to do so, but would Erik be upset? But honestly, what was there to object to? It gave her and his daughter a link in common.

"I'd like to tell you something. Is that all right with you?"

Anika nodded and reached for the water.

Callie's heart pounded hard for some reason she couldn't fathom. "I grew up in a big house near a huge lake. I had a kind, caring mama and papa that I loved dearly." She thought about mentioning her little sister but decided not to. "We were very happy, much like I bet you were with your parents."

The child's forehead crinkled.

"But something dreadful happened. They got sick, and both of them died."

Anika's pretty eyes widened. She held up two fingers.

"Yes. Papa died first, and then Mama shortly after. I think she didn't want to live without him."

Anika squeezed her hands together, probably remembering her own loss.

"At first I kept things inside and wouldn't talk about them, not even to the woman who had been my nanny, but I've discovered that if you talk about the things that frighten you, it helps to make them go away. It does take time, but things will get better."

The intense expression on Anika's face worried her. Was she thinking of her mother's death?

"Then my uncle moved into our house, and he told me I couldn't stay there anymore. So, that's why I left home and came here."

Anika scooted over and laid her head in Callie's lap. Running her hand over Anika's wispy hair, Callie prayed for God to help the little girl find peace and not be afraid to talk again. Callie had to believe that the fright of all Anika had witnessed and experienced was what held her silent.

Perhaps knowing that Callie had lost her mother also would help the blossom of a bond growing between them to bloom fully. After a short minute, Anika sat up and tugged on Callie's hand.

"Time to pick flowers? You go ahead and start while I clean up here."

In a matter of minutes, a beautiful bouquet rested in the water jar, and they headed home. As they approached the house, Callie saw Erik standing on the back porch watching them. Her heart bucked, and she found it hard to breathe. Why did she have such an odd reaction to seeing her employer?

Anika spied her papa and raced toward him, waving her hand. She pointed back to Callie and gestured like she was eating.

Erik walked out to meet her and lifted her up. "Did you enjoy your outing?"

The child nodded vigorously.

"I see you picked some lovely flowers for us to enjoy. How sweet of you two." He kissed his daughter's cheek. "Why don't you run in and see your aunt. I need to talk to Callie for a moment."

Anika frowned but slid down and disappeared into the house.

Erik walked up to her and held out his hand. "Could I carry those for you?"

With mouth too dry to speak, she passed the jar to him and croaked out a thank-you. Just when she needed the water, the flowers were enjoying it. He set the bouquet on the porch, looked out across the field for a long moment, then back at her.

Callie could tell something was bothering him. He sighed, then caught her gaze. A muscle flicked along his jawline. "I have some news."

Her mind raced. What could he possibly have to tell her that was disturbing him so badly?

"Harvey Butler is back in town."

Callie knew the man would return sooner or later, but why should that upset Erik? "And?"

"It turns out that he and Alma May were not suitable, and they are getting their marriage annulled."

She frowned. "How could they discover they were not well-suited in so few days?"

Erik shrugged. "I do not know the answer to that, but that is not what concerns me." He rubbed one hand across his chin and stared at her again. Those incredible blue eyes turned her insides to mush. "Harvey has learned that you are here, and talk about town is that he intends to win you as his bride. He says it is only fair since he paid for you to come to Sowers."

Chapter 5

Callie gasped, her mind racing with disturbing thoughts, foremost of all—would she be forced to marry a man she had no feelings for? "Am I obligated to marry him? What about *our* agreement? Are you voiding that?"

Erik took hold of Callie's shoulders, effectively silencing her. "Take a breath. Relax. We still have an agreement unless you change your mind."

He released her and stepped back. His words instantly calmed her. He wasn't turning her out. "Thank you."

"I am a man of my word. You can trust that."

She smiled, then sobered. "Mr. Butler sent me the money to travel out here. What if he insists I pay him back?" She didn't want Erik to know that she didn't have anywhere near that, not even after he paid her small salary.

"The way I see it, your contract with Harvey was voided when he chose to marry someone else. It does not matter that the marriage did not work out. A gentleman would not have treated you so poorly or left you alone to discover such devastating news."

She found herself wishing that Erik had been the one who'd sent for her. Yes, he had agreed to marry her, but that was only to have a mother for his daughter and a cook and housekeeper. If only he truly wanted her to become his wife.

She forced her thoughts back to Mr. Butler instead of foolish wishes. "I think I should at least hear what he has to say. After all, he did save me from a forced marriage."

Erik frowned. "What do you mean? Who was forcing you?"

Callie dipped her head and stared at the ground.

Erik shook his head. "Never mind. I should not have asked that. I am sorry."

She turned toward him and touched his arm. "No. It's only fair that you know." Her cheeks warmed at having to share her dreadful story. She told him about her parents' deaths and then Uncle Roger moving in and claiming all that she thought was hers.

"Did your father not have a will?"

"He did, but he was an old-fashioned thinker. He believed that women didn't have a place in business. He was kind and loving, don't get me wrong. He thought he was providing for me. Had I married, my father's business and the house would have belonged to my husband. Father provided well for Mother and me and thought my husband would do the same. He only made Uncle Roger his heir in case he died before I married." She sighed, thinking how Father never realized that his brother had far less integrity than he himself did.

"Father believed my uncle would provide for me and oversee the business until I married. Instead, Uncle Roger had everything put into his name and then ordered me to find a husband. When I didn't, he said I'd have to marry his friend—a man older than Father." She gazed into Erik's troubled eyes. "I couldn't do that."

"I would think marrying a stranger would be worse."

She shook her head. "Not to me. Mr. Krenz frightened me whenever he got me alone." She shuddered. "Also, I fear if I had married him, I would have still been under Uncle Roger's control. At least Mr. Butler was my choice."

A muscle ticked in Erik's jaw.

Callie shrugged. "It seemed a better choice at the time. And maybe I was excited a bit by the adventure of coming to a strange land."

A smile softened his tense expression. "That is something I can understand. I left my parents and siblings to come here to start a ranch. I also took Inge away from her family."

"Couldn't you have started a ranch in Kansas?"

"Probably, except that the winters here are far less severe and better for cattle. But I had a strong desire to come to Texas. I was enchanted with the cowboys I saw when I was young and longed to be one."

"Are you sorry you came here?"

He shook his head. "Although I am sorry for what happened to Inge. She was kind and loving, even though she could be a might obstinate."

"I see a bit of that determination in your daughter."

"Yes, that is true. To be fair, though, I can be stubborn myself."

She cocked her head, enjoying this private chat with him. "I can't say that I've witnessed that, so I won't comment on it."

He chuckled. "If you stick around long enough, you will."

Callie watched a beautiful black and yellow butterfly with blue on its lower edges land on the bouquet of flowers. She sucked in a breath.

Erik turned to see what she was looking at. "That's a tiger swallowtail.

Magnificent, is it not? God has blessed Texas with much beauty."

She glanced up and caught him staring at her, not the butterfly. Her cheeks flamed. Surely he hadn't meant her. He held her gaze until she looked away.

"Callie, I know you have not known me long, but I hope that you will choose to stay with Anika and me and not go back to Harvey. We need you."

She opened her mouth, but nothing came out. She cleared her throat, certain she had mistaken his meaning. He needed a cook and caregiver, not *her* in particular. Disappointment swamped her. "I. . .um. . .promise I will pray about what to do. I do feel I am in Mr. Butler's debt, and it's only fair to hear him out. But you came to my rescue, so I'm in your debt too."

He frowned. "You owe me nothing. I do not do things just to get repaid." He touched the brim of his hat and walked away.

Callie hadn't meant to hurt his feelings, but the truth was, she did owe both men. She wouldn't be in Texas if not for Mr. Butler. And who knows where she would have ended up if not for Erik.

Someone was bound to get upset. There was no way she could please both men.

The coolest breeze Callie had experienced since arriving in Texas caressed her face as she rode into the churchyard with Erik and Anika. She wished Janna had come too, but she wanted to rest and start preparations since she was going home this week. Callie dreaded that day. Janna had become a good friend in a short time.

Callie glanced sideways at Erik, who sat tall on the wagon bench, looking quite dapper in his Sunday suit. Her heart flip-flopped when he glanced her way and smiled. She turned away, hoping the turmoil in her stomach would settle before they entered the sanctuary.

She studied the tiny church, wondering what the inside was like. She used to love Sundays, going to services at the big Christian church only four blocks from their home. Afterward they would dine with friends, but that was before her parents died. Several weeks after Uncle Roger moved in, she quit going because he only seemed to attend so he could introduce her to his associates. She well knew he was attempting to find her a husband and had little interest in the service. Instead of attending on Sunday, she'd stay in her room, reading her Bible and praying.

Erik pulled the wagon to a stop, set the brake, then hopped down. Anika slid over, and he lifted her down. Callie froze, trying to remember how she had dismounted the first time. Before she made a move, Erik stood beside the wagon with his hands raised.

"Bend down and put your hands on my shoulders. I will do the rest."

Her cheeks heated at the thought of being so close to her employer, but then, if things went as planned, he would soon be her husband. Besides, wasn't bending forward better than backing down from the wagon and giving him a full view of her posterior?

She rose and did as ordered, realizing too late how close that brought her face to Erik's. Her eyes locked with his clear blue ones, making it hard for her to breathe. His hands wrapped around her waist, then he easily lowered her to the ground. They stood there a moment, her hands on his shoulders and his on her waist, just inches apart. Slowly, his lips pulled into a smile. Callie was afraid if he let go, she'd fall on her wobbly legs.

Callie felt a yank on her skirt and looked down. Anika waved toward the church.

"Oh my, the music has started." Callie's cheeks felt overly warm as she touched one.

Erik stepped back, a twinkle in his eyes, and held out his arm. "Shall we go?"

"Um. . .yes, certainly."

As they entered the small church, Callie realized they were already in the sanctuary. There was no vestibule here, but rather an open area where she suspected people could gather before the service. She was thankful the congregation was already seated, and she hoped that anyone who looked her way and noted her red face would attribute it to the sun or wind.

She removed her bonnet and Anika's as Erik did his hat and placed them on two of the empty pegs that lined the wall. A man several rows up turned around, staring at them. Callie noted his curious expression. He rudely kept staring. She looked away and entered the pew Erik gestured to. Anika reached up, and Erik lifted her into his arms and followed.

The church had just the one main aisle down the middle with pews on either side and two narrower aisles along the walls. Callie's eyes were drawn to the pretty stained glass windows. Although they weren't nearly as magnificent as the ones in her home church, they were lovely in their simplicity.

She focused on the front and noticed several people peeking back at them and smiling, but the man she'd noticed earlier kept glancing her way. He was of average height and thin, but the most notable thing about him was his oversized handlebar moustache.

Callie glanced at Erik. He held out a songbook, leaned closer, and whispered, "Harvey Butler is staring at you."

She wasn't sure what she had expected, but it was far different than the man across the aisle. How many hours a day did he spend perfecting that moustache?

The pleasant baritone of Erik's voice drew her away from Mr. Butler. She didn't recognize the song, which had a tune a bit livelier than what they sang back in Sandusky. After the third hymn, they sat.

Pastor Sanders stood up front and talked about the children of Israel and how God set them free from captivity in Egypt by rolling back the waters of the Red Sea and allowing them to cross on dry land. What a miracle that was! God could have allowed them to trudge through inches of mud, but in His love and mercy, He dried the bottom of a riverbed that had been underwater for centuries. Then after the Israelites crossed, the waters rolled back, drowning Pharaoh's army.

Anika fidgeted and bumped into Callie. Erik lifted his daughter onto his lap and whispered something. She leaned against him and closed her eyes. Callie wondered if that was a weekly occurrence.

"God's people were finally free," Pastor Sanders said, pulling her gaze to the front again. "After several hundred years of living as slaves, they were free. A new life awaited them. God has a new life for each of you too. Second Corinthians 5:17 states, 'Therefore if any man be in Christ, he is a new creature: old things are passed away; behold, all things are become new.' "

Pastor Sanders rested his hands on the pulpit and stared out at the congregation. "Each one of you can become a new creature. Shed the sins of the past and open your heart to God. A new life of peace and joy awaits you. Let us pray."

The pastor wished them a good week, then escorted his wife down the aisle to the church entrance. The conversation rose to a loud timbre in the small building. Still holding Anika, who slept on his shoulder, Erik stepped into the aisle. He held out his hand. Callie slipped in front of him and followed the line of people slowly exiting.

At the door, Pastor and Mrs. Sanders wished each person farewell. When Callie reached the smiling couple, Mrs. Sanders reached for her hands and squeezed them. "How are you faring, Miss Webster?"

"Very well, thank you. I thoroughly enjoyed your sermon, Pastor Sanders."

"That's kind of you to say. Welcome to our small community. How is Mrs. Allen doing?"

"Janna is well," Callie said. "She is leaving for home this week, and since she'll be traveling, she felt the need to rest today."

The pastor nodded. "We enjoyed her worshipping with us while she was here and wish her safe travels."

"Thank you, sir." Erik slid beside Callie and shook the pastor's hand, then guided her toward the wagon.

Two women Callie thought were probably in their late thirties approached. Their dresses were nice but looked casual compared to the fancy garments ladies wore at her former church. Still, she felt more comfortable in her simple gray skirt and white shirtwaist than she ever had in the fancier dresses. She smiled.

The dark-haired woman returned her smile. "I'm Lilah Thompson, and this is Sue Ann Meriweather." The blond woman nodded. "We want to welcome you to Sowers and invite you to come to our sewing circle on the first Tuesday of each month. We meet at Sue Ann's house, which is just a mile west of town."

Sue Ann tucked a wayward strand of hair behind her ear. "I know you just arrived and are still getting settled, but we wanted you to know that you're welcome to come if you'd like and if you can work it into your schedule. Of course, Mrs. Allen is welcome to attend also if she's feeling up to it."

"That's very kind of you to invite us. I will see how things go. I'd like to attend if I'm able." She didn't feel it was her place to mention that Janna was leaving soon.

Lilah's gaze shifted to Erik. "Good to see you, Mr. Kessler."

Smiling, he tipped his hat. "You too, ladies. Thank you for welcoming Miss Webster so kindly."

Sue Ann giggled and turned red. Callie wondered if the woman had set her bonnet for Erik. If that was the case, it was odd she'd invite his housekeeper to her house.

As the women walked away, Erik held his sleeping daughter in one arm and offered his other one to Callie. He assisted her onto the wagon bench, then handed Anika to her. He untied the horses and joined her. Callie stared out at the crowd. People stood in small groups talking to one another. Other families had already started out for home. She liked the feel of this small town. Maybe in time she would get to know many of these people.

She thought about what the pastor had said about a new life. She'd long ago given her heart to God, and although times hadn't always been easy, she always believed in Him. Had God brought her to Sowers to start a new life with Erik and Anika?

Callie looked past Erik and gasped.

Harvey Butler dodged past several people, nearly knocking one down. His gaze focused on her as he rushed toward them.

Chapter 6

Two days. Erik—bless the man—had bought her a reprieve from talking with Mr. Butler until Tuesday afternoon. She pounded down the lump of dough, rolled it into a ball, then thumped it several more times.

"That dough is not going to rise if you beat it up much more." Janna laughed. "Why don't you put it in the pan and tell me what is bothering you."

"I'm sure you know." Callie sighed and did as Janna suggested, then covered the dough with a cloth. She washed her hands and dried them. "Mr. Butler is coming here on Tuesday, and I don't know what to say to him."

Janna poured water into the dirty dough bowl. "Shall we leave this for a few minutes and go sit on the porch?"

Tired after the trip to town, then preparing Sunday dinner and supper, Callie gladly agreed. "Just let me check on Anika to make sure she's still in bed."

A few minutes later, she joined Janna on the porch swing. The lantern cast a soft glow on the porch as twilight settled. "Sound asleep."

"That is good. Sometimes when she has a long nap, she will have trouble getting to sleep."

"Are you excited to be going home?"

"Yes. I can hardly believe I will see Ben again in just four days. I have missed Fader and Moder and my siblings also."

"I miss my parents."

Janna touched her hand. "I am sorry. Is that what has you so addled?"

"No. Not really. I merely thought of them when you mentioned yours. I'm concerned that I don't know what to say to Mr. Butler. I feel like I'm under some obligation since he paid for me to come here."

Janna gently pushed the swing into motion, creating a soft creak every time they swung forward. The sound of crickets and tree frogs filled the yard. "I understand that, but it seems to me that since he stood you up and married someone else, your agreement with him has ended."

"What if he doesn't feel that way?"

"Even if he plans to get his marriage annulled, he is still married at the moment. What can he offer you now?"

Callie pondered that thought. Mr. Butler must be married. She doubted anyone could get an annulment so quickly.

"Besides, my brother has made you a far better offer. Not only do you get this nice house and a sweet daughter who needs you very much, but you get my brother. He is a kind, honorable man you can trust. And you have to admit that he is a fine-looking man." She glanced sideways at Callie and giggled. "Did Sue Ann Meriweather make eyes at him this morning?"

Callie gasped. "So I didn't imagine her interest."

"She is a nice woman, but she is at least eight years older than Erik. He has never shown any interest in her other than friendship."

Callie cleared her throat. "I hear Harvey Butler will soon be available."

Janna snorted, then burst out laughing, and Callie joined her.

"Well, that is a pleasant sound if I ever heard one." Erik stepped onto the porch.

Janna chuckled as she swatted her hand toward her brother. "Ja, I sounded like a little pig."

Callie giggled.

"What is so funny?" He leaned his hip against the porch rail.

"It was merely ladies' talk." Janna dragged her feet, stopping the swing, then rose. "I will finish cleaning the kitchen, then I am going to bed." She patted her stomach. "This little one needs its rest."

"Why don't you go on to bed. I'll see to the kitchen," Callie said.

"Are you sure you don't mind?"

"Of course not. I'll see you in the morning."

"Sleep well. Tomorrow is laundry day."

Callie groaned. "Don't remind me."

Janna snickered as she entered the house and shut the door. Callie wondered if she should go on in, but Erik still leaned on the railing.

"I love this time of day," he said. "My work is done, and I can relax for an hour or two before retiring." He rose, then moved toward her and sat on the swing.

Callie stiffened, surprised by his action, but inwardly pleased. For several moments they sat there, gently swaying. He smelled of outdoors, hay, and horses—oddly enough, not an unpleasant scent.

"I have been praying about Harvey's visit," he said.

"You have?"

"For many months I have prayed that God would send a woman to help Anika and me. I have asked all the women in town, and short of leaving my daughter with one of them at their homes, nothing has worked out. When I saw you sitting there in town, alone and looking so dejected, I felt prompted to speak with you." He placed his arm behind her and turned toward her. "I believe you are the answer to my prayers, Callie. I hope you will choose to stay with us."

She sucked in a breath. Was he confirming the very thing she'd wondered—that God sent her to Texas to help him? "I'm not sure I've ever been someone's answer to prayer."

"I had begun to believe God was not going to respond, but He was simply waiting for the perfect timing, as He often does."

"Janna said that Mr. Butler is still married. I know from things my papa said that the legal system works slowly, so it may be quite a while before he is free to marry again."

"That is most likely correct."

"I feel that frees me from the obligation of marrying him, but what do I do about the money I owe him?"

"I am more than willing to pay him back so you will be free of his debt."

"No! Then I will merely be more indebted to you."

He pressed his arm around her shoulder. "Callie, you will never owe me anything. What I give, I give freely with no expectation of reimbursement."

Tears burned her eyes. Erik Kessler truly was a good man.

"I would like you to stay here because I hope you have grown fond of Anika, and that maybe you can tolerate me. If you choose to marry me, I will not pressure you for anything until you feel you are ready."

"Thank you, Erik. And so you know, I tolerate you just fine."

The pressure of his hand increased for a moment. "That is good."

"Ja, good." Callie smiled.

"I like you, Callie. More than a little. I believe we will make a good match."

"Could you be there when I talk with Mr. Butler?"

"He will not like it, but I would be happy to stand by your side."

"Thank you." After a long moment, she boldly leaned her head against his shoulder and stared out at the night sky. Thousands of twinkling stars dotted the heavens.

This was where she wanted to be, here with Erik and Anika. *Please, God, work things out with Mr. Butler so I can stay here and be Erik's wife and Anika's mother.*

Janna cut off the top of a fresh-picked strawberry, then sliced it and dropped it in the bowl on her lap. "You are biting your nails again."

The porch swing rocked as Callie shifted and dropped her hands into her lap. "I wouldn't do that if you'd let me help you and keep my hands occupied."

"You do not want to be all sticky when Mr. Butler arrives."

"I honestly don't care. Does that sound dreadful?"

"Not at all. You are nervous."

Callie stared in the direction of town, half relieved Mr. Butler hadn't arrived and half wishing he would hurry up and get there so they could get their meeting over and done with. She glanced at the barn. The doors were open but no one was around. Erik had promised to be present, but she hadn't seen him since lunchtime. That was two hours ago. Did he forget?

"God tells us not to worry but to trust in Him. Being anxious only hurts us. My stomach churns when I am worrying."

"Mine is doing that now." Callie pressed her hand against her abdomen. "I wish he'd hurry. I was hoping to conclude our meeting before Anika wakes up from her nap. I don't want to worry her that I may be leaving too." She stared out at the lovely day, pleasantly warm but not hot. A yellow butterfly flitted around the colorful flowers in front of the porch.

Janna looked at her, eyes wide. "So you are considering leaving?"

"I'm not particularly thinking about it. but what if Mr. Butler forces my hand? I do owe him a goodly amount of money, and I agreed to be his bride."

"You cannot marry a man who is already married."

"That is true. But what if he gets his marriage annulled?"

Janna grinned. "You know what I think?"

"What?"

"If you are already married to my brother, there would be nothing Mr. Butler could do."

Smiling, Callie gently nudged her friend's shoulder. "You sure are tenacious."

Janna shrugged. "I probably should not say this, but Erik will be so disappointed if you leave. I think his heart is set on you marrying him. He has not shown interest in a woman since Inge died."

Callie's heart flip-flopped. Was it possible Erik was growing to care for her as a man would a wife?

"Here comes Mr. Butler." Janna dropped her knife in the bowl of strawberries.

Callie tensed. She wasn't ready to talk to him. And where was Erik?

Janna rose. "I will be in the kitchen if you need me. I hope things go well. I will be praying for you."

"Thank you."

Callie rose and stood next to the railing. She glanced down when she felt a pain in her hands and realized she was gripping the wood so tightly that her knuckles were white. She released it, then paced the porch. Finally, she dropped into one of the two rocking chairs. She didn't want Mr. Butler to think she was anxious for him to arrive.

She glanced every way looking for Erik. Where was he?

Mr. Butler rode into the yard and dismounted, his eyes watching her like a hawk. She wished she could run into the house, but that would only prolong things.

He tied his horse to the hitching post, then stopped at the bottom of the steps, gawking. A slow smile lifted his moustache. He reached up and twirled one end. "Afternoon, Miss Webster."

"Mr. Butler." Her heart pounded as if she'd run a footrace.

"You're looking quite lovely today."

"Thank you. Would you care to sit?"

"Don't mind if I do." He walked up the steps and took the chair next to her.

The quick clopping of horse hooves echoed through the yard, and Erik rode around the side of the house on his big black horse. He stopped the horse, slid off, then dropped the reins. Callie's relief was immense as he loped up the steps. "Afternoon, Harvey."

"Kessler."

Erik leaned against the porch, facing them, and winked at Callie. She ducked her head. Never had she had two men interested in her. She didn't like conflict and seriously doubted that things would end today without any.

Mr. Butler hopped up. "Look here, Kessler, this is a private matter."

"Miss Webster requested I be here."

Mr. Butler's head swiveled her way. His scowl told her he wasn't pleased. He turned back to Erik. "How is a man supposed to woo a woman with another man present?"

Erik crossed his arms. "The way I see it, you are in no position to be courting. You are a married man, am I correct?"

"Well. . .at the moment, but that will soon change. And then I will expect Miss Webster to honor her commitment."

Callie glanced at Erik, more than willing to let him speak for her.

"Her commitment ended when she arrived in town and found you already married."

"That's not true! Marrying Alma May was an unfortunate mistake. I'll be free of her soon, and then Miss Webster and I will marry as planned."

"That is not going to happen. You abandoned and humiliated Miss Webster. Left her prey for the town ruffians." Erik straightened, bringing him a full two inches taller than Mr. Butler. "Besides, you cannot expect her to wait for you when she has no feelings for you."

"How would you know that?" Harvey stood just three feet from Erik.

Callie rose and moved over by the front door.

"How could she develop feelings for you when she had never even met you?"

"We wrote letters." Harvey lifted his chin.

"Just two." Callie held up a pair of fingers.

"Regardless, your agreement with Miss Webster has ended since you are married."

"But she owes me twenty-two dollars for traveling expenses."

"You voided the contract by your actions, so the way I see it, Miss Webster does not owe you a thing."

An ugly sneer lifted one side of Mr. Butler's face. "Oh, I see. You want her for yourself."

"What I want is irrelevant. Why do you not ask Miss Webster what she wants?"

Callie's heart bucked as Mr. Butler turned his hardened gaze on her. "And what is it you want, Callie, dear?"

She opened her mouth to respond, but her voice wouldn't cooperate. This man intimidated her, just as Mr. Krenz had. What a blessing that God had spared her from marrying either one. She cleared her voice, reaching deep within for the gumption she knew was there. "I cannot marry you, since you are already married."

Mr. Butler slammed his hat on his head. "We will see about that."

The front door opened, and Anika stepped out. She trotted toward her father, then halted suddenly. She slowly turned toward Mr. Butler and started screaming. Erik reached for her, but she bolted into the house.

Chapter 7

The moment Mr. Butler left the porch, Callie rushed inside, following Erik. They found Anika in her room on the bed, sobbing in Janna's arms. Erik's sister looked up with a baffled expression and mouthed, *What happened?*

Erik shook his head and sat beside them. Anika crawled into his lap and buried her face in his shirt. He gently brushed his hand down her head. "What is wrong, Schätzli? Please tell me so I can help."

Anika shook her head.

Erik glanced up and shrugged.

"Why did she scream? What in the world happened?" Janna patted her niece's back, obviously hurting for the frightened girl.

"She came outside and headed for Erik, but then she saw Mr. Butler. He's what set her off. I wonder if that is why she hides her face in church."

"I have noticed that she is afraid of him. I thought it was perhaps because of his large moustache." Janna pursed her lips, brows furrowed.

Erik placed a kiss on his daughter's head. "I believe she is afraid of him because he was on the stagecoach with Inge the day she died. I have always wondered how she ended up dead and Harvey did not get a scratch."

"Do you think he reminds her of what happened?" Callie asked softly, her heart aching for the little girl she'd come to love. She longed to hold and comfort her, but Anika needed her father right now.

Erik sighed. "I suppose we will never know unless she starts talking again. You two go on out, and I will rock her for a while."

"Ja, and we will pray for her."

Callie followed Janna out, then closed the door. "That breaks my heart."

"Perhaps seeing Mr. Butler so unexpectedly made Anika remember her mother's murder, and that is what scared her."

"I wish I knew. Shall we sit on the porch and pray for a bit?"

"Ja. I wonder if I should stay longer. I hate to leave with Anika so upset and things unsettled."

Callie sat in one of the rockers. "You should go home before it gets too hard for you to travel. Ben has been very patient allowing you to stay this long."

"I wish our homes were closer." Janna turned toward Callie. "So, are you staying here, or will you wait to see what happens with Mr. Butler?"

"He seems so hard toward the woman he's married to now. Why did he marry Alma May if he didn't love her? I fear that if I did marry him—not that I want to—he might tire of me just as quickly. And then where would I be?"

"That would not be good. In truth, Mr. Butler has always made me a little uneasy, but I did not want to tell you that before you talked with him."

"He makes me nervous too." Callie huffed a derisive laugh.

"I wonder if Alma May has returned to Sowers—or perhaps she is somewhere working on getting the annulment."

"It would be hard to come back after what happened."

"Ja. Well. . .I know what you should do."

Callie laid her head back. "And I know what you're going to say. I have to admit, I'm leaning that way."

"Good! I will like having you for a sister. We should pray now."

"Yes, we should."

Callie prayed for Anika, for God to grant her peace and to be able to talk again. After a while, her prayers turned to Erik. Was it God's will for them to marry? It seemed to be the far better option, but she wanted to be sure in her heart.

Everything about Erik seemed to be good. She especially liked how he so gently comforted his frightened daughter and how he stood up to Mr. Butler and defended her without backing down a speck. No man other than her father had ever done that.

When she thought of Erik and his kindness to her, her heart swelled. Was it merely gratitude she felt, or was it the beginnings of love?

Wednesday evening, Callie cleaned the kitchen after supper while Janna packed the last of her belongings. How she dreaded the thought of her friend leaving, even though she knew it was time. Janna needed to be with her husband these last few months before their child was born.

Still, she would miss her. She'd had a few close friends while growing up, but after her parents died, Callie stayed home and avoided visiting others. It was too painful to see her friends with their mothers, interacting and laughing, while she would never have that closeness again. Eventually they quit calling.

Shortly after her uncle moved in, everything changed. He sold off some of the family's antiques, which her ancestors had bought in the early 1700s. It broke her heart, but that was only the beginning. His declaration that she must marry was the final straw. He might destroy memories of her past, but she wouldn't allow him to ruin her future.

"Callie?"

She jumped at Erik's closeness.

"I did not mean to frighten you. I am sorry."

"It's not your fault." She dried her hands on a towel and hung it up. "I was merely lost in thought."

"Good thoughts, I hope."

"Not really." She shook her head. "How is Anika?"

"Sleeping—finally. Seeing Mr. Butler sure upset her. I always leave her at the Sanders's house when I go to town because she refuses to go any farther into Sowers. When her mother was alive, Anika loved our trips to town. She used to enjoy church also, but now she sleeps through the services." He ducked his head and sighed. "My little girl has changed so much."

"I'm praying God will heal her and help her get over witnessing such a tragedy."

His head lifted, and his eyes sparkled. "Thank you. You are very kind." He cleared his throat. "I wonder if you would care to take a walk with me."

Her hand lifted to her hair. What a sight she must be after cooking and washing dishes. Still, her heart took flight at the thought of spending time alone with Erik. She untied her apron, then turned to face him. "Yes, that would be nice."

His charming smile made her stomach flutter like moths around a porch lantern. He held out his arm, and she looped hers through it, trying to still its trembling. Determined not to reveal her nervousness to Erik, she summoned her willpower and walked with him to the door. He opened it and stepped aside for her to exit, and then they resumed their closeness at the bottom of the steps.

She strolled beside him, enjoying the cooler temperatures of the evening. It was still warm enough that she didn't need her shawl. If she concentrated, she might hear the waters of Lake Erie splashing against the shore in her mind, but instead, a Texas night bird cried out, and insects of all manner serenaded them.

When they reached the corral, Erik released her arm. He leaned back against the railing and stared at her in the waning light. Behind him the final rays of the deep orange sunset blended with the navy sky of twilight.

"I thought we should talk since Janna is leaving tomorrow."

Callie nodded. There were so many things to be settled.

"Have you decided whether you want to stay here, or are you planning to marry Mr. Butler when he is free?"

He sure didn't beat around the bush, but she liked that. He said what he meant, and he wasn't wishy-washy. She knew in her heart what she desired. "What do you want?"

His eyebrows lifted in surprise. "Me? It's your decision."

"But I'd really like to know your thoughts."

He straightened. "I do not think Harvey Butler deserves you. He had his chance." Erik stepped closer and took her hand. "I realize we have not known one another long, Callie, but I believe you are the answer to my many prayers."

"For a housekeeper and caregiver for Anika?"

"Yes, that."

Her heart plummeted.

He stepped closer. "And for a wife for me." He lifted his free hand and tucked a strand of hair behind her ear. "In the short time I have known you, I have learned you are a caring, conscientious woman. My heart knows that you are meant to be with us."

Tears burned Callie's eyes. Her heart said the same thing. Harvey Butler may have brought her to Texas, but Erik Kessler was the man she wanted to spend the rest of her life with. She nodded. "It would be my delight to marry you."

His wide grin brightened the evening. "I would like to kiss you, but I will not dishonor you by doing so until you are my wife. May I hold you for a moment?"

Callie smiled and fell into his arms, tears running down her cheeks. Twice God had spared her from marrying a dreadful man. How was she so blessed to win the heart of a good man like Erik Kessler?

"So, we will take Janna to town early, then get married so she can attend our wedding, ja?"

Callie's mind raced. She didn't have enough funds to buy a wedding dress or time to make one, so she'd have to wear something she already had. And with Janna leaving, the proper thing would be to marry right away. "All right. We will marry tomorrow."

He squeezed her, then leaned back. "Thank you, Callie. I think we will have a fine life together."

"Me too."

He ran his finger down her cheek, and she saw the longing in his eyes. Erik was lonely. Well. . .after tomorrow, she would see to it that he was never lonely again.

The May sun shone bright in the cloudless sky as Erik assisted Callie to the ground outside the church in Sowers. He turned and lifted Anika down and then helped Janna. The ride to town had been a tight squeeze with all three adults and one child on the bench.

Callie brushed dust off the lovely lavender dress Janna had given her for a wedding gift, hating the way her hands shook. What did she have to be nervous about? She was marrying a wonderful man. God had truly blessed her in bringing her to Texas. Never could she have imagined her life turning out so well. And soon she'd have a sweet daughter. Imagine that.

Janna hurried to the back of the wagon and plucked the bouquet of flowers they'd picked earlier from the jar of water. She wrapped them in a towel, then handed them to Callie, a huge smile on her face. "When I came to Texas to help Erik, I never expected to be getting a new sister." She clapped her hands. "I am so excited! Just wait until I tell Moder."

"The news will make her happy." Erik nodded, his smile twinkling in his eyes. He bent down and picked up his daughter. "Are you ready to get a new mama, Schätzli?"

Anika nodded and smiled at Callie.

Erik had told her about his chat with his daughter, explaining how they were getting married and that Callie would be living with them. Once he told Anika that they would always love and remember her mother, she had been happy about the wedding. Callie didn't know what she would have done if Anika had objected to their marriage. *Please, Lord, show me how to help Anika heal and talk again. Help me to be a good mother and wife.*

Erik gave his daughter a hug. "I must put you down to escort these lovely ladies inside. Could you carry the flowers?"

Anika nodded so hard her braids flopped against her shoulders. She accepted the colorful bouquet from Callie, then held them out in front of her as if afraid she might damage them.

Callie accepted Erik's right arm, her heart thundering so loud she was surprised the others couldn't hear it. She walked into the church with a confidence that her parents would not only have approved of Erik but would have loved him. If only they could be here, then today would be perfect. She didn't miss the irony of her wish, knowing that if they were still alive, she'd never have met her soon-to-be husband.

Pastor and Mrs. Sanders were waiting at the front of the church. Erik had ridden to town earlier this morning to make sure the couple was free to do a wedding. He had shared how delighted the pastor and his wife were to learn the news. Mrs. Bailey, the piano player, sat up front with a big grin on her face.

Janna released Erik's arm, took the flowers from Anika, and handed them to Callie. She passed a small basket filled with freshly plucked flower petals to her niece. "Now, remember what I told you. Walk slowly down the aisle toward the pastor and drop the flower petals as you go. I will sit in the second row, and you can join me when you are finished, ja?" Anika nodded, and Janna hurried to her seat.

The pianist began playing Wagner's "Bridal Chorus." Anika skipped around Callie, then started a bit quicker than she should down the short aisle, tossing clumps of flowers in little piles.

Erik smiled at Callie and patted her hand. "Are you ready?"

"Yes," Callie whispered, her insides fluttering with a mixture of excitement and nervousness.

Together they stepped forward and walked toward their new future.

In less than ten minutes, Callie's life had changed forever. She was now Mrs. Erik Kessler. Callie Kessler.

"Erik, you may kiss your bride."

He turned to face her with a more serious expression than she expected. He cocked his head and lifted his eyebrows, as if asking permission to kiss her. Callie smiled.

Erik's lips pulled into a wide grin, but as he leaned down, all breath fled Callie's lungs. His lips were warmer—softer—than she'd imagined. He applied a gentle, delicious pressure, but he wasn't forceful. She couldn't resist reaching out to touch his solid chest. Far too soon he leaned back, but the pleased look in his gaze told her the kiss had been as delightful for him as it had been for her. Did he realize it was her first kiss?

Janna squealed and clapped, and Anika joined her, as did Mrs. Sanders and Mrs. Bailey.

The pastor stuck out his hand to Erik. "Let me be the first to congratulate you."

"Thank you, sir. We appreciate you doing the service on such short notice. We wanted to get married before Janna left so she could attend the ceremony."

Anika tugged on Erik's pant leg, and he bent down and picked her up, then gave her a kiss on her cheek.

"You have a lovely family." Mrs. Sanders joined her husband. "I've prepared lunch, and we hope you will join us."

Erik glanced at Callie, and she nodded. He looked back at Janna, and she did the same. "It looks like we are all in agreement. Since we have over an hour before the stage arrives, we would be honored to dine with you."

"Wonderful. Mrs. Bailey, would you care to join us?" the pastor asked.

The woman rose from her bench, shaking her head. "Thank you for the invitation, Pastor, but Mr. Bailey will be expecting me home to get his lunch on the table."

"Very well. Thank you for coming today."

"It was my pleasure." She smiled as she collected her music and hurried down the aisle.

Mrs. Sanders chuckled. "The town will soon know of your marriage. Mrs. Bailey is a dear woman, but she can't keep any news to herself."

"It is good the men of this town know that Callie is a married woman." Erik's eyes held a teasing glint.

Grinning wide, Callie held on to Erik's arm as they made their way outside.

They gathered in a small group with Anika skipping around them. Mrs. Sanders touched Janna's shoulder. "We've enjoyed having you visit and look forward to seeing you in the future."

"Thank you." Janna walked ahead with Mr. and Mrs. Sanders.

Callie tried to grasp the fact that she was married. Uttering several lines of promises with Erik before the pastor had changed everything. She didn't feel any different, but she knew she was.

At the Sanders's porch, Anika started wiggling, and Erik set her down. She tugged on his pants again, and he glanced down.

Anika motioned toward the back of the house.

"I'll take her." Callie reached for Anika's hand, then headed around the house. She could hardly believe this sweet child was now her stepdaughter. She glanced up at the lovely sky. A few fluffy clouds drifted lazily against the blue, reminding her of Erik's eyes—her husband's eyes. If only Janna weren't leaving, the day would be perfect.

She opened the door of the privy for Anika and then stood outside, waiting for her to finish. She tried to grasp the fact that she was actually married. She may never see her home in Sandusky again, but Uncle Roger couldn't hurt her anymore.

At the sound of footsteps behind her, she turned, expecting to see Erik. But instead, Harvey Butler stood four feet away, his forehead puckered in a deep frown.

"Is it true?"

"Is what true?" Callie glanced toward the house, hoping Erik would decide to check on them. Would Anika recognize Mr. Butler's voice and be frightened again? She leaned against the door so the girl couldn't get out.

"You married that—that yellow-haired, funny-talkin' foreigner even though we have an agreement?"

"Our arrangement is void since you are married. And, well, I am too." It felt good to have another reason not to have to worry about Mr. Butler coming to call on her again. The man made her feel as if spiders were crawling all over her. She rubbed her arms.

"We'll see about that." Mr. Butler rushed toward her. Callie had nowhere to go. She couldn't run for the house, not with Anika still in the privy. Suddenly, Mr. Butler grabbed her and slung her over his shoulder. Callie could barely breathe. She tried to suck in a breath so she could scream, but all she could manage was a squeak.

She lifted her head, watching the privy. The door opened slowly and Anika peered out, eyes wide. She started running toward the house but then stopped suddenly and turned to follow.

No! No! No! Go back. Callie wanted to scream out the words, but she didn't dare alert Mr. Butler to the girl's presence.

Father, please. Help me. Protect Anika.

Chapter 8

M r. Butler carried Callie down the steps of a root cellar, then lowered her to the ground. "You'll stay here until I decide what to do with you. And don't worry about hollerin'. This place is far enough away from town that nobody will hear you."

She shuddered and quickly glanced around the cellar while the door was open. There wasn't much to see. The room was only about six feet on each side. Three barrels lined one wall. A couple of burlap bags with red lettering lay in a pile in one corner, and a shovel leaned against the wall on her right.

Mr. Butler stomped up the stairs, then slammed the door shut. Callie coughed from the dust stirred up and shivered as the room was engulfed in darkness. Fingers of light stretched through cracks in the door, barely illuminating the top steps.

She slowly moved up the stairs, hoping to get an idea of where she was. Her heart dropped. All she could see through the slits was the sky. One crack was wide enough that she could stick two fingers out. She tugged hard on the wood, but it didn't give.

Callie sank onto the steps. How would Erik ever find her here? She knew that he would search for her, but what would he do if he didn't find her? Would he take Anika and return home without her?

Tears burned her eyes. She finally had a home and people who cared for her, but she stood close to losing it all. She wouldn't give up though. "Help me, Lord."

Something skittered outside, and a shadow blocked out most of the light. Callie's heart bucked. Had Mr. Butler returned already? If he put her on a horse and took her away, could she ever find her way back?

Something touched her shoulder. Callie yelped as she scrambled down the steps. She spun around and squinted at the door. Was that a hand? Anika?

In her fright, she'd forgotten the child had been following them. Hope soared through her as she scurried back up the stairway.

"Anika, sweetie. I'm all right, but please go find your father and show him where

I am. Can you do that?"

The hand disappeared.

"Watch out for Mr. Butler. Don't let him catch you."

For a brief moment, she heard footsteps running, then silence. Inspired with hope, Callie turned, and with her back against the door, she pushed with all her might. It creaked but didn't budge. She tried again and again, but to no avail. Tired and discouraged, she sat down to wait for Erik. "Please, heavenly Father, help Anika get back to her father safely. And help her remember how to find me."

Erik wondered what was keeping his girls. Anika never took so long to visit the privy, especially when it was time to eat. He peeked out the back window but didn't see them.

The meal Mrs. Sanders and Janna were dishing up smelled delicious. His stomach rumbled, reminding him that he'd skipped breakfast in his rush to ride to town early this morning and make the wedding arrangements.

Janna placed a platter of sliced beef on the table. "What do you suppose is keeping them?"

"I do not know. Maybe I should check to make sure everything is all right."

"They'll be along in a moment," the pastor said.

"Ja. Probably." But in his gut, Erik felt something was wrong. He started for the door, when he heard someone fumbling with the handle. His heart calmed when he saw the top of Anika's head through the lacy curtain.

The door suddenly flew open, and the second he saw his daughter's wide-eyed expression, Erik knew something was wrong. He hurried to her as she ran to him. She pointed toward the door, shaking her hand vigorously.

"Slow down, Schätzli. What is the matter?"

Tears coursed down her cheeks. Anika ran her index finger over her upper lip rapidly—an action she'd never done before—then she hugged herself and shuddered and pointed outside again.

He realized Callie hadn't returned. Had something happened to her? He rushed outside to the privy, praying a rattlesnake hadn't bitten her. But Callie was nowhere to be seen. He knocked on the privy. When he got no answer, he opened the door. Where was she? He got a sudden knot in his belly. Had she changed her mind about marrying him and run away? *Please, God. No.*

Anika raced around the house, followed by the pastor and his wife and a slower-moving Janna.

"What has happened?" Pastor Sanders asked. "Where is Callie?"

241

Erik shook his head, unable to voice his dreadful thought.

Anika tugged on his pants. She pointed away from town.

He knelt down and gently grasped her shoulders. "I don't understand. Did Callie. . .go somewhere?"

Anika shook her head, continuing to point. Erik glanced up at his sister's worried expression.

"P–Papa!" Anika stuttered.

Erik's gaze shot back to his daughter's face.

"M–Mr. B–But–ter took her."

Janna gasped.

"Mr. Butler took Callie?"

Anika nodded.

"Do you know where she is?"

She took his hand and tugged. Erik started forward, then glanced at the pastor. "Could you gather some men in case we have trouble with Harvey?"

Pastor Sanders shook his head. "I'm coming with you." He turned to his wife. "Frances, go get some men to help us."

"Consider it done, dear." She faced Erik. "Go! Find your bride, Erik."

"I've got a couple of rifles in the house." The pastor raced for the house, and Erik followed, carrying Anika.

Please, Father, let us find Callie before she is harmed or taken away from me.

A shadow once again blocked the shafts of light filtering into Callie's prison. Had Erik come to her rescue already? The lock rattled. A shiver snaked down Callie's spine. If Erik were outside, wouldn't he call out to her? That meant Mr. Butler had returned. She rushed to the back of the cellar, planning to fight the man. Suddenly, she remembered the shovel and raced back to grab it.

Instead of returning to the back of the cellar, she pressed into the corner where the shovel had been, near the stairs. If Mr. Butler entered the small room far enough, she might be able to clobber him and get away.

"C'mon out, Callie. There's no place for you to run."

She cringed at the nasally sound of his voice, but she refused to move. If he wanted her, he could come get her.

"I know you'd hate for that snivelin' Kessler kid to get hurt, so you'd best get up here."

Callie's stomach clenched. He had Anika?

All hope of being saved fled as she sagged against the wall. If he had Anika, she had no choice but to the leave the cellar. She started to toss the shovel down but changed her mind and hauled it up with her.

As she neared the top, she tried to keep the shovel on the side away from Mr. Butler. She noticed immediately that Anika was nowhere to be seen. Two horses stood a few feet behind Mr. Butler, and he had a gun aimed at her.

The fool had tricked her. Sudden anger coursed through her at all the pain this man had caused. She swung the shovel around hard, slamming Mr. Butler in the elbow, knocking the gun to the ground.

He cried out and scrambled across the dirt for his weapon. One of the horses squealed and bolted, and the other one followed.

She'd never reach the nearest building before Mr. Butler got to his gun, so she raced toward the weapon. He reached out to grab it, but she banged the back of the shovel against his hand.

He yelped again, then cursed and climbed to his feet. Callie wanted to flee, but she faced him, shovel in hand. He growled and charged.

She backed up but stepped on her skirts and fell, landing hard on her backside. The shovel flew from her hands.

Mr. Butler stood over her, breathing hard, an expression of gloating anger on his face. "I'll have fun taming you, Miss Webster."

"It's Mrs. Kessler, remember." Callie hiked her chin. "My husband will hunt you down and haul your sorry hide to jail, where you'll spend the rest of your days."

The man had the gall to laugh out loud. "Just like his wife's killer is doing?"

Callie knew no one had been arrested for Inge's murder. "What do *you* know about it? You were on the stage. You saw the man who shot her, didn't you?"

His smirk was the only answer Callie needed. She tried to rise, but her skirts held her bound.

"Why do you think that foreigner's kid screams every time she sees me?"

Callie gasped. "*You* shot her mother?"

"No one ever suspected that an upstanding citizen of Sowers was part of an outlaw gang." He chuckled again. "And I scared the chatter right out of that kid. Should've killed her too, but I had a rare moment of compassion. Stupid of me."

Callie trembled with a mixture of anger and fear. She looked up again and found herself staring into the barrel of his gun.

"Alma May got in my way too. So I had to take care of her. I am now free to marry again."

"Too bad I'm not."

He tugged at his moustache. "I've changed my mind about you. You're too much trouble."

He stepped forward, blocking the sun from her eyes, and aimed his gun.

Callie's heart hammered. Poor Eric. He was about to lose his second wife. What would that do to him? And Anika?

A shot rang out. Callie jerked but felt no pain.

Mr. Butler's eyes widened. The gun fell from his hand, and he dropped to his knees, a stunned expression on his face. A circle of crimson stained his white shirt. His eyes closed as he fell forward, his head landing a foot from Callie's shoes.

She looked up. Erik stood there, rifle in hand, reminding her of a warrior from a novel she'd read. He handed his rifle to the pastor and rushed forward. He checked Mr. Butler's pulse. "He's gone."

He hurried to Callie's side and knelt next to her. "Are you hurt?"

She closed her eyes and blew out a steadying breath. "No. But if you'd arrived a few seconds later, I'd be the one lying here unmoving."

He helped her up and held her close. Nothing had ever felt so good. After a long moment, he moved back a half step and stared down at her. "I was so afraid I had lost you."

"If I have anything to do with it, you won't lose me for a very long time."

He grinned. Then his eyes smoldered with a matching desire she felt welling up inside her. He leaned down, kissed her cheek, and trailed little kisses to her lips. After a long moment of pure bliss, Callie leaned back to catch her breath. She glanced at the pastor, whose lips turned up in a pleasant grin. Heat blistered Callie's cheeks.

Behind him, Anika ran toward them, followed by several men from town. Callie bent down and reached for the girl as she flew into her arms. Anika hugged her neck tightly and cried, "Mama!"

Callie's gaze locked with Erik's.

He grinned and nodded. "She started talking so she could tell me what happened to you. Anika is the real hero today."

Epilogue

W e're almost there!" Anika knelt on the seat, pressing her face to the train window.

"Are you nervous?" Erik laid his hand over Callie's.

She shifted on the seat to face him. "A little, but I'm also eager to meet your parents. Your mother's letters have been such a blessing." Especially the family recipes the older woman had shared, which enabled Callie to prepare some of Erik's favorite dishes and desserts.

He trailed a finger down her cheek. "Do not worry. They will love you. They are so excited that we are coming to help celebrate their thirty-fifth anniversary."

"I sure hope they like me." She couldn't help wondering if Erik's parents would compare her to Inge, but that concern was overpowered with excitement. "I can hardly wait to see Ben and Janna's baby."

"Ja, me too. Being an uncle does not seem real since I have yet to hold my nephew."

"You will soon."

The train shuddered as it slowed. Brakes screeched. The Olathe depot crept into view, and the train slowly stopped.

Anika spun around. "We're here!" She scooted off her seat and stepped into the aisle.

Callie reached out to snag the little girl she loved so much. "Just a minute, young lady."

"But I'm so excited to see baby Joseph."

"We are too. But we must gather our things first." Erik reached for the satchel that held their food. "Do not forget your dolly."

"Oh! Poor Betsy." Anika crawled across the bench to retrieve her favorite toy.

Callie reached for her daughter. "Let me fix your cloak, sweetie. It's crooked. We don't want you getting sick. Remember, the weather in Kansas is much colder than Texas."

"I believe we are ready." Erik stepped into the crowd. Callie slipped in front of him holding Anika's hand.

They made their way to the door, then plodded down the steps to the platform, where a blast of chilly air greeted them.

"There they are!"

Callie glanced to her left at the sound of Janna's voice. When she spotted her sister-in-law, she hurried toward her. Anika pulled her hand loose and ran straight for Ben, who held baby Joseph.

Janna tugged Callie into a hug, then stepped back and looked down. Her eyes widened. "You're expecting?"

"How can you tell?" Callie glanced down to look at the front of her dress.

"Your face is glowing. I was not sure, but you just confirmed it."

"Sneaky. I see motherhood hasn't changed you much."

Janna squeezed Callie's hand. "It's so much fun. Except for losing sleep when Joseph is hungry at night, and. . .well, diapers." She grinned. "Come and meet my parents. They're so excited to finally get to meet you."

Janna started forward, but Callie tugged her back. "Please don't tell your parents about the baby just yet. Erik wants to reveal our news once we're at the house."

"Of course. I would not dream of spoiling your surprise."

Callie followed Janna through the crowd to where an older couple waited. Both were taller than her and looked a bit apprehensive. Were they concerned that Erik had married the wrong woman—or that she might not like them? Callie smiled and hurried forward, hoping to waylay any fears they might have. Erik's hand at her back gave her emotional support.

"Moder, Fader, this is Callie, my lovely wife."

Both of them smiled. Mrs. Kessler reached out to touch Callie's hand. "Welcome to the family, my dear. I cannot tell you how happy we are to finally meet you."

Callie stepped forward and gave her mother-in-law a gentle hug. "Me too. We've been counting the days until we'd all be together."

Her father-in-law smiled at her but didn't reach out, so Callie moved back to Erik's side. He had warned her that his father wasn't overly affectionate, although he never doubted his love.

With her arm looped through Erik's, she followed Janna off the train platform and into the large carriage. She never dreamed when she came to Texas that she would find such a wonderful family to love. And now she was going to be a mother.

Thank the good Lord that she'd arrived in Sowers a day late and a dollar short.

Bestselling author **Vickie McDonough** grew up wanting to marry a rancher but instead married a computer geek who is scared of horses. She now lives out her dreams in her fictional stories about ranchers, cowboys, lawmen, and others living in the Old West. Vickie is the award-winning author of more than forty published books and novellas. Her novels include the fun and feisty Texas Boardinghouse Brides series and the Land Rush Dreams series. Vickie and her husband, Robert, have four grown sons, one of whom is married, and a precocious ten-year-old granddaughter. When she's not writing, Vickie enjoys reading, antiquing, watching movies, and traveling. To learn more about Vickie's books or to sign up for her newsletter, visit her website at www.vickiemcdonough.com.

The Groom She Thought She'd Left Behind

by Darlene Panzera

Chapter 1

The blue sunlit sky and late summer foliage with fragrant pink and white roses blooming outside Emily Pembrooke's family estate would have made it a perfect day for a wedding—if she were not the bride.

Now twenty-two years of age, Emily had dreamed of her wedding day for as long as she could remember. How she would wear her mother's exquisitely hand-sewn white satin dress with its beaded bodice and intricately woven lace train. How she'd walk up the aisle of Boston's Old North Church with the four friends from Miss Porter's Finishing School she'd asked to be her bridesmaids. How her sister, Susannah, would be her maid of honor and her two little nieces, her flower girls. But not once had Emily considered the notion she wouldn't be acquainted with the groom.

Of course, she and Christian Gould had exchanged letters after she'd accepted the wealthy business investor's proposal in early June. And she knew her marriage to Mr. Gould would be mutually beneficial. Her family had fallen into desperate times financially—a residual result of the Panic of 1893 three years before—and Christian Gould sought a wife with a family name of old ancestral English heritage to gain him entrance into the preeminent social circles he desired. Pembrooke, indeed, was such a name, as it could be traced back to sixteenth-century nobility. It had become Emily's most valuable asset.

In return her fiancé had promised to care for her beloved family's needs so she would no longer have to worry about their welfare and her father would bear no shame. Her dear father, for whom she held the utmost respect, supported the match and had reverently stated that her marriage to Christian Gould was "*a most fortuitous provision that could only have been orchestrated by God himself.*"

Emily was not as convinced that God was involved. For if God cared for her and her parents and her younger siblings, Susannah and Thomas Jr., why would He have allowed them to become so financially desperate in the first place? Why would a loving God want her to feel riddled with anxiety and pressured to submit to an arranged marriage to a man she didn't know? Still, she held the hope that love would grow in time and her marriage to Mr. Gould would become more than just a convenient business transaction.

"Come, Emily," her sister called, exuberance dancing within the lilting high-pitched tone of her voice. "You must see the carriages your future husband has sent to escort us to the church."

Taking Emily's hand, Susannah pulled her behind the thick full-length curtains half drawn in the parlor, much like she'd done when they were both children playing hide-and-seek with Thomas. From there they could look out through the wide bay window and see the barouche carriages parked outside in the circular driveway.

Each of the three exquisite shiny black vehicles featured two double seats facing each other and a collapsible canvas half hood that had been folded down on this fine day. Drivers dressed in formal black coats and top hats perched on the ornate, high box seats in front, and a majestic pair of large black horses with long black manes and tails stood ready to pull each carriage. The cart horse and wagon Emily had driven around her aunt and uncle's country estate were an embarrassment by comparison.

"Only the best for Christian Gould's new bride," Susannah boasted. "Oh, I *do* hope he makes you happy."

"His letters to me have been very cordial," Emily said, not wanting to concern her sister with the fact that his written words had also been excruciatingly dry and impersonal.

Susannah let out a dreamy sigh. "If only you could have met him in person before taking your vows."

Emily hadn't seen the need. Once she'd accepted the terms of the proposal, there was no going back. Besides, she'd been happy to remain overseas with her aunt and uncle and their six children at their rural homestead in the English countryside for as long as she could. She'd already been living with them two years, quietly fulfilling the role of governess, and she knew that after she left, her days of living free from the rigid constraints of society would come to an end. Thankfully, after Emily agreed to the arranged marriage, her elated father had allowed her three more idyllic months before she had to board a ship back to the States. While her parents had eagerly agreed to take care of all the necessary preparations leading up to the nuptial ceremony, Emily had savored her precious last days of freedom.

"Why, Christian Gould could be a fat old toad for all you know," Susannah teased.

Emily smiled, her lips tight. "I trust your judgment. You said he was handsome, did you not?"

"He *is* handsome," Susannah said with a quick nod, "if you like men with a beard and a moustache."

"Most gentlemen do have beards and moustaches." She playfully nudged her sister with her elbow. "You'd best get used to it if you want to marry one day."

Laughter from Emily's bridesmaids drifted in from the hall. No doubt the women were headed toward the front door to see the fancy carriages for themselves. Emily moved to step out from behind the curtains to join them, as it was almost time to leave, but froze when she overheard some of their comments.

"Christian Gould may have money—Emily certainly won't be lacking for that—and she'll get to live in a grand house on a fine estate, but if you ask me, the man is an absolute *rake*!"

The other bridesmaids giggled, and in a low voice another said, "He's untrustworthy, for sure. I heard he's been seen in the company of six women this past month alone, and his attention toward them has been anything but indifferent."

"Poor Emily. No doubt he'll continue his philandering ways after the wedding ceremony."

"It's also been rumored he has no desire for children."

"Does Emily know?"

"I haven't had the heart to tell her."

"Nor I," said another.

Emily's heart lurched. *No children?*

Beside her, Susannah let out a small gasp. Emily whispered tersely, "Did you know about this? Is it true what they say?"

"I—I do not know Mr. Gould's stance on children," her sister said, her voice hesitant. "But it *is* rumored he. . .has an eye for attractive women. However," she was quick to add, "the rumors could be fueled by idle gossip, spurred by jealousy, and nothing more."

"Idle gossip," Emily whispered, a dull ache forming in the pit of her stomach. "Of course."

Her resolve faltered as she joined the others, and they stepped outside toward the open carriages waiting to transport them to the church. While the bridesmaids were directed into the foremost conveyance, Emily's family was escorted into the second. She gathered her skirt in one hand and prepared to join them, when one of the immaculately groomed young coachmen stepped forward to block her path.

"Excuse me, miss, but the bride is to take the carriage behind this one."

Emily glanced at the third vehicle, which sat empty except for the trunk carrying her clothing and few treasured possessions. A reminder that after she and Christian Gould exchanged vows, she would not return to the Pembrooke estate.

She looked back at the coachman. "But I wish to ride in the same carriage as my father."

"I've had implicit instructions from the groom," he insisted.

Peering over the coachman's shoulder, her father encouraged, "Do as you're told, child."

Didn't she always? When had she ever not done *exactly* as she'd been told?

Both her mother and her father shot her an apprehensive look, reminding her how much they were counting on her to help save the family from financial ruin. She nodded to ease their fears. She wouldn't let them down. *Would she?*

The first and second carriages pulled away and, accepting her fate, as she'd done when accepting Christian Gould's proposal, Emily followed the last coachman to the remaining carriage where she sat on an oversized burgundy cushioned seat and steeled herself for the perfunctory ride to the church.

Alone.

Was this a forewarning of what she'd soon have to endure? Frequent nights alone. . .while her husband was who knew where with who knew whom?

"Does the carriage meet with your satisfaction, miss?"

Emily turned toward the voice and realized the coachman awaited her reply. "It's. . .spacious."

Spacious enough to fit six children in around her. Children she might never have.

"Is there anything else you require?" the coachman asked. "A lap blanket perhaps? Or . . .a sniff of lavender?"

Emily shook her head. "A sniff of—no. Why would I need lavender?"

"To help calm your nerves?" he prompted.

A distinct queasiness had indeed begun to churn her stomach, but she doubted lavender would have any effect. "No, I don't need anything."

"Then. . .do you mind releasing my hand?"

Emily's gaze flew from the coachman's amused expression to her fingers, still clenched tightly over his. She must have latched onto him when ascending the carriage steps and forgotten to let go. Heat sprang into her cheeks as she pulled her hand away. "Forgive me."

The coachman grinned as he climbed up onto the box seat before her and took hold of the horses' reins. "You must be excited to marry Christian Gould."

When she didn't respond, he glanced back at her. "Aren't you?"

She lifted her gaze to meet his and stared at the question in his eyes. "I—I don't know how I feel."

With a slight frown, the coachman turned around and clucked his tongue, signaling the team of horses to walk. "You need not worry, miss. I am sure you will find Mr. Gould quite agreeable as your future husband."

And if she did not?

"I hear you've spent the last two years abroad," he continued. "Did you enjoy your time there?"

Immensely.

"Mr. Gould is also very fond of travel," the coachman informed her. "Not overseas though. I fear he's prone to sea sickness."

Her heart sank. Did that mean her new husband would never take her to visit her aunt and uncle and nieces and nephews in England? Emily tried to ignore the incessant *clip-clop* of the horses' hooves thundering in her ears, each beat reminding her of the commitment she would be making when they arrived at the church.

"Is there anywhere here in the States you would like to visit?"

Emily pulled her gaze away from the wrought-iron gates lining the cobblestone street and locked onto the back of the coachman's light brown hair, which stuck out beneath the black top hat matching his formal dress coat. Did all of Christian Gould's coachmen ramble on like this? She was certain it wasn't proper etiquette for the coachman to continue to chat with her in this manner.

"I—I suppose there are nice places to visit in the US as well." Although, at the moment, she couldn't think of any and she did not want to converse about travel.

However, perhaps she could use his desire to talk to her advantage.

Leaning forward, she decided to ask a few questions of her own. "Is Christian Gould a good employer?"

"The very best," the coachman was quick to boast. "He is a kindhearted, generous, trustworthy gentleman, very respected in Boston society."

Emily frowned. "My bridesmaids say otherwise."

The coachman glanced back at her again, his expression indignant. "Oh? What did they say?"

"Things that it would not be well for me to repeat."

"I hear many things too," the coachman said slowly, then shifted his jaw. "Perhaps I can help put your mind at ease and tell you whether or not the rumors are true."

Emily drew a deep breath and realized this might be her only chance to find out the truth. "Well, this may be improper for me to say, but my bridesmaids' words lead me to believe Christian Gould may be the opposite of what his first name suggests."

"Can you be more specific?"

"They say. . .he is an untrustworthy, philandering *rake!*"

The coachman seemed to relax, his mouth curving into a smile. "He most definitely is *not*."

"How do you know? You are a man, and men do not speak of such things."

A deep, throaty chuckle burst from his lips, and the glint in his gray-green eyes implied he thought she was funny. "You just do not know him."

"You're right," Emily agreed, surprised by his staunch loyalty to his employer. "I don't."

Her mother's words sprang back to her from the day before. *"It's not so bad. Your father and I had an arranged marriage, and we've managed to make the best of it."*

Except Emily suddenly realized she didn't want to "make the best of it." She wanted the kind of love her aunt and uncle had in England with their six children. She wanted a marriage that would make her happy.

Dear God, is that so much to ask? Where are You when I need You? Is this really Your will for my life?

"You'll have plenty of time to get to know each other after the ceremony," the coachman supplied, his voice smug.

"Yes," she said softly. "Because marriage is. . .*forever*, a binding commitment not to be taken lightly, but to honor for the rest of our lives."

"Indeed."

The back of her throat closed, and she swallowed hard to dislodge the lump threatening to choke the life right out of her, or what little life she might have after she went through with this marriage.

Had she made a terrible mistake? Not yet, she hadn't. A small voice in the back of her head told her there was still time. Except her family, her friends, all the elite of Boston society, would already be at the church waiting for her. . .including Christian Gould.

Her heart fluttered crazily as she thought of her mother and father, and the apprehensive looks they gave her right before their carriage pulled away. Didn't the Bible say to "honor thy father and thy mother?" They'd be extremely disappointed if she disobeyed that command and didn't keep her part of the bargain.

The redbrick building with its tall white steeple and colorful stained glass windows suddenly loomed into view, and she began to tremble. Five minutes more and they'd be pulling up to the entrance of the Old North Church.

"Wait!" she shrieked, springing forward out of her seat. "I—I don't think I can do this."

"Do what?"

Her breath came so fast and shallow she could hardly breathe. "Get married!"

She launched forward, stood on the empty bench seat across from her, and snatched the horses' reins from the coachman's hands, her mind focused only on one thing. Putting as much distance between herself and the church as possible.

"Whoa, there! You can't just—" The coachman made a grab for the reins, but when she spun the carriage around, he toppled backward.

"I'm afraid I can, and I will!" she declared.

For she would not marry a man she didn't love, no matter the cost. She'd find another way to support her family. There had to be another way. One she could live with.

One that would allow her to hold on to her dreams for the future.

Chapter 2

Christian opened his eyes, blinked twice, and sat up with a start. Wincing, he reached up to touch the back of his throbbing head. It took a moment for him to realize he was on the floor of the carriage. *His* carriage. And he remembered—he'd been flung backward, off the box seat. It took him another moment to notice the driver now sitting on top of the box seat wore a white wedding dress and was none other than his bride-to-be. As she rocked to the side, steering the trotting horses onto Tremont Street, he glimpsed the twenty-two-foot tall bronze Brewer fountain and expansive green lawn of the Boston Commons, about a mile away from the church.

She'd actually stolen the reins! He'd be the laughingstock of Boston society if the local gossips ever got wind of this, but the feisty, blue-eyed brunette moved fast, and he'd been ill-prepared for the sharp turn she'd negotiated.

"Miss Pembrooke, I must insist you stop the carriage at once," he said, clutching the edge of the seat to steady himself.

She glanced over her shoulder at him with a look of surprise, as if she'd forgotten he was there. Then, returning her attention to the horses, she pulled back on the leather straps and called out, "Whoa! Easy boys."

A second after his team of black Friesian geldings came to a halt, she spun around on the box seat and said, "I'm sorry. I should have let you off sooner. You may go."

"Go where?"

"Back to the church, of course. Although, I'm afraid you'll have to do it on foot. I'm going to require the use of Mr. Gould's carriage a while longer."

He stared at her, the folly of his "plan" beginning to sink in. "I can't go back to the church without you."

"Accepting the proposed arranged marriage was my father's idea, not mine. I no longer think I can save my family by marrying someone I do not know and, moreover, don't love," she said, lifting her chin. "Especially not one with such a questionable reputation."

"You won't even give him the benefit of the doubt?"

"I'm afraid it's too late for that."

"But your friends and family and the other guests are all at the church waiting."

"Yes, I know." A deep frown creased her forehead, and she lowered her gaze. "I fear that neither my father nor Mr. Gould will ever forgive me."

She was more beautiful than the image she'd sent along to him with her letters from overseas. Still, he'd had his own doubts about the marriage, and prior to the ceremony he'd surprised his coachman when he said he intended to pick up his appointed bride himself. Christian had borrowed the standard coachman's attire and shaved off his moustache and beard hoping she wouldn't recognize him, and she hadn't. Neither had anyone else.

The railroad financiers he sought to do business with required he have ties to either "old money," backed by European currency, since the run on gold had made the US dollar unstable, or an "old English name," which at the very least lent prestige. Since the majority of his family's wealth did not meet those requirements, he had no other option but to go for the latter.

Like many who sought to recoup money lost in investments during the Panic of 1893, Christian feared they were entering a second wave that some were already calling the Panic of 1896, and he needed this deal. Not only to uphold his position in society but to enable his family to keep Ridgeview, their 2.5-million-dollar summer home in the Berkshires they'd just finished building the year before the economy soured.

His mother would be upset if they had to lose it, but Christian would be even more so. He'd always loved the Berkshire mountain region of western Massachusetts, even as a young boy visiting his friend's country estate. It was the one place, if he was forced to admit it, that he'd always felt he could leave the pressures from being the only son of prominent parents in polite society behind.

The vast financial gain he expected from the railroad deal would both solve his own monetary woes and allow him to help support the family of his bride. If he so desired.

After disguising himself as a coachman, he'd decided that if he found Miss Pembrooke's appearance and demeanor satisfactory, he could change into his wedding clothes at the church. And if he did not. . .he'd back out of the arrangement.

He just hadn't expected her to back out first.

"My dear," he said, his voice suddenly hoarse. "I cannot allow you to do this."

"I'm not asking for your permission." She gave him an apologetic look. "Now, if you would be so kind as to jump off. . ."

"I cannot. Indeed, I fear for your welfare. Especially in your present state of mind."

"There is nothing wrong with my present state of mind," she retorted with a scowl. "Either jump off or come with me, but I'm—I'm leaving!"

The notion she'd rather run than marry him gnawed at his ego. She didn't even know him. And therein lay the problem. He'd been so preoccupied with his business accounts that he had not taken care to abolish the outrageous rumors swirling about the gossip train when he should have. His mother had warned him, quoting Proverbs 22:1, "A good name is rather to be chosen than great riches." Of course there was nothing he could do about that now.

Climbing up onto the seat closest to her, Christian noted the stubborn look of resolve on Miss Pembrooke's face and asked, "Where will you go?"

"I do not believe it is any of your concern," she said, her face filled with defiance. "That is my personal business."

"Seeing as how you've kidnapped me, it seems I am already involved in your personal business," he said, unable to contain his perplexity over the entire situation. "And I think I have every right to know—"

"*Kidnapped?*" she asked, quirking a brow.

"And knocked me unconscious."

Miss Pembrooke's eyes widened. "That was unintentional."

"Nevertheless, a result of your carelessness when you turned the carriage around."

"I was not careless!" she shot back. "I know how to drive a team of horses. You were just not holding on."

"How could I?" he demanded. "You stole the reins out of my hands."

"Yes," she said, her tone softening. "I did. I suppose I should have entrusted your skills as a coachman."

"My skills as a coach—" He broke off when he remembered she did not know to whom she was speaking. As far as she was concerned, he was nothing more than a servant.

Miss Pembrooke's expression grew contrite. "By taking over the reins, I may have endangered your reputation."

"You've endangered more than that," he countered, thinking of the prestigious investment he would lose if she did not marry him.

"I suppose you could have a concussion." She narrowed her eyes, appeared to study him, then held up her gloved hand. "How many fingers do you see?"

The fact that this beautiful young woman could so stubbornly oppose him and yet be genuinely concerned for his welfare at the same time soothed his pride enough for his indignation to ebb. "I see two."

"Thank goodness for that," Miss Pembrooke declared, and after a moment's pause, she sighed. "As for where I should go. . .I do not know. I cannot go back home without a way to contribute to my family's expenses. I'd be too ashamed. My father still works, but he counted on this wedding to get our family out of debt, and by now. . .he must know I've let him down. I cannot afford passage overseas to return to my governess position at my uncle's estate in England either. No, I suppose I will have to find employment elsewhere, perhaps in a factory."

He couldn't help but stare at her. "You, a lady of society, with the Pembrooke name on your side no less, intend to work as a common laborer?"

She nodded so vigorously her veil slipped off her upswept dark coiffure of curls and fell to her lap. Squeezing the lacy material in her hands like a washrag, she said, "I'll do whatever it takes to help support my family."

"Except marry Christian Gould."

"Yes, anything but that."

He held her gaze, not sure what he should do.

As if she could read his mind, Miss Pembrooke pursed her delicate pink lips and another flair of defiance lit her dark blue eyes. "In fact, if you would be so kind as to drive Mr. Gould's carriage back to his estate, I'm sure I can manage from here."

Leave her stranded? "This is ludicrous!" he sputtered. "I can't just leave you here alone, unprotected, with no money and no place to go."

"I appreciate your chivalry, but I assure you," she said, giving him a direct look, "I will be fine."

"No, I cannot—" he protested.

"Why is that?" she asked, lifting her chin. Then her expression softened. "Oh dear. You fear you will be fired, don't you? And I suppose that would be all my fault."

Christian stood gaping at her for several long seconds before the absurdity of it all made him grin. "I never intend to work as a coachman again anyway."

"No?" Her eyes grew wide. "What will you do?"

One minute she could be feisty and the next she could be full of concern. He wasn't sure which side of her he liked better, as both left him intrigued. Should he tell her who he was? No. First he wanted to get to know her better. Win her trust. Convince her that his "boss" wasn't the disreputable louse she believed him to be.

"Let me help you," he said, eager to do anything that might allow him the chance to change her mind and convince her to marry him before the month's end. After that, his window of opportunity to get into the new railroad venture would be lost. "I know this area," he assured her. "And I have connections. By nightfall, I guarantee I can find us both a place to stay."

Her brows lifted in surprise, then her face took on a thoughtful expression. "I'll want to go somewhere. . .out of the public eye, where people will not readily recognize me."

He nodded. "We can go to the Berkshires. There is a beautiful estate in Stockbridge," he coaxed. "With a lake, trees, and an orchard of McIntosh apples. They employ many hired hands and—I have friends there."

"You'll help me find a job?" Excitement tinged her words.

"If that is your desire."

"I've never been to the Berkshire region, but I hear it takes several hours to get there by train." She gave him a fretful look of remorse. "And. . .I fear the fare is more than I can afford."

Christian pulled a small coin pouch from the inside pocket of his coachman's jacket. "I can cover your expenses."

She shook her head. "Sir, I will not take charity."

"You can repay me. . .at a later date," he replied.

"It simply isn't proper for a young lady to travel alone with a man without a chaperone," she insisted. "I scarcely know you any more than I do—"

"The groom you left behind?" he asked, breaking into another grin. When she nodded, he said, "We could pose as brother and sister. That should stop people's tongues from wagging."

Her brows drew together, forming a sharp V. "Excuse me, sir, but I do not believe in deception!"

"Didn't you already deceive Christian Gould and all the people at the church when you chose to run away?"

"I suppose I did," she said, dropping her gaze.

"I can drive," he prompted. "And get us to the station in time to board the two o'clock train."

She gave him a wary look, as if still unsure. Then the anxiety on her face lessened and she smiled. "You don't like my driving?"

"Afraid not," he said, again rubbing a hand over the sore lump on the back of his head. "Are we agreed?"

She answered him with another smile. "First, I'll need to change out of this dress."

Bunching the material of her white satin skirts in one hand, she climbed off the box seat and circled around to the back of the carriage. Following her, Christian watched as she opened her trunk and pulled out a plain, bluish-gray day dress and a scuffed pair of black leather boots.

"You mean to change here?" he asked, unable to mask his surprise. "In the park?"

"Of course not." She laughed as if he'd made a jest, then pointed up the street. "In the Parker House Hotel."

"Unassisted by your maids?"

"I can do a good many things unassisted," she assured him.

Knowing she had been born into a life of privilege, he had a hard time believing that to be true, but as he envisioned the spirited, stubborn beauty before him trying to perform the duties of a servant, he knew one thing for certain.

He would like to see her try.

After Miss Pembrooke's insistence that they pay a driver to return the carriage to the Gould estate so no one would think her a thief, and once she'd sent a message to her family telling them her tentative plan, the trip from Boston to Stockbridge had been blessedly uneventful.

Reclaiming her trunk off the baggage car, Christian then hired a hackney coach to take them the final distance to Maple Glen, owned by Stephen and Alice Belmont. It was when he knocked at the door of the servants' entrance and was unexpectedly greeted by the butler that he had his first taste of trepidation. If he were to be recognized now, all his efforts trying to appease Miss Pembrooke would be for naught.

"Christian—" So surprised was the aging butler to see him, dressed as a coachman besides, that when Mr. Norris sputtered his first name it came out as barely a whisper. Then with his eyes widening, his voice rose as he continued, "—Gilbert Lawrence—"

Alarmed, Christian shook his head in warning, and when Mr. Norris spotted Miss Pembrooke approaching a few steps behind, the intuitive white-haired man wisely dropped his voice back down to a whisper as he finished, "—Gould. What in blazes are you up to?"

Mr. Norris would have been severely reprimanded for greeting any other gentleman in such a manner, but the old man had been part of Christian's life since he and Stephen were children and knew more of their exploits than even their own fathers. The trusted butler had kept their secrets but had also exercised his authority to box their ears a time or two when they deserved it, and spoke to them, even after they grew, as if they were children of his own.

"It's in my best interest not to draw undue attention," Christian confided.

"I see." Mr. Norris gave Miss Pembrooke's plain, homespun blue-gray clothing a sweeping gaze as well. "How can I assist?"

"I've come to speak to Mr. Belmont, if he'll see me."

Christian searched the old man's expression, hoping for a tell-tale sign of what to expect when he and Stephen came face-to-face. The last time they'd met, Christian had voiced his disapproval of Stephen's choice for a bride, and they hadn't parted on good terms.

Mr. Norris gave him a hesitant look, one that let him know Stephen still held a grudge. Then, returning to his role as butler, he straightened his stance and said, "I will inquire within."

As soon as Mr. Norris retreated inside, closing the door on them while they awaited a response, Miss Pembrooke stepped forward. "I'm sorry, I couldn't help but overhear the butler speaking to you. Is that your name? Gilbert Lawrence?"

It was—in part. He nodded. "Yes."

She gave him a quizzical look. "You hesitated."

"I have several names," he confided.

Miss Pembrooke smiled. "So do I. My sister calls me Em. And my father calls me Emiline after my grandma."

"What should I call you?" Christian prompted.

"Emily."

"Emily Pembrooke," he teased, "it is a pleasure to officially make your acquaintance."

A rosy hue blossomed into her cheeks as she averted her gaze and said apologetically, "Forgive me for not initiating proper introductions earlier. My thoughts were consumed with—"

"Running from the altar?"

The color in her cheeks deepened. "Yes, that."

"Calling me 'Gilbert Lawrence' would be a whole lot nicer than simply being referred to as 'sir' or 'coachman' the way you have all afternoon."

Emily nodded. "Mr. Lawrence, I—"

"Not Mr. Lawrence," Christian interrupted and grinned. "If we are to pretend to be brother and sister, you should call me Gilbert."

"Very well then, *Gilbert*," she said, smiling. "It's been a pleasure to meet you too."

The butler returned a few moments later to report that Mr. Belmont would indeed see them, but Gilbert asked her to wait outside. Her newly adopted "brother" was a mischievous young man, to be sure, but he'd kept his word and paid her train fare and the required transport to Maple Glen, the grand Berkshire estate he'd described—a place where, he'd told her, he'd worked once before. Perhaps he hoped to use that to their advantage, and to that end, she decided to trust him.

Twisting her hands together nervously, she gazed up at the large white house on the hillside that had twice as many windows as her family's residence in Boston. The owner had to be very rich, as rich as Christian Gould. With a small pang in her stomach, she wondered for the umpteenth time if she'd made a mistake when she decided to run.

What if her bridesmaids had been wrong about Christian Gould? What if she had left a perfectly good groom behind. . .out of fear? Nervous jitters?

Even if he was a good man, if she had gone through with the wedding, she still wouldn't have married for love. And that would most definitely have been a mistake. She knew that now. While sitting on the train, she'd recalled how her uncle Joseph would look lovingly at her aunt Rebecca, and Emily decided that in the future, she wouldn't even consider marriage until a man looked at her that same way. Her relatives didn't need money to be happy, and neither did she. She only needed enough to help support her family, and to support herself, until a man she deemed worthy did come along.

Unless it was God's will she become a spinster.

Frowning, she pushed the unpleasant thought aside and fixed her gaze on the door through which Gilbert Lawrence had entered to inquire about possible employment. While marrying Mr. Gould would have provided her family with money to spare, the truth was that with her father's work negotiating contracts between the steel manufacturers and her extra added meager earnings, the family would survive. But what would she do if the Belmonts had no use for her? How would she be able to help support her family? Where would she go from here? She walked around the gardens, unable to sit still as she waited for Gilbert to return and give her the news.

She'd either be hired—or she wouldn't. It was as simple as that.

But oh how she'd love to work at this lovely summer estate with all its big beautiful buildings, white trellised walkways, marble fountains, and fine greenery. Heat coursed into her cheeks as she also thought of the exceedingly helpful, vibrant young man who had brought her here.

Gilbert Lawrence was not unpleasant in appearance to cast her gaze upon either.

Chapter 3

The interior of the Belmonts' "cottage" on the country estate they'd named Maple Glen had not changed since Christian's last visit a year ago. The French-inspired green silk velvet upholstery and draperies were designed in Louis XIV style. Carved wood and gold gilt wall panels represented scenes from classical mythology. And the water fountains and marble statues had been brought in from Europe by Stephen's parents, who had commissioned the family's summer cottage to be built and furnished nine years earlier.

Although many would call the "cottages" of the upper-class palaces or mansions, the forty-two-room, thirty-five-thousand-square-feet retreat had only cost two million, much less than their main residence back in Boston.

Of course, the land had been in the Belmont family long before the summer-house was built. Back when Christian and Stephen were boys, Maple Glen had been a working "gentlemen's farm." Fruits and vegetables were still grown and sent back to their Boston estate.

He'd heard Stephen's parents were not to arrive for another few days, even though most of the socially elite had already descended upon their Berkshire cottages for the six-week season, which started at the end of August and lasted through September.

As Christian followed the butler down the hall, Stephen's wife of six months, Alice Belmont, came out of the parlor and stopped short at the sight of him. A soft gasp escaped her lips, and her face took on the expression of a startled doe.

"Mr. Gould is here to see Mr. Belmont," the butler explained a bit hastily. Perhaps to save her from having to come up with a proper response, since the woman had not been raised in upper-class society as Emily had been.

Christian half expected the fair-haired woman's cheeks to redden with acute embarrassment as they had in the past after she learned that he didn't support her marriage to his best friend.

But she surprised him with a gracious nod of her head as she smiled. "Welcome to our home."

Even more remarkable was the fact that her tone held neither sarcasm nor resentment, both of which he deserved. Christian had been callously forthright in his opinion of his friend Stephen marrying beneath his station in society. And now, shamed at the humiliation he had caused them, he found himself at a loss for words, except to simply reply, "Thank you."

Christian courteously waited until she passed before he followed the butler to the study. Then, after announcing Christian's arrival, Mr. Norris gave him one last encouraging nod to wish him luck and backed out of the room, leaving him to face Stephen alone.

"What the devil are you doing here?" Stephen greeted him, a lock of his black hair falling across his forehead as he rose from his claw-footed French mahogany desk. "I thought this was your wedding day."

"I couldn't very well get married without a best man," Christian countered, and caught Stephen's quick look of regret. "Or. . .a bride."

Stephen stared at him a moment, then sputtered, "What happened? Did she run out on you?"

"She ran *with* me," Christian answered dryly.

"The two of you decided to elope?"

"It would appear so, if only the bride knew who I was. She thinks me a mere coachman."

"You do look like one." Stephen pointed toward his long, black, double-buttoned topcoat with the embellished "G" embroidery on the lapel, typical attire for all the Gould coachmen. "Why are you wearing that?"

"Because I had this crazy idea that if I switched places with the coachman driving her to the wedding, we'd have time to get acquainted before facing everyone."

Stephen chuckled. "I understand your motivation, but I still wonder. . .why you of all people, would—"

Christian gave him a rueful look, and Stephen laughed, catching on to the truth of the matter.

"You were ready to run too, weren't you?" he accused, and laughed once more. "Seems you may have met your match."

"She is a spitfire, that one," Christian agreed.

With a nod, his friend invited him to take a seat in one of the large winged-back upholstered chairs in front of the stone fireplace and sat across from him. "How could she not recognize you?"

"She's spent the last couple of years in England and just arrived back in the States a fortnight ago. Hardly enough time to even see my picture in the newspapers. And even if she did, she would have seen me with a beard and moustache. And certainly not dressed like this." Christian took off the topcoat he'd borrowed from his coachman and slung it over his arm, revealing the white workman's shirt he wore with the black trousers and black suspenders. "The different social classes seem to be stuck in her head and make her oblivious to the truth."

"Like someone else I know," Stephen said, arching a brow.

Christian nodded, suppressing the ache in his gut. "I'm sorry for our quarrel last spring. I was wrong to suggest you were making a mistake by proposing to Alice."

"No one has ever made me happier than she has," Stephen said, giving him a direct look. "And the fact she once worked as a maid on my father's estate does nothing to diminish the insurmountable love I have for her. Or my respect."

"Then she also has my respect," Christian promised. "As well as my deepest apologies."

Stephen regarded him for a moment, then smiled. "Imagine what your runaway bride would say if she knew who you were. Seems you are going to need to win her respect, and quick too, before she finds out the truth."

"You're right," Christian agreed. "Miss Emily Pembrooke heard rumors that convinced her Christian Gould was not someone she wanted to marry, and I need to change her mind."

Stephen arched a brow. "How do you plan to do that?"

"Before I left Boston, I sent word to my parents to inform our guests that the bride had become ill and the wedding would be postponed until she is feeling better. Which, for the most part, is quite true, but I also need your help," Christian admitted.

Stephen nodded with amusement. "What can I do?"

"Hire us to work here on your estate."

Stephen eyed him as if he'd lost his mind. "Hire. . .*you?*"

"Emily is determined to find a job and send money home to her family. I need time to win her over and convince her to go forward with the wedding."

"Surely you must be jesting."

"I will pay her wages," Christian insisted. "And every expense we both incur while we are here."

"Most of our staff are new this season, but there are a few, like Mr. Norris, the head housekeeper, and the cook, who know who you are," Stephen warned.

"Can they be trusted to hold their tongues?"

"They won't lie, but neither will they say anything to give you away."

"Well," Christian said with a grin, "that's something in my favor."

"But what shall they call you?" Stephen asked, giving him a pensive look.

"Emily overheard Mr. Norris address me when we arrived. She now thinks I am Gilbert Lawrence and that we are pretending to be brother and sister in order to procure employment."

"This just gets better and better," Stephen mused. "And when Miss Pembrooke finds out the truth, what then? Do you suppose she'll still have you?"

Christian shook his head. "I'm not certain of anything at this point."

"But why her?" Stephen asked, shaking his head. "With all the women you have to choose from who clamor for your attention, why go to all this trouble to marry this one?"

Christian hesitated, and Stephen slapped his thigh again and smirked. "You like her!"

"I've only just met Miss Pembrooke for the first time this morning."

"But you do like her," Stephen said, his voice smug. "That look in your eye gives you away."

Christian remained silent, content to let his friend think whatever he wanted. No need to bring up the business deal at this point. Better to let Stephen believe his desperation to win Miss Pembrooke's hand in marriage was a matter of the heart since it was something to which his friend could relate. Christian asked once again, "Will you help me?"

Stephen leaned back in his chair, and his smile broadened. "I'll have a jolly time watching this."

He nodded. "I reckon you will."

"To think I get to treat you like a servant." Stephen shook his head and laughed. "Tell you to saddle my horse, fetch my slippers."

"I'll work in the stable," Christian agreed. "But I won't fetch your slippers."

"If you work for me, you'll have to do everything you're told," Stephen proclaimed. He let out another good-natured laugh.

Christian couldn't bring himself to share in his friend's mirth. But surely both Stephen and Alice would forgive him for his haughty attitude after this. God too, hopefully.

Raising his gaze heavenward and accepting his penance with as much dignity as he could muster, he thought of Emily and the hopeful expression on her face when he'd promised to help her find employment. She was depending on him. And he would not let her down.

After a fitful night's sleep, Emily woke with a start when a firm hand touched her shoulder.

"Time for your chores," a crotchety old woman's voice commanded.

The head housekeeper.

Emily sat up and glanced about the small attic room she'd been assigned to share with three other women the night before. Climbing down the ladder of her bunk bed, she noticed them bustling about, pulling on white aprons over their black dresses. The maids had introduced themselves as Charlotte, Hester, and Phoebe, but it was the head housekeeper, Mrs. Williams, who looked at her as if she was as foolish a girl as one ever did see.

"Here's your uniform," Mrs. Williams said, handing her the traditional garments. "Cook will have a biscuit set out for your breakfast in the back room of the kitchen, but don't tarry long. They will be expecting you in the stables at six o'clock sharp."

Stables? Emily thought she must have misheard the old woman. She rubbed her eyes, realizing it was before dawn and wishing she could go back to sleep. But she did as she was told, and it wasn't until she had gone outside and Gilbert handed her a pitchfork that she realized she had heard correctly and she had been hired as a stable hand.

"Last night when you returned from speaking with the Belmonts and said they'd agreed to give us stable jobs," she said, staring at him, "I thought you meant 'stable' as in steady. Secure. I didn't think you meant we had to work in an actual horse stable!"

Gilbert shifted his jaw. "You asked if I could help find you a job, and I did."

They hadn't had much time to discuss the details. The housekeeper had come to show them to their rooms and, tired from the day's events, Emily had lain down and fallen asleep without any dinner. But she should have known better than to trust the coachman.

Turning her head, she caught the older man mucking out the stall behind them and the young boy whom she supposed to be the man's son both trying to hide a smirk.

"I am most certain that women are not allowed to do this," Emily protested.

Gilbert ran his hand affectionately down the neck of the brown horse beside them and asked, "Why not?"

"For one thing," she said, backing away and almost stumbling when the horse swung his head around toward her, "it's dangerous. These animals must weigh over two thousand pounds, and—"

"About one thousand," Gilbert corrected. "A little more for the larger ones."

"And I'm sure they bite," Emily said, watching the horse curl its lips at her. The beast was either laughing. . .or preparing to eat her whole.

"This here is Blaze," Gilbert introduced. "He's just wondering why you smell so sweet."

"But I—I don't know much about horses."

"You said you knew how to drive them."

"Driving a team and attending to their needs are not the same," she argued. After she drove a carriage, she'd hand off the reins to a stable hand to take care of the rest.

"Don't worry, I'll teach you."

Why did Gilbert have to sound so glib? "Thank you, dear *brother*, for being so helpful, but I'm sure there must be another option."

"Well. . ." Gilbert said, a glint of humor in his eyes as he gave another shrug. "I suppose you could hop a train back to Boston and beg Christian Gould to take you back."

Emily gasped. "How dare you—I would never!"

"Are you sure?"

Emily glanced over at the boy, who had leaned in to listen. She guessed him to be about twelve years of age, only slightly younger than her own brother, Thomas, which made her think of the rest of her family—and the embarrassment she must have caused them when she didn't show up at the church.

"Yes, I'm sure," she said, more to herself than Gilbert. Then, drawing in a shaky breath, she forced a smile. "Where can I find a pitchfork?"

Emily tried. She really did. She'd watched Gilbert scoop out the dirty straw, all the while holding her breath as much as possible so she wouldn't breathe in the putrid smell of horse dung. And she'd stuck her own pitchfork in, several times, and dumped the contents into the wheelbarrow. But when Stephen Belmont surprised them with an unexpected visit to "meet the new help," Emily accidently got a little too close to one of the horses, and the thousand-pound beast stepped on her foot.

The pressure lasted only an instant before the horse jumped back, but the pain accompanying the burst of shooting stars flitting across the sea of darkness before her eyes seemed eternal.

A high-pitched yelp rang in her ears. Her own? She wasn't sure, but the sound seemed vaguely familiar. Then two strong sets of hands guided her toward the doorway where she could gulp in a breath of fresh air.

"Emily, are you all right?"

Gilbert. Her dear "brother," Gilbert. She focused on his face. His handsome clean-shaven face with strong lines, a firm chin, and. . .those ever-watchful gray-green eyes.

She was also aware of another set of eyes, much darker and more of a hazel hue. The eyes of her employer, Mr. Stephen Belmont!

Alarmed that he should see her in such a state, she nodded vigorously. "I'm fine, absolutely fine. Don't worry, I can do this."

Both men looked skeptical, so she attempted a smile but burst into tears instead. "I mean," she amended, "I will be able to, just as soon as I find my pitchfork."

Luckily Mr. Belmont did not fire her on the spot. He did, however, think she was unfit for the job and had a word or two to say to Gilbert for allowing her to step foot in the stable in the first place.

"Tomorrow morning, why don't we have Emily report to the cook for kitchen duty," their employer suggested.

Emily agreed. "Thank you, Mr. Belmont. I would love to work in the kitchen."

She meant every word, but as soon as Mr. Belmont left, Gilbert leaned toward her and whispered with concern, "Have you ever worked in a kitchen?"

Emily shook her head and confided, "No, of course not. But after this, how hard could it be?"

Chapter 4

She was wrong. Working in the kitchen was every bit as hard as using a pitch-fork in the stable to muck out dung-laden straw. And the head cook turned out to be a whole lot less concerned for her well-being than Gilbert. Not to mention Emily still had her sore foot to contend with, which had turned a nasty black and blue.

During the latter part of the afternoon, her arms strained as she carried the heavy soup kettle across the kitchen.

"Stop hobbling and stand up straight," Cook shouted, "before ye spill the broth."

Too late. The kettle tipped over, and some of the chicken vegetable soup spilled onto the floor, forming a puddle around her feet.

"I'll get a mop to clean this up," Emily promised, and hurried forward.

"Careful not to slip—"

Emily's injured foot went out from beneath her. As she went down, she knocked over a pile of empty metal pans sitting on a low table in the corner. The noise was like the reverberating trill of a dozen brass cymbals as the pans toppled onto the ground around her.

Painfully scrambling to her feet, she wiped her hands on her apron. Then, meet-ing Cook's unsympathetic gaze, Emily winced, heat flaming her cheeks, and she said, "I'm—I'm so sorry."

"You'll be sorry, when I send ye to bed tonight without any supper," Cook prom-ised in her thick Irish accent. The plump red-haired woman waved a long-handled spoon at her. "What are ye doin' here anyway? You don't belong here. Especially not in my kitchen. Why don't ye go on back where ye came from instead of pretendin' to be somethin' yer not?"

For a moment, Emily thought Cook knew her secret, that she was really the daughter of a prominent Boston socialite. But that was impossible. The only one who knew the truth was Gilbert, and if he'd said anything, no one would believe him. What proper lady would ever follow her coachman into the rural mountains of western Massachusetts to willingly become a servant and put herself under the direction of someone like Cook?

"Now look what ye done!" Cook rushed over to the oven to fan away a pillar of smoke. "You've distracted me from lookin' after supper for the mister and missus."

A faint gasp turned Emily's head toward the open doorway, where a tall blond woman in an elegant pink evening gown with enormous leg-of-mutton puffed sleeves stepped back out of sight. With an inward groan, Emily realized she must be Mrs. Belmont, who would be certain to tell her husband that the new kitchen maid was to blame when the food on their plates arrived seasoned with black char.

"Quit yer dawdling. Clean up yer mess, and be quick about it," squalled the cook.

Emily had never felt so inept. When attending Mrs. Porter's Finishing School, she'd been at the top of her class. She'd been taught to believe that she could become a woman of great value and make a difference in the world. Her Aunt Rebecca in England had also encouraged her to dream and believe in herself, and trusted her implicitly with the care of the children. Even in church Emily had been told there was a God in heaven who valued her enough to send His Son Jesus to die for her and redeem her soul.

If only she'd trust in Him and the plans He had for her.

His plans. When she'd run from the altar, had she substituted God's plans for her life with her own? Was it a lack of faith in God's ability to work everything out that had landed her in the position she found herself in now?

She hadn't prayed in a very long while. Not a real prayer. But when Cook kept her word and sent Emily away without any supper, she got down on her knees beside the flower garden and bowed her head.

"Now what are ye doin'?" Cook's harsh voice intruded. "Get up off the ground before ye soil yer skirt. Mrs. Belmont has requested ye bring a tray of food to her private parlor."

"Yes ma'am," Emily replied, and hurried to do Cook's bidding, her prayer unspoken.

Emily entered Mrs. Belmont's lavish parlor and set the tray of freshly baked chicken, potatoes, and carrots onto the marble table while trying to ignore the hunger pangs aroused by the food's savory aroma.

"Would you like anything else?" Emily asked. The slim woman looked no older than herself. A reminder that she could be living in such luxury if she hadn't run from her groom.

"Yes," Mrs. Belmont said with a nod, and smiled. "I'd like for you to sit down."

Emily glanced at the empty chair beside her. "I—I'm afraid I do not understand."

"The food is for you. I overheard what Cook said to you earlier, and one of the other maids confirmed you've had nothing to eat."

"It's my own fault," Emily said with a shake of her head. "Cook was right. I'm not much help in the kitchen, and I deserved her wrath."

"No one deserves her wrath," Mrs. Belmont confided. "The only reason we keep her is because my father-in-law adores her apple pies. Now sit down and eat before she sees you. Cook would be quite angry if she knew who the food was really for."

Christian retrieved a brush from the stable, then crouched down near the outside well pump to scrub the horses' water buckets.

"You're doing it all wrong," Martin informed him. The twelve-year-old handed him a different brush. "This one will clean the slime off better."

Martin Fuller had been showing him what to do all day, and to Christian's frustration, the small, skinny stableboy could wash buckets, muck stalls, and do almost everything in and around the stables better and faster than he could.

To make matters worse, the boy's father, the stable master, had assigned so many chores there hadn't been any time yet today to speak to Emily. And it was almost dusk.

Richard Fuller walked over and narrowed his gaze upon him. "Where did you say you came from?"

"Boston," Christian replied, scrubbing the bucket with the new brush. Martin was right. It did help.

"You've never tended horses before though, have you?"

Christian shrugged. "I've helped."

"*Helped*." Richard's dark, bushy brows drew together in a tight line. "Earlier you didn't know how to harness Mr. Belmont's team of horses to the carriage."

He could tack up a single horse well enough, but to fasten the straps and buckles that harness *four* horses together had been an unsurmountable challenge.

"I will learn," Christian promised.

Richard continued to scowl. "Your hands are too smooth to be a stable hand."

The Fullers had been hired just three months earlier and did not know him. Christian hoped to keep it that way. The less they knew, the less they could tell Emily.

"I might not have your experience," he told the stout little man, "but I need this job."

Finally, the hard look on Richard's face eased. "Don't we all. This recession has even the rich running scared."

Christian thought of Emily—and himself. "Yes, it does."

"Though I reckon there will still be a fair amount of them coming to the Belmont ball this weekend," Richard said, handing him another water bucket. "That's why we need every horse and carriage stall scrubbed down. We need to get ready for the incoming guests."

Ball?

Christian hurried through the rest of his chores, then found Mr. Norris and asked him to send a message to Stephen. Twenty minutes later, Stephen met him outside behind the garden shed.

"You didn't tell me you were having a ball," Christian exploded. "Who's invited?"

Stephen gave him a mischievous grin. "A few of the Vanderbilts, Cabots, Lowells, Astors, and about two dozen other families you know."

"Is this how you think to help me?"

"I had no choice," Stephen said, lowering his voice. "Mrs. Langhorne specifically asked if we could host a ball for her cousin's birthday."

"Why can't she host her own ball?" Christian demanded.

"She said she's having her summerhouse remodeled. Although I suspect that isn't quite true. She approached me last spring and said it was a pity that Alice and I had not been invited to more parties since we married."

Christian frowned. The wealthy were fickle in their friendships, and when Stephen had married beneath him, they hadn't taken kindly to Alice, just as he had warned him.

"I think Mrs. Langhorne desires to help us," Stephen admitted. "She knows that with her presence, the others will come and will have to accept Alice as one of their own. After such a grand gesture, I couldn't possibly refuse. Besides, think of what this means to Alice."

"I'm sorry," Christian said, a knot forming in his throat. "I too should have stood up to them. I should have defended you. . .and Alice from those vicious vultures. Now I suppose they will shun Emily too when they discover she isn't sick after all, but ran away."

"And here I thought you would be more worried about yourself," Stephen mused.

"This isn't funny," Christian said, his stomach turning. "What if someone recognizes us?"

"They won't," Stephen promised. "I sent word to Mrs. Langhorne the morning after you arrived and asked her if we might host a *masquerade* ball. Everyone will be in masks. Even our staff."

Christian released his breath. "Thank you."

"Don't thank me," Stephen said, giving him a direct look. "Thank Alice. The masks were her idea."

Christian finally got a chance to speak to Emily just before the staff retired for bed. He'd spied her standing on the far side of the stone terrace overlooking a view of the Housatonic River.

His heart lifted when she turned to face him. Her long dark hair, which he had only seen upswept, now fell to her shoulders in waves, giving her face a softer look. More vulnerable. Unless that was due to the tiredness that surrounded her eyes.

"How was your day?" he greeted.

"Not very good, I'm afraid." She gave him a rueful look and showed him the palms of her hands. "I've got blisters."

Grinning, he turned over his own hands. "Me too."

"I will never take any of my servants for granted ever again," she vowed.

Christian nodded. "Nor I."

She gave him a curious look. "What?"

With a jolt, he realized his blunder. "I meant, we should value those around us."

"Oh yes," she said. "Of course."

He gave her a sidelong look, admiring her beauty. Hoping to see her smile, because she truly had a wonderful smile, he teased, "Surely you had better luck in the kitchen than you did in the stable?"

"I'm afraid not," she said, releasing a sigh. "Cook doesn't want me, and Mrs. Williams, the head housekeeper, doesn't want me either. I overheard Mrs. Belmont tell Mrs. Williams that I am to work with the maids tomorrow, and when she protested, Mrs. Belmont responded by saying, 'Goodness sakes! How can she possibly mess up changing the bedsheets?' Too bad the Belmonts do not have any children. I know I could be a good governess."

"We should leave at once," he told her. "We can find employment elsewhere."

"You would come with me?" she asked, her eyes wide. "Why?"

"The Belmonts are having a ball this weekend, and several prominent families will be in attendance. You and I can leave before any of them show up."

"Don't worry, Gilbert. No one will recognize us. The maids tell me it is to be a masquerade ball."

"You could still be recognized," he warned her. "We could go somewhere else, slip back into Boston—"

"Is that what you want?" she challenged. "To go back to work for Mr. Gould?"

He'd very much like to go back to work *as* Mr. Gould.

"I would like to try to protect your reputation," he said honestly.

Emily frowned. "I thank you for your assistance, Mr. Lawrence, but I do not need you to protect me, nor do I intend to leave this beautiful place."

"I thought you said the cook and the housekeeper do not want you here."

"They don't," Emily admitted. "But in the days ahead I am determined to show them I can be of value. Besides, I think I have made a new friend."

Christian smiled. "Me?"

"No," she said, shaking her head, then blushed. "Though, I suppose we are now friends. However, I was referring to Alice."

"Alice?"

"Mrs. Belmont," Emily clarified. "When she learned the cook did not allow me any dinner, she had a special meal prepared for me. She's so. . .very kind."

Christian suppressed an inward groan. Now he truly would have to thank her.

And pray her idea of wearing masks to hide their identities worked.

Chapter 5

Emily spent the next three days helping the other maids, Charlotte, Hester, and Phoebe, clean curtains, sweep floors, and polish furniture, all in preparation for Friday night's ball. The morning of the big event, the housekeeper had them changing all the bedsheets.

"Faster, Emily," Mrs. Williams exclaimed. "There is other work to be done after this."

"Yes, ma'am."

Emily pulled the sheets off the beds in the next three rooms and stuffed them into the laundry basket. Then she took the basket down the stairs to the head laundress for washing, picked up another basket of linens, and headed back up the stairs to remake the beds before the housekeeper could yell at her again.

Thankfully, Charlotte, the maid who bunked beneath her in the attic loft, offered to help.

"I'll tuck in this end if you tuck that one," Emily said, nodding toward the opposite side of the four-poster guest bed.

Charlotte nodded, but before Emily could fold the embroidered hem of the linen sheet under the mattress, the maid let out a startled shriek. "Emily, these sheets are dirty."

Emily's gaze fell upon the dark soiled smudge on the pillow case, and she realized Charlotte was right.

Pulling the other linens from the basket, Charlotte exclaimed, "All of the sheets in this basket are dirty."

"I must have picked up the wrong basket," Emily whispered, her body tense.

Hester and Phoebe poked their heads through the doorway.

"Did someone scream?" Hester asked.

Before Emily could respond, Phoebe spotted the soiled sheet in her hand and demanded, "What are you doing in here? I already changed the sheets in these rooms. Where are the *clean* sheets I put on the beds?"

Emily stared at her. "I—I guess they were the sheets I took down to the laundress."

"Hurry, Emily," Charlotte urged. "You must find the clean sheets before they are re-washed, or they won't dry in time and there won't be enough for all the beds tonight!"

Her heart racing, Emily sped back down the stairs, through the kitchen, and into the laundry room where the head laundress and two of her assistants stood beside the porcelain oblong tubs, their hands in the water.

"Excuse me," Emily interrupted. "It seems there has been a mistake. Where is the basket I brought down here a few minutes ago?"

The laundress and her assistants glanced at one another, then the head laundress nodded toward the long table on the other side of the room beside the stove with the various heating irons. "The basket is over there."

Emily rushed to the basket but discovered it was empty. Turning back around, she asked, "And the sheets?"

"Right here," one of the assistants said, pulling a wad of the wet white fabric out of the water in her tub.

"Oh no." Emily's stomach clenched. "What am I going to do?"

"I'll tell you what you can do," Mrs. Williams stormed, entering the room behind her. "You can pack your bags and find a different place of employment!"

Tears filled Emily's eyes as she went back up the stairs to say goodbye to Charlotte, Hester, and Phoebe. She'd done her best over the past week to fit in, but it seemed she wasn't cut out to perform any of the tasks she usually took for granted. Tasks performed by others. Was she so helpless that she could do nothing but marry and rely on other people to serve her needs? She'd expected more of herself. She'd hoped she could learn. But in the end, she was nothing but a failure.

On her way down the upstairs hall, she paused by the open door of Alice Belmont's dressing room. The woman sat in a chair with a mirror in her hand and a distinct look of dissatisfaction on her face. A young maid Emily wasn't familiar with was trying to style Alice's beautiful blond locks, but instead of elegance, the flowers pinned into the upswept coiffure stuck out at odd angles like straw out of a scarecrow.

"I'm sorry, miss," the girl whimpered in a shrill voice. "I'll start over."

"Please do," Alice told her. "Perhaps you could try a simple wreath of flowers instead?"

Emily thought of her own hairstyle a week before, the day she was to marry

Christian Gould. She'd wanted to wear a wreath of daisies and tiny white roses threaded with strings of pearls atop her head as she walked down the aisle, but her mother had argued that it would interfere with the placement of her veil.

Emily knew she should continue on her way but hesitated a moment more as she watched the maid attempt to rework the flowers. Clearly, the young woman was doing it all wrong.

Stepping through the doorway, Emily asked, "Can I help?"

"I do not know how to make a wreath," the maid admitted.

"I do," Emily assured her and looked at Alice. "May I?"

Alice looked surprised to see her but nodded. And within a half hour, Emily had not only created a simple but elegant floral wreath, but had fastened it atop Alice's blond curls using a set of sapphire-studded combs.

"Beautiful," Stephen Belmont said, coming in through the adjoining room, his eyes shining with approval.

Alice smiled. "She did a marvelous job, did she not?"

"I'll tell you what she did!" Mrs. Williams stormed into the room from the hallway, then stopped short when she saw Stephen. "Pardon me, Mr. Belmont, for my intrusion, but I wish to speak to Mrs. Belmont about the. . .new addition to our staff."

The housekeeper gave Emily a haughty look, and for a moment Emily wished she'd taken Gilbert up on his offer to leave when she'd had the chance.

"I would like to speak to you too, Mrs. Williams," Alice replied. "I do not believe Emily is suited for the work she has been assigned."

"I couldn't agree with you more," Mrs. Williams said, nodding.

"From this moment on," Alice announced, another smile touching her lips, "Emily will assume a new role—if it pleases her. She is to be my own personal lady's maid."

Emily's spirits lifted. She'd do anything to stay at Maple Glen. And who better to recommend the latest fashion trends than another lady? One who had just come back from London, no less, where many of the styles originated. Why, the position was perfect!

Christian knew he'd have to work hard if he chose to keep up the role of coachman. More than once he'd bitten his tongue and swallowed his pride this week just so he could stay close to Emily and get to know her. But he had not anticipated having to endure the wrath of the head stable master.

"Who do you think you are?" the irate man demanded. "You think you're too good to shovel manure like the rest of us? Where were you yesterday when you were supposed to be helping my boy and the other stable hands with the stalls?"

He'd been talking with Emily. He hadn't meant to ditch his duties, but when he'd seen her by the wood-slatted fence beating the dust out of a rug with a broom, he couldn't help himself. He needed to hear her voice. Watch her smile. See her look at him with appreciation for who he was instead of how much money he was worth.

He hadn't been disappointed. But he had neglected to finish his chores.

"I have half a mind to speak to Mr. Belmont and have you fired," Richard Fuller continued. "But we need every stable hand on duty tonight as the carriages come in."

Christian nodded. "I won't let you down."

However, later that evening after the ball was in full swing, Mr. Norris came down to the carriage house to inform him that Emily had been recruited to serve punch, and Christian feared he might have to break that promise.

"She's off to the side of the main ballroom," the old butler said, the tight lines around his mouth betraying his worry. "And she's wearing a mask like the other staff. But she doesn't look like the other staff."

Christian motioned the butler outside, took a quick glance around to ensure they were alone, and asked, "How so?"

"The graceful way she moves gives her away."

"Has anyone else noticed?"

"Not yet," Mr. Norris assured him. "But I fear it's only a matter of time."

Christian scowled and his fingers clenched the leather horse bridle he realized he still held in his hand. "Who assigned Emily to work the refreshment table?"

"The housekeeper. I told Mrs. Williams not to, but she insisted they were short-handed. But I think the woman wants Emily exposed. . .so she'll have to leave."

A stone's throw away, Richard Fuller emerged out of the shadowed entrance of the carriage house, and with a jolt of alarm, Christian wondered how much the man had overheard. Apparently enough to guess "Gilbert Lawrence" wasn't who he said he was. The stable master stepped toward him with a new look of understanding in his eyes, took the bridle out of his hands, and with a simple nod toward the big house, said, "Go."

Christian didn't hesitate. Hurrying across the lawn, he entered the main house through the servants' entrance, borrowed a black mask from one of the kitchen staff, and made his way into the grand ballroom.

At least thirty couples, dressed to the hilt in their frock coats and stylish ball gowns, were on the dance floor, blocking the path between him and Emily. He paused on the outskirts of the spectacle, judging whether he should weave his way around the musicians or cut through those conversing with one another on the other side of the room.

He spotted Stephen and Alice, unmistakable with their matching white swan feathered masks, and chose the latter, hoping they would be easier to slip past than the dozen or so violinists and other members of the orchestra. Stephen gave him a curious look as he went by, but Christian managed to dodge most of the attendees, until one woman with a dark blue feathered mask covering the upper half of her face stopped him in his tracks.

"Christian Gould?"

He recognized her voice at once. The soft teasing tone of Nancy Langhorne, who at just seventeen had turned quite a few heads with both her beauty and her wit at recent social gatherings. She'd also taken a fancy to him, during the months preceding his engagement to Miss Pembrooke. Of all the people at the ball, of course she would be the one to catch him.

Careful to keep his voice low, he asked, "How did you recognize me?"

"You move your jaw from side to side whenever you're frustrated," the young woman confided. "A dead giveaway, despite the mask, the clean shave, and your inadequate attire."

Christian followed her gaze and glanced down at his work trousers and casual waistcoat, then swallowed hard, unable to avoid the truth.

He'd been caught.

Emily helped two other maids serve drinks at the refreshment table in the west wing and tapped her foot in time with the music, yearning for the first time since arriving at the Belmont estate to join in the upper-class festivities. She loved music and dancing more than any other form of entertainment and hadn't realized how much she missed it—until this night.

She wondered if the servants ever had the opportunity to dance, perhaps outside in the moonlight. Or in the garden overlooking the river. The night before, while dressing for bed, Charlotte had said that if the opportunity arose, she wouldn't mind dancing with Richard Fuller. The other maids had giggled, but if Emily were to dance with someone—well, the only one she could think of to be her partner was Gilbert.

The other men at Maple Glen were not nearly as handsome nor half as jovial as the coachman she'd accompanied from Boston. Yes, if the opportunity arose, she'd dance with Gilbert. Although that wasn't likely to happen this night. Most of the guests would not be retiring from the festivities until well past midnight, and neither would she. For the next several hours she'd be stuck serving punch and forced to listen to more drab talk from the men discussing the economic downturn, the J. P. Morgan bailout the year before, and the upcoming presidential election.

But her interest perked up when three young ladies came to her table for a cup of punch.

"I hope he asks me to dance," one of the women squealed under her breath. "He's so handsome, and worth millions."

"Gertrude!" the lady beside her exclaimed. "The man is still engaged!"

"He wasn't expected to be here," whispered the third. "He wore a mask, but everyone knows these masks can't really hide who you are. I overheard him speaking to Nancy Langhorne. I must say, I wouldn't mind a dance with him myself."

"Who?" asked another woman joining them.

The first three women smiled as they chorused, "Christian Gould."

With a gasp that turned the heads of all four women, Emily dropped the ladle back into the punch bowl, splashing droplets of red juice in every direction. Repulsed by the splatter and fearful the juice would stain their elegant evening gowns, the group of women departed her table at once. That left Emily free to step out from her position and search the masked faces of the couples filling the massive ballroom.

He was here?

Trembling, she wondered what she would do if Christian Gould came to her table. Would the mask truly be enough to hide her identity? It certainly hadn't been enough to hide his. She couldn't take the chance. She had to leave. She had to find Gilbert.

Emily turned and had not taken two steps when she ran right into him. "Gilbert, he's here! Christian Gould is here!"

"I know," Gilbert said, taking her arm. "Let's get you out of the public eye."

"If I leave my post, I could be fired," Emily exclaimed. Her heart raced as she drew in a couple quick, shallow breaths. "But if I stay, Christian Gould may overhear someone call me by name and recognize me from the photographed portrait I sent him."

"You're safe with me," Gilbert promised. "I won't let anyone find out who you are."

"Rumors could spread," she continued, as he led her into the coatroom. "They'd wonder what I'm doing here, why I ran from the church, why I couldn't marry for money."

"I will not let them ruin your reputation."

Emily looked up into his gray-green eyes, drawing comfort from his words, his calm assurance, and realized how much she'd come to rely on him over the past week. . .how much taller he was than her. . .how close they now stood together.

"Thank you, Gil," she said, as he took hold of her hand. "If I ever do marry, I'll marry for—"

Gilbert nodded, lifted the mask up over his head to reveal his face, and with one of the most tender looks of understanding Emily had ever seen, he said, "Love."

The word hung between them, pulling them even closer together. . .

Until Stephen Belmont burst into the coatroom.

Raising his brows, their employer gave each of them a startled look, then his hushed voice spat, "What the devil are you doing in here?"

Chapter 6

Emily's stomach wrenched tight as Mr. Belmont led her and Gilbert into his study. Gilbert didn't seem as concerned as she was that they might be fired. Maybe because with his connections it would be much easier for him than for her to get another job. She waited until their employer closed the door and then clasped her hands together and decided to plunge right in with an apology.

"Mr. Belmont, forgive us for abandoning our posts, especially at such a prestigious event as your lovely ball. It was very wrong. I'm so sorry."

Stephen smirked and shot a look at Gilbert. "There had been some talk about where you were, which, I must admit, concerned me. That is why I came looking for you. But I think I was even more surprised by what I saw when I found you in the coatroom."

Heat seared her cheeks. "That was my fault, sir, not his."

"Oh?" Mr. Belmont asked, as if mildly amused. "Enlighten me."

"I—I had been under duress, and Gilbert was kind enough to assure me that everything was going to be all right."

"We were talking," Gilbert added. "Nothing more."

"Nothing more?" Mr. Belmont countered, arching his brow. "The way you were looking at her seemed like more than 'brotherly affection' to me."

Gilbert's jaw shifted to the left as he narrowed his gaze on the man. But there was no sense denying it. Mr. Belmont was right. They hadn't been upfront about who they were—or about what might have happened if he hadn't interrupted. Emily was convinced that if they had stayed in the coatroom a moment more, Gilbert would have kissed her.

"We aren't brother and sister," Emily confessed, and hung her head. "I'm sorry to have led you to believe otherwise."

"You came to me looking for employment under false pretenses," Mr. Belmont accused. "However, because of your expertise in styling my wife's hair this evening and helping her look absolutely radiant for our guests, I suppose I can forgive you."

Emily released her breath. "Thank you, sir."

"You can wait upstairs until Mrs. Belmont needs further assistance," he instructed. "But Gilbert, I'd like to have an additional word with you if I may—in private."

Emily tensed as she glanced at Gilbert, then back at Mr. Belmont. "Surely you will let Gilbert stay too?"

Mr. Belmont smiled. "Yes, Emily. Gilbert can stay too. If he behaves himself."

Christian waited by the threshold of the study until he was sure Emily had left, then closed the door and marched back across the room. "Did you have to embarrass her?"

"I doubt she was overly embarrassed," Stephen mused. "She was too busy defending you."

"She does seem to take a proactive approach to getting what she wants."

Stephen broke into a smile. "So do you. Never in my lifetime did I ever think to see you go to such extremes for the sake of a woman."

"Emily is not just any woman," Christian insisted, taking a seat in front of his friend's desk. "She's a Pembrooke."

The night before, Christian had finally filled Stephen in on the details of the original agreement he'd made with Emily and her family.

Stephen nodded. "Ah yes, she has the old English name you need for acceptance into the railroad investment. What if I told you there was another way?"

"What do you mean?"

Stephen walked around the other side of the desk, withdrew a telegram from a drawer, and handed it over. "This came for you this morning."

The message had come from Christian's father in Boston. With a sense of foreboding, he read:

I'VE SPOKEN TO MR. JAMES WINTHROP, A DIRECT DESCENDANT OF THE ENGLISH WINTHROPS, WHOSE ANCESTRY CAN BE TRACED BACK TO THE SIXTEENTH CENTURY, *Stop* HIS DAUGHTER, MISS MARY WINTHROP, WOULD BE MOST AGREEABLE TO ACCEPT YOUR PROPOSAL OF MARRIAGE UPON YOUR IMMEDIATE RETURN, *Stop* THE REVEREND ASSURES ME THE CEREMONY CAN TAKE PLACE WITHIN THE WEEK, THUS ALLOWING US TO MOVE FORWARD WITH THE RAILROAD INVESTMENT BY THE APPROACHING DEADLINE, *Stop*

Christian squeezed his eyes shut, trying to quell the unease gathering in the back of his mind, then looked at Stephen.

"So you see," his friend said with a mischievous smile, "you are free to return to Boston at once and marry a woman who can give you everything you want."

Christian shook his head, his throat tight. "Not everything."

Stephen's smile widened into a grin. "Yes, well, the new bride may not champion your rights to employment like Miss Pembrooke, but if you gain access into the league of investors behind the railroad deal, you'll never have to work another day in your life."

"You know I've never been averse to a little hard work," Christian said, leaning back in his chair. "Helping Mr. Fuller and his son in the stable the last few days has made me remember how much I used to love sneaking out to help our grooms with the horses as a boy. Although the exertion is more than I'm used to, being outdoors most of the day is a far cry better than being cooped up behind my desk negotiating contracts."

"I thought we agreed your employment here would be temporary," Stephen teased.

"And I thought you promised Miss Pembrooke you wouldn't fire me," Christian said, dropping the telegram back on the desk.

"And what of Miss Winthrop?" Stephen taunted. "Think of all you could gain. . ."

Christian leaned forward in his chair. "Remember what you said when I told you that you had nothing to gain by marrying Alice?"

Stephen nodded. "I said I had *everything* to gain. Without her, nothing made sense."

Christian gave him a direct look. "That's how I feel about Emily."

"Be careful," Stephen warned, "or she'll steal more than just the reins away from you. She'll steal your heart."

Christian laughed. "I'm afraid she already has."

"And your father?"

Christian nodded toward the paper on the desk. "Please send a return telegram with my thanks for his trouble in seeking another arrangement, but that I will have to decline."

After Stephen took his leave to return to the ball, Christian lingered in the hallway as he thought about how disappointed his parents would be if he lost the railroad investment. His family might have to sell off the summer home, but their overall net worth wouldn't dip more than they could handle. And with a woman like Emily by his side, Christian was sure that in the future he'd be inspired to create a few new deals of his own.

All he needed was Emily.

And to thank Alice for befriending her. He'd put off facing Alice long enough, and now he deemed it time to set things right. He found the blond woman, her white swan mask removed, at the bottom of the stairwell preparing to ascend the steps to her room.

"Mrs. Belmont, may I have a word?" Christian asked as he approached.

She hesitated, as if unsure whether he could be trusted, for which he was truly sorry. Then she nodded and lifted her chin in confidence. "You may."

"I would like to humbly offer my sincerest apologies and beg your forgiveness for the manner in which I reacted to your marriage to my dearest friend last spring. I have never seen Stephen happier, and I credit that all to you."

Alice's expression relaxed as she smiled. "Thank you. I appreciate you saying so. It grieved Stephen a great deal for the two of you to be at odds all these months, and I know he is happy to have you and Miss Pembrooke here visiting us."

"If only it truly were a social call," Christian said, lowering his voice. "I am grateful for your insistence the staff wear masks at the ball, and for befriending Emily and taking her in as your personal lady's maid."

"It's been a pleasure to make her acquaintance," Alice confided. "I do hope everything works out in your favor."

"As do I," Christian said with a grin.

And to show he truly held no further ill-will between them, he bent forward and kissed her gloved hand before saying goodnight.

Just when she thought God cared about her. . . Just when she thought He had brought her to this place to fulfill her dreams to find a husband she could truly love. . . Just when she had begun to imagine that man might be Gilbert. . .

Emily stepped out onto the upstairs balcony, looked down, and saw Gilbert kiss another woman's hand!

She shook her head, berating herself for being a fool. She should have known better. Hadn't she learned by now that the only one she could count on to look out for her was herself? That's why she needed to take control, make her own way.

Except she'd just done her best to convince Mr. Belmont to allow them to stay and feared Gilbert was going to get caught and change Mr. Belmont's mind. *I won't let him ruin it*, she vowed.

After helping Alice out of her ball gown, Emily crept downstairs, marched down to the carriage house beside the stables, and knocked on the door to what she thought was Gilbert's sleeping quarters.

Martin answered the door instead.

"I'm sorry to awaken you," Emily told the sleepy-eyed boy. "I was looking for Gilbert. Have you seen him?"

The boy's father appeared in the doorway behind his son and pointed. "Behind you."

As they closed the door, Emily spun around, and indeed there he was, his magnificent tall frame outlined in the moonlight as he strutted across the lawn from the big house with his gait as suave as a peacock.

"Where have you been?" she demanded.

Gilbert let out a low chuckle. "Do I detect a note of impatience?"

"Yes, I'm impatient," Emily scolded. "I've been working all day and night. I'm tired, and I want to go to bed like everyone else around here but can't sleep a wink until I set things straight between us."

"Emily," he said in a low, husky voice. "Is this about what happened in the coatroom?"

"No, this isn't about the coatroom!" she exclaimed. "It's about your overt hand kissing with Mrs. Belmont at the bottom of the stairwell. What if Mr. Belmont had walked in and seen you like I did? After I pleaded with him to let us stay?"

"Is your job the only thing that concerns you?" he asked, his tone tinged with amusement.

Why would he be amused?

"Of course, I'm concerned about my job. What else should I be concerned about?"

Christian took a step closer. "For a moment, it sounded as if you might be just the tiniest bit jealous."

"Why on earth would I be jealous?" she said, wrapping her arms across her chest. "That's ridiculous."

"Yes," Gilbert agreed, the humor still in his voice. "Because Alice and I are just friends."

"I thought you said the upper and lower classes do not mix," Emily reminded him. "Why would she want to be friends with a mere coachman?"

"Why would you?" Gilbert retorted, reminding her that she was also a lady of the upper class.

Or had been.

Gilbert laughed, a deep throaty laugh, as if he were enjoying himself. "Emily, remember I told you I had friends at the Belmont estate? Alice is one of those friends."

"She was your 'connection' that helped get us the jobs?" Emily asked. "I thought it was the butler."

Gilbert nodded. "Mr. Norris is a friend too."

"I don't understand," Emily said, shaking her head. "How did you all meet?"

"Both Mr. Norris and I were here a couple of years ago when Alice worked as a maid," Gilbert explained.

Emily gasped. "Alice was a maid? Then she understands what it is like to have to work. That must be why she is so nice to me."

"And it was because she was nice to you that I kissed her hand," Gilbert said, his voice warm. "To thank her."

Emily smiled. "And here I thought you were an amorous philanderer like Christian Gould."

"Christian Gould is no more a philanderer than I am," Gilbert assured her. "During the festivities of the ball tonight, I learned that Mr. Gould received an offer to marry another woman with the old English name he needs to cinch the railroad deal. . .and he turned it down."

Emily frowned. "My father said that deal meant everything to him. Why would he turn it down?"

"He's still hoping to marry you."

"But he hasn't heard from me. He doesn't know where I am." She thought of his sudden appearance at the Belmont ball. "Does he?"

"He may," Gilbert admitted.

"I didn't think of it before, but he could have checked the passenger lists for the outbound trains. However, that still doesn't explain. . . Why me?"

"Maybe he sees something in you he doesn't see in anyone else."

Emily shook her head. "We never met."

"Surely you corresponded?" he asked.

"A few letters only."

"If he turned down marriage with another woman," Gilbert said, his expression earnest, "in hopes that you might return to Boston with a change of heart, then he must have seen more in your letters than you realized."

"I can't imagine what."

"I do," Gilbert said, taking her hand in his. "You see people for who they are. You always try your best, are willing to stand up for others, and are certainly not afraid to voice your opinions or take control when you deem it necessary. You value love over money. . .and friendship over social status. . .or you'd never be standing here speaking to me."

"Or. . .the reason for our friendship may be because. . .I am no longer a true lady," Emily confessed. "We're both working-class citizens."

"You'll always be a true lady to me," Gilbert told her. "Even if you do get a little jealous and refuse to admit it."

She would have laughed, except the tone of his voice was so sincere it made her feel as if they were back in the coatroom, and her pulse kicked up a notch.

"I suppose I might have been a little jealous," she conceded. "You've never kissed my hand."

Gilbert grinned, then giving her a look that shot heat up into her cheeks, he grasped her fingers and raised them to his lips.

Chapter 7

After working around the clock to ensure the ball was a success for the Belmonts and their guests, the majority of the staff had been graciously allowed to sleep until nearly noon the next day.

Except for Christian, who had been told by the stable master that he had to tend to the horses' morning feed. He didn't mind, as he couldn't sleep much anyway after his discussion with Emily the night before.

She'd seen him kiss Alice's hand—and she'd been jealous. Other women had been jealous over him before. Sometimes he would be speaking to a woman and another would drop her handkerchief right in front of him, hoping he'd pick it up. Or several ladies at once would bat their eyes at him above their fans to fight for his attention. Or they might try to trick him into a dance, insisting he'd promised each of them at an earlier event when he'd done no such thing.

But not one of them had cared about *him*, only his bank account and rich estate. And in his younger years, he'd had his heart broken more than once when he'd ventured to think otherwise. But Emily did not believe he had so much as a penny tied to his name. And she liked him anyway. She liked him enough to be jealous when she thought he'd been flirting with another woman. Which meant she truly cared—at least a little.

His heart beat with rapid anticipation as he performed his chores. The Belmonts had given the entire staff the afternoon off to go on a picnic with the leftover food from the ball. And there was nothing he'd like better than to spend time along the shore of the lake with Emily and do his best to win her whole heart.

The carriages arrived at Stockbridge Bowl, also known as Lake Mahkeenac, at two thirty. The Bowl was surrounded by the sloping hills of the Taconic Range to the west and north, the Berkshire Hills to the east, and Monument Mountain seven miles to the south. Not only was it a great place for picnics, but for swimming and boating as well.

Christian tethered the team of horses to the hitching post and then helped

Emily, the housekeeper, and the three other maids alight from the carriage steps so they wouldn't trip over their long A-line skirts. The stable master and his son had driven another carriage carrying the head cook and laundress and their assistants. And another stable hand drove the carriage with Mr. Norris, the gardeners, and a few of the other staff, making it a grand party indeed.

By the time all the food had been set out on blankets, Christian was famished. The meal consisted of roast beef, Cornish game hen, slices of homemade bread, cheese, and fruit, all of which he'd eaten before, but never had anything tasted so good. Nor had the music ever been more delightful to his ears. For instead of an orchestra, they had Emily, who had brought along a wooden flute given to her by a traveling musician when she'd stayed at her aunt and uncle's home in England.

As she played, the maids clapped in time to the rhythm, and even the house-keeper broke into a smile, making it clear that Emily had won everyone's hearts, including his own.

One song in particular, a soft, lilting melody that fit right in with the beauty of the green lawn leading down to the edge of the lake, the sparkles of sunshine reflected on the clear blue water, and the rise of the hills towering over the tops of the trees dotting the distant shore had even the cook humming along.

The old woman wiped tears from her eyes and said, "That was my favorite song when I was a young girl. My mother used to sing it in the kitchen when she baked."

Emily's face lit up as Mr. Norris also added his praise. "My granddaughter told me she wants a flute for Christmas," he said. "I tried to whittle her one, but I couldn't get the holes lined up right."

"Give her this one," Emily offered.

The old butler shook his head. "Oh no, dear, I couldn't."

"I have two," she insisted. "I'd be thrilled to know I've made your granddaughter happy by giving her one of them."

Mr. Norris gave her the biggest smile Christian had ever seen as he took the flute and gave her a slight bow. "Thank you for your kindness."

Christian had been told Mrs. Norris had passed away, but he never knew the man he referred to as a friend had a granddaughter. In fact, now that he thought about it, he didn't know very much about him at all. Even after all the times Mr. Norris had helped him and Stephen whenever they managed to get themselves into trouble. With a pang of guilt, Christian realized he needed to take lessons from Emily and learn to be more giving instead of always being concerned about what he could gain.

"Is there anything you miss from your life in Boston that you don't have here?" Christian asked when he'd finally managed to pull her away from the others.

She stood with him by the water's edge watching young Martin row out into the middle of the lake, and smiled. "I do miss chocolate. I saw trays of chocolate candies at the ball but didn't dare take one. They were for guests only."

"I would have snatched one for you if you had asked," Christian declared, to which she laughed.

"I wouldn't have wanted to get you in trouble!"

"You could have had all the finest chocolates you wanted if you'd married Christian Gould," he teased.

"Last night you said he gave up another offer of marriage hoping I might return, even though in doing so he would miss out on his opportunity to invest in the new railroad. But I want more than chocolates. . . . Do you think that is selfish?"

"No," he assured her. "That's not selfish. That's smart. Stephen and Alice married for love, and look how happy they are."

"They do seem happy, but you should not speak of them so informally," she scolded. "Even if Alice is your friend."

"Did you know that Christian Gould is also their friend?"

"That would explain why he was at the ball," Emily said with a nod. "In addition to possibly wanting to find me."

"His family has a house in the Berkshires as well." Taking a thin gold telescope from his pocket, he extended the lens and handed it to her. "Over there on the opposite shore," he said, pointing. "Do you see that big white house with the black shutters and sprawling green lawn?"

She lifted the telescope to her eye. "Yes."

"That's Ridgeview."

"It reminds me of my aunt and uncle's place in England," she said softly. "All six of their children would be running all over that lawn. Another reason I didn't marry Christian Gould is because I heard he didn't want children."

"That's not true," Gilbert said, aghast that such rumors had been circulating. "He does want children. He's just been too busy to settle down."

"I wonder if he is there right now," Emily mused.

"You weren't the only one with doubts before the wedding, Emily. Christian Gould had doubts too. . . ."

"I don't want to talk about Mr. Gould," she said, dropping the telescope to look at him. "Tell me something about you. Are both your parents living, Gil?"

"Yes," he assured her. "Living and trying to pressure me about as much as your parents have been pressuring you."

Emily frowned. "What are your parents pressuring you to do?"

"Same as you. Get married."

"I sent my first earnings from Mr. Belmont to my father the day before yesterday," she confided. "And let my family know where I am staying. I pray they are not angry with me. I do miss them and hope to receive a return telegram soon."

"Are you sure you don't want to go back to Boston?" he asked, studying her worried expression.

She raised the telescope to her eye one more time and looked out across the lake. "No, I believe I could happily stay here for—Gil! Look!"

Emily thrust the telescope into his hands and pointed, but he didn't need a telescope to see that Martin's small rowboat was half sunk and the boy was in the water waving his arms for help.

Christian glanced about and saw the others had noticed the boy's plight, but there was no sign of the father. Mr. Fuller must have gone back to the carriages to check on the horses.

"He's going to drown!" one of the maids squealed.

Meeting Emily's fear-filled gaze, Christian didn't hesitate. He kicked off his shoes and dove into the water. He hadn't had the opportunity to swim all summer, but he was a strong swimmer, and with a series of broad strokes, he reached the boy in a matter of seconds.

"I've got you, Martin," he said, wrapping one arm around him to keep his head above water.

The boy didn't fight but allowed Christian to pull him in toward the shore. They were almost there when Mr. Fuller came running down the embankment and splashed into the water.

"Martin, are you all right?" Mr. Fuller shouted, lifting the child into his arms.

Eyes wide, his shivering son nodded. "The boat hit a rock and the bottom splintered. Water came gushing through."

Mr. Fuller lifted his gaze. "Gilbert," he said, his voice hoarse. "Thank you. . .for saving my boy."

The back of Christian's throat knotted. He'd also been relieved to get Martin back on dry land. But it was the way Emily ran forward and took his arm as if *he* needed help from the water—and looked at him as if he were her hero—that made him truly understand what Richard Fuller must be feeling at the moment.

For if he lost her now, he might never recover.

The following morning being a Sunday, Emily sat beside Charlotte, Hester, and Phoebe in church but couldn't help squirming in her seat while listening to the sermon. The minister recounted the biblical story of Jonah and how the Hebrew prophet thought he could run from God.

Had she done the same?

Jonah hadn't liked God's plan and decided to take control and do what he wanted—run the other way. In the end, he'd found himself swallowed alive, stuck inside the belly of a great fish.

While Emily hadn't shared his same fate, she did feel she was stuck in an impossible situation. Earlier that morning, she'd received a telegram from her father pleading for her to come home. He said he never meant to make her do something she didn't want to do but had truly believed God helped orchestrate the agreement they'd made with Mr. Gould. The agreement she broke when she ran.

But if she returned to Boston, she'd have to leave Gilbert.

Later that day, while helping Alice change from her church clothes into her less formal Sunday afternoon tea dress, Emily couldn't suppress the mounting anxiety bubbling up inside her any longer and dared to ask about marriage between the upper and lower social classes.

"People can be extremely prejudiced," Alice warned her. "If you do not conform to their ways of thinking and behaving, they can be inconsiderate with their words and blackball you from every societal affair."

"Is that what happened to you?" Emily asked, tightening the laces on the back of her employer's dress.

"For a while," Alice admitted. "I worked here as a maid in the Belmonts' summerhouse for three years before Stephen proposed. Certain individuals did not take kindly to the thought of him marrying the hired help. But with the senior Mr. and Mrs. Belmont's influence, and women like Mrs. Langhorne, opinions have started to change."

"But are you happy?" Emily pressed.

Alice smiled. "Stephen and I are very happy. And soon to be parents."

Emily stared at Alice's stomach. "You're with child? Should I loosen your stays?"

"Not yet." Alice looked down at her waist and smiled again. "But perhaps in another few weeks."

"I have experience as a governess," Emily exclaimed. "In addition to lady's maid, I could help care for the children."

Alice laughed. "I think you may soon find you'll be too busy caring for your own."

Emily's cheeks suddenly grew warm. "Marriage comes before children. And I do not even have a proper suitor."

"Don't you?" Alice teased.

Emily smiled, aware she was referring to Gilbert. "He hasn't made it official."

However, when Emily stepped out of Alice's room, the housekeeper informed her that Gilbert waited for her in the garden. When she joined him there, he handed her a small box of chocolates.

"When I went into town today on an errand for Mr. Belmont, I passed by the chocolatier," he said, smiling. "And of course, I thought of you."

"But Gil, they're so expensive!" she exclaimed, gazing at the luscious dark sweets topped with creamy white chocolate swirls. "They must have cost a fortune."

"Your happiness means more to me than money," he said, taking her hand. "Especially if I have the honor of being your beau?"

Giddy with joy, Emily knew in her heart that she was more than willing to give up the prospect of ever returning to proper society for a chance at the happiness they could share together. Smiling up at him, she nodded.

"Yes, Gilbert, I'd be very pleased to have you be my beau."

Chapter 8

The following Saturday afternoon, Emily tried to sit still while Charlotte brushed the knots out of her hair.

"No one ever believed you were related," the maid assured her. "You don't look at all alike, and then there is the besotted way the two of you look at each other."

Emily caught her breath. "We do not—"

"Yes, you do," Charlotte insisted, and the other maids giggled.

Hester and Phoebe had also gathered around her, offering their opinions on what she should wear when she met up with Gilbert later that evening. He'd asked her to join him on the garden terrace overlooking the river, as he had something very important to discuss. And when Mrs. Williams found out, she'd immediately offered to chaperone "to keep everything respectful."

"I wonder if he will bring you more chocolates," Hester teased. "Or flowers, or ribbons, or beaded jewelry."

Emily smiled. Each day that week her dashing new beau had sent her some token of affection, much to the other maids' anticipated delight.

"Maybe he wants to read her a love poem beside the river," Phoebe crooned.

Charlotte laughed. "Or ask her to marry him."

"Charlotte!" Emily exclaimed, her whole face tingling. "I've only known Gilbert Lawrence two weeks."

"Long enough to fall in love," Phoebe said gaily, and sighed. "Surely this is a match made in heaven."

Emily bit her lip. That was what her father had believed when he'd tried to match her up with Christian Gould. But her father must have been mistaken. It wasn't always easy to decipher God's will. She certainly hadn't been able to see it. But now that He'd brought Gilbert into her life, she was sure God did care about her, and she'd started to pray again. In fact, she'd gotten down on her knees each day this week to thank Him. Maybe in time her father would also come to see that Gilbert truly was the one God had meant for her to marry all along.

Which reminded her. . . She still needed to send a telegram to Mr. Gould telling him he need not wait for her any longer, that her heart belonged to another.

"Too bad Mrs. Williams insists on being a chaperone," Hester said, hanging over the back of her chair. "Mr. Lawrence may have wanted to kiss you."

The jovial laughter that ensued was abruptly brought to a halt when a sharp knock rapped upon the door and Mrs. Williams entered uninvited, her face drawn as she handed Emily a telegram.

"This came for you," the housekeeper informed her. "Mrs. Belmont said I should bring it up to you straightaway."

Charlotte dropped her hands from Emily's hair and took a step back. Hester and Phoebe did the same, as if sensing she might need space.

No doubt it was bad news. Emily swallowed the dread welling in the back of her throat as she took the telegram from the envelope and looked at the name of the sender.

"It's from my sister, Susannah," Emily told them. Reading further, she gasped, brought her hand up to cover her mouth, then before the welling tears could blur her vision completely, she looked at their worried faces. "My father has suffered a heart attack. . .and the doctor questions whether he will recover."

Leaving Mrs. Williams and the three maids behind, Emily ran down the stairs, out the back door, and all the way up the road to the redbrick church with white trim where she'd attended the service the previous Sunday. Although Mrs. Williams must have seen it while hovering over her shoulder, Emily had not told the maids the rest of the message. . .

The part that said Mr. Gould would still be willing to marry her if she returned.

Trying the handle of the church door and finding it locked, Emily wandered across the front lawn toward the children's chime tower, a twenty-five-feet peaked stone structure that chimed nursery rhymes on the hour, chimes she'd hoped her own children would one day hear.

But not if she went back to Boston.

Apparently, when she did not show up for the wedding, Christian Gould had informed the public that the wedding would be postponed to a later date when she was feeling better.

As if she had taken ill and needed to recover!

Her sister said Mr. Gould had done it to protect her, to save her reputation, so that she could still return to Boston and marry him with no fear of disgrace, and that he would still honor his portion of their original agreement.

Well, she did not feel any better about marrying Christian Gould, but now that her father's heart was failing, who would support the family? Although their finances had been in disarray, her father had still negotiated business deals between the steel manufacturers and only needed her wages to supplement his income. But if he were unable to work. . .

She did not see how she could come up with the money to support her family on her own.

They'd be destitute. Disgraced. Ousted from their home. All because she refused to marry Christian Gould.

Unless she reconsidered and took him up on his offer.

She could live happily as a servant the rest of her life, but her beloved mother and younger sister and brother couldn't. They hadn't spent time in the rural countryside like she had at her uncle and aunt's estate in England, and even with that helpful experience, Emily still had trouble performing her duties at Maple Glen. And although she detested having to marry for money, how could she be happy with Gilbert, knowing she had placed her family in such a predicament?

Dear Lord, what am I to do?

The sermon she'd heard at church the week before came flooding back to haunt her. The one about Jonah and how he had arrogantly thought his way was best, that he could run.

"You can't run from God," the reverend had emphasized, and quoted Proverbs 3:5–6: "Trust in the Lord with all thine heart; and lean not unto thine own understanding. In all thy ways acknowledge him, and he shall direct thy paths."

Dropping to her knees, tears streaming down her cheeks, Emily realized she had wanted to run because she didn't trust God, and she didn't trust Him because she didn't really know Him.

Clasping her hands together, she prayed, "Dear God, please help me to know You more. I've been selfish. Arrogant. Instead of thinking of others, I've only been thinking of myself. I wanted to take control and do what I wanted, then hoped You would bless my plans. Instead, I should have trusted You."

With a heavy heart, Emily realized she hadn't even given God a chance. But from now on she would pray before making hasty decisions, and even when she didn't understand how certain situations could work out for good, she would trust the plans God had for her.

My life is in Your hands, Lord. Do with it as You will.

Hoping God had heard, she gathered her strength, wiped her tears, and headed back to Maple Glen. After all, it was half past six.

And Gilbert waited for her.

Once Mrs. Williams took up her position as chaperone on the upper portion of the garden terrace, Emily forced herself to walk across the wide expanse of lawn below. She caught her breath at the scene before her.

Beside the stone half wall, a white-linen-covered table had been set with a glass vase of beautiful flowers—roses, lilies, gladiolas, and daisies. A tray of delectable desserts—including elegantly decorated chocolates—had been spread before two crystal fluted glasses and a matching pitcher of pink lemonade. And interspersed between these items at least a dozen white candles flickered like tiny glistening stars, beckoning her forward with their glow.

Gilbert stood by the steps that led down to the river and turned with a smile as she approached. "I must say you look lovely this evening."

Did she? Emily had forgotten that Charlotte had curled her hair and the other maids had helped press her prettiest dress. She glanced down and brushed a piece of moss off the midsection of her skirt, something she must have picked up when she'd knelt at the children's chime tower to pray.

"Thank you," she said, forcing the words from her mouth. She took in his attire, noting he was handsomely dressed in his white dress shirt, blue trousers, and matching vest. "You sport quite a fine image yourself."

Christian's smile broadened. "I've taken the liberty of persuading Cook to dish up some special treats. I hope you approve. There's even chocolate on the menu."

Emily shook her head. "It all looks delicious. . .but I don't think I can eat a bite."

"Please," Gilbert urged, picking up a pastry puff and handing it to her. "At least try this."

Her hands shook as she raised the small golden triangle to her mouth for a taste, and the vibrant flavor of the raspberry filling slid over her tongue. For a moment, she closed her eyes. It was sweet. And so was Gilbert for wanting to please her so. But he needed to know the contents of the telegram.

"Gilbert, there's something I have to tell you."

"And I you," he said with a warmth that sent an ache straight through her very soul. "Would you care to sit?"

Gilbert pulled out a chair for her, but she shook her head. "No, I—I'd rather stand." However, her legs trembled beneath her skirts, and fearing she might collapse, she changed her mind. "All right, I'll sit."

After she was seated, Gilbert sat beside her. "I've looked forward to this moment all day," he confessed. "I couldn't wait to see you. Every moment I've spent in your presence these last few weeks has been. . .an absolute pleasure. I don't even mind the stable work because I think of you and all the conversations we've shared, your laughter, steadfast resolve, the way your face lights up when you're happy."

"I've enjoyed our time together as well," Emily admitted, wringing her hands. "Which makes it even harder for me to say this, but—"

"You do not have to say anything but *yes*," Gilbert said dropping down onto one knee and withdrawing a small black jeweler's case from the inside of his pants pocket. "When you first told me that you would only marry for love, I didn't quite understand. I didn't value how important love was. . .until I met you."

Oh no! Charlotte was right. Gilbert was going to propose. "Gil—"

He flipped open the lid of the case, and she stared at the large diamond ring, her heart thundering in her chest. *Why, it must have cost him his whole life's savings!*

"I'd like nothing more than to marry you," Gilbert continued, "and have you become my wife. But first there's an. . .uncorrected misunderstanding. . .that I need to clear up. Something I should have told you the first day we met. I'm not who you think I am, I'm—"

"You are a very good man," Emily said, pushing out of her chair to stand. "But I can't marry you."

The devastated look on Gilbert's face as he slowly rose to his feet tore at her insides and pierced her heart all over again. Never had she seen anyone look so helplessly vulnerable as he did when he met her gaze.

His jaw shifted, the way it did whenever he was flustered, a trait she'd come to find endearing. Now it only reminded her of everything between them that would be lost.

"May I ask why?" Gilbert said, his voice low. "Is it because you think me a mere servant?"

"No, of course not!" she assured him. "This has nothing to do with social class. And I *do* care for you."

The pain reflected in his eyes lessened. "Then why won't you marry me?"

She opened her mouth to tell him about the telegram, about her father's heart attack and how it would affect her family if she didn't honor Christian Gould's proposal. But how could she tell him she had to marry another man?

"I'm sorry, Gil," Emily said, shaking her head. "I just. . .*can't.*"

And before he could stop her, she turned, picked up her skirts, and ran back up to the house.

Christian stood on the terrace a good long while, looking out over the river. Then he directed the housekeeper to remove the decorative items from the garden terrace and went to search for Stephen. The butler informed him that his friend was in the library.

"She turned me down," Christian said, striding into the room. "I proposed to Emily, and she turned me down."

Stephen closed the book he'd been reading and placed it on the end table beside his chair. "Did you tell her who you are?"

"She didn't give me a chance. I was all set to tell her the truth, but she said she couldn't marry me, stood up, and ran. Everything was going so well. I don't understand what could have happened. Maybe I'm just not meant to get married."

"I'm sorry," Stephen said, rising from his seat. He came over and clasped him on the shoulder. "What can I do to help?"

"Nothing, I'm afraid." Christian paced in front of the floor-to-ceiling bookcase, his throat tight as he fought to lock down his emotions. "I shouldn't have deceived her."

"She's the one who misunderstood when the butler said your name," Stephen reminded him. "And she's the one who assumed you were a coachman and insisted on finding work to support her family. All you did was go along for the ride."

"I should have told her my full name," Christian said, angry with himself for believing this whole charade would somehow work out for good.

"No one is perfect," Stephen said with a frown. "We all make mistakes."

Christian turned to give him a direct look. "Except I fear I'm going to suffer the consequences of this one until the end of my days. I just wish she'd told me why she couldn't marry me."

"I'll tell you why," Alice said, rushing into the room waving a telegram. "Her father had a heart attack, and she's returning to Boston to marry Christian Gould!"

"To marry—" Stephen raised his brows and looked at him.

"Where is she now?" Christian asked, already on his way toward the door.

"She asked Mr. Fuller to drive her to the train station," Alice informed him. "I sent Charlotte along with her so she wouldn't be traveling alone."

"This time she's *truly* left me behind!" Christian sputtered with exasperation, then smiled. "But not for long. Call me another carriage. I must make haste and return to Boston as quickly as I can."

Chapter 9

Emily had wanted to tell Gilbert about the telegram but just couldn't bring herself to do it. Her emotions were already a mess, and if Gilbert had begged her to stay, she didn't know how she'd be able to keep her commitment to Mr. Gould, no matter the consequences.

Another tear slipped down her cheek, and Charlotte, who sat beside her on the train, handed her a new handkerchief.

"You are doing the right thing," the maid assured her. "For your family."

Emily nodded. "Yes, but it doesn't make it any easier."

"Women do not often have easy choices," Charlotte told her. "Maybe if we had the legal right to vote, things could change. With new laws, women might get paid the same wages as men for the same job, but right now we're not. Certain jobs aren't even open to women, making it hard for us to support ourselves and our families."

"It doesn't seem fair," Emily grumbled.

"No," Charlotte agreed. "But do not give up hope. Sometimes things do work out in our favor."

"Have you ever met Mr. Gould?" Emily asked.

Charlotte shook her head. "No. I've only been at Maple Glen two months. But Hester and Phoebe met him last year when he came to visit, and they said you may find you like Mr. Gould as much as you do your dear Gilbert."

"I know I must remain optimistic," Emily said, brushing away another tear. "Although I am not sure how."

"Trust in the Lord."

"With all my heart," Emily said, remembering the Bible quote. "Except I do not feel I have any heart left."

"You do," Charlotte soothed. "Or it wouldn't ache so much."

It was late when Emily and Charlotte disembarked in Boston. Still, they managed to arrive at the Pembrooke estate before midnight. No one had been expecting her, but a flurry of lights and padded footsteps flew down the stairs as soon as she came through the front door.

"Emily!" her mother cried, hugging her tight. "I'm so glad you've come."

The reunion with her parents, Susannah, and Thomas Jr. was bittersweet. She loved her family dearly, but seeing the condition her father was in and knowing what she must do brought more tears to her eyes.

However, the following day, Emily was surprised to discover that her father was well attended not only by the doctor, but by three nurses. She also noted that several of her family's staff who'd previously been let go had been rehired, and the outside grounds looked immaculate with freshly trimmed bushes and weeded garden boxes. For dinner the cook placed a succulent hen, herbed potatoes, and other carefully prepared vegetable dishes on the table.

"How can we afford all this?" Emily asked, leaning toward her sister.

"We've received a generous weekly stipend from Mr. Gould over the last several weeks," Susannah whispered.

Emily's heart nearly skipped a beat. "Even though there was no guarantee that I would return?"

Her sister nodded. "Even with no guarantee."

More good news arrived a day later when the doctor informed them that he believed her father would pull through, although he would be on bed rest for quite some time. Emily thanked the doctor, wondering what would have happened if Mr. Gould had not enabled her father to receive such care.

How could she ever repay his kindness?

She glanced at the calendar on the wall in her father's study, realized how much time had passed since their original wedding date, and took out a pen and piece of stationery to write Christian Gould a much overdue letter.

The second afternoon after his return to Boston, Christian stood in the aisle of the stables on his own family's estate, much to the consternation of his head stable hand.

"Is there anything you are looking for in particular?" the burly man asked, a nervous tremor in his voice.

"No," Christian said, opening one of the stalls and running a hand down the neck of a dark bay thoroughbred. "I just wanted to see the horses."

"We brush them down each day and make sure their hooves are trimmed, and those needing shoes had them checked by the farrier only yesterday," the stable master prattled on.

"Their coats are immaculate," Christian said. He leaned his shoulder into the animal's side, picked up one of its back feet, and examined the hoof. "Who did the trim on this horse?"

The stable master hesitated. "Why, I—I did, sir."

"Excellent."

Christian gently placed the hoof back down, then came out of the stall, careful to reclose the gated half door and slide the lock. They didn't need any of the horses getting loose like they had one night at Maple Glen. But that was before he'd learned the finer details of equestrian care.

Smiling, he walked toward the wide-eyed man in charge and grasped hold of his shoulder. "I can see you are doing a splendid job taking care of the horses. Thank you for all your hard work. I know it isn't easy."

The stable master stared at him, then flushed a deep crimson. "I'll continue to do my best, sir. You needn't worry."

"I'm not worried," Christian assured him. "In fact, I'm going to see to it that you receive an increase in pay."

"An increase?" The stable master shot a nervous look at the three stable hands hovering nearby.

Christian followed his gaze and grinned. "You're all going to receive a pay raise."

"Thank you, sir," the stable master said, beaming.

And as the other three men came forward, their caps in their hands, to voice their appreciation, Christian realized they looked at him in a way they never had before.

With respect.

His heart thumped. Visiting the stable made him think of Emily, and he was half tempted to take a horse and ride over to the Pembrooke estate to see her when a courier brought him a letter penned by her own hand.

Dear Mr. Gould,

I must humbly ask your forgiveness for any embarrassment my actions may have caused these last few weeks. You have been patient beyond measure and most generous to my family in spite of my behavior, which is quite undeserved. To show my appreciation, I will marry you the day after next, if you so desire, as it is the last day of the month and your last day to meet the requirements for inclusion in the railroad investment. I would hate for you to lose it on my account after you have shown so much kindness toward me and my family.

Sincerely,

Emily Pembrooke

Wednesday dawned even lovelier than the first time Emily had put on the white satin and lace wedding dress. Except this time she had Charlotte pin a floral wreath atop her head of upswept curls, like the one she'd created for Alice Belmont.

She realized now that life wasn't always about getting what she wanted, and that she needed to look out for the needs of others, but she could at least allow herself this *one* little indulgence. And her mother had not uttered one word of complaint on how the new style would interfere with the gauzy veil.

Once ready, Emily went to her father's bedside and kissed his cheek, then followed her mother, Susannah, Thomas Jr., and the bridesmaids out to Mr. Gould's waiting carriages.

For a moment, Emily paused, overcome by the memory of stepping into one of the black carriages with the large gold-lettered *G* on the side—with Gilbert. Except the coachman dressed in the black top hat and suit wasn't Gil, but a much older man. And he didn't direct her to ride in a carriage off by herself but directed her to sit inside the coach with her family.

The coachman did, however, provide her with a return letter from her future husband, which she was to read before reaching the church. Removing the elegantly embossed stationery from the envelope, her gaze fell upon the lettering.

Dearest Emily,

Please know that I once had doubts too, which, like you, led me to take matters into my own hands to make sure we were making the best decision. I do not doubt any longer and look forward to us spending the rest of our lives together. But please be advised that appearances can be deceiving.

Sincerely yours,
Christian

Emily frowned and showed the letter to her sister. "What do you think he means by 'appearances can be deceiving'?"

"Judge a person by their heart instead of how they look?" Susannah suggested.

"Do you suppose something happened to mar his outward appearance?" Emily asked.

"I heard he shaved off his beard," Thomas Jr. announced.

"And I would think he'd look far better for it," her mother said with a nod. "I do not approve of beards, even though most consider them fashionable."

Emily agreed with her, as Gilbert had been clean shaven.

She supposed it must also be fashionable to crowd the streets to see if the woman marrying Christian Gould would once again "not feel well" or would show up this time. There seemed to be a lot more people standing around staring at her carriage when it arrived in front of the church than had been invited. Especially taking into account the short notice. She imagined she'd become quite the curiosity, drawing forth those who heard the rumor she'd been seen driving a carriage through town on her last wedding day.

Well, if they expected her to run, they'd be sorely disappointed, because she'd made up her mind to go through with the wedding no matter what obstacles she faced this day.

Her mother descended the steps of the carriage first, followed by Thomas Jr. and Susannah, her maid of honor. Her bridesmaids had already arrived and were standing by the front door of the church, as were. . .Stephen and Alice Belmont!

What were they doing here?

Her pulse raced, and she caught her breath. They were friends of Christian Gould. Of course he would have invited them. But would the Belmonts tell him she'd been working for them these last few weeks? That she'd preferred the work of a servant than marriage to him? What if they told Mr. Gould about her relationship with Gilbert and he found out she'd run away with his own coachman! Would Christian Gould still want to marry her?

Dear God, I will not run. I will trust in You.

She drew in a deep breath to calm her nerves, as the memory of Gilbert's face, his endearing proposal, and other memories from their time together pierced her heart. Worse than marrying someone she didn't love was having to walk away from the one she did. But her family needed her help, and she couldn't abandon them.

Picking up the hem of her skirts, she walked forward prepared to meet her fate.

Chapter 10

Christian took out his handkerchief and wiped the sweat off his brow. Then he peeked out the side window of the church for the umpteenth time.

What if she didn't come? Shaking his head, he paced back and forth in the small chamber off to the right of the main church sanctuary. He hadn't had enough time with her. He should have told her who he was. What if she got angry and ran out of the church, out of his life, never to return? One of the first things she'd said to him when they met was that she did not believe in deception.

"She's here," Stephen informed him, striding into the room.

"And the rings?" Christian asked.

Stephen patted the front pocket of his tuxedo. "Ready."

"And the reverend?"

"All set."

The door to the chamber opened and Alice stepped inside to help pin the rose boutonnieres to their lapels. "White for the groom. Stephen, yours is the red."

"I should have gone to her house and talked with her in private before the ceremony," Christian said, regret knotting his stomach. "But my father sent me on an urgent last-minute errand to New York to meet with a buyer for our summerhouse in the Berkshires, and I didn't get back until just this morning."

Stephen frowned. "I didn't think you'd have to sell anything if Emily married you by the deadline for the railroad investment."

"Just a precaution," Christian informed him. "In case. . .she doesn't."

The soft music from the pipe organ in the sanctuary changed to the stronger strains of Wagner's "Bridal Chorus," signaling the start of the wedding processional, and Alice said, "It's time."

"Good luck," Stephen said, meeting his gaze.

Christian's pulse quickened in his chest. He needed more than luck. He closed his eyes and said a quick prayer.

Emily's nieces hadn't been able to make a return trip from England, especially on such short notice, so she did not have any flower girls. However, her bridesmaids from Mrs. Porter's finishing school looked lovely as they slowly walked down the aisle, one by one, each holding a bouquet of red and white roses to match the men's boutonnieres. Susannah gave her a quick kiss on the cheek and then went next.

Emily had hoped to walk down the aisle with her father, but because of his frail condition, she found herself—alone.

The queasy feeling in her stomach did not abate but picked up in tempo with the music as everyone in the church pews stood and turned to stare at her.

Including Alice Belmont, who stood off to one side and offered a smile of encouragement. But where was her husband?

Just as Emily took her first step down the aisle, Stephen Belmont and Thomas Jr. joined the reverend by the altar at the front of the church, both wearing the red boutonnieres designated for the groomsmen. Startled, she realized Christian Gould must have asked Mr. Belmont to be his best man.

But where was the groom? Shouldn't he be up there beside them by now? What if he didn't show?

No, she mustn't think such thoughts!

She took a few more steps. She was now halfway up the aisle. Still no groom in sight.

Then a man with brown hair in black formal wear stepped out from behind Mr. Belmont and Thomas Jr. and met her gaze.

Gilbert! He'd come for her!

Dear God, he'd come for her. And he was speaking to the reverend. Oh my! Was he going to try to stop the wedding?

She froze. Surely her heart stopped beating as well, and her breath caught in her throat.

Then Gilbert turned fully around, and for the first time she saw he wore an elegant tuxedo that only a rich man could afford—and the white boutonniere meant for the groom.

He held his hand out to her, but where was Christian? Bewildered by the strange turn of events, she continued forward.

Trust in the Lord with all thine heart; and lean not unto thine own understanding.

She glanced at her mother, Susannah, Alice, then Stephen, and the other people on either side of the aisle. Didn't anyone else think it odd that Gilbert was filling in for Christian Gould?

Apparently not, for most of them were smiling. . .

One more step, then Gilbert took her hand in his and gave it a gentle squeeze, but the look on his face was filled with anxiety.

"Appearances can be deceiving," he whispered.

Emily recalled the same line from Christian Gould's letter and her brother's comment that Christian had shaved off his beard. Gilbert was clean shaven too.

With no other groom in sight, she stared at him, as if seeing him for the first time. Especially when the reverend welcomed the crowd and spouted the opening lines of the ceremony.

Was Gilbert. . .Christian Gould?

He squeezed her hand again as the reverend asked, "Do you, Emiline Jane Pembrooke, take Christian Gilbert Lawrence Gould to be your lawfully wedded husband?"

Her mouth fell open as she remembered the first time they'd met, his request she ride alone in a separate carriage, all the improper questions. The butler's greeting at the Belmonts', which she now realized she must have only heard in part. She thought of the masquerade ball, where someone had seen him and how *Gilbert* had vowed to protect her and pulled her in close. Then on the garden terrace, he'd knelt and proposed but said he needed to clear up a misunderstanding, that he wasn't the man she thought he was. . . .

Emily looked at Christian and relaxed when she saw the same love in his eyes she'd seen in Gilbert. Her Gilbert.

Why did he let her think he was the coachman? Maybe for the same reason she'd stolen the reins and run away. The first part of his letter floated back to her, the part saying he'd had doubts too, but that he didn't doubt anymore.

She didn't either.

Smiling, she said, "I do."

Christian blew out a deep breath and grinned. A few steps to his right, Stephen and her brother grinned as well.

"And do you, Christian Gilbert Lawrence Gould," the reverend continued, "take Emiline Jane Pembrooke to be your lawfully wedded wife?"

Christian nodded. "Yes. I truly do. For richer or for poorer."

"In sickness and in health," Emily agreed.

"Till God takes us, one from the other," Christian finished.

The sincerity in his husky voice, combined with the way he was looking at her, melted all her remaining concerns and warmed her with dreams for the future.

Dreams she'd once thought she would have to give up forever.

"Thank you, Lord," she whispered, her heart overflowing with gratitude and awe for the way He had managed to make everything work out for good.

After the reverend pronounced them husband and wife, Christian leaned down as if to kiss her, and she smiled, having secretly anticipated this moment since the night of the Belmont ball. But he stopped when he drew within just inches of her mouth.

"I was never more afraid of anything in my life than the moment you hesitated before saying yes," he confided. "I'm so sorry I didn't tell you who I was right from the beginning."

"As I recall," Emily countered, "I didn't give you much of a chance. And if I did find out who you were, we wouldn't know each other the way we do now, would we?"

"No, we would not." Her new husband grinned. "I love you, Emily. Only you."

Her spirit soaring as she thought of spending the rest of her life with her loving husband and their future children, Emily replied, "I love you too, Christian Gilbert Lawrence Gould. All of you."

Christian let out a low chuckle, then cupped her face in his hands, bent his head, and pressed his warm lips against hers, delivering a heart-pounding kiss so tender and sincere that it stole her breath and made her believe God really did know best. Prayers could be answered.

And dreams really could come true.

Darlene Panzera is a multipublished author, speaker, and writing coach of both sweet contemporary and Christian inspirational romance. Her career launched with *The Bet*, a novella included in bestselling author Debbie Macomber's *Family Affair*, which led her to publish nine more titles with Avon Impulse, a division of Harper-Collins. The final installment of her newest three-book series, Montana Hearts, debuted May 2016. Darlene is also a member of Romance Writers of America and serves on the board of the Northwest Christian Writers Association. When not writing, she loves spending time with her husband and three kids, serving her church, teaching at conferences, and feeding her horse carrots. Learn more about Darlene at her website: www.darlenepanzera.com

The Flyaway Bride

by Jenness Walker

Acknowledgments

A big thank-you goes to my first readers. I have the best critical friends out there, and I love them for it. Extra thanks go to Elizabeth, who gifted me a favorite line to use in this story—one that apparently made my editor's week, and I couldn't even take credit for it! Thank you to my local coffee shop who cheerfully kept the sweet tea flowing during much of the writing of this story. Thanks to my lovely agent, Tamela Hancock Murray, and to my writer friends who mean so much. And finally, a huge thank-you to my family: Jason, I'm not sure I could do it without you. Kamden, I could do it faster without you, but I love you anyway.

Chapter 1

Ohio
1877

None of this courtship had gone the way it was supposed to.

Josey Middleton paced another circle in front of the nearly empty train depot. No one who appeared to be Everett Kane magically appeared. There was only Josey and a raggedy dog turning its head to and fro to follow her progress.

Things couldn't just go as planned for once, now could they? Mr. Kane couldn't show up where he said he'd be waiting, declare his eternal love, and whisk her to a church smelling of roses and peonies. No, that would be far too easy, and nothing about this had been easy.

Nothing, except falling in love. And, well, that had been an accident.

But her true love wasn't here. Even after she'd left everything in her small town and bounced along in a hired wagon for hours while imagining a dozen different ways that their first in-person meeting would go.

Not meeting him hadn't come up in those wildly romantic scenarios.

Josey chewed on her lip and squinted at the sun.

Mr. Kane may have faced some unexpected delays on his business trip to Pennsylvania, or even before he'd left Colorado. Or he might even—God forbid—have encountered an untimely accident, and here she waited at a train depot, chafing at the delay and hoping for a life much different than the one she'd lived up to this point. All while he breathed his last in one of those vast western ravines.

Oh dear. Panicking didn't suit her. Josey raised her chin and took in a deep breath of fresh Ohio air. She really needed to get ahold of herself and figure out a plan. To do that, she needed to hear Mr. Kane's voice in her head once again.

"All right, Rags." Stopping at the bench, Josey nudged the dog, making room for herself on the bench it guarded. "If you can bring yourself to share your seat, I'll share the last of the biscuits I brought from home."

As the stray gulped down the snack, Josey sat and pulled Mr. Kane's last letter from her reticule, carefully smoothing it against her travel skirt before skimming down the page.

319

I find myself whiling away the hours, awaiting the arrival of the post. My time is no longer my own. It is held hostage by your beloved letters and the fate of the mail coach. I long to know more about you, and each letter does not tell enough. I need you here with me. My dearest, your words have won my heart. I pray that you feel the same.

"There you go, Rags." Josey pointed to the paper. "*My* words won him. I want that fact to be crystal clear, in case you have any questions."

It didn't appear to make any difference to Rags. The next section wouldn't either—the part where he spoke of travel instructions and money for her fare. And best of all, a proposal in words not too flowery nor too plain. Perfect words—all except for one. A very small one she'd rather forget, despite the growing discomfort in her belly.

Because really, what was in a name?

"You see, Rags, these letters, they're not technically written to me."

"I'm not sure if'n you realize this, ma'am," a hushed voice said from behind her, "but that there be a dog."

Josey startled and swiveled to see a young boy leaning around the corner, his eyes sad and his face streaked with dirt.

"All the same," he continued, a little louder now, "I have questions, even if Penny don't."

"Penny?" Josey asked.

"Ain't my dog, but I'm plumb certain she don't like Rags. Ain't classy enough."

Josey watched the dog lick its paws, then move on to other parts. "Classy, indeed."

"Anyhow. . ." The boy crept closer, settling on the floor beside her. "Why'd ya swipe some gal's letters?"

Her cheeks burned. "Is there somewhere you need to be, young man?"

She almost missed the slight tremble of his chin. "Yes, ma'am. But there ain't nuthin' I can do about it right now. 'Sides, Preacher John says confession is good for the soul."

"Do you have something to confess?"

"Tell me yours first, then we'll see."

Biting back a chuckle, Josey nodded. "Agreed. But you and Penny are sworn to secrecy."

"Ma'am, you surely *do* need to confess. Preacher John says no swearin' neither."

"Duly noted." Josey checked inside her bag, wishing she had some food to offer the boy, if for no other reason than to keep his mouth busy chewing instead of being impertinent. "All right. It's a long story, starting when Sammy Jo at the general store back home told my sister about her nephew or cousin—I never can quite remember the connection—and his investments in Colorado. Jenny always wanted to marry someone who'd take her on an adventure, and Mr. Kane sounded like he'd do just fine."

She should stop, but the words kept tumbling out, as if practicing for the real confession to come. Glancing around to make sure she was indeed only talking to a boy and a dog this time, she continued.

"Jenny has no patience for letter writing but somehow managed to begin a correspondence. She wanted my help. She's all the family I have left, so how could I not? But Mr. Kane's letters were so wonderful, and. . .and then he proposed."

The part that should thrill her to her toes. All those letters she'd dictated to win over the witty, brilliant, accomplished Everett Kane bore fruit. Mr. Kane had fallen in love.

Unfortunately, so had Josey.

"I see." The boy hugged his knees to his chest. "This is a stumper."

"A stumper indeed. He asked me to marry him, but it isn't really me, is it? It's Jenny." And Jenny, well. . .

"What did your sis say?"

"She doesn't know. Never got the chance to tell her." Chewing on her lip, Josey carefully refolded the letter. Just before the arrival of the last message, Jenny added a whole new twist to this rather complicated courtship. Now Josey was left holding the pieces, ready to hand them over to Mr. Kane and let him figure out what to do next.

Except he wasn't here. It was just her, a dog, a boy, and a hot summer sun.

"You should tell 'im."

"As hard as it will be, I concur. I could write him a letter—a final one in my own handwriting, explaining everything." But who knew when Mr. Kane would get it, or how he would react? He'd been deceived. Not purposely, no. But Jenny wasn't who he'd thought she was, and she wasn't his any longer.

"I guess I assumed this kind of news shouldn't be trusted to the hands of strangers." She trembled at the thought of facing his wrath. Or worse—his disappointment. But washing her hands of the whole affair seemed wrong. Heartless. And when it came to Everett Kane, she was *all* heart. If she could only meet him and tell him the truth, maybe he'd see Josey was the one he loved, after all.

If she could only find him.

"Preacher John don't need no letter. You can tell 'im yourself."

Josey blinked. "Tell who what?"

"Preacher John. Your confession." The boy shook his head and huffed his impatience. "He can tell you what you should do. And seein' as you don't understand a dog cain't talk, and you've got some stealin' and swearin' proclivities, I'd say you can use all the help you can get."

"You may be right." She hid a smile behind a cough. "What's your name, young man?"

The boy hugged his scrawny legs closer and sucked a deep breath into his lungs. "My name is Tommy, and I reckon it's my turn to confess."

"Very well. Do go on."

"I'm lost."

She waited. Penny yawned. "That's it?" Josey finally asked.

"Well, yeah. Maybe it don't sound as bad as yours, because yours is awful bad, I reckon. But I ran away from my family this morning, ready to make my own way in the world. Stowed away on the train—I got caught at it, so doing it again'll be a mite trickier—then realized I'd left without lunch, and Becca ate my breakfast bacon, which is why I ran away in the first place, and here I am hungry enough to eat a whole possum, without a penny to my name, disappointed to learn that grown-ups *still* steal from their siblings."

Now she really wished she'd saved a biscuit for him. "Are you telling me you don't know how to get home?"

"Ain't that what I just said?"

"You said a lot of things, Tommy."

"It's just that when I get a chance to talk, I grab it with both hands and run. Don't get much opportunity back home."

"Ah. That explains it. Well, I was supposed to meet someone here, as you overheard me telling Penny. But maybe the person I'm really supposed to meet today is you."

"I ain't gonna propose, ma'am, if'n that's what you're gettin' at."

"No, Tommy, I. . ." She gave up and laughed in spite of the towheaded boy's obvious consternation. "I'm just saying that you, um, helped me. So maybe now I can help you." It was a risk. Mr. Kane had instructed her to meet here, after all. But *here* had no lodgings, and it had a little boy who needed a little assistance. "You see, it seems I will be continuing on to the next station and could use a good, strong escort."

"You mean it?"

"I mean it."

"Well. . .okay. But only so I can show you where to find Preacher John."

"Tommy, it's my sincerest wish that I will find myself standing in front of a preacher very, very soon."

Of all things for Everett Kane to be late for, picking up his bride-to-be was the worst. Especially since she wasn't here.

He watched strangers file off the train. Two rough-looking men. A family of four. A wisp of a lady with a hunched back and gray bun. A mother with her son and mangy-looking dog. A young couple—newlyweds, by the looks of them.

Anxiety gripped him. Had something ill befallen Jenny? Maybe she'd never received his telegram to meet here instead of the station closer to her hometown. Or had she decided to reject his proposal? Something he'd never allowed—*couldn't* allow himself to consider.

What if she'd never received his proposal in the first place? What had he been thinking to trust something so important to the postal system?

He should have traveled on to her town. Looking back, it would have been the right thing, the decent thing, the commonsense thing to do. But he'd been blind to anything except his eagerness to marry the woman whose words had stolen his heart, and as soon as possible. Their paths would cross on his way back to Colorado from his business trip. Meeting partway seemed the ideal solution.

Until now, when she was nowhere to be found.

A harried-looking woman let out a shriek as she jumped up from a nearby bench, nearly dropping her baby into her husband's arms as he unfolded his long legs to stand beside her and a passel of children. The young boy and dog from the train ran to her, his mother—no, aunt?—trailing behind with a smile on her plain face.

Everett couldn't guess how Jenny would greet him, though he'd imagined their first meeting many times. Would she become shy? Behave as though they were strangers? Would he need to start over with the wooing process? Would she find his appearance pleasing enough? Would she—

He ran a hand over his beard as the plain woman turned from the family to the station agent, spoke briefly—and probably uselessly, considering how his last conversation with the man had gone—and with a visible sigh, followed the family to a waiting wagon.

Concerned, he studied them as they held another discussion, and then the woman climbed on board with her reticule, the dog wagging its tail from its perch at the young boy's side. Several of his siblings piled in beside her. The darkening sky made it difficult to interpret her expression as she cast one more look toward the near-empty platform.

The wagon pulled away, and Everett turned his attention back to the station agent. One more conversation with the man, then he'd search for somewhere to sleep. If he could sleep, that is. He whispered a prayer for Jenny's protection and that they'd find each other soon.

Telling himself he felt better, Everett stepped up to the station agent's window. "Excuse me again, sir."

The harried-looking man barely acknowledged him as the telegraph machine rattled on. "What is it this time?"

"Just checking again to see if you have any messages for me." There'd been none waiting for him when he'd asked earlier, but he could hope.

"I'm so busy receiving 'em I can't get 'em delivered." He grumbled something about sick runners and inconvenient schedules and the B&O Railroad, adding a few impolite words on the end.

Everett frowned but kept his tone even. "I am sorry you're overwhelmed. If you haven't received any for me—"

"I don't know if one came in for my own mother. My fingers are tired, and thanks to you distracting me, this vital message for the sheriff now reads, 'Pack it up, Ethel.' "

With that, the telegraph operator turned his chair around, dismissing him.

Everett glowered at the man's back before dropping a greenback onto the wooden counter. "I apologize for inconveniencing you, but I need another message sent to my fiancée in case she missed the train at the last station."

The man glanced back and paused, sliding his eyes between the money and Everett before handing over a piece of paper. "Fine. Write it here."

Squelching the pointless urge to hide his note, Everett took the pen and scratched Jenny's name across the top.

"Wait." The operator squinted at the paper. "Middleton?"

"Yes." Everett's heart quickened. "Have you received a message from her?"

"No, but a lady was here earlier, asking if I had anything for Jenny Middleton." The operator tapped his finger against the money still on his desk.

Impossible. He'd been right here. "What did she look like?"

"Dark hair, kinda plain, with fiery eyes."

Everett hid a smirk. If her conversation with the operator went the same way Everett's had, no wonder her eyes flashed. "Where did she go?"

The operator shrugged, his fingers still twitching against the money in an involuntary version of Morse code. "She had a boy with her—the one that couple lost, sitting at that bench over yonder. No wonder, with twelve kids."

There'd only been nine at Everett's count, but that didn't matter. He'd stared right at Jenny, watched her leave, wondered at her story—and let her go.

He'd lost the love of his life before he'd even found her.

Chapter 2

The next morning, Tommy Pittman clambered from the wagon bed to the seat beside Josey as his father halted the horse in front of the depot.

"You sure you gotta leave, Miss Josey? You still ain't got a chance to meet Preacher John."

"There's someone else I need to meet now, but it was a pleasure spending time with you and your family, Tommy."

Mr. Pittman smiled and offered another round of thanks for helping the boy find his way home. Penny stuck close to Tommy. It appeared Josey had lost both travel companions.

The boy wrapped his arms around her neck and gave a squeeze. "Since you gotta go, I promise to take good care of Puddles."

She squeezed back. "Who is Puddles?"

He pointed at the stray and the puddle dangerously near Josey's reticule.

She snatched it to safety and shook her head. "You'll have your hands full."

Giving a sage nod, Tommy stood tall. "I'm up for it. And if'n you and your fella don't work out, you know where to find me."

"Why, Master Tommy, is that a proposal?"

"It's true that you're a mite elderly, but one good turn deserves another."

Mr. Pittman chuckled, and they bid her farewell while Josey tried to decide whether to laugh or cry. As she stood there, alone, two choices awaited her.

Continue on, persevering in her search for Mr. Kane. Blindly choosing hope.

Or return home.

If she had any pride, she'd choose the latter. Between her travels yesterday and the small amount of sleep she'd managed last night after nearly being pushed off the mattress by four small sets of very cold feet, she looked nearly as ragged as Rags-Penny-Puddles, and sported an aroma reminiscent of the dog as well.

As she'd only planned to meet Mr. Kane and explain the situation before returning home—either with her tail tucked between her legs or to pack her few treasures for a journey to happily ever after—her reticule was small and sadly lacking in supplies. She was woefully unprepared to make a good impression.

And yet she was this close. *This close!* To turn around without doing all she could to meet the man who turned her lonely heart into all those foolish things Jenny used to go on about but Josey never believed—well, it was inconceivable.

So that settled it. She'd press on to find Mr. Kane, all the way to Colorado if she needed to.

After checking the schedule and buying a ticket that would take her one stop closer to Mr. Kane's home, Josey studied the street. The general store was a short stroll down the dirt road. She could make it there and back in no time at all. But would she miss Mr. Kane again? Another discreet sniff made her decision for her, and she hurried down the walk and through the heavy wooden door.

At the store, she selected items necessary to continue—only what she could afford with her own carefully hoarded money. Mr. Kane's funds she intended to return, as they were not sent to *her* if someone insisted on getting letter-of-the-law about it. The money was sewn into a hidden pocket in her petticoat for safekeeping.

She stood near the counter, debating between a splurge on lilac- or rose-scented soap when a long whistle sounded. A *train* whistle.

Oh dear.

How had he missed her?

Everett walked through the train cars, studying each passenger. The brunette was nowhere to be seen. After bunking in an overly full boardinghouse, he'd almost been too late for this train. Had there been an earlier one? The station agent insisted Jenny purchased a ticket. She should be here.

But she wasn't.

Ignoring the coy looks from a young lady with an overly embellished hat that reminded him of one of Jenny's letters, he strode through the next car and tried to decide on his next move. Stay here and search the town? Go to the next station and see if Jenny had somehow arrived ahead of him?

Why had he not taken the time to go to her home?

The train began to tremble. Searching for the right decision, Everett glanced out a window, then did a double take. A woman hurried toward the platform, snatching up packages as she dropped them again and again.

Could she be. . .?

Another rumble. A long whistle.

Jenny Middleton. It had to be. And she wasn't going to make it.

Everett rushed through the car and whipped open the door of the caboose as the train lurched forward. Peering around the side, he found she'd managed to wrap the parcels in her shawl and was making much faster progress. She'd nearly reached the train when it began to pick up speed.

Two cars passed her. Three.

Everett had just determined to jump down and join her when she began to run. With one hand pressing her hat to her head, her reticule and shawl-wrapped parcels bouncing over her shoulder, and a determined set to her lips, she ran.

Grinning, Everett made ready as the caboose pulled even with her. "Throw the bags!"

Her eyes lit, and she tossed them to the platform of the caboose. With his foot, he pushed them to safety, then he reached for her. "Take my hand!"

"Don't. . .drop. . .me!" she panted. Then with a final burst of speed, she grabbed hold and scrambled for footing as he swung her up.

Jenny Middleton. At last.

He smiled into her face and wondered at her flushed cheeks. From the exertion alone, or due to a charming blush? Did she recognize him—if not his face, his heart, which belonged to her?

He opened his mouth to greet her, but she stepped back, smoothed her clothing, and offered a reserved smile that didn't hide the mischievous glint in her eyes. Green eyes. Sweet and warm and lively.

"Thank you for rescuing me." She had to shout to be heard over the rumbling train.

"My pleasure, Miss—"

"Middleton," she supplied before he could finish.

"Miss Middleton." The address felt so formal on his lips. In his mind, she'd been Jenny—*his* Jenny—for so long now. He took her hand—the hand he'd dreamed of holding—and gave a slight bow, then lifted his gaze, wanting to see her expression.

She lowered her lashes, definitely blushing this time.

"I am Everett," he said.

She cocked her head as if straining to hear, her eyes tracking back to him. "Just Rhett, did you say?" She gave a teasing smile. "Again, thank you for your assistance, Mr. Rhett. Shall we go inside where we don't have to yell or hang on for dear life?"

Motioning for her to precede him, he opened the door and waited as she gathered her belongings. All the while trying to ignore the sinking feeling in his chest. Something was wrong. He couldn't put his finger on it, but. . .

Trepidation tempered his joy at finding her. She hadn't answered any of the telegrams he'd sent. She'd appeared with a random child and gone home with a strange family. She'd nearly missed the train—the reason being, it seemed, because she'd emptied out the general store. Was she flighty? Addled? A spendthrift?

He hated to even think it, but how much had Aunt Sammy Jo told Jenny about the state of his accounts? About his investments in hotels and cattle and shipping? He'd hinted in his letters that he'd done well enough to support her comfortably. But was she after more?

No. He couldn't believe that of her. Yet the fact that she'd misunderstood his name could be a blessing, allowing him a little time to get to know the *real* Jenny Middleton, to see if, deep down, she was truly the woman he'd fallen in love with through her letters.

Or maybe he was just upset she hadn't been able to pick him out of the crowd. No matter that he hadn't known who she was when he'd almost crossed paths with her yesterday. It wasn't fair of him to expect that of her.

But it still stung.

Either way, Everett found himself refraining from correcting his name as he followed her down the aisle and helped her find a seat, then, with her permission, settled across from her.

"Are you sure you're quite all right?" he asked. "That was a close call."

"Perfectly fine, I assure you. Although I haven't had that much excitement since. . ." She frowned. "Well, since Becca Pittman found a frog in our sheets early this morning. And before that, when—let's just say yesterday was exciting. But, well. . ." Her cheeks reddened again, making the hearty sprinkling of freckles across them all but disappear. "Normally I don't live a very exciting life."

She and her sister worked in a milliner's shop that was run by an elderly lady who tended to overfeather everything, and was frequented by quirky customers such as Mrs. Meecham and Mrs. Stuart, who competed to see who walked away with the largest creation on their heads.

Had she minded terribly leaving that familiar routine in order to join him in a place so far away? Everett remembered most details of Jenny's letters. She wrote in wonderful word pictures, creating scenes that lived in his head so vividly it was as if they were his own memories. Had the words flowed? Or had she labored over them like he had, crumpling up precious paper in each attempt before settling on the missives that finally winged their way across the continent?

"What about you, Mr.. . .?" she asked, seeming to fumble for a name.

Right. He'd only given her one. Did he lie and make up a surname, or confess?

"Do you live an exciting life?"

"You can just call me Rhett. And sometimes. If you count travel exciting."

"So far I would have to say yes, then. Unequivocally." She laughed. It was a soft, throaty chuckle, full of wry humor. No horsey, overly loud guffaw. No high-pitched, nerve-grating giggle.

He liked it even more than he'd imagined. Her hair, on the other hand. . .

A smile broke through his musings. It seemed, after her exertion, the brown wisps had taken on a life of their own. Not straight but not exactly curly, the soft-looking strands escaped Jenny's coiffure and the confines of her dainty hat, which sat slightly off-kilter. He'd not caught her at her best. And maybe that was as it should be.

Who are you really, Jenny Middleton? Without pretense. Without a need to impress. Without any masks.

He looked forward to finding out.

Her heart should not still be thumping this hard. Yes, she'd hopped on a train, of all things. The excitement and adventure and physical strain would make any woman short of breath. But this—this was something more. Blushing, she avoided staring at the man across from her, instead allowing her gaze to roam the train car. Even so, her eyes kept wandering back to him.

No one could deny her rescuer was handsome. Medium height with muscles that had strained the sleeves of his coat as he'd hauled her onto the train, his hands warm and strong. He had a square forehead. Thick, dark hair. A well-trimmed beard. Brown eyes that warmed and twinkled and held some sort of knowing glint.

Josey dug through her reticule and found a fan, and her fingers slid across the fine paper of the stack of letters she kept close. Oh dear. Her journey had hardly begun, and she was already getting distracted.

No, that wasn't true. She admired Mr. *Just* Rhett, because what woman would not? But her heart belonged to Everett Kane. Always.

Even if the fact that he hadn't come made her heart skip beats for a different reason.

What if he'd seen her—knew who she was supposed to be—and found her sadly lacking? She wasn't as pretty as her sister. What if her plain face and lack of grace had turned him away? What if he'd decided he didn't want Jenny after all? Or what if he realized she was a stand-in and knew with one glance that he could never love the frizzy-haired Middleton?

Or worse by far, what if he no longer walked this earth altogether?

There she went, stumbling into morbidity again. Fanning herself, she forced her breathing to steady. *Breathe in.* Mr. Kane still lived—she would have felt the loss if he did not. *Breathe out.* Mr. Kane still loved her. Surely he did. He only needed a few facts explained before they lived happily ever after.

Oh Josey.

Hiding her face, she tapped the fan against her forehead. Her father had always accused his daughters of being impulsive, cautioned them against that similar part of their very different personalities.

Look at us now, Papa. Josey winced. *If you could only see us now.*

"Is something wrong, Miss Middleton?"

Oh dear. She'd been making faces again, hadn't she? Jenny always teased her mercilessly about the way Josey's thoughts played across her face clear as day. Yet somehow Jenny never guessed at Josey's growing feelings for Mr. Kane.

Or. . .had she? Could that have factored into Jenny's recent actions? Josey's brow furrowed at the sudden suspicion.

"Miss Middleton?"

Her eyes flew open to find her rescuer frowning at her. "I am well, thank you. Just. . .tired."

"Ah, yes. Thanks to Becca Pittman, I presume?"

She laughed, and his face relaxed.

"I'm sure there's a story there."

"Why, of course," she said. "I'm afraid that with me, there is always a story."

Did she imagine his eyes narrowing slightly? "Is that so?"

"That's what my family claims."

Rhett ran his thumb and forefinger over his beard. "What family do you have?" He asked an awful lot of questions.

Josey studied him in turn. "What is it you said you do, Mr. Rhett? Are you a businessman? Gambler? Marshal?"

He blinked twice, then rubbed his chin again before lowering his hand. "I'm between. . .things at the moment."

Drifter, then. Soon they'd part ways and she'd no longer be distracted by his nosy questions. Or his piercing eyes and strong shoulders.

Inside her head, Josey's conscience cleared its throat. *Everett Kane.* She tipped her chin up, imagining the man behind the letters. She couldn't wait to meet him. Mostly. After her first confession, anyway.

"Where will your journey end?" she asked. She was not one to have her head turned by a handsome face. Hadn't she proved that with shallow Frank and arrogant Elmer? She required something much more substantial. Character. Humor. Love. And—

"I'm headed out west. St. Louis first. Kansas City and beyond."

Did "beyond" include Colorado? Josey swallowed. So she may see more of him than she'd assumed. Why did that unsettle her? Squirming, she grasped at an excuse to avoid more probing questions. "I wish you pleasant travels. Thank you again for your assistance, but I do believe I must rest now."

"Becca?" he asked wryly.

"Yes. Silly girl." With that, she turned her face to the window and closed her eyes. Mostly.

Chapter 3

If he wasn't mistaken, Jenny was peeking.

Not at him, unfortunately. No, her eyes had opened to the tiniest of slits, and he was quite sure she stared out the window, taking in the landscape as it changed from town to countryside.

She hadn't traveled much. She and her sister had been raised as small-town girls, according to her letters. Why was it that he now questioned their verity? At any rate, she'd blocked him out, using her exhaustion as an excuse.

His questions made her uncomfortable, or was it just him, in general? Because she had something to hide—or because she was being loyal to her fiancé, not realizing she sat across from him?

Everett watched the trees race by for a moment before returning his attention to the brunette. The sun played across her face, and he studied the shadows and contours. It was oval in shape, her chin maybe a touch too small. But her lips were full, her nose straight and well formed, her neck slender, and the rest of her—well, he forced himself not to examine her too thoroughly. She may be on the plain side, but she was by no means unpleasant.

Her eyelids flickered, and he shifted, feeling a blush stain his own cheeks this time. She wasn't cattle for him to size up and bid on at auction. Her appearance really didn't matter, not when her heart spoke to him with pen and ink. But it was gratifying to know his right-hand man had been wrong.

"She's going to be an absolute hag, Kane." Horace wore a gleeful smile. "Why else would she travel across the country to marry someone she's never met?"

"Women do it all the time, for all sorts of reasons."

"Most of them having to do with snaggleteeth and crossed eyes, I'd wager."

Everett refused to dignify that remark with a response.

"You'll see, Kane. And you'll owe me a raise."

"I'll not wager on my future bride." Not that he was a gambling man in any case.

333

Horace, on the other hand. . . "Your favorite horse, then."

"Moose? Absolutely not."

"You fear I'm right. Admit it."

Somehow Everett had been goaded into agreeing to the bet. Deep down maybe he questioned if Horace spoke truth. If Jenny was as beautiful a soul as he thought her to be, why had no one claimed her before now?

Of course, she may wonder the same about him.

He'd never pictured finding love through correspondence, had scoffed at the idea of mail-order brides. The first letter to Jenny had been written as a favor—a short missive giving the daughter of a friend of his aunt an overview of life in Colorado, as requested. Aunt Sammy Jo explained that the young woman was restless and threatening to hop a train headed out west where she knew not a soul. Deter her, his aunt requested. Or befriend her so she'll have a protector if she made good on her plans.

A wry smile tugged at Everett's lips. Maybe Aunt Sammy Jo had been the one with plans all along. Whatever the case, instead of driving Jenny away, Everett eventually found himself all but begging her to join him.

For some reason, she'd agreed. At least he assumed she had. She was here, wasn't she? She'd chosen him.

And Moose was safe from Horace's stables.

The light began to fade, and Miss Middleton's eyelids eventually quit twitching as she truly fell asleep. Everett watched her another lingering moment as dark lashes settled against her cheeks. Then, assured it was safe, he pulled her last letter from his pocket. It was nearly unreadable in places where he'd folded and refolded it. Everett traced a finger over her words, reading again what he knew by heart.

When I was young, I dreamed of being married. Of wearing my mother's veil—the closest I'll get to having her with me for that happy event. Of a church filled with flowers of all kinds. I imagined a grand honeymoon across the sea with a trousseau that required its own cabin on the voyage. The pomp and circumstance was what I equated with love.

For many reasons, my dreams have changed as I've grown older. Love now has a different appearance. It's filled with quiet nights and everyday moments. Reading by the fire, laughing softly at shared memories, eating simple meals or elaborate—it matters not. Just that they're eaten together. The only flowers needed are the ones admired on the bushes where they grow, while we walk side by side.

Now, to me. . .I'm quite certain love looks a lot like you.

Those weren't the words of a fortune hunter. Couldn't be. Nor a spendthrift, nor someone who would flit away as soon as someone or something more exciting came along. Jenny was no flyaway bride. Her words were true words, loyal and wise.

And he was doing her a disservice by testing her like this.

Everett smoothed the paper into a square once again and slid it into his vest pocket. When she awakened, he would tell her his name again. His full name. He'd propose in person at the next stop, buy her a room full of flowers, and find someone to marry them. Just as he'd intended when he'd sent that impulsive final letter. Due to time constraints and logistics, it wouldn't be the large church wedding she'd dreamed of as a girl, but they would be husband and wife, and he'd spend the rest of his life attempting to surpass her ideal of a sweet, lifelong love.

The train rumbled around a bend, then blew a whistle as its wheels began to squeal.

Jenny's eyes sprang open to catch him watching her. She gave a self-conscious smile, patted her hair, then turned again toward the window.

Now was the time, before they disembarked and he lost her again.

"Miss Middleton," he began, his mouth dry as guilt pricked again. "There's something you should know."

But it was as if she didn't hear him. Gasping, she reached up to touch the glass. "Oh dear," she said. "What's happening?"

Everett swiveled and moved closer. Lights from the city shone in the distance, but a fire sparked much closer, and as the train ground its brakes turning into another bend, he realized they were headed right toward it.

Chapter 4

Josey gripped the windowsill as the train screeched to a halt before it reached its platform. More fire danced up ahead. Shadowy forms carried torches. An occasional shot rang out. Glass shattered. Someone screamed.

Rhett leaned near, his presence somehow comforting. "I've heard about unrest. Strikes. Disgruntled railroad workers after B&O docked their wages again," he said. "I didn't realize it had spread this far into Ohio."

Josey couldn't tear her eyes away. She'd heard stories as well but hadn't paid much attention. Why would she, when she'd been resigned to live out her life in her hometown—her only travel the dusty walk between work, the boardinghouse, and church?

"Now what do we do?" A rock hit the glass near her, and she flinched.

Rhett grabbed her arm, pulling her back. "Now we get off this train and as far away from the riot as possible."

He was right, but Josey held on to the arm of her seat, biting her lip. How would she ever find Mr. Kane in all of this?

The sound of a woman's sobs snapped her back to the present situation. "Of course. Shall we go out the same way we came in?" She held back a snicker. This was hardly the time for humor.

Rhett flashed a grin. "I'd say our exit may be almost as exciting as your entrance."

"It seems I'm making up for the lack of adventure in my life." Josey gathered her purchases, tucking them into her reticule and shawl the best she could.

Rhett watched for a moment, lips drawing downward beneath his beard. "I'm afraid we'll have to return for your trunk later."

"No need." Josey tested the weight of the bag. Her purchases had been necessary but perhaps premature. She hadn't realized she'd be playing the role of packhorse on this impromptu trip. "I didn't bring one."

A quick glimpse of Rhett showed a deepening frown, but a larger stone hit the window, erupting the train car into another volley of shrieks and exclamations of dismay. This was no time to attempt to decipher what troubled the handsome stranger. The frightened passengers needed someone to conduct them to safety.

As no one else seemed to be stepping up, Josey nodded to the seats across the aisle. "I'll take that side. You take the rest."

Not waiting to see if Rhett followed her lead, Josey comforted an elderly couple, assisting them to their feet and toward the back exit. Then she slipped over to a young lady who quaked under a blanket.

"There, there now," Josey said softly. "It can't be as bad as all that."

"Oh yes," the woman sniffed. "Yes, it can."

Sobs broke out, and as the blanket shifted, Jose noticed the rounded condition of her midsection.

"He told me to go stay with his mother. 'Like it or not, you're going, Florence,' he says. 'You'll be safer there,' he says. 'Closer to the doctor.' " She pointed a shaky finger at the window. "This is not 'safer.' And I—" Gasping, she grabbed at her belly, eyes squeezing shut. "And I am. . .not. . .at his mother's."

Oh dear.

"I'll get you there," Josey found herself promising. Never mind that she had never been to this city and her funds were rapidly dwindling. "But first I need to get you off this train. Now, take my arm."

As best she could, Josey added the woman's bag to her own pile of goods, then aided her down the aisle. Rhett stood on the ground, his own valise at his side, ready to assist.

"Miss Florence, meet Mr. Rhett. Between the two of us, we'll get you there in plenty of time."

"Plenty of time?" Rhett asked out of the corner of his mouth.

Josey just smiled. And prayed.

Once Florence was safely on the ground, her helper turned to Josey, his expression solemn. Earnest. As if he were about to give an explanation for why they needed to part ways.

"Miss Middleton, first there's something—"

As he spoke, she found herself searching for reasons to convince him to stay, but Florence moaned, cutting him off quite effectively.

Oddly relieved, Josey turned from him and focused on the mother-to-be. "I daresay the little one is coming. Let's mosey on to its granny's home, shall we?"

Out of the corner of her eye, she saw Rhett's eyebrows climb nearly to his hairline, but he hoisted as many of their belongings as he could before moving to the other side of Florence, ready to assist if needed.

How he was needed. He'd rescued her once. She hoped he'd stick around long enough to help her rescue this woman and her baby. Josey wrapped an arm around Florence and moved off the tracks toward the city. Toward chaos. And hopefully toward Mr. Everett Kane.

Her gaze strayed to Rhett, and she found herself hoping Mr. Kane was just a little bit like him.

Everett admired Jenny's cool-headedness as they navigated through angry railroad workers and militia. They followed Florence's rough mental map, hauling the pregnant lady over debris and down alleyways, and made it to Florence's mother-in-law's stone two-story home without a scratch. Well, Everett and Florence, anyway. Jenny sported a claw mark or two, thanks to an ill-advised attempt to pet a cat in passing.

Once at the house, at Florence's request, Jenny continued upstairs to assist with the imminent birth. Everett paced back and forth like an anxious father before taking himself outdoors. They'd need food. Maybe a place to stay. He'd search for provisions and a way to continue their journey now that the trains were unreliable.

Maybe he'd manage to find someone to perform the ceremony while he was at it. If so, he'd send Jenny a message. Buy flowers. Make his confession. And if she would still have him, they could marry on the morrow. Perhaps Florence would even feel well enough to witness the happy event, although maybe he was being overly optimistic.

Did Jenny carry her mother's veil in that bulging reticule of hers? Or was it in the trunk that apparently had not made this last train ride? Whatever the case, whatever their state, Everett prayed he'd be marrying his brave, enchanting Jenny on the morrow.

Except one wrong turn led him closer to the depot and the confrontation between railroad workers and the militia. Seeing flames, he stepped back, ready to retreat—but not quickly enough.

Baby Harry arrived with a squall to rival the noise outside. Once he'd been cleaned up and Florence fell asleep, Josey held the sweet bundle in timid arms. It had been quite a while since she'd contemplated the thought of motherhood. She'd reconciled herself to eventually becoming a favorite aunt. She would have been a good one. But a mother? The thought terrified and thrilled her. Humming softly, she studied the baby's perfect face. Did he take after Florence? Would he grow to be a miniature version of his father?

If Josey ever had a child, what would he or she look like?

Before their long-distance courtship began—before her sister had entreated Josey for help—Jenny had once seen a small portrait of Mr. Kane. She'd described him in her quick, flippant way: "*dark hair, dark eyes, clean shaven, and so very handsome.*"

So brown hair would be a given, and Josey imagined hazel eyes—glowing golden brown or green depending on the light—and not a freckle in sight on the child's chubby little cheeks.

Josey hadn't even met Mr. Kane. She presumed far too much. *Jenny* was the one he'd agreed to write. The one who'd begged Mr. Kane's aunt to set up the correspondence in the first place. She was the pretty one, the fun-loving, adventurous one with the charming laugh, fluttering eyelashes, and graceful, carefree ways. She was the one men had flocked around, vying for her attention.

But Jenny was also the one who'd lost patience with writing letters, with waiting for the long-distance relationship to turn into excitement and forever. She was the one who'd decided to pursue a different adventure—running off to elope with a bridge builder instead. Leaving Josey with the proposal, a guilty conscience, and the knowledge that Mr. Kane had been fooled—and that Josey had helped.

Josey's face flamed. Yes, dreaming of having his babies might be premature.

She gave Florence's child a soft kiss before settling him in a basket, snug and warm beside his mama. Then she tiptoed from the bedroom and down the stairs. Mrs. Bamberger would be back up to check on the two of them shortly.

The lady of the house—a stern, capable widow—had insisted on booting her youngest son, Walter, from the second bedroom to provide a place for Josey. For Rhett they supplied a pallet on the pantry floor.

Maybe there he'd be able to scavenge some dinner for them both, since Josey realized she hadn't eaten since breakfast. But the first floor was empty, and the porch deserted as well.

Rhett was gone.

Disappointment stole her appetite. Oh, she had no reason to expect him to stay. He'd gone above and beyond, helping her make the train and then assisting two strangers to safety. But there'd been no goodbye, no chance to express her gratitude. To find out where he was from, where precisely he was going—if she'd ever see him again.

Josey ran a hand over her face and dropped into a plum-colored wingback chair. It appeared she'd gone from somewhat content spinster to fickle woman who didn't know her own mind. Rhett or Everett Kane?

Not that it mattered, because neither was here now.

Resting her head against the back of the chair, Josey stared at the ceiling. Maybe exhaustion was talking, but she couldn't help the sliver of doubt creeping in. Was this a fool's mission? What if she made it all the way out to Colorado only to be politely dismissed? Or even turned away in disgust?

Josey rubbed at her chest, just above her heart, as if that would alleviate the sudden heaviness.

She'd stay here tonight, then be on her way tomorrow. Alone.

Chapter 5

The first thing he noticed was the smell of soggy yeast bread. Then the uncomfortable position he lay in. And then the pain—an insistent throbbing over his left temple where the rock had hit.

Everett pushed himself to a sitting position, wincing as the throbbing increased tenfold. After he recovered enough, he took stock of his surroundings. The violence seemed to have settled some, at least in this section of town. He appeared to be uninjured, with the exception of his head wound and some minor cuts and bruises. His packages had been rummaged through. The food he'd purchased, trampled or taken. His pocket watch was gone, along with most of the contents of his wallet.

The hidden compartments in his vest appeared uncompromised. Those funds should be sufficient for traveling home but nothing else. He'd need Western Union to wire funds from back home. Wouldn't Horace revel in rubbing that in?

But now he just had to get back to Jenny. With a wary look around, he stood, steadying himself against a fence before taking an uneasy step forward. By the time he reached the Bambergers' home, he'd almost gotten used to the sledgehammer inside his head. The dizziness was another matter. After bracing himself against a porch post, he made his way to the front door and knocked. No one answered, as the sun had yet to rise, so he cautiously let himself in.

The fireplace in the parlor was dark. Everett limped over and sat on the hearth, then gathered the energy to wedge another couple logs and a bit of kindling into the ash and start a fire. The cool of the summer night had managed to chill him through.

Only then did he notice he wasn't alone in the room. Jenny sat on the chair across from him, her breathing even and slow. Her hair tumbled loose over one shoulder, almost reaching her waist.

Everett stared, imagining the texture. Tucked into a chignon or some such, her hair may not be the envy of women. But without having to fight the constraints of pins and braids, it fell in long, soft waves, begging to be touched.

He moved closer, unable to help himself. Sleep became her. Awake, she seemed confident, comfortable with herself and around others. People gravitated toward her, and no wonder. She was happy, likable, helpful.

But asleep, she'd relaxed completely. Curled up into herself—her feet tucked under her skirt and hands under her chin. Letting down her guard along with her hair, and appearing vulnerable for once, especially with the faintest of streaks down both cheeks. Had she cried herself to sleep?

His heart panged at the thought, and he reached for her, catching himself just before he could caress her face. She wasn't his yet.

But she would be.

"Goodnight, my love," he whispered. Then he stoked the fire a final time and limped his way to his pallet in the pantry.

The cries of the baby jerked Josey awake. Groggily, she made her way up the stairs to the bedroom where Florence lay, and helped soothe and change little Harry until Mrs. Bamberger roused enough to take over. Turning to go, Josey lingered near the door, watching the sweet scene as mother and newborn child fell a little more in love. Would she ever have a moment like that, with a warm, cooing bundle—the evidence of love—tucked close to her heart?

She hoped so. But it surely seemed she was taking the long way around.

Mrs. Bamberger motioned her over. "I can't thank you and your young man enough for all you did to help my Florence."

"Oh, he's not mine." She smiled, tamping down conflicting emotions. "We just met along the way. I'm afraid he left—"

"He returned early this morning and is still asleep in the pantry." The woman's smile thinned a little. "Where he was *supposed* to sleep."

Josey blinked at the news, self-consciously brushing at her wrinkled clothing. The ones she'd slept in, in the parlor, where Rhett surely would have seen her.

"Thank you for your hospitality," she managed. "I intended to return to the room you so kindly provided, but I'm afraid exhaustion took over before I made it there."

The older woman's reproving expression softened. "It was a long day for all of you. Again, thank you. You're welcome to stay until my other son can make it here, and then I'm afraid we're full up."

Josey nodded her appreciation and stepped back into the hallway. She hoped she wouldn't be here long. There were travel plans to make, a valise to buy, and—

"By the way. . ." Mrs. Bamberger followed, closing the door softly behind her. "Someone slipped a message to Walter. Said it was for you." After fumbling in her apron pocket, she handed over a wrinkled note with a familiar scrawl.

Swallowing hard, Josey took it and nodded again, not trusting her voice. She nearly tripped down the stairs in her hurry to read it.

Please meet me at Sweetbriar Chapel at half past eight in the morning. Will explain everything. All my love. EK

She sank onto the bottom step, her smile so big it hurt her cheeks. Mr. Kane lived! He was here! How he'd found her was a mystery, but he had indeed. Maybe he'd asked after her around the telegraph station? Walter had headed out shortly after their arrival to send a telegram to Florence's husband. Maybe they'd crossed paths at that point. An answer to prayer.

Though Mr. Kane's love was pledged to J. Middleton, Josey could pretend for the moment that the first initial stood for her own name, not that of the prettier Middleton sister.

But it didn't. . .and Mr. Kane wanted to meet at a church.

Suddenly picturing herself wearing her mother's veil—which wasn't in her reticule anyway—and standing at the altar, Josey could almost hear her own guilt-ridden voice squeaking out a protest when the preacher asked if anyone objected to the marriage.

Oh dear.

She chewed her lip a moment before running her finger over his initials. They'd figure things out. Right? He was alive and *here*, and she would meet the love of her life very soon.

An image of Rhett flashed in her mind—his strong hand held out, grinning at her from the back of the moving train. She hurriedly pushed the memory aside. He'd been a godsend. A helper along the way. But he was still a stranger.

Handsome. Kind.

But a stranger.

Again, she caressed the page, then folded it to slide inside the envelope containing the last letter. Everett Kane was the man she loved, and in just a few hours she'd find out if he could love her too.

Shortly before the appointed time, Josey tucked the end of her braid into place. She'd done the best she could with no time for elaborate measures. A loose braid coiled around a low bun, and wisps of curls framed her face. It looked nice enough now, although it likely wouldn't last the walk to the chapel. She'd changed into the blue day dress she'd purchased at the last stop and wrapped her red shawl around her shoulders.

Her reflection showed a shabbily dressed woman of average height and build. Average in everything, really, but with green eyes sparkling with hope. She offered a tremulous smile. Hopefully Mr. Kane would see the heart he'd fallen in love with. The real J. Middleton.

Dear God, let him love me.

After hiding the envelope with the letter and message inside her bodice, she drew a fortifying breath and headed for the stairs.

"Miss Middleton." Mrs. Bamberger nodded a greeting as Josey passed her in the hallway. "I see you're ready to meet your beau."

The woman had read the message. Of course she had.

"Well, let me send you off with some advice. I may be an old widow, but I still know some things."

Josey flushed, shooting a look down the stairs. No movement.

"I don't know who this mysterious EK is, but I do know your young man in the pantry would be my choice if I were you. Or, honestly, even if I were *me*. I am a widow, after all." Had a giggle just escaped Mrs. Bamberger's stern lips?

Josey felt the very tips of her ears turn warm. "He's not my—"

"Maybe not, but he should be."

"Mr. Rhett seems to be a good man, but—"

"But nothing. And those shoulders! Land sakes! Mark my words, if you let him get away, it'll be a lifelong regret. Although. . .well. . ." Mumbling something about *some*one's advanced age and not having that long to regret choices, the older woman turned and slipped back into the other bedroom.

Uncertain whether or not she'd just been insulted, Josey stared at the door as it creaked closed and the baby began to cry anew. After a confused moment, she descended the stairs and set her reticule by the door.

Attempting to ignore Mrs. Bamberger's words, she cracked open the pantry door. Rhett lay on the floor, partially covered with a ratty quilt, his coat and vest folded for a pillow. He faced the wall, a jar of pickles mere inches from his nose. Still sleeping, his breathing heavy.

Where had he gone? And where would he go now?

She watched for a moment, even clearing her throat a tiny bit in hopes he'd wake up. The only movement was the rise and fall of those broad shoulders.

It felt wrong leaving without telling him goodbye. Yet what would she say? Maybe this was for the best.

Goodbye, Rhett. Godspeed.

Resolutely turning her back, she left to find the chapel. To find her happily ever after.

Lunchtime found Josey wandering in the graveyard behind the chapel—an appropriate setting, considering she felt as if she'd just buried her dreams.

Mr. Kane had not made his appearance. Maybe something happened. Again. Maybe he was just very late. More likely, he'd come, taken one look, and changed his mind. She'd wondered before. Now she was near certain.

What now? After her earlier conversation with Mrs. Bamberger, the idea of returning to the house sent shivers of humiliation through her entire body.

She could travel back home. Should do so, in fact, but did anything await her there? Jenny should be in New York by now, deliriously happy with her new husband. Making hats had never been something Josey enjoyed, and who knew if her job had been held for her. And her room at the boardinghouse? She hadn't intended to be gone this long. Without dipping into the funds Mr. Kane sent, she would doubtless be late on her rent.

Sighing, she settled onto a fallen log and stared at the headstones, not even working up a smile at the clever epitaphs. She could only imagine hers joining them.

Here lies Josey, the freckled old maid.
Back at home she should have stayed.
Instead she's here, with no one dear,
and the gravedigger's yet to be paid.

Well. It was something to consider anyway.

"Oh Josey." Plucking a petal from a daisy, she allowed herself to wallow. "You've really done it now."

"Miss Middleton?" Florence's brother-in-law hollered from the path. "Is that you?"

Hastily wiping her face, she stood to meet him. "Yes, Walter. Is everything all right?"

The youth dashed toward her, panting. "Mother sent me to find you. It's Mr. Rhett. He's very ill, and the doctor still hasn't arrived to check on Florence and the baby."

Josey swept her bag into her arms and hurried toward the street, then hesitated. If she left and Mr. Kane was only late, she might miss her chance to catch up with him. Finally and forever.

But Rhett had been there when she needed him, and now he needed her. Quickening her steps, she followed the boy home.

He couldn't remember his name. Or at least the name they called him didn't sound quite right. How hard had he been hit?

Now *that*, he remembered. Coming around a corner, arms full, heart happy. Then the split-second realization, as a stray rock careened his way, that he couldn't move fast enough.

Other details remained fuzzy. Why he was in this house to begin with. Why happiness floated around the edges of his consciousness despite his pain, and why in the world he'd awakened hugging a dusty jar of pickles to his chest.

If he thought hard enough, he'd surely remember, but right now all he wanted to do was fall back into a sleep deep enough for the pounding in his head and the uneasiness of his stomach to disappear.

The pantry door opened slightly, allowing a wedge of light to violate his dark cocoon. He growled but couldn't find the willpower to turn away.

"Mr. Rhett?"

That name again.

"What happened?"

The voice though. *That* was familiar. Without opening his eyes, he could suddenly picture the reason he'd been happy.

Jenny Middleton. Sweet smile, freckled nose, kind eyes, wild hair, and a heart of gold. He'd planned to marry her today. Instead, he probably sported a black eye, no longer had funds on hand to lavish her with gifts, and may never again be able to stand up without feeling like vomiting.

"Oh dear."

The door opened wider, and he grimaced as the light turned the back of his eyelids fiery red.

"They said they couldn't wake you up. That you didn't seem to recognize your name." Gentle hands touched his jaw, turning his head slightly, and a finger brushed the skin near his wound. "Oh dear," she said again. "Rhett, do you know me?"

Despite the pain, his lips curled slightly. He knew she loved lavender. Her favorite food was watermelon, and as a young girl she'd beat most of the boys in a seed-spitting contest. A feat unappreciated by her family. He knew both of her parents had since passed on, with only an older sister left.

"I know you." Cautiously, he raised his hand to grasp hers. She let out a surprised gasp but didn't pull away.

"Mrs. Bamberger sent Walter to tell me you were ill. How were you injured?"

Forcing his eyes open, he squinted up at her. Through the blur he could tell her hair was windblown, and were her eyes reddened? She'd been crying. Again.

"Where did you go?"

She released his hand and fidgeted with something. "A fruitless errand, it seems, but I'm fairly certain we were talking about you."

His vision finally cleared. What he could see of her hair was intricately woven in a way he hadn't seen her wear it as of yet. She'd changed her dress. Its blue tones drew out the storm in her eyes. The sound of paper crinkling as she shifted her position brought it all back. The message he'd sent. The appointment today where he'd planned to reveal his full name—which certainly wasn't Rhett—and beg her to marry him then and there.

The appointment he'd surely missed.

No wonder she'd been crying. Yet here she was, putting her own feelings aside to care for a random traveling companion. Just as she'd put her safety and agenda aside to watch over a pregnant stranger and a lost boy before that.

His bride was an angel.

"Maybe I should ask where *you* went?" She backed away, attempting to maintain a proper distance in the small storage space. "You didn't stick around long enough to meet the baby you worked so hard to save."

While explaining about the rock, Everett worked himself into a sitting position. Jenny fussed over him, genuine concern in her eyes. And maybe something else? He felt it in the way her hands lingered a little long on his shoulder, on the way she smoothed his hair clear of his injury.

Or at least he hoped so, hoped she could love him.

He opened his mouth to introduce himself properly. Everett Kane—he remembered now. But he cut himself off. With barely enough money on him to get them back to Colorado, much less pay for the wedding and the lodgings and gifts she deserved, he dared not risk the possibility of seeing love turn to pity. After waiting so long to meet Jenny, he would not come to her empty-handed.

No, he must be patient a little longer, and hope and pray she'd be patient as well.

Chapter 6

Josey pulled herself together and assisted Rhett to his feet. Trying not to notice how it felt to wrap her arm snug around him, to have the warm, solid weight of his arm draped around her shoulders, she pointed him toward the parlor.

Wringing her hands, Mrs. Bamberger hovered nearby, her normally severe composure fractured as she fretted over this and that. "Don't get blood on my sofa, please," and "Are you sure it's nothing contagious? He seems quite ill. Should he be quarantined?"

Her favor—so quickly won—seemed to have been lost just as easily. The baby wailed, and Josey sighed in relief as Mrs. Bamberger left them alone.

"She'll never rest easy with me here," Rhett said.

Josey hated to admit he was right. "The doctor should arrive soon to check on Florence. We'll see if he says you're able to travel."

She was ready, for sure, but at this point she wouldn't get far. She needed to secure some sort of transportation.

"Where are you headed, again?" Josey settled another cold cloth on his forehead and watched him wince. No complaints, but his head still pained him. What would be the smoothest alternative to the railroad?

"West."

"Just 'west,' Mr. Just Rhett?" She raised her brows.

Curious how he weighed his answer. "I'm. . .searching for something."

She knew that feeling. She was living it.

Maybe it wasn't meant to be.

"You don't know what that something is?" She struggled to keep her voice even.

With effort, he turned his head and gave the slightest smile. "I think I know."

Her breath caught, and heat flooded her face. *He did* not *mean you*, she silently chanted until her cheeks cooled. Whatever he meant, he could not have been flirting. Or if he was, he surely didn't mean it. Men weren't drawn to her, not in that way. There was only one man who'd fallen for her—Josey masquerading as Jenny, that is—and apparently he'd changed his mind.

The heavy feeling returned to her stomach, the ache to her heart.

"What's your final destination?" Rhett asked.

Josey absently reached to smooth the papers tucked over her heart. Caught herself and adjusted her collar instead. "I'm not sure anymore."

"Really?" His voice took on an unfamiliar quality. Gruff. A little. . .hurt, almost? "What changed? You seemed quite determined yesterday as you charged after the train."

"Was that only yesterday?"

He chuckled.

She didn't. "Yesterday I believed I was on my way to meeting the man I love. The man I was going to marry."

When she didn't continue, Rhett prompted her, his voice soft. "And now you're not sure?"

"How can I be? I'm here, but he is not. That's twice now he's failed to come when he said he would." Anger and hurt strained her voice as she curled back up in the chair she'd slept in last night. She should not be sitting so informally in front of this stranger. Shouldn't be confiding in him, sharing her heartache, her dreams. But something about Rhett made her more comfortable in her own skin.

Made her feel almost as if she'd come home.

"Miss Middleton—" His voice seemed pained.

Abruptly, she straightened, aware she'd crossed into dangerous territory. She agreed with Mrs. Bamberger that Rhett was a good man—she sensed it deep down. She couldn't help admiring him, but he wasn't settled. He was a stranger. She'd obviously made him uncomfortable with her honesty. And, most of all, he wasn't her Mr. Kane.

At the thought, a twinge in the general vicinity of her heart caught her by surprise. She tamped it down hurriedly, springing to her feet. She would not betray Mr. Kane. *Everett.* Though it looked as if he'd deserted her, there was a chance there was more to the story. That he was in trouble—or that he'd discovered the switch. If either were the case, she needed to pursue her mission. To make certain he was all right or to explain what had happened and beg his forgiveness.

Their correspondence meant enough to her that he deserved the benefit of the doubt. She would not betray him.

But could she face him, suspecting he'd rejected her so soundly?

"What's wrong, J—Miss Middleton?"

Rhett moved from his half-reclining position, the damp rag held in his hand as he studied her with furrowed brow. His hair was disheveled in the most endearing way. His eyes were warm—a rich and sweet cinnamon—and concerned about *her*, when his own pain must be great.

She needed to assure herself he was well, and then she needed him to be gone. And right now, well, she needed some air.

Josey darted across the room.

"Miss Middleton?"

"Going to find the doctor," she called over her shoulder, glancing back to where he stood now, half in shadows. His tall form cut a handsome figure even in his torn and stained clothing. She took one last look.

Then she closed the door.

It didn't take long to find Doc Sullivan. The many injuries of the night before made for several stops along the way, but he assured Josey the Bamberger home was next.

She wanted to make sure Rhett was okay, that he'd be back to his original strength so he could continue to play rescuer and protector. A role he'd worn so well in the short time she'd known him, for which she would be forever grateful. But she couldn't very well stay, could she?

After discreetly counting her remaining bills, she turned toward Main Street. She must find a way to arrange transportation to—somewhere. And soon.

Colorado. Maybe. She wasn't sure.

Wherever she went, it needed to be away from Rhett, even if that knowledge hurt just a little.

After the doctor proclaimed him well enough and the baby and mother doing splendidly, after Mrs. Bamberger sent him another dozen glares and long-suffering sighs, after the noonday sun beat down and continued its journey, and after the pain in Everett's head settled enough to allow him to think clearly, he realized Jenny wasn't coming back.

Nausea rose, and not due to the head injury. If he lost her here, would he be able to find her again? With the uncertainty he'd instilled in her by not meeting this morning, she seemed hesitant to continue the journey. Would she return home? Did she have enough money left to do so?

Too many questions. He had to find her. Now.

Taking his leave of a relieved Mrs. Bamberger, Everett limped along to the train station. Jenny likely wouldn't choose to travel that way after all they'd experienced. But—if anything remained of it—the rails seemed the logical place to begin, even if it made his temple ache more with each step closer.

No rocks flew his way this afternoon. The town seemed to have calmed down, although tendrils of smoke still rose from the direction he headed. Foot traffic was light, but a lad rushed past, brushing up against him. Everett automatically reached to protect the wallet that had been emptied the night before.

What he really needed was the Colt six-shooter tucked inside the trunk he'd abandoned when they'd fled the train. Especially as he rounded the corner and saw the tracks laid out in front of him, with a car on its side, blocking the path.

Clenching his jaw at the sight, he trudged on to the depot and found it deserted and in shambles. He relaxed slowly. No train service meant Jenny hadn't gotten out that way. Was there a chance she was still in the town? Lying in an alley with a head wound, perhaps?

Cold chills broke out, even though the fighting in town seemed to have settled. What had he been thinking, asking her to meet him? If he'd thought at all, he would have realized that unless her sister agreed to travel with her, she'd likely have to come unchaperoned. No protector. No companion. Not immediately making it clear who he was—it was unforgivable.

Yet he hoped she'd find it in her heart to do just that. *If* he could find her.

The river was next. Everett followed the road to the water as the sun slipped a little further in its path behind the earth. Packet boats carried passengers, mail, and other cargo at a snail's pace through the canals and waterways, often pulled by horses on the bank. Though the boats in this area traveled south, not west, there could be a chance Jenny decided to catch a ride.

A flash of red in the bushes along the river caught his eye. Veering toward it, he found a scrap of fabric much like the shawl Jenny wore the last he saw her. Dread coursed through him as he saw another glimpse behind a nearby tree. He moved toward it to find someone huddled beneath the wrap, shivering. Crying.

"Jenny?" he said softly as he approached.

The figure let out a small shriek and scrambled to her feet. Too small to be Jenny. Eyes too gray and face too pale.

Everett stiffened, surprise stealing his voice.

She gathered her shabby skirts, preparing to run.

"Wait!" He stepped closer, hands raised.

The girl flinched, as if she expected him to hit her.

He froze and slowly lowered his arms. "I'm not going to hurt you, miss. I would just like to know where you came across that shawl. I'm looking for a friend who has one very similar."

She shrank against the tree trunk and stared in his direction, warily taking in every detail. "Were you in a fight?"

"Not exactly." Everett touched his head. "You could say I walked into a rock."

The girl couldn't be more than fourteen. Shadows darkened one cheek—or were those bruises?

He desperately wanted to ask about Jenny again, but first: "Is anything amiss? Are you lost?"

Her prominent chin quivered. She asked in a small voice, "What was your friend's name?"

"Miss Middleton."

Sinking to the ground, she resumed her sobbing, and Everett resumed his fretting.

"She's gonna die, and it will be all my fault!" Her wailing picked up a decibel or two, until the river caught her attention. Clapping a hand over her mouth, she regained enough control for Everett to hear himself think.

"Whatever are you going on about?"

"She took my place on the boat. My papa—" She touched her shadowed cheek, and Everett's jaw clenched tight. "I do the cooking when he has passengers. But today I—I had to get away." The tears fell harder. "She helped me, and now. . ."

"I can help her." He hoped. No, he prayed. "Just tell me how long ago they left. What the boat looks—"

"There." She pointed at the water. A long, narrow vessel reached a bend in the river, a team of horses helping to pull it along from the bank. "It's already left. I'm so sorry."

"Quickly. Is there a bridge nearby? One your father's boat will travel under?" It wouldn't travel fast. Four miles an hour or less, he'd guess.

The girl gave an affirmative answer, then forlornly sank to the ground and hugged her knees to her chest.

Everett itched to go. Traveling would take longer, be more difficult with his injuries. But Jenny risked herself for this young girl. Everett would make sure her efforts had been worth it.

"What's your name?"

"Mildred."

"May I call you Millie?"

Another wail. "*She* asked me that too."

He found a warm smile for the girl, deciding to take that as a yes. "I'll look after Miss Middleton. Let me worry about her, you hear me, Millie? Now, do you have somewhere to go?"

In answer, she bit her lip.

Jenny hadn't figured that detail out already? Oh dear.

Another smile flickered across his face as her oft-used expression worked its way into his thoughts. The amusement quickly died as that affirmed his assumption that the situation must have seemed desperate indeed.

"I have an idea." Fumbling in his pocket, he retrieved his last letter from Jenny—the only paper he had on hand. Removing the envelope, he scratched a note onto it along with the address he'd left earlier. "Go here. Ask for Mrs. Bamberger. Hand her this, then tell her your story."

The widow may not be happy with a girl in need showing up unannounced, but she'd grumbled several times about needing help. Well, he aimed to please.

"They may not be able to pay you, but you'll have somewhere safe to go for the moment."

Millie took the envelope from him and held it in both hands. "Thank you, mister." She sniffled, then started to unwrap the shawl.

"Keep it," Everett said. "She obviously wanted you to have it." He stared after the boat, then back at Millie. He should escort her to the Bamberger residence, make sure she arrived safely.

As if reading his mind, Millie shook her head. "I'll be fine, mister, now that I have somewhere to go. Just get on that boat before my pa figures out it ain't me in the kitchen."

Chapter 7

If Josey had been thinking, she would have asked Millie for her recipes. But she'd been so afraid the drunk captain would come back to the market to find his daughter, or that Millie would change her mind about getting to safety, she'd half shoved the girl away without even a word of farewell.

Now in the sweltering kitchen of the packet boat, Josey had peeled her fifteenth potato, nicked her finger twice, and still come up empty as she racked her brain for the instructions to make Granny's famous stew. Even if she escaped the notice of the captain, she'd likely be in danger of her fellow passengers once the food was served.

Oh dear. Whatever had she been thinking?

She hadn't. Just like when she set off on this ill-fated adventure to begin with.

Sniffing, she reached for the onions. Might as well have an excuse if more tears were in her future. Goodness, what was she going to do? She'd been lonely before but content enough. Now she'd chased off on some foolhardy mission and—

Fretting wouldn't fix anything.

She prayed as she chopped the first onion. Prayed some more as she peeled the second. Kept praying as she minced the third.

And then Rhett exploded into the small kitchen, nearly knocking her into the fire. "Are you hurt?" he nearly shouted as he reached her, holding her out in front of him as he raked her with his gaze.

Josey stood mute as his brows furrowed. His mouth tightened in the fury she felt building inside him and stiffening his arms.

"What has he done—?"

"How did you get on board?" she interrupted, thoroughly confused.

"Jumped." He flicked a hand toward the window.

She glanced in that direction, then her gaze darted back to him as he plucked at the skirt of her apron.

"Where are you injured?"

Batting his hands away, she scrutinized him in turn. "I believe you're the one with the injury."

He seemed hardy enough. His clothes were damp with sweat but not soaked. It appeared he hadn't swum after her. Whatever the method, the exercise left him with wild eyes, a ruddy complexion under his beard, and his hair once again disheveled.

Basically, it made him intensely handsome.

"You came after me?" Hope affected her voice, choking it slightly.

Oh dear.

"Yes. Now. . ." He patted her arms, held her waist, framed her face as he tipped it gently one way, then the other in his examination. "Tell me where you're hurt, and I'll get you off this boat."

"But why?"

"Is it not clear?" His gaze found hers, the wildness softening into something that made her insides quiver.

Oh. Oh. Dear.

"No, it's not." In desperation, she pretended to misunderstand him. "I'm fine, as you can see, and I have passengers to feed."

"If you're fine"—his voice was gentle but held a note of steel as he wiped away her tears with his thumbs—"then why do I find you weeping and your clothes bloodied?" He held up the edge of her apron once again.

Sudden laughter welled up inside, breaking the tension as it burst forth. She may have giggled overly much, but his glowering made it hard to stop. Pointing to the pile of chopped onions and the knife, then holding up her hands for him to examine, she watched as comprehension dawned.

"He didn't hurt you?"

"No." She abruptly sobered as the relief—the concern—in his voice nearly made her want to weep again. "All injuries so far have been self-inflicted."

He didn't laugh. "I thought you were lost. Or dead."

"So you jumped off a cliff?"

He smirked. "If you call that riverbank a cliff, just wait until you get out west. But no. I jumped off a bridge as the boat passed a couple feet below. Hardly a hero's feat."

There hadn't been any bridges visible when she'd boarded, and Rhett had been nowhere in sight either. Judging by his muddy boots and sweaty clothing, he'd run very far or very fast. With a head injury. For her.

The mysterious Rhett managed to make it harder and harder not to fall in love with him.

"I would say it's somewhat heroic." The words came out breathy. Had he noticed? Josey unsuccessfully tried to push away Mrs. Bamberger's words of advice.

"Then let me continue my heroism by rescuing the damsel. Do you have your things with you? What's left of them, I mean?"

"I'm not leaving."

Rhett bolstered her courage by his very presence. Probably not his intention, by the way his mouth opened but no words came out.

"As I said before, I have passengers I promised to feed."

"Millie insisted you were in extreme danger."

"And so I will be if I don't get these people their supper. Do you know how to make stew?"

It appeared he wanted to argue, if the sudden mottling on his face and tightly clenched teeth indicated the frustration she assumed it did. Instead, he gave one final look out the window, then scrounged up another knife to chop carrots.

"The meat should go in the pot first." He pointed to the kettle and the water that had just come to a boil, then began peeling and cutting vegetables with slow but practiced movements.

"You actually *do* know how to make stew." She should have figured. Rhett was certainly a jack-of-all-trades.

"I've spent a lot of time on the trail or fending for myself at home."

"Home?" Josey kept her hands busy following his instructions, trying not to appear so surprised. So curious. "Where's that?"

The silence took on a weight, one she couldn't decipher the reason for. Glancing up, she found him studying her, as if trying to discern whether she could be trusted with his secrets.

She suddenly hoped he found her worthy. Guilt made her break eye contact.

"Miss Middleton—"

The door burst open, barely missing Josey.

"Mildred!" a man roared.

Stifling a shriek, Josey froze. Half hidden between the door and the flour barrel, she fastened her wide-eyed stare on Rhett as he rose and turned to face the threat.

"Who are you, and where's my good-for-nothing daughter?" The captain huffed and stomped closer to Rhett, seeming not to notice the paring knife now held in Rhett's fist.

"I'm helping her," Rhett said.

Pressing her fingers to her mouth, Josey endeavored to stay silent—not one of her strengths. If she swooned, surely it was because she held her breath, not because as Rhett played the hero—again!—she couldn't helping noticing how brawny his arms looked with his sleeves rolled up past his elbows. How his eyes glinted like the steel in his hand. And how his voice didn't shake like her knees were doing right now. Instead, it remained steady, deep, calm—and a tinge dangerous.

In fact, it was hard not to notice everything about him and wish, just a little, that she'd met him before Jenny received that first exquisite letter from Mr. Kane.

Oh dear. It seemed her plan to run away from Rhett—to stay loyal to her first love—may very well have backfired.

"She doesn't need help." The captain advanced another step. One glance to the side and he'd see her. "Where is she?"

"Not sure." Rhett casually settled back onto the stool, drawing the angle of the man's gaze away from Josey.

She took the opportunity to crouch lower, nearly knocking over a jar of preserves.

"I just know I'm supposed to finish chopping carrots and get them into the pot," Rhett continued. "I promised to help make my famous trail stew. Your passengers will be impressed with the fare, I'm sure."

"Humph." Crossing his arms, the captain glowered another moment. "Make sure to tell Mildred I need my pipe. And you—" He shook a finger at Rhett. "If you ruin my dinner, I'll toss you into the river myself."

Rhett laughed. The sound stopped abruptly as the captain swung around and Josey found herself staring straight into his bloodshot eyes.

"Um, hello." She slowly straightened.

He sputtered, yelled again for Millie, and brought his florid face inches from Josey's. "Where is my daughter?"

"I'm sure I don't know." Josey's voice came out squeaky.

"Then why. Are. You. Wearing. *This*?" One beefy hand gripped her arm. The other fingered her shawl as his breath curdled the contents of her stomach.

"We switched. My red shawl looked quite fetching with her coloring." Josey sought out Rhett as he inched closer. "Did you notice? I meant to mention it to her—"

"Are you daft, girl?" the captain roared.

"Possibly, but right now I'm mostly worried about the stew. It would be a shame to overcook the meat."

To her surprise, he let go. Rhett backed off, lowering the knife.

"Fine. Cook dinner. Serve it. And send Millie to me. *Not* in that order."

"Well, technically, the cooking and serving should be in that—" Josey pinched her lips closed as Rhett rolled his eyes.

"You two are up to something." Millie's father glared from her to Rhett and back again. "Whatever it is, if I don't like it, you're *both* getting dunked."

"Yes, Captain." Josey's head bobbed too emphatically, thumping against the cabinet behind her.

With a final glare and shake of his head, the man left the room.

Josey wilted, and Rhett reached a knife-free hand to catch her.

"Save the stew, Mr. Rhett," she muttered against his shirt. "Because I'm afraid saving *me* is going to be out of the question."

"You were brilliant," he said, and it almost felt as if he pressed a kiss against her head before slowly—maybe even reluctantly?—letting go. "Did he injure you?"

The warmth and care in his voice wrapped around her heart, sending shivers through her. She rubbed her arms. "I'm fine." She'd surely be bruised in the morning. Poor Millie.

"Lucky for him," Rhett grumbled as he added tomato preserves to the kettle.

The shivers turned to butterflies, but reality sank in. This needed to be it—the end of the line for them—for so many reasons.

"Tell me how to finish up the stew, please."

He looked up at her abrupt request, brows raised. A smile teased at his lips, and suddenly she found herself trying to picture his mouth without the beard surrounding it. Oh, it was a nice beard. Well-kept. Handsome. It wasn't that she hated it. Just that she was—curious.

She should not be curious.

"It's a secret recipe," he said. "Developed over time and refined over many miles, and many, many campfires. I don't share it with just anyone."

"Please, Rhett." The panic thickened, made her forget the formality of adding "Mr." to his address. "You need to tell me how to finish the stew. And then—then you need to leave."

"*We* need to leave, you mean," Everett corrected. Of course that's what she meant. Jenny might be impulsive, but she wasn't an imbecile.

"No. After dinner I'll hide. . .somewhere. But I need to be on this boat."

"You're being ridiculous."

"I'm being—" She sniffed and turned away. "I'm being practical. You need to get off because you're heading west, and this boat is not."

He'd realized that, of course, but had assumed her sense of direction might not be that keen, or in her hurry to help a poor soul, she'd rushed in without thinking about the destination at all.

Dread crawled along his spine. "Isn't that where you're going?"

"Like I said before, I don't know anymore." Conflicting emotions swirled in her eyes as she lifted them to meet his. "I just don't know."

"I thought you loved the man."

"I never said that."

"You didn't?" He was certain she had. Not in person. Not in their limited discussion. But in her letters she'd made her feelings clear.

Everett patted his pocket for the familiar feel of that last correspondence. Had he read more into it? Put extra sentiment between the lines? Oh bother. He couldn't pull it out to read in front of her, not without confessing. And now wasn't the time for that if she was busy second-guessing their relationship.

"So you don't love him?"

She sniffled. "I didn't say that either."

"But you're not going to Colorado."

Wait. Had she ever told "Rhett" her final destination? He held his breath, waiting to be called out.

She hadn't seemed to notice his slipup. Just stared at her biscuit dough, misery etched on her face. "Maybe. Maybe not. I need to get a few things settled in my mind first."

That didn't sound good. Not good at all.

The captain's voice sounded from above, roaring slurred orders. Were they preparing to pass under another bridge? That would make it an ideal time to flee.

Leaning forward, Everett gripped the flour-covered table. "Wouldn't it be better to settle your mind in a more, well, *settled* spot? Not floating along, destination unknown, with an angry drunk hovering about?"

She avoided his eyes and set to shaping the biscuits. "You make good points. Except there are hungry passengers, a perfectly delicious stew to finish, and. . .and. . ."

"Say it. You can tell me."

With a sigh, she set down the biscuit cutter. "The truth is, I need space."

His brow furrowed.

"You're going to make me spell it out? Fine." Raising her chin, she glared for a moment, then tackled her work with more vigor than necessary. "I need to get away. From *you*."

It was a good thing he'd been hanging on to the table, because her words packed a greater punch than the captain could ever manage.

"Let me get you off the boat," he said hoarsely, then cleared his throat and tried again. "Let me make sure you're safe, and then. . .then I have something to tell you. If you still want to part ways, well, I'll abide by your decision." Maybe. He'd try.

It would be the hardest thing he'd ever done.

"Fine, but I'm not going anywhere until after—"

"After supper. Understood." Rhett rubbed the back of his neck and stared out the window. He couldn't keep the secret anymore. Hadn't really meant to in the first place. "Jenny, I—"

She whirled on him, eyes wide and stark. "What did you call me?"

"I'm sorry. Miss Middleton." He was butchering this. She'd never given "Rhett" leave to use her given name. Had she even told him what it was?

"What. Did. You. Call. Me?" Her finger stabbed his chest.

Apparently she had not. "Jenny. Let me explain."

"Not now." She slammed the half-finished biscuits into the woodstove and darted toward the door. "I need air."

Before he could stop her, Jenny slipped into the main cabin beyond. He tried to follow—to give her the space she required but still manage to keep her safe—but she was fast. She scooted past chatty passengers and gained a few curious looks before she crawled up to the roof and out of sight.

But not so far away that he couldn't hear the captain shout for his daughter.

"Still just me, Captain," Jenny called as she came back into view, but her retreat was blocked when one of the captain's men joined Everett at the bottom of the ladder.

"Excuse me." Everett smiled civilly and set his foot on the first rung. When there was no resistance, he continued to the top.

Jenny's slender form wobbled in the center of the roof, struggling to keep her footing as she decided how to escape both of them. Her back was to him—and to the rapidly approaching bridge.

"Low bridge!" A crewman shouted.

The passengers up top ducked, but, focused on the captain's approach, Jenny swayed in place, not heeding the warning. Everett sprinted toward her, then nearly jerked to a halt as well, because in the captain's hand was a gun. And it was trained on Jenny.

Chapter 8

This wasn't how Josey had pictured dying. While more exciting than what she'd had in mind, she would have preferred to at least meet Mr. Kane first.

"What did you do to my daughter?" The captain growled as he took a step closer.

"Not what *you* did to her, that's for sure," Josey growled back at him.

"Miss Middleton!" Rhett sounded desperate and so far away. "Get down!"

"I'll teach you for meddlin'." The gun lifted, its barrel a dark, evil eye staring into Josey's soul.

She should have prayed more about her decisions of late. She should have been more kind when she said goodbye to her sister. Had Jenny eloped partly for Josey's sake? To give her a chance with Everett Kane? She'd never know now.

She should have heard Rhett out.

Maybe.

The captain's finger twitched. A solid weight hit Josey from behind, wrapping around her, and suddenly she was rolling and tumbling and falling as a blast rang in her ears.

And then nothing. The world muted as she sank beneath murky water, until finally something propelled her to the surface. Sputtering and gasping, she treaded water as Rhett's face came into view.

His hair stuck to his head in short waves. His white shirt and dark vest clung to his muscular chest—the chest she'd been clasped to as he valiantly swept her out of harm's way.

He'd saved her. Again.

"Jenny?"

With a cry, she shoved away and paddled for shore as fast as her clumsy strokes allowed. He followed, smoothly keeping up with her, attempting to assist as she scrambled up the bank in her sodden clothes.

The most perfect, gentlemanly, handsome, heroic *liar* she'd ever met.

"Miss Middleton. *Please.*" His rich voice was husky with desperation. Concern.

In the growing darkness, she trudged to a nearby tree and collapsed to the ground beneath it, pulling her legs up underneath her dress. The few things she'd brought on this unfortunate journey were still on the boat.

And the letters—Mr. Kane's beautiful letters—all lost to her, except what was tucked in her bodice, and even that was most assuredly ruined.

It was almost too much.

Rhett sat beside her, his movements tentative, so unlike his usual confident manner. For once he kept quiet, allowing her to stew.

Which reminded her. . . "My biscuits are burning. I never got to try your stew or feed the other passengers."

"They'll be all right."

"No, they only bake for twelve minutes. They're definitely burning."

"The passengers, J—Miss Middleton. I meant the passengers."

"If you say so."

Rhett's voice lowered. "He was going to shoot you."

She hugged her knees to her chest, watching the boat as it inched its way down the river. Taking with it her letters, her escape—her hope. She'd been half in love with Rhett. Completely in love with Mr. Kane.

Now she was confused, lost, and finding it hard to trust the man sitting beside her. "I never told you my name was Jenny," she finally said, her voice soft and shaky.

Rhett leaned forward to better see her.

She turned her face away.

"I was going to tell you. I *tried* to tell you—"

"How long have you worked for him?"

A long pause. A cautious, "What?"

"Oh come on, Rhett. He sent you to meet me, or spy on me, or. . .I don't know. Were you supposed to report in? Let him know if I was suitable? Because *I never told you* my name was Jenny. *He's* the only one who would have done that."

"You. . .you think I *work* for him? This man you've been writing?"

"What did you tell Mr. Kane?" Josey swiped at a tear as her voice rose. "What made him stay away after he *promised* to come?"

Rhett's throat worked as he stared in shock. Probably never figured he'd be caught.

Well, he'd certainly fooled her. Did his job include testing her loyalty? Because she'd nearly failed that. She loved Mr. Kane's words—had fallen in love with the man himself because of them. But Rhett's heart— Well, she'd gone and fallen for that as well, hadn't she?

And, in doing so, had likely lost them both.

Rhett began to speak, but she cut him off with a swish of her drenched skirts as she rose. "Never mind. I don't want to know. Thank you for saving my life once more. Now I think I'll find my own way back home."

She'd taken a few steps before he called out, "Jenny. Miss Middleton."

Josey halted, her back to him.

His words were quiet. Subdued but steady. "Come with me. We'll find a place to rest for the night, then you can meet with Everett Kane."

"I've heard that before. More than once."

"I give you my word. Whether that's good enough is up to you. But. . .I give you my word."

Everett had wanted to call her by name for so long. Not just Jenny, but *his* Jenny. How had it gone so terribly wrong?

She trudged along beside him with none of the cheerful chatter he'd grown accustomed to. He'd traveled hundreds of miles to meet her. She'd been worth every penny, every hardship, every second. But the misunderstanding and his thoughtlessness may well have broken her heart, ruining any chance of happiness they may have had. While he'd been enjoying getting to know her in person, she'd been struggling with insecurity over Mr. Kane's affections, and possibly even guilt over being drawn to someone else.

Or was he the only one who'd felt the connection between them?

The path narrowed, and his arm brushed against hers until she jerked away and fell further behind. Yes, even angry she felt it. He had to believe that.

The sun had nearly disappeared by the time they reached town. Everett saw Jen—Miss Middleton settled at an inn, as much as she could be with no belongings. Down below, he arranged for a bath and food and anything else he could think of to assure her comfort. Then, since she refused to see him, all that remained was for him to fret over her reaction to his news tomorrow.

If she'd only stay through the night.

He'd sleep in the hallway just in case.

How could she hate Rhett when he'd even seen to having her dress washed while she slept?

Josey stared at her reflection in the mirror. Dark circles shadowed her eyes, but sleeplessness gave her time to work her hair into intricate twists and braids, which turned out quite presentably, if she said so herself. Partially thanks to the toiletries Rhett arranged to be delivered. How he'd paid for everything, she had no idea.

Her gaze traveled lower and she smoothed her dress. The river water left muddy stains in several places, but it would do. She had no choice, after all. She'd meet the man of her dreams in an imperfect gown, but at least her hair smelled of lavender after the hot bath last night.

Again, thanks to Rhett's consideration.

Who was she fooling? She'd met the man of her dreams already. Rhett might not even be able to write, much less pen exquisite letters. Who knew? But he was everything in real life—and more—that she'd dreamed Mr. Kane would be. Except for the fact that it was all based on a lie.

Just like she was.

Oh dear.

Early this morning, she'd hit him with the door when she tried to slip out for a moment. Had he slept there because he'd spent the last of his money on her? Or because he feared she'd run away?

She'd certainly considered it.

Instead, she'd remembered the money sewn into her petticoat and had retrieved it to tuck into his pocket instead. Mr. Kane certainly owed the man that much, at least.

Rhett hadn't awakened, and she'd stared a little too long as his chest rose and fell. Wanting to smooth his hair back once more, to memorize every inch of his face, maybe even to hold his hand. Resisting, she retreated to her room once again.

Now she picked up her waterlogged letter from its spot near the fire and tried to make out the smeared ink. She had memorized the words, but quoting it wasn't the same as studying the letters Mr. Kane had labored over with his own hand.

Maybe she didn't want to meet him. Maybe the dream of him would wash out, just like the ink.

Someone knocked on the door. Straightening her shoulders, Josey opened it. Rhett smiled slightly, his eyes warm but cautious as he held out a folded piece of paper. As she took it, he leaned down and his beard tickled her hand as the warmth of his lips brushed against her palm.

Before she could react, he strode to the end of the hall. Had the kiss been a goodbye? Would she ever see him again?

Maybe she'd overreacted. Maybe pride played too large a role in her response to him last night. How could she choose between the two, if either of them even wanted her? Josey clutched the note tightly, suddenly realizing she'd followed Rhett to the top of the stairs.

He didn't look back, making the choice for her.

Fighting unexpected tears, she retreated to her room and smoothed out the note. Mr. Kane's handwriting once again scrawled across a scrap of paper, asking her to meet him in the dining room for breakfast in an hour. No church this time.

She didn't know whether she was devastated or relieved. Nevertheless, she'd give him one final chance to show. And if he didn't?

Tempted to crumple the note, Josey folded it carefully instead. She only had this and the waterlogged letter left. The others aboard the packet ship probably burned along with her biscuits.

When the time came, she gathered up Millie's shawl along with her courage and made her way to the dining room. There Rhett waited at a table near the window. He looked different somehow. His clothes were ill-fitting around his shoulders, but new. His hair was clean and carefully combed. It took a moment to realize he was clean shaven, and he was every bit as handsome as she suspected he'd be.

But what was he doing? Josey frowned in his direction. Did he wait to give her another excuse why Mr. Kane wasn't here? Because the room was nearly empty, and she didn't see anyone who looked like a wealthy businessman from Colorado. A family sat in the corner. A lone traveler puffed on a pipe by the fireplace, his bald pate shining as if he'd polished it this morning. A waitress bustled by him, sending him a glare as smoke blew in her direction.

Josey stopped in the middle of the dining room. She couldn't do this. Couldn't hear any more excuses, couldn't suffer through any more pity in Rhett's gold-flecked eyes. Couldn't—

"Excuse me, miss." Someone jostled past her on his way to the front door. A man dressed like a cowboy.

Could he be. . .?

Rhett stood and moved in her direction as the door swung open to admit a bulky fellow with a star pinned to his vest. The cowboy halted abruptly and whirled, dodging around Josey.

Oh dear. This wasn't good.

Especially when the pipe-smoking traveler moved in to help corner the cowboy, leaving Josey in the middle of the circle with a wild-eyed desperado. He jerked her to him, tight against his chest. She caught the scent of horse, sweat, and salt pork before a gun to her head made her senses go numb.

This was not the way she'd imagined meeting Mr. Kane.

Chapter 9

Everett glared at the second ruffian who dared threaten his fiancée in as many days.

Not today. Not after all they'd been through. Not when the truth was about to be told, a decision about to be made.

Only a few yards away. If he'd told Jenny in the hall, just spit out the truth, this wouldn't be happening. She'd be safe, hopefully in his arms, and they'd be looking for someone to perform a wedding.

"Stay back!" the cowboy yelled. "I'll shoot!"

"What then, Curly?" the lawman asked, advancing a step.

"Then this pretty gal is dead, with no one to blame but yourself. I guess you'd prefer that not be the case. So get back outside, fork a horse, and leave me alone."

The sheriff hesitated, but the helpful bystander had already faded into the woodwork, deciding things had gotten over his head.

"Do it," Everett ordered, praying he'd obey. The lawman's priority would be the criminal. Everett's priority was the sweet woman with the freckles standing out in stark relief against her ashen skin.

The one he should have married already.

Tension crackled as the lawman debated, finally stepping back into the sunlight and allowing the door to shut.

The room had emptied, leaving only the ruffian, Jenny, and Everett, who kept his eyes steady on the criminal, his hands in plain sight.

"There's a back entrance." Everett infused as much calm as possible into his voice, for Jenny's sake as much as the cowboy's. "Release Miss Middleton, and you will not be stopped. You can make your escape that way."

The man snorted. "I won't make it three feet without a hostage."

"Then take me." A step closer. Close enough to grab Jenny's arm in a quick lunge. Not close enough to help her escape the shot that would surely follow.

"Ain't happenin', and that's the long and short of it." With a quick glance around,

Curly backed toward the stairs, dragging Jenny with him.

"I'm sure we can come to a satisfactory solution." Everett followed slowly.

"I'd like to weigh in on that solution," Jenny sounded breathless but not terrified.

That should have surprised him, but after the trip they'd had so far, it only made him smile.

"You see, I'm here to meet someone," she continued. "I'm assuming you're not Mr. Everett Kane?"

A huff of a laugh. Another half-dragging step closer to the stairway. "Curly Rogers, at your service, ma'am."

"Figures." Jenny sighed. "How many times can a woman get jilted?"

"Jilted?" Everett couldn't help himself. "You're the one who hopped on a boat going the wrong way!"

"After Mr. Kane forsook me on the church steps, of all places."

Rhett's head still throbbed, come to think of it, but he couldn't give that excuse. Not yet. "You're the one who didn't wait at the train depot in the first place."

"I did." Her gaze shifted, then glared defiantly. "For a while."

Curly cleared his throat. "I hate to interrupt this lively discussion, but—"

"What do you think, Curly?" Everett interrupted. Jenny had managed to distract the cowboy, whether or not that had been her intention. If they could just keep him guessing. "Is Miss Middleton a runaway bride?"

Josey huffed. "How can I be a runaway bride when he never asked me to marry him?"

Everett blinked. "But he did."

"Who did?" Curly asked.

"Everett Kane." Jenny answered, suddenly avoiding looking in Everett's direction. Something was off, and now he was the distracted one.

"That's easy enough to figure," Curly said as they reached the back door.

"Oh really?" Jenny sounded genuinely curious.

"Sure 'nough." He swung his finger to point at Everett. "Go ahead 'n ask her, Kane."

"What?" She laughed. "You're mistaken, Curly. That's. . .that's. . ." Her voice faded when Everett didn't join in the laughter or jump to correct the outlaw.

"That's Everett Kane," Curly assured her, adjusting his grip on his six-shooter. "I saw him at the bank early this morning. Only recognized him just now, or we might've found a solution earlier."

And here came the blackmail. Although at the moment, dealing with the outlaw would be preferable to seeing the realization—the betrayal—dawn on Jenny's face. Again.

"In fact, I'm certain we can all walk away happier than a dead pig in the sunshine if Kane here would stake my trip back West."

He'd do it. Do anything if it meant—

"Pretty sure you're wrong, Curly." Jenny again. "I know *I'm* not very happy."

"Are you certain this is a good time to discuss—" Everett began.

"Since it hasn't come up before, I believe I'll take the truth when I can get it."

"I'm confused," the outlaw said. "Kane, did you propose to the gal?"

"I did."

"You did not," Jenny insisted.

"Jenny—"

"Stop calling me that!"

"Awful formal, ain't we? Since you're gettin' hitched and all?"

"Shut up, Curly."

"Jenny—"

"I'm. Not. Jenny!"

In the sudden silence, Miss Middleton stomped on Curly's toe, spun, grabbed the weapon, and aimed it at the man's buckskin vest. Jaw hanging low, Curly didn't put up a fight, even when Everett tackled him and secured his arms with a curtain tie.

Panting slightly, Everett sat on top of the man's chest and stared at the woman he loved. "You're Jenny Middleton. You met me at the train station even if you didn't know it was me. You were heading to Colorado. You. . ." She'd said she loved him. Hadn't she?

The woman—whoever she was—sank to the bottom step. "I'm *Josey*. Jenny's older sister. I was going to tell you when I met you, except I never met you. Officially. Mr. Kane."

"I'm awful confused," Curly said, his voice raspy.

"You stole your sister's letters?" Everett's voice raised. "A proposal meant for her?" How could he have so misjudged the woman whose face had haunted his dreams ever since he'd met her? The one he'd admired for her courage and kindness? Honesty had surely factored in there somewhere.

Her chin raised in indignation. "Of course not! I mean, not exactly."

"Still confused," Curly said.

"And you," Jen—Josey said hotly, as she adjusted her grip on the weapon. "Was this whole thing all an audition? A test for your future bride?"

"Not at all. I'll explain. But first, can you put the gun down?"

"No, I—oh." She nearly dropped the revolver in her haste to get rid of it. "You were never writing Jenny. I mean, it was her handwriting, her name, her idea. But never her words. *I'm* the one who told her what to write. *I'm* the one who memorized your letters. Most of the stories are mine. And. . .and *I'm* the one who fell in love with you."

"What happened to Jenny?" Curly again. Thinking when Everett seemed to be at a loss.

"She got tired of waiting for Mr. Kane to rescue her from a life she wasn't happy with. She eloped the night before Mr. Kane's proposal arrived." Her gaze sought Everett's. "I wanted to meet you. To tell you the truth in person. And to, well. . ." Cheeks reddening, she turned away.

"To declare her undying love. That is, if you was decent to look at."

"Curly!"

"What? You two obviously need help with the communication bit."

"It's true," Josey said. "You have some explaining to do as well."

"I introduced myself. Told you right away, on the back of the train. But it was too loud, and when you misunderstood, I thought it might be good to make sure you were. . ." He cleared his throat. "Well, make sure you were who you'd represented yourself to be. From your letters."

A dozen questions crossed her face. He could read them on her brow. But only one crossed her lips. Faint, shy, tentative. "And?"

"And what?"

Curly groaned. "She's askin' what you thought of who you found. Sakes alive, you're a mite weak north of the ears, ain't you?"

"I found. . ." He swallowed hard and searched for the right words. Ones that would express his feelings—his real, deep down feelings. Not the shallow hurt and frustration over learning she wasn't who he thought she had presented herself to be. Because he knew he'd overcome those, as surely as he knew she hadn't meant to deceive him.

But he was too slow. Miss Middleton leaped to her feet and fled up the stairs, and Everett was stuck waiting on the slowest lawman to ever hunt a bad guy.

Chapter 10

Angrily swiping at tears, Josey gathered her ever-shrinking collection of belongings before collapsing on the bed. To leave, she'd have to marshal her courage and descend the stairs, facing Everett Kane once again. If she stayed, he'd confront her. Try to smooth things over. Let her down easily.

He hadn't meant to reject her. She knew that well enough. He'd conducted himself honorably, shown kindness to those around him, and was prone to rescue her from whatever mess she landed herself in. If she gave him the chance, he'd try to rescue her now—either by marrying her even though he obviously preferred otherwise, or by buying her off. Finding a home and job for her since she'd very likely lost hers back in Pennsylvania.

But that wasn't what she wanted. She wanted the Everett Kane from the letters. The observant, witty, wise, God-fearing man she'd come to treasure. And she wanted the Rhett from her travels. The handsome, caring, charming protector she'd come to rely on. To look up to. To love.

She didn't have to choose between the two, after all.

Except now she didn't get to choose at all.

A high-pitched yowl behind the curtain caught her attention. With a final quavering sigh, Josey crossed the room to find the window opened to a balcony. How had she not noticed? A kitten perched on the branches of a tree just beyond, shaking and peering at the ground. A quick jump and it'd be safe on her balcony, escaping the danger, but it was frozen in place.

Josey could relate. But here it was—her escape. If she truly wished it.

No. No, she didn't. But she didn't want Rhett's pity either. Strengthening her resolve, Josey crossed the balcony and hefted herself over the rail, grabbing the closest tree limb for balance. Shimmying out onto it, she dared not look below.

"Come on, kitty. Let's go find home."

A few minutes later, the two made it safely to the ground, although Josey's hairstyle had suffered irreparable harm. She raised her chin, pulled the remaining pins free, and resolved not to care. No one else did, it appeared, considering she'd been rejected each time she'd taken extra time to look presentable.

Well, now she had a cat. She supposed that should be some consolation. The kitten squirmed, clawing its way down until it broke free.

And then she didn't even have that.

Josey watched as it disappeared under a porch, then she stared at the sky. "What are you trying to tell me, God?"

That she needed to let go? Well, wasn't that what she was doing? Freeing Everett. Leaving Everett.

"He's trying to tell you I'm not fond of cats." Everett's voice was rich, deep, but not how she imagined God sounded. One of his angels maybe. "Or maybe He figures a dainty pet like that one wouldn't make the trip to Colorado."

Josey turned slowly, tucking her wild hair behind an ear. Everett stood under the tree she'd climbed down, his clothes in disarray from scuffling with Curly. He took a tentative step toward her as if fearing she'd turn and run like the cat.

She considered it.

"Come with me, Jen—Josey." He flushed.

"You're a good man, Mr. Kane." It felt strange to be so formal with him—this man who'd dragged her from the water. Whose brow she'd smoothed and checked for fever. "But I will not be the object of your pity."

"Oh, I don't pity you." He chuckled. "I pity anyone who stands in your way."

The words felt like a slap. Cheeks hot, Josey took a step backward, closer to a passing wagon. To a rescue she needed even more than she'd anticipated.

"Miss Middleton, no." His face sobered instantly, and he sprang to her side. "Aw, Josey. When it comes to words, it appears I'm much better on paper. Please allow me to start over. To convey to you how I really feel."

"To be honest, Mr. Kane"—tears hovered behind her words—"I'm not sure how many more of your words I can bear."

How many times had he made her cry?

Everett brushed her hair back, loving the softness of it just as he'd imagined he would. "Please. Allow me another try." Cupping her cheek, he stared into her wide eyes. "When I found you, *Josey* Middleton, I found *more* than I imagined or hoped. I still don't completely understand how I've been calling the woman I love by the wrong name all this time, but. . .I love you. *You.* The woman standing in front of me. The one who takes care of those around her, finds the good and the humorous in any situation, stays true to her word—or her sister's word. I'm not—" His brow furrowed, and he shrugged. "Anyway. I pity those who stand against you, because you fight for what's right, what's good, and who can win against that? I want to stand *beside* you. Always."

Taking her hand, he slowly moved to kneel in front of her. "Josey Middleton, would you do me the great honor of becoming my wife?"

A commotion behind him drew her gaze before she could reply.

"I heard it, Miss Josey." Curly gave a whoop. "The man *did* propose!"

"Curly Rogers!" the sheriff shouted. "Get back here and get your hands in the air!"

"Give 'im an answer, already!"

Everett coughed lightly. "For once, I agree with the outlaw."

A hint of a smile finally crossed Josey's face, and she focused on him once again.

"If you can forgive Curly for holding a gun to your head—"

"It wasn't loaded," Josey said.

Everett wasn't sure he wanted to know how she'd figured that out.

"It weren't loaded," Curly confirmed.

"Curly?" Everett hollered. "Don't you have somewhere to be?"

"Shore 'nough. See ya in Mexico!"

Another whoop, a shout from the lawman, and a gasp from Josey.

Everett winced. "Poor choice of words again?"

She snorted—actually snorted—then doubled over with a peal of laughter. He'd take that as a good sign, except it delayed her answer further.

"Josey?"

With a long sigh, she sobered, still bent close to where he knelt. "Did you mean everything you said?" Her bright eyes were wide and bright and near enough for him to count three different shades of green. "Truly?"

"Every written word. Every spoken word that I didn't butcher. All of them except when I called you by the wrong name, of course. My apologies, Miss Middleton."

"But you just did it again."

His brow wrinkled. He was certain he'd said—

"Because my name isn't Middleton."

His eyes closed, but she rushed on.

"Oh dear. I was trying to be clever but—now who needs to be using pen and paper? Here. Wait just a moment." She pulled out a crumpled paper stained with water and ink.

Everett recognized it. The stationery had the same look as the one in his breast pocket, with the same river stains and similar worn creases. She'd carried one of his letters, treasured it, as he had hers.

She patted the pocket of her skirt, as if checking for a pen. He had none to offer—his extending pencil was likely stuck in the mud at the bottom of the river.

"Fiddlesticks." Spotting a twig, she swept it up and turned it onto the dirt and began to write. Biting her rosy lip, she stepped aside so her words were in full view.

Dear Rhett,

You are looking at the future Mrs. Kane, if you will have me. Will you?

Yours,

Josey

"Shorter than your usual missives."

"I'm learning that sometimes. . .things happen. Best to just get it out there."

He tugged the stick from her hands, his fingers brushing hers. Her handwriting was exquisite, even in the dirt. Not because it was perfect in form—it had fewer embellishments than her sister's, and the letters weren't uniform in size like his own. But they were joyful—overflowing with life and energy as they spilled across the ground.

"No one actually calls me Rhett. Just so you know." He figured he should throw that out there—full disclosure this time around.

"One person does. She's quite smitten with it."

"Well, as long as she calls me by the right name when we say our vows. . ."

"Will that be very soon?" She bit her lip.

"The sooner the better. I'm learning that sometimes things happen."

Josey leaned closer, her adorably freckled face inches from his. "Sometimes they actually do," she murmured.

Then she kissed him.

Jenness Walker lives in South Carolina with her website-designer husband, their toddler, and their hungry hound. Her lifelong love of books is evidenced by her day jobs, which have included freelance editing, managing an independent Christian bookstore, and even cleaning a library. Jenness's short stories have appeared in *Grit* and *Woman's World* magazines as well as in Guidepost's *A Cup of Christmas Cheer* collections. She is a former American Christian Fiction Writers Genesis contest winner and Carol Award finalist, and her debut novel, *Double Take*, received 4.5 stars and a Top Pick rating from *RT Book Reviews*.

The Irish Bride

by Renee Yancy

Dedication

To my good friend Wendy Veino,
who has been there since I started writing fourteen years ago.
You are the best!

Chapter 1

The music had disappeared. The wild fiddle notes that danced across the cotters' fields each summer evening had vanished like the smoke from their winter fires.

That was the first clue.

The second omen was the stench. Acre after acre of potatoes rotting in the fields overnight, fetid black masses that only the day before had been fine, stout specimens. A bumper crop, Da had said.

Now famine gripped Ireland in its bloody jaws, and her father had lost his race against time.

Deanie Devane huddled under the lap blankets in the carriage with her maid, Oonagh. Their hasty departure from the estate of Killkerrin hadn't allowed time to heat the soapstone bricks for their feet, and her father had forbidden the groom to light the lanterns outside the carriage. Her bad leg ached in the bitter cold of the worst winter in memory. She shivered, wondering again why her father had insisted on secrecy as they left for Dublin in the wee hours of the night, leaving Killkerrin for America where her uncle lived.

Leaving the memory of Michael.

Deanie closed her eyes. She didn't want to think about him, but whether she willed it or not, his face rose in her mind. The groundskeeper's son, Michael Quinn, with his deep blue eyes and curly black hair. They'd known each other since they were five. He had been her *m'anamchara*. Friend of the heart.

As a child with no mother to keep her at home, she'd had the run of the estate. She and Michael had explored every nook and cranny of Killkerrin during the long summer evenings after he'd finished his work in the estate's office. They caught fish and cooked them for supper, climbed trees to peer into birds' nests, and investigated the ancient standing stones in a hidden grove of oak trees.

As they grew older, they shared their dreams for the future. And then, lying close together on the heather one warm summer evening, they had shared a kiss.

And everything had changed.

Perhaps her father caught wind of it. Running in for supper one twilight evening, he had met her at the door. Taken in her windblown hair and flushed cheeks. He had gazed over her head into the gathering darkness beyond. Deanie had frozen stock-still. Could her father see Michael hovering in the shadows?

Papa had closed and locked the door. Then he turned and smiled at her. "It's about time to leave off the runnin' around, aye, Bernadine? You're a young lady now, almost ready to marry. Time to stay home and learn a few things about women's work. I realize I have been remiss."

Her father's word was law in the Devane household. He had given her unlimited freedom, and then had taken it away. For the rest of the year, she'd been kept busy with cookery lessons and the like. She watched out the house windows for Michael, but he never appeared. And then Maggie, the old cook, said Michael Quinn had left Killkerrin to seek his fortune elsewhere.

He had never come to say goodbye. Her heart still hadn't gotten over that.

The horses squealed, yanking her out of her reverie. The carriage jerked to an abrupt halt, and she tumbled to the floor in a jumble of blankets, with Oonagh tangled next to her. Her father helped them up and rapped his cane on the front wall of the carriage. "Drive on, Tom. Quickly!"

Deanie's gut clenched at the jarring note of strain in her father's voice. Or was it fear? But she'd never seen her father afraid of anything.

A wavering orange glow penetrated the lace window curtains. The grunts of a struggle and harsh voices outside brought Da out of his seat, reaching inside his jacket. Deanie stared at the Colt revolver stuck in his belt. Why was her father armed? She'd never seen him carry a gun before.

"Ho!" Thomas shouted. "Let go!"

The carriage compartment jostled while the horses whinnied and stamped the frozen earth. The horsewhip cracked and something heavy hit the ground with a muffled thud.

"Off with you!" cried Colin, her father's valet.

The carriage pitched forward and then again violently halted as a swell of angry voices rose and hands slapped against the sides, rocking it on its springs.

Deanie gasped. "Da, what's happenin'?"

He held his finger to his lips. Oonagh whimpered and buried her head under the blankets. A menacing voice shouted outside. "Come out, Devane!"

The splintering crack of breaking glass pierced the air, and a hand ripped the window curtain away. A man with a bloody rag tied around his head peered through the broken window, and a leering smile split his face when he spied her father in the torchlight. Beads of sweat broke out on Da's forehead.

"Here he is, lads!" the man yelled over his shoulder. "Take him!"

Oonagh cowered in the corner, shrieking like a steam whistle.

"Da, what do they want?" Deanie turned on her maid. "Be still, Oonagh, for heaven's sake."

The man knocked the rest of the glass out of the window frame with a stick, thrust an arm through the window, and groped toward the lock securing the door.

"Be off, you miserable cur!" Her father raised his cane and smashed the handle on the man's hand as he tried to turn the lock. Blood spurted from the man's shattered fingers and he fell away from the window, howling like a banshee.

"Drive on!" Her father dropped his cane, braced his feet, and held the door latch closed against the men outside trying to open it. He drew his revolver. "Faith and begorra, Thomas, drive on!"

Neither Thomas nor Colin, who'd been sitting on the box with the groom, answered.

Da stuck the Colt against the door and fired through it. Orange flame spilled from the end of the barrel and the acrid reek of gunpowder filled the carriage. Dazed, Deanie clapped her hands over her ringing ears. Da fired again and scrabbled to keep the lock turned. The carriage careened on its springs as men swarmed over it and jerked the door open. One ruffian caught her father's arm and tore the Colt away. Rough hands pulled him from the carriage, and he disappeared into the seething mass mob as it lurched away, leaving Deanie trembling in the sudden silence.

"Da!" She scrambled to get out of the carriage.

"No, miss!" Oonagh threw her slight body in front of Deanie. "For sure they'll kill you too!"

What was happening?

"Stay here!" Deanie jumped out of the carriage and missed the step, crashing to her knees. Pain shot up her bad leg. Off the road, a hundred feet away, a bonfire threw sparks into the night sky. The mob of men milled around it, shouting and cursing.

Deanie put out her hand to push herself up, touched something wet, and recoiled at the body of a man under the carriage, half his face shot away. The sickening smell of blood filled her nostrils, and a wave of nausea surged into her throat. Thomas had slumped over on the driver's seat. Colin lay on the ground, unmoving. Deanie limped toward the fire as fast as her bad leg would let her, her heart hammering in her throat.

"Thought you'd get away with it, Devane?" a man shouted. "Razin' our huts! Sendin' our families away!"

"You turned us out to die!" bellowed another man, brandishing a torch.

Deanie gasped. Two men had her father gripped between them, shaking him hard with each jeering shout. His hat had been knocked off, and blood ran down his face, black in the firelight.

"Thought you'd get off easy, did you? Creepin' away in the darkness like the rat you are!"

"You'll pay, Devane!" Another man raised the Colt in his hand.

A shot rang out.

Deanie screamed and pushed through the throng. The crowd went silent at her approach and parted to let her through. Her father lay writhing on the ground, and she dropped to her knees beside him.

"Da," she whispered, tears running down her cheeks. Blood seeped from the bullet hole in his chest.

"Bernadine," he panted, one hand rising to touch her face. His fingers gripped the back of her neck, and he put his lips against her ear.

"In your bag," he whispered faintly, "the bottom—" He broke off and turned his face aside to cough.

The men murmured behind her, their feet shifting in the stony grass.

"In the bottom," he whispered again, "the gold. . .hurry. . ."

"I'm not leavin' you, Da. I'm not!"

"Go, Bernadine. . ." His face contorted in a spasm, and foamy blood bubbled up out of his mouth. He heaved one gasping breath, and then his body shuddered and became still.

"Da!" she sobbed, shaking him. "Da!"

The firelight disappeared as the ring of men pressed closer and a hard hand clamped on her shoulder. "You'd best get out of here, miss." The hand closed around her arm and dragged her to her feet.

Another man bristled in his face. "And who are you to say, Malone? Her father's dead, but we can still get somethin' out of her, 'ey?"

"She's done nothing to deserve that, O'Doul." Malone locked her arm tighter, the smell of his sweat rank. "Let her go."

"She's his get, isn't she?" Another man in a leather jerkin, taller than the rest, looked down into her face and smiled coldly. "And a whole lot prettier, sure."

"I may be starvin', but I've got enough juice left for that. C'mon!" O'Doul threw his stick into the fire and grabbed her other arm. Deanie screamed as he tried to jerk her away and Malone wrenched her back toward him.

A gunshot reverberated through the smoky air. Fifty paces away, Colin stood with her father's hunting rifle aimed at the men. Blood ran from his nose. "Get back!"

When the men didn't move, he looked down the sight. "Get your hands up, lads. Now!"

The men muttered and slid away, raising their hands.

Colin jerked his head at Deanie. "Get back to the carriage." He widened his stance and dug his heels into the mud.

"But—my father—"

"Go *now*, Miss Devane!"

She went. The carriage seemed a long way off. Somehow she managed to put one foot in front of the other and broke into a ragged run. Thomas stood by the open carriage door. Blood ran from a cut over his eye. Her legs shook so that when she reached the step, her knees buckled, and Thomas had to lift and shove her in. He slammed the door shut, and the carriage jostled as he climbed to his seat.

"Oh miss," Oonagh wailed. "Have they killed himself, then?"

Deanie nodded, breathing hard, and Oonagh broke into a keening moan. A moment later, footsteps thudded toward the carriage, and Colin swung the door open and put a foot on the sill.

"Go!" he shouted to Thomas.

Colin swung himself into the carriage as it jerked forward, then slammed the door shut and lodged the rifle through the broken window. He peered out at the road ahead. Thomas had given the horses their head, and the carriage wheels seemed to barely touch the ground as they flew through the night, leaving the angry mob behind.

Colin left the rifle resting on the windowsill and looked at the two of them. "Well." He pulled a handkerchief from his pocket to wipe his bloody face.

Deanie stared at the immaculate white linen with the familiar initials embroidered in black silk.

JPD. James Patrick Devane.

She reached out and snatched the handkerchief from his fingers. Only then did she notice what he was wearing. The scream welled up in her throat, and she clamped her lips together to stifle it. Colin wore one of her father's suits. Even the cairngorm stickpin in his cravat belonged to her father.

"Why did they kill him?" She tried to swallow the hysteria in her voice. Oonagh had sunk into a heap on the floor. She reached down to touch the girl's quivering shoulder. "Come and sit with me now."

Oonagh raised a tearstained face. Deanie patted the seat next to her, and Oonagh sank onto the cushion beside her.

Deanie faced Colin. "Why did they kill him?" Painful spasms of nausea rolled over her, and she clapped her hand over her mouth and waited until she could speak again. Tears filled her eyes and streamed down her face. "What did he do?"

Colin wiped his face on his sleeve. "Miss Devane, I will explain when we reach Dublin. But I need to be watchful right now."

He glanced out the window again, searching the darkness in both directions, then moved across the seat to look out the other one, his knuckles tight on the rifle.

The familiar scent of bergamot rose from the handkerchief she was holding, and a fresh jolt of agony tore through her. *Oh Da, Da, what have you done?*

She put her arms around Oonagh and tried to swallow the lump in her throat. What were they going to do now?

Oonagh whimpered in Deanie's lap for the remainder of the ride to Dublin. Frigid air whistled through the shattered window as, over and over, Deanie replayed her father's murder in her head. Each time she arrived at the same conclusion. The father she knew couldn't have committed the crimes the spalpeens had accused him of.

Sometime after midnight the carriage stopped before a modest boardinghouse. Snow fell in heavy flakes that carpeted the frozen ground and cast a hush over the street.

Colin got out and wet a handkerchief in the snow to clean the dried blood off his face.

Then he reached up to assist her. "Say nothing when we check in, Miss Devane."

She nodded, not trusting her voice, and stumbled from the carriage, her bruised knees now stiff and clumsy. Colin steadied her and glanced back into the carriage where Oonagh slept on the seat under the pile of blankets. "We'll leave her for now."

Deanie followed Colin into the reception room and waited while he spoke with the desk clerk. They were shown upstairs to two rooms, small but well-kept and clean. A yawning maid brought hot water in a pitcher and lit the lamps while Thomas brought their luggage.

Colin left and returned with Oonagh in his arms. He laid her on one of the beds and turned to Deanie. "There's a sitting room downstairs, across from the desk. Mrs. Gallagher said we might have the use of it for a bit. I will meet you there in a quarter of an hour."

Numbly, Deanie nodded. Her bones ached after the jolting carriage ride, and she longed to fall into the other bed and wake up in the morning to find this had all been a terrible nightmare. Instead, she moved to the dresser and poured water in the basin to bathe her gritty eyes, avoiding the mirror. She pulled off Oonagh's shoes and covered her with a blanket. Oonagh was an orphan. Two years ago James Devane had found her crying at the side of the road and brought her home to be Deanie's maid, but in truth she was more like a little sister.

Colin hadn't yet arrived when she descended the stairs and entered the tiny parlor. A peat fire burned in the grate, and she drew a footstool close to it to warm her hands, comforted by its familiar homey scent. Then she noticed the dark stains that crusted the bodice of her ruined dress, and she shuddered. Her father's blood.

Colin entered the room and closed the door, then pulled an armchair around to face her. He lowered his lanky frame into it and laid his hands on his knees. His nose had swollen, and his eyelids were puffed and blackened. A frown creased his lean face.

"Tell me, then," she said when he hesitated, "and spare nothing."

Colin loosened his collar. "You know your father has been planning this emigration for several years. Every coin he could save went to this venture. And then last year. . ." He cleared his throat. "Your father did some terrible things. . .to the tenant farmers and spalpeens. . ." He reached into a pocket and withdrew a leather flask. "Excuse me, miss." He twisted the cork out and took a long swallow of the whiskey.

Deanie clenched her fists. "Is it bottled courage you need now, Colin? To tell me the rest?"

Shamefaced, he stowed the flask away.

"What has he done?" Hysteria lingered at the edge of her words, and with an effort, she lowered her voice. "Get on with it."

Colin sighed. "There was more profit to be made from growing wheat and grazing cattle and sheep. But the plots of the tenant farmers broke up the estate land, although God in His heaven knows they hadn't paid rent for months, even years. Your father evicted them and paid their passage on a ship to Quebec. To a new life in Canada. Over eight hundred of them." He pressed his lips together.

"Why to Canada?"

"America wouldn't accept them."

"Why not?"

Colin closed his eyes and held up his hand. He fished out the flask and had another long pull of the whiskey.

Deanie crossed her arms over her chest to stop the shaking that had begun in her middle and spread to her arms and legs.

"The ships. . ." His lips trembled. "They're called. . .coffin ships."

Deanie stared at Colin, trying to make sense of his words. "Coffin. . .?"

Colin swallowed hard. "Because most of the spalpeens are dead on board when they arrive."

She shook her head. "It can't be true."

Colin's voice dropped to a whisper. "It's true, miss. He drove them off the land. Men with clubs forced them out and razed their huts to the ground. Families. Even the old widows." Colin turned away and stared into the fire. "They had nowhere to go. And it was cold, so cold. Many died the first week."

A sob tore out of her throat. The angry men on the road. *Thought you'd get away with it, Devane?*

"That's why we left after dark?"

"Yes." His shoulders slumped. "Denis Mahon in County Roscommon sent his tenants off the same way. A month later he was ambushed on his estate and shot to death. Your father knew it could happen to him. That determined his precautions."

Her father. A murderer.

"Where are we going, Colin? And how can we go now that he's dead?"

"Your father made arrangements for me to go on in his place if anything happened." He drew a deep breath. "In Liverpool I will see you safely off to your uncle in America." His fingers tightened on the flask. "Whatever else he has done, Miss Devane, you must believe he loved you. And wanted to protect you."

She covered her face with her hands, trembling. Yes, her loving father had protected her. But at what cost?

Chapter 2

In the early morning darkness, the Devane carriage made its way along the River Liffey Road toward Dublin port. Strange bundles and bags lined the lane, and as the pale light of dawn crept over the horizon, some of the bundles moved. A bare arm protruded from one mess of rags and raised stick-thin fingers toward the carriage, pleading. Tattered men, women, and children—some nearly naked in the cold—stumbled to their feet and cried out for bread. A wailing baby sat on the frozen ground, mucous dripping from his nose.

Oonagh moaned and closed her eyes, pressing tight against Deanie. Some of the figures lay unmoving on the ground, frozen in the awful postures of their death throes. Ragged children clung to the dead bodies of their mothers. Fathers raised hollowed eyes to the carriage while they crouched over the corpses of their children.

"Don't look, Miss Devane." Colin took her arm. "We're nearly there."

But each dead or dying figure imprinted itself into her brain as her heart pounded and her breath came in short gasps. There were hundreds of them. Bile rose in her throat, and she gagged, groping for her handkerchief. She pressed it to her mouth as the carriage slowed and stopped. Colin got out quickly and helped them down, turning them away from the terrible sight.

Deanie twisted out of his grasp. A few feet away, the emaciated body of a young girl lay frozen. She couldn't have been more than thirteen. Her red hair spilled bright against the snow, contrasting with the green stains around her mouth. Near her the snow had been clawed away to reveal the grass underneath. The girl had eaten it before she died. Deanie groped for the carriage wheel and leaned over to vomit, tears streaming down her face.

Oonagh touched her shoulder. "Don't cry, *mo chuisle*, I can't bear it."

Deanie nodded, choking back the sobs. "I can't bear it either."

"Miss Devane, we mustn't linger." Colin glanced about them. "Come."

Deanie wiped her eyes and took Oonagh's hand.

With Colin acting in place of her father, they took the packet boat from Dublin to Liverpool. Thomas had been allowed to keep the carriage as payment for his help in the escape and planned to return to his ancestral village far to the south of Ireland in County Kerry. Two of Colin's brothers met them when they disembarked, big, burly, and armed with truncheons. A teeming gang of men pressed down upon them as soon as they stepped off the gangplank, barking and yelling of boardinghouses, pubs, and inns for travelers. One befuddled young Irishman was taken by the arms and forced away.

Oonagh whimpered at her side.

"Hold tight to me." Deanie clutched her hand.

Colin and his brothers surrounded the girls and forced their way through the horde, smashing their truncheons with abandon to make a way through the mass of bodies. Deanie gagged at the stink of unwashed bodies mingled with the stench of rotten fish and held her reticule close as they were jostled back and forth. Finally, they reached a place on the dock where the crowd thinned, and they were left alone.

"Thank you," Deanie said, her voice unsteady. The two young women would never have made it through the threatening mass of men if not for Colin and his brothers.

Colin nodded. "Your father arranged for them to come and paid them well."

Indeed. Her father always planned everything well. Except his own death. She winced. Left unshriven and unburied in the dirt outside Dublin. Who knew what the angry spalpeens had done to his body after she and Oonagh escaped?

Oonagh snatched her hat off and wailed. "Oh oh oh, my hat!"

Deanie's father had given Oonagh leave to choose a hat from a Dublin shop. She had pored over the catalog for days and selected a blue felt bonnet that matched her eyes, with a scarlet feather in the brim. Now the feather, broken in the scuffle off the boat, drooped forlornly over the brim.

After a modest lunch in an overheated hotel dining room, Colin walked them to Waterloo Dock, where the ship that would take them from Liverpool to America lay at anchor. The packet boat they had traveled on to Liverpool paled in comparison to this gargantuan ship, the RMS *Cambria*. It had a huge paddle wheel, with three red-painted masts, and a wood hull. The saltire cross of St. Andrew flew from one of the masts, white against blue.

"RMS?"

"Royal Mail Ship," Colin said. "They carry London's mail to America and transport passengers." He dropped his voice. "Your father investigated thoroughly before he booked passage, Miss Devane. You're traveling first class. You'll be very comfortable."

As opposed to the spalpeens he had thrown out of their hovels to die in the cold. She swallowed hard and pushed the thought away.

Other first-class passengers stood nearby, and Deanie examined them to distract herself from the knowledge that she and Oonagh were about to cross the ocean to a strange and foreign land, to an uncle she barely remembered. They wouldn't be having peat fires in America, and already she missed their humble scent.

A different group of passengers huddled together at the other end of the pier while seagulls wheeled overhead. Clad in familiar nondescript browns and grays, these women in head scarves clutched infants to their breasts and carried cloth bundles on their backs. Men and young lads in caps and tattered jackets toted mattress rolls and blankets tied in bundles. Forks and knives poked out of their shabby bags, and pots and pans strung together on rope were looped over the men's shoulders. A few had wicker cages containing a chicken or two. Wizened grandmothers, clad in black, stooped over their baggage, their work-worn hands grasping canes made from gnarled tree branches.

Colin followed her gaze. "The steerage passengers."

"Steerage?"

"They are emigrating too, Miss Devane."

"Thrown out in the same way as our spalpeens?"

Colin frowned and nodded. She turned away from the pained look on his face. It wasn't *his* father who had committed murder. A stab went through her chest at the thought, and she winced. How could Da have done what Colin said? The father she had known had always been kind and thoughtful. And now he was no longer here to tell her he wasn't guilty of the crimes he was accused of. She would never see his dear face again.

She caught sight of a ragged figure lingering on the next dock. Something about the tilt of his head and his tall frame was familiar and— "Michael! Michael Quinn!"

The figure turned at the shout. It was him. Wasn't it? Her heart beat madly as she waved and took a few steps closer. The young man stared at her, then pulled his cap down over his eyes and melted away into the crowd. A deep spear of sorrow went through her. Before the whole world fell apart in one black night on the road to Dublin, she had thought of him every day without fail.

Oonagh and Colin had turned at her shout.

"Where?" Colin searched in the direction Deanie faced. "Was it him, Miss Devane?"

"I don't know. I thought so."

She turned and searched the wharf, eyed every person, searched the ships. No sign of him. If it had been him at all. But oh how her heart had leaped for joy. "I must have been mistaken."

Now he was gone, as her father was gone. And an unknown future lay ahead. If only she could toss the grim thoughts into the air like chaff separated from the wheat. At the other end of the ship, pigs were being driven up the gangplank, followed by three bellowing milk cows. Crates of squawking chickens and other fowl were passed aboard. A man with a clipboard stood at the foot of the gangplank to check them off as they passed him.

Deanie had never seen so much food in one place. Trays bearing a score of calves' heads arrived, followed by bins of turnips and beets. Sundry other green-stuffs made their way on board, followed by crates of raisins, almonds, figs, and prunes. Some crates had SPAIN and GREECE stamped on them. Sides of beef. Bushels of potatoes, yams, and parsnips. Cartons of oranges and apples. Crocks of butter, wheels of cheeses in wax shells, and kegs of beer. Nausea curled at the back of her throat. How many starving people in Ireland would this bounty feed?

Deanie glanced at Colin. "How long did you say the trip to America will take?"

"Twelve days if all goes well."

Oonagh's eyes goggled. "Is all that food for us?"

"I would think so," Colin said. "The steerage passengers bring some of their own food, and the shipping company supplies them with a pound of biscuit each day."

Deanie started. "That's all? A pound of biscuit?" Colin must have assisted her father with the preparations to evict the spalpeens, and she held back the hot words that rose to her lips unbidden. It was over and done with. There was no use taking her anger out on Colin.

"How many first-class passengers are there?"

"Twenty."

"All those provisions for twenty people?"

"The second-class passengers will receive some of it."

While the spalpeens received a pound of biscuit a day?

Again she thought of her father's body lying in the mud in Ireland, robbed of the Blessed Sacrament of the Last Rites. A shudder went through her. Perhaps it was fitting that his body lay unshriven in the frozen dirt like so many other Irish dead.

Oonagh shouted. "Look, Miss Deanie!" A crane twisted overhead with a cargo net full of trunks and valises. It moved across the sky and then stopped, poised over the ship. At a signal from one of the sailors, the net released the luggage into the hold of the ship.

Deanie felt a touch on her sleeve. "I must leave you now, Miss Devane." Colin held out his hand. "The ship's staff will look out for you. It's all been arranged. My own ship leaves soon for Southampton, and I must rejoin my brothers."

"Wait." Deanie clutched his coat sleeve and turned him away from Oonagh. "Maybe. . .this is a mistake, Colin. I can't go to America. I want to go home."

Colin shook his head. "There's nothing for you there, miss." He gently disentangled her hand. "Only a tainted family name and your father's crimes. In America you'll make a fresh start with your uncle, and no one will be the wiser."

Deanie choked back a sob and turned her face away. Colin didn't understand. She would never be able to forget what her father had done. The horrific knowledge he had saddled her with would follow her to the end of her life.

"Come now." Colin gathered her and Oonagh close to speak the traditional blessing over them. "May the road rise up to meet you. May the wind always be at your back."

Tears stung Deanie's eyes at the familiar words.

"May the sun shine warm upon your face and the rains fall soft upon your fields." His voice broke. "And until we meet again, may God hold you in the palm of His hand."

He dropped a soft kiss on their heads, and then he was gone.

Oonagh broke into sobs. Deanie drew her close and exhaled hard as their last link with home walked way.

Chapter 3

The first-class stateroom that would be their home for the next fortnight held two narrow bunks built into the wall, one atop the other. The room was twelve feet long and eight feet wide, with barely enough room for a tiny stand with a washbowl and pitcher against one short wall, secured by a double railing. A brass-framed mirror hung above it. Several iron hooks hung on the opposite wall for their cloaks. And a low bench, thinly padded, with a porthole above and a space underneath for their valises, sat opposite the bunks. Each end of the cramped compartment had an oil lamp on the wall ensconced in its own metal railing.

When Deanie stretched her arms wide, she could almost span the width of the cabin. And even here in the first-class cabin, the stench of oil pervaded the air.

There was a knock at the door, and a steward poked his head in. "Almost time for the roll call, miss." He touched his cap. "You're exempt as first-class passengers, but you might find it interesting. You can go up to the quarterdeck now if you like."

Deanie flinched at the thought of mingling with the other passengers, always acutely conscious of her limp. It was the first thing people noticed about her. But the tiny cabin already seemed stifling.

"Would you like to see it, Oonagh?" The girl shrugged, and her lips trembled. A tear rolled down her cheek. She'd barely spoken since Colin had left.

Deanie put an arm around her slender shoulders. "The Lord is with us. It will be all right. You'll see."

But would it?

Deanie sighed, weary with thinking of it. "Come, let's go up on deck."

They made their way through the hallway to the stairs leading upward. Other first-class passengers joined them. Once on the main deck, a second staircase led to the quarterdeck. Below them hundreds of steerage passengers assembled on the main deck in ragged lines, their tattered belongings piled around them.

A tremor went through the ship, and Oonagh clutched her stomach, her eyes wide. "Ooh." She reached out to grasp the rail.

"It's the tugboats, miss," a voice said behind her. A tall gentleman who looked vaguely familiar, with a high domed forehead and a bulbous nose, smiled kindly at Oonagh. He gestured toward the bow with his pipe. "Starting to pull the ship away from the wharf."

Deanie nodded. "Thank you."

"Is this your first trip across the ocean, miss?"

"It is."

He bowed to her. "May I introduce myself? Phineas Taylor Barnum, at your service."

"Oh!" Three years ago, that name had been plastered all over Dublin. "*The* P. T. Barnum?"

He chuckled. "The very same."

"How wonderful to meet you. I am Bernadine Devane, lately of County Offaly, Ireland. And my maid, Oonagh O'Connell."

Oonagh dropped a little curtsy. "Oh Mr. Barnum." She clasped her hands together eagerly. "Is Tom Thumb with you?"

At that moment, a droll little face peeped between Mr. Barnum's trousered legs.

Barnum laughed and pushed the small figure forward. "There you are, you scamp. I want to introduce you to Miss Devane, and her maid, Miss O'Connell."

The miniature fellow doffed his cap and swept a deep bow. "Charles Sherwood Stratton, at your service," he piped in a tiny voice.

"This is my protégé, Miss Devane, also known to the public as General Tom Thumb."

Deanie inclined her head and dipped a small curtsy. "How nice to make your acquaintance, Mr. Stratton."

"Oh, call me Tom," he said breezily. "Everyone else does."

He was a charming little person, with rosy cheeks and a snub of a nose, dressed in a military uniform with a double row of bright brass buttons and shiny patent-leather boots. Replacing his cap, he adjusted the brim to a jaunty angle and did an impromptu jig.

Oonagh's eyes sparkled, and she clapped her hands. "Oh, how cunning you are!"

"Did you see the show while we were in Ireland?" Tom asked.

"Unfortunately, no." Deanie shook her head regretfully. "But I read all about it in the papers. How you entered Dublin in a special coach pulled by the smallest ponies in Ireland."

Tom nodded. "I'm going to have a whole stable of ponies when we get back to America."

Tom and Oonagh moved to the rail to peer overboard.

"So, you are immigrating to America?"

"Yes."

"I hear the situation in Ireland is very bad."

Deanie smiled grimly. "That word can't describe the horror of what is happening there, Mr. Barnum. People are dying by the hundreds daily."

And yet she had escaped the horror. Because of what her father had done.

"Will you be making your permanent home in Boston then?"

"Yes, with my uncle."

"Ah," he said pensively. "There are many Irish in Boston."

A clattering of feet sounded below. The crew members convened on deck before the captain, carrying poles, hammers, and chisels. Some poles were tipped with a long nail, and Deanie frowned.

"The search for stowaways must commence before the passage tickets are collected," Mr. Barnum said. "A normal part of a ship getting under way."

"Stowaways?"

"Yes." Barnum studied the deck below. "Three or four pounds for passage is out of the reach of many a poor man who would make his way to the land of opportunity. That's what the immigrants call it, Miss Devane, America, the Golden Door of Opportunity."

The captain dismissed the men. Shortly thereafter muffled shouts and cries arose from below deck. "What on earth are they doing, Mr. Barnum?"

He shrugged and flicked pipe ash over the railing. "Every nook and cranny will be probed. Casks and barrels opened. Bedclothes hammered."

Deanie gasped. "Surely you're not serious, sir."

"Unfortunately, I am, Miss Devane. Sometimes they hide amidst the luggage in the hold or come aboard in a trunk pierced with air holes, lest they suffocate."

The crew members reappeared now, driving several cringing stowaways before them. A pang went through her at the sight of the bedraggled figures. "What will happen to them?"

Mr. Barnum pulled a watch from his waistcoat and glanced at it. "If they come up with the ticket money, they'll be allowed to stay on the ship. Occasionally they will press a strong man into service on the ship if they have need of help. The others will be put on the tugboat and carried back to the wharf to stand before the magistrate for committing fraud unless someone volunteers to pay their passage."

The captain stood before one fugitive at a time, took his name, and asked if he could pay for his ticket. After much protesting, two of the men came up with the coins, hidden inside the lining of their jackets. The last man shook his head. He had a sinewy body, a laborer or a farmer perhaps, his arms roped with muscle. The captain signaled one of the crew, who took the man below.

Mr. Barnum relit his pipe, releasing a puff of sweet-scented smoke. "Now the captain will proceed to the roll call. This could take several hours. Perhaps you'd be more comfortable in your cabin?"

A series of muffled thumps interrupted him as two sailors each manhandled an oak barrel onto the deck and rolled it toward the captain.

Mr. Barnum raised an eyebrow. "They've found a few more, apparently."

The crewman applied a chisel to one barrel, and a dusty white figure emerged, coughing and wheezing.

The crew member holding the next barrel upended it on the deck, and Deanie gasped at the strangled cries coming from inside.

"Enough," the captain said. "Open it."

The sailor pried off the top, and a young man crawled out, gagging. He unfolded his thin arms and legs and revealed himself to be taller than the captain. Deanie's heart started to beat faster.

The captain examined the white-shrouded figures before him. "Are you able to pay the fare?"

The older man shook his head, sending puffs of flour into the air. One of the sailors gave him a quick once-over, feeling the man's pockets and pants legs, and then shook his head at the captain.

Only the shivering young man was left, his bony wrists protruding several inches from the sleeves of his threadbare jacket, and his body stick-thin under the coating of flour.

The captain fixed him with a stern look. "Have you the ticket fare, boy? Quickly now!"

The boy shook his head dejectedly. Puffs of flour fell from his head, revealing black hair. Deanie caught her breath and pressed closer to the rail. Michael?

"Your name?"

"Michael Quinn."

Next to her Oonagh gasped and clapped her hand over her mouth.

The captain contemplated the boy and then looked toward the passengers. "Is there any among you who would care to pay for these men's steerage tickets?"

There was a muttering and shifting of feet, but no volunteer stepped forward. Deanie moved to the brass railing and clutched it tight, frozen in place. Michael glanced upward, and the desperation in his pinched face made her heart spasm.

The captain nodded to a crew member. "Put them on the tug."

Two of the crew laid hands on the older man and Michael and pushed them toward the rail, preparing to transfer him.

Deanie found her voice. "Wait!"

The other passengers on the quarterdeck turned as one to stare at Deanie. Maybe first-class passengers never did this? "I–I will pay their passage, Captain."

She fumbled with the reticule attached to her belt and retrieved her coin purse, ignoring the inquisitive looks from the other passengers.

She turned to Mr. Barnum. "Would you ask the captain the cost for second-class fare?"

Colin had said the steerage passengers received a pound of biscuit a day, along with whatever food they could bring on board. Clearly both men were destitute, and obviously there weren't any provisions in the barrels with them.

A murmur went up from the passengers behind her.

Mr. Barnum nodded. "Price for second-class tickets, sir?" His booming voice carried easily to the captain below.

The captain hesitated, glancing at the two men's bedraggled figures. "I'm afraid that's not possible, sir. It must be steerage. Six pounds even for the two of them."

P. T. Barnum shrugged and turned to Deanie. "Miss Devane, I'm afraid they aren't quite second-class status. The captain may have a mutiny on his hands if the men are placed with those passengers." He gave a slight jerk of his head to indicate the men and women clustered to the right of Michael, as far away from him as it was possible to get. They were soberly clad, farmers and merchants possibly, respectable middle-class people like herself. And several of them gawked at her with disapproval plain on their faces.

All conversation had stopped, and the passengers on the quarterdeck now stared at Deanie and Mr. Barnum, with some of the ladies whispering behind their hands to each other. Michael and the other man waited, their hopeful gazes fixed on her.

She dug in her purse for the fare. "Would you be so kind?"

Mr. Barnum took the proffered coins. "Certainly."

He tossed the money to the deck below. The captain bowed to her and accepted the payment. The men were sent below, but not before each shot her a pitiful look of gratitude.

Mr. Barnum smiled at her. "That was most compassionate of you, Miss Devane. If they survive the voyage, they might make a fresh start in America, thanks to you."

Tom Thumb doffed his cap and swept her a low bow. "Nicely done, miss."

Mr. Barnum took a thin gold case out of his waistcoat and drew out a card.

With a pen, he wrote something on the back and handed it to her. "We'll be in Boston for the spring, at the Concert Hall. I'd like you both to be my guests. Come and see me after the show."

Deanie turned the card over. *Two Free Admissions* written in bold script, and underneath, in smaller letters, *Backstage Pass.*

"That would be lovely. Thank you, Mr. Barnum."

But she didn't deserve their congratulations. Her father had turned his back on hundreds of his own people, abandoning them to starvation and hopelessness.

Somehow she had to atone for that.

One of the calves' heads made an appearance at dinner that evening in the first-class dining cabin, with a baked apple in its mouth and olives for eyes. But Deanie had no appetite. Nor did Oonagh, and as soon as possible they said goodnight and hurried back to the refuge of their stateroom where Oonagh cried herself to sleep, still clutching the worn leather bag that held her few possessions.

Sleep eluded Deanie, teasing her with a hint of release and then retreating. On the wall across from the bunks, a St. Patrick medal swung from the tack where Oonagh had placed it. The ship's engines throbbed upward from the bowels of the ship through the wooden slats of the bed. Without sleep to take her away, all the questions came swirling back, pushing with insistent hands at the corners of her mind.

She turned onto her side, trying to get comfortable in the narrow bunk, and remembered her father's words on the roadside moments before his death.

"In the bottom of your bag—"

She climbed down and pulled the flowered portmanteau from underneath the bench where the steward had placed it. Her father had ordered it especially for her from Dublin, a sturdy bag with compartments and pockets, and her initials monogrammed on one side.

She heaved it onto the top bunk and climbed back up. Opening the bag, she lifted out the stationery and writing materials, a paisley shawl, and her Bible. But it still felt heavy. Then she spied a ribbon loop, placed her finger inside, and the bottom lifted like the lid on a chest.

The hidden compartment held a letter addressed to her, her father's last will and testament, a black velvet ring box, and many small packets of twisted paper. She opened one and gold gleamed within. A British sovereign. She counted the packets. Three hundred sovereigns, to be exact. A small fortune.

She opened the letter and winced at her father's distinctive script slanting across the page.

Dearest Bernadine,

If you are reading this, then I am dead and no longer able to protect you. By now Colin will have told you what I have done to preserve your inheritance. I don't ask you to forgive me. I did what I needed to do to give you a new life in America.

My will has left you the sole inheritor of my fortune, which over time I have transferred to your uncle's bank in Boston. You may need to engage the services of an attorney to help you obtain it. I have enclosed three hundred sovereigns for your use in the event that a substantial period of time may elapse before you can obtain access to your inheritance.

Lastly, in the tradition of our beloved Ireland, I leave you your mother's wedding ring, as a remembrance of happier times.

Ever your loving,
Father

It was signed and dated the day before they left the village. Deanie dropped the letter and pushed her fist against her mouth to stifle the sobs. Oh Da, Da! When Oonagh stirred below, Deanie took one last gulp and placed the will in her reticule.

Inside the velvet jewel box, her mother's gold Claddagh ring winked back at her. Two hands holding a heart. The hands signified friendship, and the heart, love. A crown surmounted the hands and heart, depicting loyalty. Love and friendship forever. Her mother had worn it on her left hand, with the crown facing away, denoting her marriage relationship.

Deanie plucked the ring from its white satin nest and peered at the words engraved inside the band: GRÁ GEAL MO CHROÍ. Bright and shining love.

Her father had been a romantic.

She slid the ring onto the fourth finger of her left hand. Perhaps it would offer some protection from curious passengers if they thought she was a widow traveling alone.

Because right now she couldn't afford to be interested in love.

Chapter 4

The next morning Deanie washed and dressed while Oonagh lay in her bunk, her complexion a greenish pallor.

"Ooh, my belly." Oonagh rocked back and forth in the bunk. "It won't stop churnin'."

"I'll bring you back some tea. And maybe a bannock?"

Oonagh groaned. "I can't eat."

Their old cook, Maggie, used to tie a bunch of fresh mint leaves around her wrist if she felt poorly. No chance of obtaining them now. Perhaps there was a ship's doctor she could consult.

"I'm going to breakfast, Oonagh, and I'll see what can be done for you. Try to rest."

The girl turned over in her bunk, clutching her St. Patrick medal.

Deanie let herself out of the stateroom, thankful for her own strong stomach. The breakfast menu was almost as bewildering as supper the night before. She'd never imagined how many different foods could be offered for breakfast, from mutton chops to sheep's kidneys, and even Yarmouth bloaters, the gamey-tasting fish her father had loved. She settled for tea and oatmeal with currant bread toast and ordered oatcakes for Oonagh and a pot of tea to be sent later.

Mr. Barnum sat at a corner table reading a newspaper and had nodded to her when she came in. Little Tom was nowhere to be seen. When she had finished her porridge and drunk her tea, she wrapped the oatcakes in her napkin. The bright sun dazzled her eyes when she emerged onto the deck, and she stopped at the rail, enjoying the fresh breeze after the heavy cooking odors in the dining room.

"Pssst."

Deanie turned and searched the deck, but she stood alone.

"Pssst. Over here."

Michael crouched behind a stack of deck chairs piled against the wall. She hurried over, standing in the recess between the deck chairs and the wall.

"I've been watching for you, Deanie." He still had flour in his hair. "I don't know how to thank you."

"No thanks needed. You'd have done it for me, aye?" Deanie gazed into his blue eyes, the left one with its smattering of gold against the blue, as if a fairy had touched him with a wee paintbrush. She had always loved the way the sun caught it. Her heart beat fast as they stared at one another, and the two years between them fell away like dew vanished in the morning.

Michael's lips trembled. "I never thought to see you again."

"Nor I you. That was you skulking about the docks, wasn't it?"

"Yes, waiting for the crew member to nail me into the barrel."

"Why did you turn away when I called your name?"

He hung his head. "I was ashamed for you to see me like this." He took her hand. "But I'll repay you. Somehow."

Her pulse jumped at the touch of his fingers. "I don't care about that. Why didn't you come to say goodbye when you left Killkerrin?"

His eyes widened. "I tried. Several times. But someone always stopped me." He shook his head. "You father protecting you, most likely."

She stiffened at the mention of her father. "You need to eat." She jerked her hand away. "You're fearfully thin. As much as you can. Fatten yourself up before we get to America. Do you hear me?"

Michael gazed into her face. "I do. I will."

A steward passed and shot a curious glance at Deanie huddled against the deck chairs. Michael shrank back into his shelter when the steward returned.

"Everything all right, miss?" He looked concerned, and no wonder. She must look daft, standing here shivering. "Cold? Can I fetch you a blanket?"

"Oh no. I'm fine. Just getting a wee bit of air." She smiled at the man.

He shrugged and left.

"I shouldn't be here." Michael straightened. "I'd better get below deck before they find me. No tellin' what would happen then. Probably throw me overboard."

"You be careful."

"You go," Michael said. "I'll creep back when I can."

"Wait." She clutched his shabby sleeve. Now that she had him, she didn't want to let him go again. "When we land in Boston, I'll introduce you to my uncle and persuade him to help you."

"That would be grand, Deanie. And then, perhaps, I may have something to offer you."

They stared at each other as hope rose within her. The sound of footsteps on deck made her draw back. Passengers were coming outside for their morning walks.

"I'll find you again," Michael whispered. "You'd better go."

Chapter 5

February 22, 1847

Pale wintry sunshine greeted Deanie and Oonagh as they prepared to disembark the RMS *Cambria*. Mist rose from the surface of the gray water as sea gulls whirled overhead.

Among a group of well-dressed people waiting at the foot of the gangplank to greet the arriving first-class passengers stood her uncle, Sean Devane. Deanie recognized him immediately, as he had the same tall imperiousness of carriage, the long-lipped mouth, and full head of silver hair as her father. She watched him search the passengers disembarking and felt a sudden urge to hide.

Behind her Oonagh whimpered. "I'm affeered, Miss Deanie. I don't want to get off the ship."

Oonagh's complexion had paled under the multitude of freckles that peppered her skin.

"I know," Deanie said gently. "I feel the same." Then she clutched her reticule tighter and took Oonagh's cold hand. "But you know we can't stay on the ship. Nothing to do but go on. At least we're together."

Her uncle's searching gaze found her then. His gaze held no warmth or hint of good humor. Unlike her father. She lifted her hand in reply and hobbled down the gangplank with Oonagh, her limp worse and her legs unsteady after eleven days at sea.

"Bernadine?"

She winced. Only her father had called her Bernadine. Bernadine Mary, for his own sainted mother. Oonagh had followed and stood silently next to Deanie.

Her uncle glanced past them at the passengers disembarking. He frowned, as if realizing for the first time that the two girls were alone. "Where is your father?"

Tears welled in Deanie's eyes. "H—he's dead. Murdered on the road to Dublin."

Her uncle's eyes widened. "What?" The mask of aloof haughtiness dropped off his face at the shock of her terse announcement but was quickly replaced by the cool impassiveness with which he had greeted her a moment ago.

Then his appraising gaze fixed on Oonagh shrinking behind Deanie's skirts. "And who is this ragamuffin?"

"My maid, Oonagh."

Uncle Sean's lip curled. "Completely unsuitable." He shook his head, muttering something under his breath, and glanced at the passengers streaming by them. "Come. This isn't a suitable place to discuss anything."

Deanie had been searching the far end of the ship where the steerage passengers were disembarking from a different exit.

"Could we wait a moment, Uncle? There's someone I want you to meet. He should be disembarking soon." She searched the crowd on the wharf behind her uncle.

"Is that so?" His eyes had narrowed when she said "he." "And who might that be?"

She spotted Michael and waved. He loped over and snatched off his cap as he reached them, out of breath. He topped her uncle by a good two inches and wore the same threadbare jacket and trousers that stopped well above the ankles. His black hair had grown past his collar, and he hadn't shaved in many days.

Uncle Sean gave Michael an incredulous once-over. "You wanted me to meet, this. . .this beggar?"

The hopeful expression on Michael's eager face dropped away. Her uncle laid a heavy hand on the young man's shoulder and gave him a rough push. "What's the meaning of this? There's no charity here, you miserable spalpeen. Be off with you now."

Michael staggered under the push, then straightened, twisting his cap in his hands.

"He's not a beggar, Uncle." Deanie stepped between them. "He worked on Killkerrin for my father, in the estate office. I hoped you might be able to find some sort of work for him."

Uncle Sean smiled coldly. "Isn't it enough that your father has already saddled me with the two of you?" He turned on Michael. "Off with you now, or I'll fetch the police and have you arrested for panhandling."

Michael's shoulders sagged, and as he turned and walked away, her heart broke. Would she ever see him again? For one wild moment, she thought of running off with him. She had the hidden gold. But what would Oonagh do? She couldn't leave her in the hands of her heartless uncle. And somehow she knew her uncle would find her. There was a ruthlessness about him. He would find them, and Michael would be arrested.

"Come along to the carriage," her uncle said, "and then I'll fetch your luggage."

Deanie cast one despairing glance behind her. Michael's tall figure had almost disappeared in the crowd.

Before her uncle could stop her, she whirled and hurried after him. "Wait! Michael, wait!" She called several times before he turned to look at her, his face set like stone.

"I'm so sorry."

His face softened, and he smiled down at her. "You've nothin' to be sorry for, Deanie." He touched her cheek gently. "When I saw you on deck that day on the ship, I thought you were an angel. An angel sent by God. I'll never forget you." He turned and walked away.

"You're goin' to give up on me that easy, are you now?" she said sharply to his retreating back. "I never took you for that sort o' man, Michael Quinn."

He turned back. "What would you have me do, Deanie?" He raised both hands and shrugged. "I have nothing to offer you."

"You've got your heart, haven't you? And the brain God gave you."

She snatched up her reticule and pulled out her coin purse, blessing the instinct that had told her to hide some of the gold sovereigns in her bag. "Take these. This will see you through. Find a good place to live. Buy some respectable clothes."

Michael stared down at the three gold coins in his hand. "Have you found the pot of gold at the end of the leprechaun's rainbow now, Deanie? I can't take this."

Beyond Michael, Deanie could see her uncle stalking toward them, his eyes flattened by rage.

Deanie closed his fingers over the coins. "You *will* take them, if you know what's good for you, boyo." She took a deep breath. "And then come and find me." A dart of panic went through her then. "I've no idea where my uncle lives. I won't know how to find you, nor you me."

Michael grinned. "I'll find you, Deanie. Don't worry. As soon as I can."

Uncle Sean reached them then and gripped Deanie's arm as Michael melted into the crowd. "What do you think you're playing at, missy?" He squeezed her arm tighter, turned her in the direction of the carriage, and marched her away.

"He's my friend. I had to try and help him." She pulled against his grip. "Let go of me."

Her uncle stopped and wrenched her around to face him. A muscle ticked in his cheek. "Don't try me, Bernadine. You're not too old for a whipping."

Deanie gasped. "You wouldn't dare."

He smiled cruelly. "Wouldn't I? It's plain to see your upbringing has been sorely lacking in civility and manners." He resumed walking toward the carriage, pulling her with him.

She wanted to say something about his own lack of manners and kindness but thought she'd better remain quiet for the moment. Michael had money now. He would survive.

The carriage waited at the edge of the dock road, and the coachman jumped down to assist at their approach.

"I will see to your luggage." The door closed, and her uncle strode back to the dock to speak to the stevedores.

Oonagh's hand crept into hers. "I wish we was back home, miss. He do look certain fierce. Not like your father at all."

"He's family, Oonagh. He'll do right by us, I'm sure." Deanie squeezed her hand. "But mind. Be quick to do as you're told."

If only she could be sure. Although she'd only known him a few short minutes, a certain implacability in him made her want to shrink away. And he didn't seem Irish at all. His speech hadn't a trace of Irish brogue. But this was her father's plan for her in the event of his death. Deanie had to hope that her uncle would have their best interests at heart.

Uncle Sean returned a moment later and climbed into the carriage, settling himself across from the two girls.

"Why do you limp?" he asked Deanie abruptly. "Are you injured?"

"No, I—"

"Speak up, then."

"I had a paralytic illness as a child, with a high fever, Uncle. It affected my leg."

"A deformity then." His lips twisted, as if in distaste.

Deanie stiffened. "I don't choose to view it as such."

"Prospective husbands might." Uncle Sean sniffed. "Although your face might make up for it."

What an appalling man. Deanie closed her eyes and breathed a prayer for strength as the groom loading the luggage jostled the carriage.

Her uncle's lips thinned in a cold grimace. "Why in the world would you give that beggar the time of day, Bernadine?" He relaxed into his seat and studied her face.

Deanie looked away and pulled at a stray thread in her skirt. "I'm sorry, Uncle."

"She paid his passage on the ship, that's why." Oonagh bristled at Uncle Sean, her thin chest heaving. "And it was a very kind thing to do, mind."

Uncle Sean snorted. "Indeed." He crossed his arms on his chest and fixed Oonagh with a steely glance. "Speak to me in that tone again, and you'll find your-self out on the street."

In that moment, the tiny hope for a warm relationship with her uncle flickered

THE Runaway BRIDES COLLECTION

and went out. Deanie shook her head at Oonagh, who shrank into the corner.

"Now tell me. What happened to your father?"

The carriage moved through the streets of Boston as a light snow fell. How odd to be back in a carriage with a man who looked so much like her father sitting across from her. But this was America, not Ireland. And this man was nothing like her father.

"Are you aware of what is happening in Ireland now, Uncle? The potato crop failing?"

"Of course."

"My father. . ." She swallowed. "He. . ." She didn't want to speak aloud what he had done. "It has been a difficult two years. The people starving."

Her uncle waited, tapping his fingers on his trouser leg.

"My father. . .apparently he. . ." Tears welled then and a surge of repressed anger tore its way to the surface. "He evicted them all, the families, the cottiers, and the spalpeens. Turned them out to die! So he could raise wheat on the land."

She dashed the tears away.

Her uncle nodded. "Go on."

"We left after midnight. I didn't understand why until we were stopped on the road by a mob of desperate men, furious at what my father had done to them and their families. Somehow they suspected he would try to steal away at night."

Deanie choked as the image of the roaring bonfire and the dark figures silhouetted against its flames rose up. And the sound of the shot. She shivered. "They dragged him out of the carriage and murdered him with his own revolver."

Tears streamed down her face, and Oonagh began to cry. Silently her uncle handed her a handkerchief, and she dabbed at her eyes.

Deanie went on. "I barely escaped from them." She shuddered, remembering the lust in the men's eyes.

Uncle Sean leaned forward. "Did he give you no instructions?"

"He told me earlier that he had deposited everything in your bank."

Uncle Sean nodded. "But he did not send anything else with you? Gold? Papers?"

"Yes." Deanie reached for her reticule. "His will." She retrieved the document and handed it to him.

Her uncle eyed the broken wax seal but said nothing. He opened it and scanned the page. "And how old are you, Bernadine?"

"Eighteen." Old enough to inherit her father's fortune.

"How did you manage to get here by yourselves if he was killed on the road to Dublin?"

"Papa gave instructions to Colin, his manservant, to escort us safely to Dublin and the packet ship to Liverpool. Colin's brothers met us in Liverpool, and with their help we boarded the *Cambria*. Colin left us there. Paid well, apparently, by my father."

She couldn't keep the bitterness from her voice.

Sean eyed her. "So, you know nothing of his papers?"

"No, Uncle." Thank God, Oonagh had been asleep when she had discovered the secret compartment in the portmanteau.

"Nothing for me? A letter?"

She shook her head.

A grimace twisted her uncle's lips. "A fine kerfuffle this is. I warned him to come earlier, but he wouldn't listen. Well. . ." He crossed his arms over his chest. "I shall see to everything."

She tried to still the quivering in her stomach and forced herself to note the scenery outside as they progressed through the city of Boston. She and Oonagh stared out the window at the tall buildings they passed. A large area of snow-covered lawns and leafless trees appeared on her right.

"That's Boston Common," her uncle said. The carriage turned onto a cobbled street lined with townhouses built of brown stone, each with a different brass door-knocker, and in front of one of these the carriage stopped.

A maid showed Deanie to a bedroom on the second floor. A tearful Oonagh had been banished immediately to the kitchen. Uncle Sean said Deanie needed a more appropriate personal maid, and he intended to choose one for her.

Deanie managed to have a private word with Oonagh. "Be patient. I will find a way to get you back with me."

Oonagh nodded, a hopeful look on her pale face.

Now Deanie stood in the elaborate bedchamber, its walls hung with blue silk moiré. A four-poster bed with matching bed hangings stood against the far wall. Sunlight streamed through lace curtains and sparked rainbows off the crystal lamps and ceiling chandelier.

Deanie held the tears back as her body tensed tight as a fiddle string. Oh to be back in the kitchen at Killkerrin with the kettle whistling on the hob instead of in this unfamiliar bedroom. She sank onto the bed and closed her eyes.

Sometime later she woke to a sharp rap on the door. Deanie sat up as a maid scurried in, then stopped and threw up her hands.

"Good Lord Amighty, Miss Bernadine, what are you doing sleeping? Dinner will be served in a few minutes, and I must have you presentable, or himself will have something to say about it!"

She hurried to the valises at the side of the large bedroom Deanie had been given.

"I'm Annie, one of the downstairs maids. I'm to assist you until your uncle procures a lady's maid for you." She opened the lid of the first trunk. "Come now. What do you have for a dinner dress?"

A large cupboard lined one wall of the room, and the maid lifted out the garments made in Dublin and hung them on padded hangers.

"Which is your dinner dress?" she said again, glancing from one dress to another and crinkling her nose.

Deanie swung her legs over the side of the bed. "The dark blue with the lace frill at the neck."

The maid pursed her lips as she examined it and then gave a decisive nod.

"Aye, the dark blue suits you with those eyes like a bluebell and hair like gold. But it's dreadfully old fashioned."

Deanie blinked. "They are all newly made, and at great expense, I might add."

"Oh aye, to be sure, but Ireland's not Boston then, is it? Come, up with you now!"

Before Deanie knew it, the maid had the dusty traveling dress off and the evening dress on, and she was sitting at the dressing table before a large mirror adorned with white plaster roses. With deft fingers, the maid took the pins out of Deanie's hair and let it fall. With long strokes she brushed the full length of it, and Deanie relaxed under her ministrations, wishing she could go to bed and not to dinner.

"They say a women's glory is her hair, and you certainly have enough of it. It's beautiful, Miss Bernadine."

The maid separated a front portion and twisted the back up into a chignon. Then she braided the front in two portions and looped them down and around the side of Deanie's face and pinned them in place.

Somewhere in the house, a clock bonged the hour of seven, and the maid jumped.

"Mercy, child, where is your jewel box?"

Deanie pointed to the portmanteau, and the maid hurried to it and extracted the rosewood box. She opened it and held it out to Deanie, who plucked the first necklace she saw, a string of pearls. The maid placed them around her neck, then ran to the door.

"Quickly now, miss. We mustn't keep himself waiting."

No, we mustn't.

Deanie made her way down the elegant double staircase. The maid had gone ahead and beckoned her to one of the pocket doors leading off the main hall.

"Here, miss." She bowed.

Her uncle stood when she entered. Another younger man stood and bowed to her, his thinning blond hair framing a square face with fine brown eyes.

"Good evening, Bernadine," her uncle said. "I trust tomorrow Annie will have you ready on time for dinner." He gave an unsmiling stare at the maid behind her, and Deanie felt its chill.

"Please, Uncle," she said. "Do not blame Annie for my tardiness. I am journey-tired and slow this evening. Please forgive me."

"This is one of my associates, Bernadine." Uncle Sean indicated the gentleman next to him. "William Fletcher."

William bowed deeply. "I am happy to make your acquaintance."

Her uncle nodded at Bentley, the butler, who stood at the end of the table in an impeccable suit and a glossy starched collar. A stream of covered silver dishes arrived, but Deanie was too tired to pay much attention, and she declined everything but a spoonful of mashed potatoes.

Her uncle raised an eyebrow. "You're not hungry, Bernadine?"

"No, Uncle." She picked at the potatoes, then put the fork back on the plate. "I can't stop thinkin' about my father—" She hesitated and glanced at Mr. Fletcher.

The young lawyer cleared his throat. "I offer my condolences, Miss Devane. On the untimely death of your parent."

"That's a nice way to phrase it." Uncle Sean snorted. "He got himself murdered is what he did."

Mr. Fletcher's cheeks reddened, and he plucked at his collar, his gaze darting between Deanie and her uncle.

The breath left Deanie's lungs at the harsh words, even though they were true. "Even so, Uncle. H–his body, lying in the mud and—" She broke off and pressed the napkin to her lips to stifle the sob. Who knew what other atrocities the mob might have done to the corpse in their anger?

"I'm looking into it," her uncle said gruffly. "I'm going to send a man to Dublin to investigate."

"And if they can find his body?"

"He'll have a funeral mass and be buried at St. Theresa's."

Relief washed through Deanie at the thought of her father lying in peace next to her mother in the family crypt. "Thank you, Uncle Sean." Perhaps her uncle wasn't quite as cold and uncaring as she had thought.

"May we move on to happier conversation now, Bernadine?" He lifted an elegant silver eyebrow and glanced at Mr. Fletcher.

She nodded, taking the hint, and turned to Mr. Fletcher. "Tell me something about yourself."

"There's not much to tell, Miss Devane—"

"Horsefeathers!" Uncle Sean shook his head. "Don't be so modest. Why, you're practically royalty." He glanced at Deanie. "His ancestor Moses Fletcher came over on the *Mayflower*."

Deanie tried to look suitably impressed, although she had no idea what he was referring to. "The *Mayflower*?"

"It was the ship that sailed from England in 1620, carrying the first settlers to the New World." Mr. Fletcher gave her a disarming smile. "Unfortunately, most of those original settlers were dead the first year." He smiled grimly. "Although my ancestor managed to father a son before he died—"

Now it was Mr. Fletcher's turn to press the napkin to his lips as he flushed as red as the roses in the centerpiece. Even the bit of scalp she could see peeking through his thinning hair was scarlet. "Please excuse me, I didn't mean, uh, that is, I . . ."

"No offense taken, Mr. Fletcher." Deanie smiled at him. Certainly the conversation in the old kitchen at Killkerrin had been far more blunt. "Tell me more about Moses."

Warming to his subject, Mr. Fletcher proceeded to divulge his family history in onerous detail and had reached the late seventeen hundreds when Deanie suddenly yawned.

"Bernadine," her uncle snapped.

She clapped her hand over her mouth "I'm so sorry. Please excuse me."

"It's my fault, Miss Devane," Mr. Fletcher said with another disarming smile. "Having such a charming audience has caused me to wax eloquent, forgetting this is the end of a long day for you."

"Thank you. And with that, Uncle, may I be excused?"

Uncle Sean nodded. Both men stood when she did, and she couldn't escape the dining room fast enough. Back in her bedroom, she threw herself full length on the bed.

"Dear Lord," she whispered, "help me get through this."

Chapter 6

March 25, 1847

Again, Miss Devane. Aaa eee iii ooo uuu."

Deanie sighed and repeated the vowels after her elocution teacher, Mrs. Tyrwhitt, a plump matron with iron-gray hair and a posture as straight as the barrel of the antique rifle hanging over the fireplace.

"Head upright." Mrs. Tyrwhitt threw her arms up, inhaling a great breath as she lowered them to her sides and thrust her chest out. "Breathe, Miss Devane. Breeeeaaathe."

Deanie restrained a giggle and focused on her posture.

"Again, child. Aaa eee iii ooo uuu. Enunciate, dear. Enunciate!"

Deanie did her best to reproduce the vowel sounds, but Mrs. Tyrwhitt sighed. "You must try harder if you ever want to lose that dreadful accent. Your uncle is paying me handsomely to rid you of it."

Deanie bristled. "I don't think anythin's wrong with my accent."

"*I*, Miss Devane. Not *Oi*. *I*. Watch."

Mrs. Tyrwhitt recited the vowels with exaggerated emphasis, and when she got to the *u*, her lips pursed like a fish. Deanie burst out laughing.

Mrs. Tyrwitt's eyes goggled, and she drew herself up stiffly. "Whatever is so amusing?"

With difficulty, Deanie calmed herself. "I'm sorry, ma'am, I didn't mean anythin' by it."

"Any*thing*, Bernadine, any*thing*. Remember to pronounce your consonants." She removed her wire-rimmed glasses and rubbed her eyes. "I think that will be enough for today. Use the mirror I gave you, if you please, and practice, practice, practice."

Mrs. Tyrwhitt gathered the papers spread about the desk and took her leave.

Deanie picked up the round mirror and peered into it. "A-e-i-o-u and fiddle-dee-dee!" She threw the mirror across the study where it hit a potted rhododendron and bounced into a corner. "Stay there," she muttered.

The grandfather clock in the hall chimed out two notes for half past the hour of six. Time to dress for dinner, at which the obsequious Will Fletcher was sure to be a guest again. According to her uncle, Will had graduated at the top of his class and was quite enamored by her.

Just grand.

She left the music room and headed down the hallway toward the staircase.

"Bernadine." Uncle Sean stood in the doorway of his study. "Would you come in here a moment, please?"

Deanie retraced her steps. A woman dressed all in black sat in the chair before Uncle Sean's desk, and she stood when Deanie entered.

"This is Mrs. Drummond. Your new maid."

The woman dipped a small curtsy and smiled tentatively. Her hair gleamed blue-black under her hat, and she possessed smooth pale skin and large gray eyes that were brilliant in the sunshine pouring through the study windows.

Deanie stared at the new maid, stunned by her beauty.

"Take her upstairs with you. She will sleep in the small bedroom off yours." Her uncle nodded, dismissing them, and sat down at his desk.

Silently, Deanie left the study, followed by Mrs. Drummond, and walked upstairs to her bedroom.

"I'm afraid I've never had a real lady's maid," Deanie said.

Mrs. Drummond's eyes widened at Deanie's voice, but she quickly composed her face back into the impassive visage she had presented downstairs.

"I will take care of everything, Miss Devane." She gestured toward the mahogany wardrobe. "May I?"

"Yes, of course."

Mrs. Drummond opened the paneled doors to reveal the new gowns and tea dresses that her uncle had commissioned for Deanie. The maid looked through each one, sometimes exclaiming over a beaded trim or silk rosette. Then she walked to Deanie's dressing table and examined the gilded brush and comb lying there and the scent that Uncle Sean had purchased for her. "And my room, Miss Devane?"

"Here." A door near the window revealed a short hallway with empty shelves on one side and a clothes rod on the other. It led to a small bedroom pleasantly furnished with rose-sprigged wallpaper and a low white-painted bed. Deanie had peeked into it before. But now she noticed two other doors in the tiny bedroom. Deanie walked to one and turned the brass doorknob to find that it led into the galleried upper hallway.

The other door connected with a bedroom even larger than her own. All its furnishings were of burgundy and gold silk, and the bed, elevated on a small platform, was carved oak. The scent of her uncle's pipe tobacco hung in the air. *This must be his room.*

She shut the door with a little too much force, locked it, and dropped the key into her pocket. She turned to find an odd look on Mrs. Drummond's face, quickly removed and a complaisant expression adopted.

"I will be quite happy here, miss."

Deanie returned to her own room while Mrs. Drummond carried her luggage into the little bedroom. The maid shut the door between them, and soon the sound of the shelves being filled with her things filtered through.

Something about Mrs. Drummond was unsettling, but Deanie couldn't put her finger on it.

Chapter 7

April 25, 1847

Two months had passed since Deanie came to live in Boston. Two months of elocution lessons, seamstress fittings, and deportment advice from Mrs. Drummond. And near daily evening dinners with her uncle and Mr. Fletcher, who seemed to hang on every word out of her mouth. Now they were in the Devane carriage, making their way to the lace shop for yet another addition to her wardrobe.

A brightly colored poster pasted on the side of a building caught her attention, and she rapped on the front wall of the closed carriage.

"Whoa," called Fergal, the groom. "Whoa now." A moment later, he opened the carriage door. "Miss?"

She pointed to the building off to her left. "I want to read that poster."

Fergal helped her and Mrs. Drummond down, and Deanie took a few steps toward it.

General Tom Thumb
the Celebrated American Dwarf
Fresh from Meeting the Royal Family of England
Exhibiting Every Day and Evening
At the Concert Hall in Boston
Corner of Hanover and Queen Streets
Presented by P. T. Barnum

Deanie turned at a child's wail. Across the cobbled street, a red-haired woman lay on the ground with a tiny child sitting next to her, clutching at her breast. The few people on that side of the street stepped around the woman and continued on their way. No one stopped to help.

As Deanie stepped off the curb, Mrs. Drummond grasped her sleeve.

"Miss Bernadine! What are you doing?" She lowered her voice and glanced about the street. "Don't go over there."

Deanie faced her maid. "Why not? She's ill or hurt. No one else has stopped to help her."

Mrs. Drummond gasped and put a restraining hand on Deanie's wrist. "There's cholera about, miss. There's no telling but what she might have it."

"And you would have me leave her there?" Deanie stared at Mrs. Drummond, seeing the real fear in her face.

The maid scowled and tightened her grip on Deanie's arm. "Your uncle bade me to keep you out of trouble, miss. I wouldn't have come over here today except that the lace he ordered is in a shop down the street."

Deanie shook off the maid's grasp and walked toward the woman, stopping a few steps away. Her face had a bluish tinge, and the fine cheekbones of her face stood out starkly. A bit of black bile had dried at the side of her mouth, and no breath stirred her chest.

A man walked by and stopped a few feet away, pulling a handkerchief from a breast pocket. He clapped it over his nose and mouth and waved her away.

"Best stay back, miss." His bloodshot eyes gazed at her over the grimy edge of the cloth.

"Do you know who she is?"

He edged backward. "I've seen her. She's a widow. Name's Mrs. Riley. That's all I know."

"Has she any family? Any friends?"

"I can't say, miss. I don't think so."

He turned to go.

"Wait," Deanie said. "What about the child?"

The man sighed. "Probably be dead by morning after another night out here."

Deanie's breath caught in her chest. The stiffness of its mother's body should have told her why the child's cries were so weak. Although the weather had warmed in the last few days and the sun shone now, the temperature would drop as night fell.

Mrs. Drummond stood across the street on the sidewalk, wringing her hands. "Miss Bernadine! Please come back."

The child had stopped wailing and lay against its mother's side, whimpering now, its fingers plucking at its mother's bodice and its blue eyes focused on Deanie.

Deanie remembered the dead girl at the side of the road in Ireland. She had died alone in the freezing night.

Not this time.

She picked up the child, and it opened its mouth to cry. "There, *mo chuisle,* there," she crooned to it. "Don't cry." She wrapped the baby in her shawl and cradled the shivering little body to her chest.

Deanie crossed the street to where her maid waited, her face such a perfect mask of affrighted indignation that it would have been funny if not for the seriousness of the situation.

"Pardon me, miss, but have you gone mad?" Mrs. Drummond edged backward, her eyes wide. "She may have cholera."

Deanie didn't reply but walked toward the waiting carriage.

Footsteps pattered behind her, and Mrs. Drummond grabbed her arm and swung her around. "Have you lost your mind? You can't bring that baby to Sea— your uncle's house! Please, Miss Bernadine, think what you're doing!"

"What do you suggest I do with the child?"

The maid's mouth dropped open. "Put it back where you found it. Someone will take it."

Deanie smiled. "Yes, someone *will* take the child." She exhaled and committed herself. "Someone like me."

She turned and walked toward the carriage, trying not to think of what her uncle would say.

The coachman jumped down off the box when he saw them approach, and his face bore the same slack-jawed expression as the maid when he saw she carried a wailing baby and not a bag of lace.

"You can't allow her into the carriage with that child!" Mrs. Drummond cried from behind her. "Stop her."

Fergal Rooney, the coachman, was as Irish as they come. "Miss," he began.

"I'll not be leavin' it to die in the street. I won't."

Fergal's face softened as he looked at the whimpering child. He reached out a large finger and gently brushed the dark curls. Then he lifted his gaze from the baby and studied Deanie.

"Beggin' your pardon, miss, but. . ." He hesitated. "Your uncle. . . If you bring that child home. . ." He ran a finger around his collar and shuffled his feet.

"I know, Fergal. He's a hard man." Who knew what Uncle Sean would do? She was almost tempted to find out. But then, might Fergal lose his job? "But what else can I do?"

"Miss." Fergal lowered his voice and stepped around the side of the carriage. "I have cousins not far from here. I could ask them to take the child."

Deanie glanced back at Mrs. Drummond, who waited on the curb with her hands on her hips. Then she took a quick peek inside the baby's diaper. It was wet, but there was no diarrhea. It was a little boy. Though he had spent a night outside with his dead mother, the baby looked well-nourished and generally healthy. The mother may have passed away from something else.

She rewrapped the baby in her shawl. "I don't think he's sick." She handed the child to the coachman. "I will give you something for them, to help with his care." She dug into her reticule for her change purse, and with another quick look behind her to check on Mrs. Drummond, she pulled out two gold sovereigns. "Here."

Fergal's eyes widened at the gold. "It's an angel you are, miss, for that will not only keep the child, it will help the entire family for a year." He pocketed the gold with his free hand, then glanced beyond Deanie, who whirled to find that Mrs. Drummond had crept up behind her. Had she seen Deanie give the gold to Fergal? Heard the clink of the coins?

Deanie stepped back. "Be off, then, Fergal. Mrs. Drummond and I will wait in the carriage."

"Where does he think he's going?" Mrs. Drummond frowned at Fergal's retreating figure.

"He knows someone who will take the child." She climbed into the carriage. After a moment's hesitation, Mrs. Drummond followed and shrank into the corner as far away from Deanie as she could get.

Deanie examined the maid's pale face. On the sidewalk, upset, she had almost said "Sean," and then cut herself off. Why would her maid be on a first-name basis with her uncle? She could think of a few reasons, and she didn't like any of them.

Her thoughts turned back to the child and his dead mother. Was there no place where they could go to receive care?

Twenty minutes later, Fergal knocked at the door of the carriage. "Safe and sound, Miss Devane."

"Thank you. Would you open the door, please?"

When he did as she asked, Deanie stepped out. "I want to sit on the perch with you on the way home."

There was a gasp from inside the carriage.

Fergal shook his head. "Miss Devane, that isn't proper for a gentlewoman such as yourself."

"I don't care. I have some questions for you."

"Nay, it won't do, miss."

Deanie gathered her skirts in one hand and put her foot on the iron step. "I'll get back in the carriage before we get close to the house."

Fergal sighed and boosted Deanie onto the box, then went around and hoisted himself up. With a sideways glance at her, he picked up the reins and clucked to the horses.

"Now, what was it you wanted to talk about, miss?"

Deanie laughed. Straight to the point. He wanted to get her back inside the carriage as quickly as he could.

"When our people are ill, Fergal, are there doctors?"

"Yes, if they can afford them. But most of the Irish here in Boston are too poor."

"So, what do they do?"

"Do? Why, nothin', miss. Except as for them who have some knowledge of plants and such. They doctor themselves, best as they can."

Deanie had been fortunate in Ireland. Her father could afford to send for the doctor whenever anyone in their family had been ill. Although the doctor had looked after her, he hadn't been able to do anything about her bad leg after the fever she'd had.

She lifted her reticule, feeling the heaviness of the gold coins inside. And she had many more at home. Her father had intended the gold for her, but she didn't want it. It didn't belong to her. It was blood money. Bloody gold, gathered at the expense of the poor souls who'd perished in the unforgiving Irish winter and died at sea in the coffin ships her father had sponsored.

"Would they come to a clinic, Fergal, a free clinic that offered care and medicine? Doctors?"

Fergal chuckled. "Certain sure, miss, if ever one appeared. But it's not likely. Who'd do that for the Irish, the most despised people in Boston?" He pointed to a shoe shop they were passing. "See that sign? In the window?"

A large white placard stood in front of the shoe and boot display.

HELP WANTED
NINA

"I see it."

"Do you know what NINA means?"

She shook her head.

"No Irish Need Apply."

Deanie gasped. "Indeed." Other shops lining the cobbled street had Help Wanted advertisements. A florist. A milliner. A glove maker. And each had NINA in the same bold black letters on their signs.

"I had no idea." How awful. "So, what do most of the Irish do for work then?"

Fergal snorted. "The same as the poor Negroes. Dig ditches. Lay track for the railroads. Work the stone quarries. The lowest, dirtiest jobs. The luckier ones might get on at a mill or textile factory and work sixteen hours a day."

Deanie thought of Annie, the housemaid who had readied her for dinner on the day she arrived at her uncle's house. "Or become a maid."

"They call 'em 'Bridgets.' "

"I'm sorry?"

"The rich people who hire the Irish girls for maids. They can't be bothered to learn their names, so they call all of them Bridget."

"Not Annie though."

Fergal chuckled. "No. I'll say that for himself. Your uncle Sean knows every one of his servants' names."

They had left the commercial area of town and entered a residential area, with homes set back from the street. Fergal stopped the carriage and jumped down from the box to help Deanie down.

"Thank you," she said, as he helped her into the carriage.

She settled into her seat and adjusted her skirts while Mrs. Drummond glared at her.

"I don't know what you think you're doing, Miss Devane, but I assure you your uncle will be quite displeased when I tell him of your actions."

"Is that the proper way for a maid to address her mistress?" Deanie studied Mrs. Drummond's flushed face. "Or is my uncle paying you to spy on me?"

Mrs. Drummond's mouth fell open, and she turned her face to the window. A few minutes later the carriage pulled up in front of the brownstone, and the maid jumped out in a swish of skirts and petticoats as soon as Fergal brought the horses to a full stop. She marched up the steps to the brownstone's front door and stopped to look back at Deanie. Then she opened the door and went in.

Deanie sighed. Doubtless the maid was running straight to her uncle to tell him that Miss Bernadine had committed an indiscretion. Picking up an abandoned baby and finding a home for him.

She didn't move when Fergal opened the carriage door. He peeked in after a moment and gave her a sympathetic smile. "So she's run off to tell himself, then, has she?"

Deanie nodded.

"Sure, and it was a grand thing you did today, miss. If there's a kerfuffle, you'll ride it out fine."

"We'll see."

She exited the carriage, but Fergal didn't release her hand immediately. He leaned in close. "Don't trust her, miss." Then he snapped back into position. "Good luck to you," he whispered.

Deanie approached the stone steps that led to the entrance of the brownstone. The faces of the downstairs maids peered at her through the curtains that covered the sidelights on either side of it. The great front door with the gleaming brass lion doorknocker opened before she touched the doorknob. Bentley, the butler, ushered her in. "Your uncle wishes to see you, miss. In his study."

More maids watched from the bannister on the upper landing of the stairway as she passed through the hall. Had Mrs. Drummond run in screaming about Deanie picking up a child on the street? How could everyone in the household already know?

At the end of the hall, the housekeeper, Mrs. Butts, stood, with a frightened Oonagh peeking around her plump figure.

Deanie moved through the carpeted hallway until she reached the last door on the left.

Her breath came faster when she rapped on the paneled door.

"Come," said her uncle's voice from within.

She turned the knob and pushed the door open.

Her uncle sat at his massive desk, his arms propped on the arms of his chair and his fingers tented before his face. Deanie advanced three steps into the room and stopped. Mrs. Drummond was nowhere to be seen.

Her uncle drummed the fingers of one hand on the desk and sighed. "What do you want of me, Bernadine?"

Deanie blinked, startled by the question.

"I have done everything to help you since you arrived in my home. I have tried to care for you as a father. Provided for you. Fed you. Clothed you." He stood up and paced the room, running his hands through his hair. "Paid for your elocution lessons."

"I never wanted them," Deanie said before she could stop herself, a fierce pain burning her throat. "I'm not ashamed of being Irish, as you are."

Her uncle's lip curled. "Perhaps I should send you back to your beloved Ireland."

Deanie shut her mouth. There was nothing to go back to in Ireland. Only the decaying remnant of a dying people and the knowledge of her father's heinous behavior toward his own countrymen.

Her uncle took a deep breath and adopted a more conciliatory tone. "I know this has been difficult for you. Your father's death. A strange new country." He smiled thinly. "An uncle you barely know. But I do want the best for you, as my niece and the child of my only brother." He cleared his throat. "I have something important to tell you. Mr. Fletcher has asked me for your hand in marriage."

Deanie burst out laughing. Mr. Fletcher, with his anxious brown eyes and thinning hair?

"This would be an excellent match for you. He has agreed to overlook the low circumstances of your birth."

"My low birth? And me own mother a direct descendant of Brian Boru a thousand years back?"

"That doesn't count for anything here, Bernadine."

"I don't want to marry him. Or anyone else, for that matter."

Her uncle shook his head. "You want to live here for the rest of your life? As a spinster."

"No." Deanie took a step closer. "May I sit?"

He gestured toward the chair. "Please."

"I have another plan, Uncle Sean."

"Oh?" He leaned forward. "And what is that?"

"I don't know what Mrs. Drummond told you—"

"That you picked up a dying child, whose mother had perished on the street from cholera."

Deanie shook her head. "The baby wasn't sick. I couldn't leave him there, Uncle." She hurried on. "But here is what I'd like to do. The poor Irish need help. They've nowhere to turn when they are ill. No money for doctors."

Her uncle's face remained impassive. Almost bored. She plunged ahead before she could lose her nerve. "I want to use my father's inheritance to build a clinic for them."

Uncle Sean jumped to his feet and stared at her as if she'd sprouted horns. "You can't be serious."

"I am completely serious."

"I won't allow it."

"But the money is mine. You've seen the will." Too late, she realized her error.

Uncle Sean sat down. "Ah, yes, the will. Now where did I put it?"

"I would like it returned to me."

"Of course. When I find it."

Deanie stood. Her uncle leaned back in his chair. "I would advise you to forget this ridiculous idea and consider Mr. Fletcher's offer of marriage." He picked up his glasses off the desktop and put them on. "And now, if you don't mind, I have work to do before dinner. Mr. Fletcher will be there. Have Mrs. Drummond do something with your hair."

He opened a folder and picked up his pen. She was dismissed.

She resisted the urge to stomp her feet, but flung the door open so hard it bounced off the wall with a crash, surprising the butler and the maids who'd been standing outside with their ears pressed to the door. They scattered like a flock of guilty chickens.

She didn't want to see Mrs. Drummond, or anyone else for that matter, as she marched through the house and out the double doors to the walled courtyard behind the brownstone. It contained a long rectangle of lawn, greening in the April sunshine. Flagstones edged the grass, and a stone path led to the back of the garden where a Japanese summerhouse made of latticed walls stood against the high stone wall, roofed with wisteria vines that promised a cool bower in the summer heat to come. There were two benches inside, and Deanie threw herself down on one of them, breathing hard.

"Finally," a male voice said. "Faith and begorra, it took you long enough!"

Chapter 8

A curly black head and a pair of shining blue eyes peered over the wall at her, and Deanie's heart jumped in her chest.

"Michael!" She glanced back at the house, then retreated farther into the garden structure so she couldn't be seen.

"I've waited out here every afternoon for a fortnight, hopin' to catch sight of you." He slung an arm and a leg over the wall and dropped into the small grassy space between it and the summerhouse. He crouched down and peered at her through the lattice. "Ye're looking fine, Deanie. A sight for sore eyes, you are."

"And you as well." His face had filled out, and he had gained some much-needed weight. "Tell me all. How do you fare?"

"I'm using the gold you gave me wisely. I have a room in the east end, a good one, with board. Took me a bit to find a job, but I did as you suggested, bought some new clothes, waited until I looked healthier."

He looked impressively healthy and handsome right now, and her heart turned a somersault.

"I was in a tea shop, and a lawyer saw my handwriting. 'Fine penmanship,' he said. Now I'm workin' for him, copying law texts." He pressed closer to the latticed wall. "I'm supporting myself now. I have a future, thanks to you."

"I'm so glad."

His hand snaked around the lattice, and she took it. Michael rubbed his thumb over the skin of her wrist, and her breath came faster.

"Deanie. . .I said before, if I'd seen you before I left Killkerrin, I would have asked you to come with me."

Deanie smiled. "And I remember thinking that in another time and another place I would have."

"We're in America now. Where anything is possible, as they say. So. . ." Michael took a deep breath. "When I've got meself more established, with a bit o' money put away, and a decent place for a lady to live, will you marry me, my love?"

"Oh yes, Michael." She pressed her face against the lattice. "I will. I will!"

A door slammed close by, and they jumped apart. The gardener had been working in the flower shed and now carried a box of seedlings toward the east wall. He never looked their way, and Deanie hoped he hadn't seen Michael.

"I must go," Michael whispered. "I will plan everything and be back a month from today. And then. . ." He smiled and didn't finish the sentence, but the promise lingered in the air.

Deanie entered the house and walked up the stairs to her room, her head bursting with thoughts. Michael had found her. The sight of him had gladdened her heart beyond anything she could have imagined. She belonged with him, and now, here in America, the land of opportunity, they would be together. And then somehow she would challenge her uncle and get her inheritance back and build her clinic for the Irish poor.

Even if her uncle denied her access to her inheritance money in the bank, she still had the gold hidden in her portmanteau. It would be enough to get started on the clinic once she was reunited with Michael.

Humming to herself, she entered her room to find Mrs. Drummond standing in front of the mirror with one of Deanie's gowns held against her. The maid gave a guilty start and hastily hung the gown in the wardrobe

"Come, miss," she said. "You'll be late for dinner."

Deanie smiled. "I don't require your services any longer. You're dismissed."

"You can't dismiss me. Your uncle hired me, not you."

"I can. And I have. Please leave my room."

"Your uncle will have something to say about this." Mrs. Drummond flounced out in a huff.

Deanie didn't care. The wardrobe door stood ajar, and through it she saw the portmanteau lying on its side. Deanie had stuffed it into the far recesses of the wardrobe when she first arrived. A warning pang went through her, and she hurried to pick it up, but the bag was far too light, and even before she looked, she knew the gold was gone.

Sure enough, the false bottom was lifted and the cavity within was empty. Deanie collapsed to the floor as the air tilted around her. Now what was she going to do? Then before she knew it, she was on her feet, flying down the staircase to the study. She didn't bother to knock, and burst in. Mrs. Drummond and her uncle jumped apart.

"Bernadine! What do you mean by this intrusion?"

Her uncle faced her, an artery at his temple throbbing. Behind him, Mrs. Drummond straightened her collar and smoothed her skirts.

"She's taken my gold. I want it back."

Uncle Sean shrugged, then nodded at Mrs. Drummond, who left the room after casting a triumphant smile at Deanie.

Her uncle took a seat at his desk. "Close the door and sit down."

She did so and perched on the edge of the leather seat.

"Why didn't you tell me about the gold?"

Because I didn't trust you.

"Well?" her uncle said when she didn't answer.

"Where is it?"

"In a safe place. Tomorrow I will deposit it in the bank."

"Under whose name?"

Uncle Sean smiled faintly. "There's no need for you to worry about such things. I will take care of it. Now go and get dressed for dinner."

Deanie made no move to get up. "She isn't really a maid, is she? You had her spy on me. Your *paramour*."

Her uncle's lips thinned as he gazed at her. "Be careful, Bernadine."

"I don't want her anywhere near me."

"I'll get you another maid."

"I don't need another maid. Let me have Oonagh." She lifted her chin and glared back at her uncle.

"You will say nothing about Mrs. Drummond to the staff?"

Deanie was sure the staff already knew about the relationship between Mrs. Drummond and her uncle. Who would she speak to about it, anyway? She nodded.

"Very well. I will have her sent up to you."

Deanie got up and left the study as the grandfather clock in the hall announced the time as half past six. When she entered her room, she went straight to the little door and checked the small room that had been Mrs. Drummond's. Her few things had already been removed. Probably into Uncle Sean's room.

A moment later there was a tap at the door and Oonagh flew in, her face lit like a jack-o'-lantern. "Oh miss, is it true? I'm to be your maid now?"

"Yes." Deanie smiled as Oonagh flew into her arms and hugged her. Having Oonagh back with her was the second point of great joy in this day, after seeing Michael and his promise for the future. Then she remembered the poster announcing Tom Thumb.

"Do you remember Mr. Barnum and Charles Stratton? From the ship?"

Oonagh giggled. "The wee little man?"

"Yes. He's in Boston. Perhaps we may go. I'll ask my uncle." Deanie sat at the dressing table and wrinkled her nose at Oonagh. "You must fix my hair. Uncle Sean has commanded."

Deanie arrived in the dining room promptly at seven. Mr. Fletcher bowed and pulled out her chair.

"Good evening, Miss Devane. You're looking quite fetching this evening." He colored pink as he said this.

"Thank you, Mr. Fletcher."

After she had made pretty conversation with Mr. Fletcher, there was a natural pause in the conversation. "I have a question, Uncle."

"Yes?"

"While I was on the ship, I met a most interesting man."

Was it her imagination, or did both her uncle and Mr. Fletcher's ears perk up? "Indeed?"

Mr. Fletcher's brown eyes and Uncle Sean's icy blue ones landed on her.

"An American entrepreneur, I think you would call him."

"His name?"

"Phineas Taylor Barnum. And his assistant and companion, Charles Stratton."

"Ah!" Mr. Fletcher smiled. "Tom Thumb, is he not?"

"Yes."

"How interesting. You met them on board the ship?"

"Yes. They were returning from a tour in Europe."

"P. T. Barnum?" Uncle Sean sneered. "That huckster?"

"He was quite proper and polite. And Tom was captivating."

Uncle Sean shook his head, disgusted.

"Mr. Barnum gave Oonagh and me tickets to his show. I'd like to go, please."

"Out of the question. No gentlewoman needs to be involved in that kind of drivel." Her uncle paused, his soup spoon halfway to his mouth. "I remember some other foolishness of his, years ago." He put the spoon down and pursed his lips. "Let me think. . . It was around the time of the Texas Revolution. Barnum was exhibiting an ancient black woman he claimed was one hundred and sixty-one years old. George Washington's nursemaid. Pah!"

"I'll admit Barnum is quite the showman, sir." Mr. Fletcher took a sip of wine. "However, the Queen of England granted Barnum and Tom Thumb a royal interview and was captivated by the lad. Altogether Queen Victoria and her court received him three times."

"Is that so?" Uncle Sean pondered this.

"Sir, I would be happy to escort Miss Devane in your stead, and this Oonagh, whoever she is."

"My maid, who came from Ireland with me."

Uncle Sean smiled. "That's generous of you, William." He shrugged. "Very well then, but it must be in the afternoon. I don't want Bernadine out at night in the city."

"What day is best for you, Miss Devane?"

"Any day. Perhaps later this week?"

He nodded. "I will see to it."

Chapter 9

The Concert Hall was a four-story building, used, as Mr. Fletcher told her, for all manner of events, from formal dinners to concerts. Now a long stream of carriages waited outside the main doors to discharge passengers. A larger version of the same poster Deanie had seen earlier that week hung on the side of the building, advertising the appearance of Charles Stratton, better known as Tom Thumb.

When their turn came, Mr. Fletcher handed Deanie down to the street, leaving his hands to linger a moment at her waist. He helped Oonagh with the same courtesy, but his attention swiveled to Deanie immediately, and he held out his arm, leaving Oonagh to follow along behind. Mr. Fletcher kept Deanie close to his side through the press of people eager to see the show. At the ticket booth, Deanie showed the pass Mr. Barnum had given her while Mr. Fletcher paid for his admission.

Deanie had never been to an event like this. An air of anticipation filled the large hall, with hundreds of people waiting to see the famous Tom Thumb. Glass display cases lined the room, filled with some of the oddities that had made Barnum famous. There were wax figures, stuffed owls, and an automaton doll who moved and played the piano in jerky movements when one pushed a button outside the case. The mummified body of the Fiji mermaid was the oddest of all, half mammal and half fish, according to the placard on the case.

At two o'clock the curtains opened and Mr. Barnum strode out, his tall, imposing figure in a tuxedo, and his luxuriant, curly hair in wings at the side of his face.

He bowed to the audience. "Good people," he began. "Tonight I have the great good fortune to present to you the distinguished miniature man, weighing only fifteen pounds and but twenty-eight inches high, who has been received with the highest marks of royal favor by Queen Victoria and all the principal crowned heads of Europe, in the very same court dress in which the Queen received him. Ladies and gentlemen, I give you General Tom Thumb!"

Tom skipped out in his elegant suit, and the crowd gasped. Deanie remembered her own astonishment when Tom had popped out from behind Mr. Barnum on the deck of the RMS *Cambria*.

"Good evening, ladies and gentlemen," he chirped in his breathy treble voice. "And welcome to the show. I'll be right with you." He waved as the curtains closed.

The small performer didn't disappoint when the curtains parted again to reveal him perched on a tiny red velvet sofa. Now he was dressed in a suit with striped pants and sported a tall stovepipe hat. The audience burst into applause, at which Tom jumped off the sofa and onto a box in the middle of the stage. He struck a pose and sang "Yankee Doodle Dandy" to the audience's great approval. The curtains closed and reopened a moment later with Tom now costumed, according to the program, as an American tar, a sailor, with flared white trousers and a neckerchief. He danced a hornpipe while carrying an American flag, bringing the audience to its feet. More marvelous costume changes came in quick succession, with Tom appearing as a Scottish Highlander, complete with plaid knee socks and a kilt, and waving a sword. Napoleon emerged to stay with the audience a bit longer, as Tom strutted back and forth across the stage in immaculate white dress uniform, gold epaulets on his navy jacket, and a bicorne hat, his right hand tucked inside his jacket like the famous French general.

The merry affectations of the little man had the audience convulsing. Deanie had never laughed so hard, and Oonagh had tears streaming down her face. Even Mr. Fletcher's normally staid demeanor had vanished, and he roared along with the rest of the crowd at Tom's antics.

Once again the curtains closed and opened to find Tom, now in some sort of elastic flesh-colored body suit, affecting poses of famous figures using props. There was Samson, with a large club, a Grecian statue, a Roman general with a crested helmet, and several poses that Deanie didn't recognize. Last of all, Tom stepped up onto the wooden box to pose as Cupid, with a pair of white-feathered wings, a tiny bow, and heart-shaped arrows.

The curtains closed to thunderous applause, and the spectators clapped long and hard for several minutes, but the little general didn't reappear.

"My goodness, my sides ache," Deanie confessed, wiping her eyes.

Oonagh clasped her hands together. "What a talented wee man! I'd like to take him home with me."

Deanie and Mr. Fletcher both laughed at the same time. The pink color in his cheeks became his plain face, and his brown eyes crackled with mirth.

"I can't remember a time when I laughed so much either," he said.

Deanie retrieved her pass and turned it over to show Mr. Fletcher where Mr. Barnum had handwritten "Backstage Pass" on it. "I forgot to tell you that Mr. Barnum gave me this on the ship. Perhaps you could come too."

Mr. Fletcher scrutinized the sprawling handwriting that ended with an even larger "P. T. Barnum" at the bottom. Before they had left for the performance, Deanie had scribbled hers and Oonagh's names at the bottom, with RMS *Cambria* underneath. They waited until most of the hall had cleared out, and Mr. Fletcher signaled one of the ushers over to show him the pass.

"I'll go backstage and see if Mr. Barnum is receiving guests today." He returned shortly and beckoned to them. "Right this way, please."

They followed him to the side of the stage where a small staircase went up to a hall with many doors.

P. T. Barnum himself came out of one of them to greet them. "Well, well," he said heartily, "if it isn't my little Irish friends from the ship." He shook Deanie's and Oonagh's hands.

"Mr. Barnum, this is a family friend, William Fletcher."

"Mighty pleased to meet you." They shook hands.

"Come in, come in. I want to hear all about your time in Boston." He ushered them ahead of himself into the room, which turned out to be a combination sitting/dressing room.

"I'll be with you directly," sang a treble voice from behind the embroidered dressing screen. A moment later, Tom Thumb appeared, now dressed in a comfortable suit and holding a cigar.

Oonagh gasped and turned red at the sight of him. He bowed to her and Deanie and shook hands with Mr. Fletcher, then seated himself on the same tiny sofa that had appeared with him onstage.

"How do you find Boston, Miss Devane? And Miss Oonagh?"

"A bit overwhelming at first," Deanie said, acutely aware of Mr. Fletcher's presence. "But I'm becoming accustomed to it now."

"And how have things worked out with your uncle?"

Deanie pasted a smile on her face. "Very well. Although he insists on lessons to rid me of what he calls my 'detestable *Oirish* accent.'"

"That's too bad." Mr. Barnum shook his head. "I think your accent is lovely."

"So do I," Mr. Fletcher said. "I wouldn't change a thing about Miss Devane."

Mr. Barnum grinned. "Smart fellow. Right you are, sir."

Mr. Fletcher's face turned scarlet, and Deanie pretended not to notice.

Mr. Barnum smoothly changed the subject. "Besides being beautiful, she is a kind young woman. Has she told you what she did for two of the Irish poor trying to escape the famine?"

"She hasn't. But I'd like to hear the story."

Tom waved his unlit cigar. "Stowaways, they were, hidden in barrels of flour."

Mr. Barnum crossed one long leg over the other. "Hadn't a penny to their name." His smile faltered for a moment. "Terrible what's happening over there in Ireland. Anyway"—he shifted in his chair, and smiled at Deanie—"this lovely young lady paid for their passage to Boston. To give them a new start in the land of opportunity."

She'd also given Michael some of her father's gold coins. At least Uncle Sean hadn't gotten all of them.

"That was indeed kind of you, Miss Devane." Mr. Fletcher nodded his approval. "And it makes me admire you even more."

Deanie raised her chin. "Most of the first-class passengers on board didn't approve." She remembered the disdainful looks and contemptuous comments whispered loud enough so she could hear them. And her uncle had certainly voiced his scorn at her actions.

Her unspoken question hung in the air between them. How would Mr. Fletcher have reacted?

He smiled, accepting the challenge. "I have not traveled abroad, Miss Devane, and have never witnessed such a thing. But I don't see how Christian men and women could act any differently. I assure you, if I had been there, I would have applauded your action and been emboldened to follow your example."

He smiled so warmly she had to smile back.

P. T. Barnum laughed. "I can see you're already becoming an American girl, ready to speak her mind. Soon I expect to hear you're working with the ladies seeking to return the right for women to vote in Massachusetts."

"I doubt my uncle would allow that."

Mr. Barnum glanced at his pocket watch. "Tom and I usually go out for an early supper before the evening show. Could I persuade you to come with us?"

Deanie stood up. "That would be lovely, but my uncle expects me at home this evening. It's been wonderful to see you and Tom again. I hope everything goes well with your new tour."

Tom hopped jauntily to his feet, and Mr. Barnum and Mr. Fletcher rose. Mr. Barnum walked them out of the concert hall to the front door and helped hand Deanie and Oonagh into the waiting carriage. "If you're ever in New York, you must come see me at the American Museum. I've employed quite a few of your countrymen there, Miss Devane."

Once inside the carriage, Mr. Fletcher turned to Deanie. "I confess this has been such a charming occasion that I don't want it to end. How would you like to get some ice cream?"

"Sure, and that would be grand, Mr. Fletcher." Oonagh clasped her hands together. "I've never tasted it. But all the girls in the kitchen talk about it. What is it, exactly?"

Mr. Fletcher smiled broadly. "It's a sweet confection made from cream, eggs, and flavoring, and then frozen. "I'd love to be the first to introduce it to you both. We'll have plenty of time to get home before dinner."

When Deanie assented, Mr. Fletcher gave an address to the coachman. Then he rolled down the windows in the carriage. Sweet spring air wafted in, redolent with the smell of the awakening earth. The trees that lined the street had a gauzy veil of green. Deanie's heart felt lighter since she had seen Michael, and every time she thought of him, of herself and him together, her heart swelled with happiness. After they were married, she would figure out a way to get Oonagh back with them.

Before long the carriage pulled up in front of a building that held a line of shops. Above one shop, a large painted sign over the lintel read ICE CREAM AND CONFECTIONARY in ornate black letters.

Mr. Fletcher helped Deanie and Oonagh out of the carriage and opened the door. A glass-fronted counter at the back of the shop held trays of candies and sweetmeats. Delicate chairs and small round tables topped with marble occupied the rest of the space, and Mr. Fletcher led them to one of these. "Allow me, ladies." He held out a chair for each of them. "I will go and order the ice cream."

Soon he returned with three silver dishes and set them down. Each dish held three scoops of ice cream. "Lemon, chocolate, and currant." He passed out spoons. "I thought you might like to try all three."

Deanie took a spoonful of the pale yellow ice cream first. Her eyes opened wide at the cold on her tongue that changed into a tangy sweetness. "Oh my," she said, and took another spoonful.

Oonagh started on the chocolate and grinned broadly after the first bite. All three were so good that Deanie didn't know which one she liked best. They passed a pleasant half hour in the ice cream parlor enjoying their first tastes of ice cream.

The ride home in the spring sunshine ended too quickly.

Oonagh exited the carriage and turned to thank Mr. Fletcher. "I don't know when I've ever had a better time. Thank you, Mr. Fletcher." She turned and went up the front steps.

Deanie smiled at him. "And I must add my thanks as well for a lovely afternoon."

"I enjoyed it very much." Mr. Fletcher touched her sleeve and then withdrew his hand. "Forgive me, but I must say something, Miss Devane." He hesitated for a moment. "I know your uncle has spoken to you of my marriage proposal."

Oh dear. Deanie didn't know where to look.

"I also know some of the difficulties you're having with your uncle."

Deanie opened her mouth to speak.

"No, don't say anything yet. Let me finish," he said. "I want you to know that you would have complete freedom to do as you wished with your inheritance. As well as complete freedom to run the household as you wish. Will you please consider it? Consider me?"

Remorse pricked her. He was a good man, an honorable man. If Michael wasn't in the picture, she might have made a good marriage to Mr. Fletcher. But her heart had always belonged to Michael.

Her uncle would be furious if she rejected Mr. Fletcher outright. She would have to pretend to consider his offer. It wasn't fair, but what else could she do? However, if he knew what she wanted to do with her inheritance money, perhaps he wouldn't press her too hard.

"Has my uncle informed you of my desire to build a clinic? For the poor?"

"He did, Miss Devane. And unlike your uncle, I think it is a plan that has great merit. I would assist you in every way possible."

"You would support me? In the face of my uncle's opposition?"

He nodded slowly. "As my wife, your welfare would be my utmost concern. And of course, you must bring Oonagh with you. Perhaps we could arrange for her to go to school."

Deanie looked up at his kind face, hating to deceive him. "You do me great honor, Mr. Fletcher. I will consider your proposal. But I must have a little time. I can give you no answer today."

"Nor did I expect one. I'm pleased that you will even consider it."

Deanie nodded to Fergal, who opened the carriage door for her.

Mr. Fletcher leaned out the window. "I will be away for a week on business. But I hope to see you on my return."

Chapter 10

Uncle Sean informed Deanie that he would be meeting with various business partners in their Boston city homes while Mr. Fletcher was away on his business trip. She would have a tray in her room or eat alone in the dining room.

Freed from the constraints of a formal dinner each evening in her uncle's presence, Deanie had the opportunity to read and walk and dream in the walled courtyard garden behind the brownstone. Every afternoon, weather permitting, she sat in the shady summerhouse with a book, hoping Michael would reappear, even though he had said he would see her in a month. The days couldn't pass fast enough.

Mr. Fletcher returned from his business trip, and his presence at the nightly dinners resumed. Now, though, his eyes held hope and expectation when he looked at her, although he hadn't spoken again about his proposal. Deanie made frivolous conversation and tried to keep things light, while mentally marking off the days until the end of May when she could end the charade.

The twenty-fifth dawned clear and bright. Deanie took special care with her toilette that morning. But she didn't want to appear too happy, lest her uncle or Oonagh suspect something. His attitude toward her had softened lately, as Deanie had outwardly become more pliant and amenable, and she wanted it to remain that way.

The faint scent of honey hung in the air when Deanie came downstairs. Annie was buffing the mahogany furniture with beeswax. The butler polished silver at the great table in the dining room. A normal day in the Devane household, except it wasn't. Not for her, anyway.

The wisteria was in full bloom now, and the graceful purple flowers covered the summerhouse. She didn't have to wait long before she heard his voice whispering her name.

"I'm here," she called back softly.

The vines rustled as he climbed over the wall and dropped into the small space between it and the summerhouse. She turned and perched at the edge of the wooden bench to let her full skirts provide additional cover.

Michael's face popped around the edge of the latticed wall, and he grinned at her. "Aw, Deanie, just the sight of you is grand. Are you well?"

"I am now that you're here." Michael's smile lit up her heart. "But my uncle hired a woman to spy on me, and she found the rest of my father's gold. My uncle has it all now, the gold, the will, and my inheritance."

Michael's face furrowed in a frown. "I'm learning from Mr. Loring at the law firm, and I don't think that's legal."

Deanie shrugged. "I can't do anything about it now."

"I'll talk to my employer to see what can be done. I've got to be back to work. Here." He slipped her an envelope. "The house will be ready in four weeks, and we can get married the same day. I've written down where we're to meet. You'll have to think of a reason to get away."

"I will." She leaned over. "Kiss me before you go." Their lips met and clung, and she didn't want to let him go.

Michael broke off. "Not much longer now, my darlin' Deanie. I love you. We'll be together soon."

"And I love you."

Quickly, he climbed over the stone wall and his boots hit the ground. She sank back on the bench as his footsteps died away in the alley, and her heart followed after him. Oh to be free. Soon to be free!

She stepped out of the summerhouse with the letter and brushed a finger over her name written in Michael's distinctive hand. She started to tuck the envelope in her pocket to read in the privacy of her bedroom, looked up, and froze.

Uncle Sean pounced on her before she could hide the letter. In a flash, he snatched it out of her hands, tore open the envelope, and scanned its contents. Then he backhanded her across the face, splitting her lip and sending her spinning onto her knees.

Deanie's face went numb. Bright red drops of blood spattered the clean gray gravel of the path.

"You ungrateful wretch—"

She shuddered at the contempt and hate in his voice. His hand clamped on her arm, and he wrenched her to her feet and dragged her toward the house, through the french doors, and into the parlor where a small fire always burned on the hearth.

Though her vision was blurred by tears, Deanie saw Annie's shocked face as her uncle shoved her into the room. Annie hastily bobbed and left.

Uncle Sean pushed her into a chair. Then he took Michael's letter and tore it into pieces, all the while his vicious gaze fixed on hers. Then, smiling, he tossed the pieces into the fire.

"No!" She threw herself onto the hearth rug, but the torn scraps had already been engulfed by the flames.

"Go to your room. Get out of my sight."

Deanie fled.

Oonagh was hanging a dress in the wardrobe when Deanie stumbled into the bedroom. "What's wrong?"

She gasped when Deanie turned.

Deanie sank onto the bed and covered her throbbing face with her hands. What was she going to do now? She had no way of finding Michael. Her future had gone up in flames.

"What did your uncle do to you?" Oonagh asked. "What?"

Deanie opened her eyes and groaned. "He struck me."

"Why?"

"He caught me talking to Michael in the garden."

Oonagh's eyes widened. "Michael Quinn?" She sat down next to Deanie. "Tell me."

The story tumbled from her lips. "Michael found me, and he asked me to marry him. We were going to figure out a way to get you out of here too." Her eyes filled with tears. "And now I don't know what will happen to us."

"We'll figure something out." Oonagh stood, her hands on her hips. "I'm going to go to the kitchen and chip some ice for your face. And if I see the master, I might just—"

"Don't. Don't say anything. He could send you away and we'd never see each other again."

Oonagh relented. "Very well." Her face troubled, she left the bedroom.

Deanie dragged herself off the bed to her dressing table. The right side of her face was bruised and swollen, and her cut lip had puffed up. Her head hurt. She had never been struck like that in her life. Her own father had never used physical punishment.

Tears welled in her eyes again, and she dashed them away. This was no time to cry. She had to think. How could she get away? Uncle Sean had all her money. If even one gold sovereign had been left, she could attempt it. But she had nothing.

She was trapped.

Oonagh returned with the ice wrapped in a linen dish towel and a small glass bottle.

"Here, take this first." Oonagh uncorked the bottle and gave her a teaspoonful. "One more." She dosed her again.

"What is it?" Deanie wrinkled her nose. "It tastes like licorice."

Oonagh held up the bottle. "Mrs. Winslow's Soothing Syrup. It's for children who are teething, but Cook said it's good for all kinds of pain. Let's get you undressed and into bed."

By the time Deanie had her nightgown on, she was feeling woozy. Once she was in bed, Oonagh cleaned the blood off her face and applied the ice pack.

She must have fallen asleep, for she woke to hear Oonagh answer the door.

"Good evening." It was the deep voice of the butler, Bentley. "Mr. Devane asks if Miss Devane is coming down to dinner. Mr. Fletcher is here."

"Miss Devane is indisposed this evening." Oonagh shook her head. "Please convey her apologies."

"Very well."

Had her uncle really expected her to appear at the dinner table tonight? She sat up, fighting tears.

"There now, don't get all bothered again." Oonagh retrieved the medicine bottle. "You need to rest."

The night passed in a hideous jumble of nightmares and pain. Her face looked worse in the morning, but the headache had gone. Oonagh brought her a breakfast tray, and Deanie was picking at the eggs when a knock sounded at the door and her uncle walked in.

Deanie's chest tightened as he advanced into the room and examined her. If he felt any regret for the injury, it wasn't evident on his smoothly impassive face.

"Get dressed when you've finished your breakfast. I have something I want you to see." He glanced at his watch. "Be ready by nine o'clock."

Deanie and Oonagh looked at each other. Now what? But Deanie didn't feel that she could disobey, and she was dressed and ready at the appointed time. She chose a bonnet with a veil to hide the bruising and cut lip.

Her uncle stood in the foyer when she came down, and she followed him outside to the carriage waiting at the curb. Deanie kept her gaze averted from her uncle as he assisted her inside and took the seat across from her.

"I have many business interests, Bernadine, and today I am going to show you one of them."

He spoke as if this were a normal day and a normal conversation, and she didn't answer. They proceeded down Beacon Street and made their way through Boston and over the Charles River bridge. The carriage drove through a part of Boston she hadn't seen before. They passed an imposing building, four stories high and flanked by a wing at each side. A high fence surrounded the property.

"That's the House of Industry." Her uncle's voice was pleasant. "Where the criminals and ne'er-do-wells are imprisoned."

He pointed out the carriage window. "And next door we have the House of Reformation and the House of Correction. But this is what I want to show you today." The carriage stopped. "The Boston Lunatic Asylum. I'm a trustee here."

A slender graveled path led to the brick building, built in the Federal style she had become familiar with in Boston, with wide chimneys and a fan-shaped window in its gable. Neatly manicured hedges flanked the path, with landscaped gardens beyond them, and here and there a bench was positioned for garden viewing.

It was a peaceful setting, but there was no peace in her heart. What purpose could he have for bringing her here?

They went in through a pedimented door and into a spacious room with fine furniture and a soft carpet underneath their feet. A china pot of buddleia and cabbage roses perfumed the room from a marble-topped table in the center. A piano stood in one corner, and on this instrument an elderly woman played softly and sang to herself.

A white-coated receptionist rose from her corner desk to greet them. "Good afternoon, Mr. Devane. Shall I ring for Dr. Katzler?"

"No, Mary, I'm not here to see him today, although you could tell him I'm here. I'd like to give my niece a tour."

Mary's surprised gaze slid to Deanie. "Yes, sir, I'll do that."

"Come this way, Bernadine. This is the women's wing." He led her down a wide hall with a polished wood floor, which opened to a roomy chamber with tall windows. Groups of women mingled here, some reading, others knitting or sewing. A few sat in rocking chairs, staring at nothing.

"They are quite forward-minded here." Uncle Sean waved his arm at the room. "They believe in fresh air, order, and routine. It's pleasant enough, is it not?" He examined her. "Although I must say you're looking a trifle pale today. Not feeling well? We'll keep our visit short then."

Incredulous, Deanie stared at her uncle. Was he serious? Acting as if everything was normal and this was an amusing way to pass a morning? Nausea flickered through her. She groped for her handkerchief and held it gingerly to her bruised lips, praying she wouldn't be sick.

He smiled and took her arm. They walked back into the reception room and went up a wide staircase to the second floor and turned left to face a large iron door with several locks, guarded by another attendant in white.

"Hello, Mr. Devane."

Her uncle nodded. "We're touring the asylum today. Would you kindly unlock the door?"

"Certainly." The attendant drew out a brass key ring and found the correct one. "Knock when you're ready to leave, Mr. Devane."

Her uncle drew her forward into another day room. Unlike the one below, all the tall windows were barred with iron. Several uniformed attendants moved about the approximately thirty women in the room. Almost every patient was engaged in some type of repetitive movement. One woman clapped her hands over and over. Another sat on the floor rubbing her head against the wall. Some had obvious physical infirmities, others sat drooling in chairs, and still another's head was covered with sores.

"Sad, is it not?" He took Deanie's arm. "But it gets worse."

Deanie pulled away. "Why are we here? What are you trying to do?" She recoiled as a woman streaked up to her, brought her face close to Deanie's, and cackled.

Uncle Sean stepped in between them. "I'm giving you an education, my dear. Come. We're not finished."

He gripped her arm and propelled her to the back of the room, where he stopped before another locked door. Once again it was opened, and they went through a dank corridor that smelled of urine and excrement. No paintings adorned these walls, nor was there any fine carpeting underfoot. Many locked doors with small barred windows lined the hall. Slowly her uncle moved down the hall, stopping before each door, and told her to look inside. They were strange bare cells with no furniture, lined with quilted cloth. And in each of them was a bedraggled figure trussed in some sort of garment that tied up the arms and restricted movement. In one cell rusty brown stains streaked the cloth. Blood?

"They're called straitjackets," her uncle said when she gasped. "Kinder than the ropes and chains formerly used on them."

He knocked on a door at the end of the hall. It was unlocked from inside and opened to reveal five beds with slats on the sides and a locked hinge top. Fearful moans and groans came from the inhabitants within, and one young woman, her eyes wild, peered through the slats at Deanie.

"Help me." She shook the slats of her cage. "I'm not crazy," she whispered. "Help me." Her fingers pushed through the cage toward Deanie.

"That's enough, Mildred." The room attendant smacked the patient's fingers with a rod. "Be quiet now." The woman whimpered and pulled her fingers inside the cage.

"These are Utica cribs, Bernadine, invented by a French doctor in Marseilles."

Deanie whirled and ran to the door as bile surged into her throat. "Open the door. Open the door!"

Then her uncle was behind her. "Calm yourself, Bernadine," he said in a soothing tone. "We're leaving now." He nodded to the attendant.

Deanie's breath was short, and her chest hurt. She had to get out of here, but her uncle gripped her arm, forcing her to a sedate pace. Once downstairs in the beautiful foyer, she whirled on her uncle.

"What is the meaning of this? Why did you bring me here?"

"Good morning, Sean." A white-haired older man in a white coat over his suit approached them and held out his hand. "Good to see you again."

"Good morning, Dr. Katzler. I'd like to introduce my niece, Miss Bernadine Devane."

The doctor bowed. "Delighted." Then he leaned closer and frowned. "Are you quite all right? You seem upset."

Deanie choked down a furious retort and tried to compose herself. "I'm perfectly fine, sir."

"You may speak openly with Dr. Katzler, Bernadine. He has much experience with melancholia and hysteria. You can trust him." Her uncle turned toward the doctor and lowered his voice. "She has unfortunately been experiencing both those symptoms lately, I'm afraid."

Deanie gaped at her uncle. "What are you saying? I am perfectly well."

Her uncle and Dr. Katzler exchanged a look.

"Now, my dear," the doctor said. "It's nothing to be ashamed about."

"I'm not ashamed!" The words came out with a hiss, and Dr. Katzler raised an eyebrow.

"Of course, you aren't." The doctor nodded. "But I'm here if you ever have need of me. We have a fine institution here, and it would be a pleasure to take care of you. Good day to both of you."

A cold sweat broke out over her body. What was her uncle planning?

"Come, Bernadine, let's get you some air." Her uncle took her arm.

Once outside she twisted out of his grasp and faced him, her chest heaving. She wanted to scream, to run away, to snatch his silver-tipped cane from him and smash him over the head with it.

Uncle Sean chuckled. "Careful. Dr. Katzler is watching."

Sure enough, the doctor had followed them and stood before the front door. He lifted a hand in farewell and went back inside.

Deanie tried to control her fury as her uncle walked her toward the waiting carriage.

She turned on him when the coachman shut the carriage door. "What are you up to?"

"I simply wanted to show you the asylum." He eyed her, and a small, cold smile crept over his face. "And to demonstrate how easy it would be to have you committed there."

Deanie went still. "You can't do that."

"But I can." He shrugged. "And I will if you refuse to do what I say."

He set his top hat on the seat beside him, then leaned back and crossed his legs. "Your father's money is in my account at the bank and has been for some time. He left it up to me to handle all these years, Unfortunately for him. And you. There is no way to prove it is your money. Tonight you will tell Mr. Fletcher that you accept his proposal. The wedding banns will be posted for two weeks, and then the ceremony will take place immediately after. If you do anything to oppose me, I will have you committed. If you try to tell Fletcher that I've stolen your money, that will work perfectly to prove that you are paranoid and delusional, further grounds to have you committed. There will be a guard outside the house and in the alley night and day." He leaned forward. "It is in your best interest to obey me, I assure you. And say nothing to your little maid about this, or I will have her confined as well."

Chapter 11

May 26, 1847

A myriad of emotions pulsed through Deanie on the nightmare carriage ride home. Disbelief, incredulity, despair. She lurched to her feet as rage flooded her, and grasped the door handle to fling herself out and be crushed by the carriage wheels.

But her uncle had foreseen this possibility and grabbed her arm. "Oh no you don't."

He laughed as he threw her down on the seat. She recoiled at his touch. Hot tears pricked her eyes, but she refused to weep in front of him. Her muddled thoughts went to Mildred, the woman imprisoned in the Utica crib. *I'm not crazy*, she had pleaded. Deanie shuddered. Had she been locked away under false pretenses?

As soon as the carriage stopped, her uncle exited and took a firm hold of her after Fergal helped her out. He had one last warning for her as they went up the stairs.

"You *will* appear at dinner this evening." Then he chuckled. "Try to put on a pleasant demeanor or you will spoil Mr. Fletcher's excellent appetite. And say nothing about your face."

Later she sat at her dressing table staring in the mirror. Oonagh had known immediately that something was wrong, but Deanie couldn't tell her.

Father in heaven, help me. Help me!

But heaven's ear seemed closed tonight.

There was a knock at the door, and Oonagh answered it. After a few words were exchanged, Oonagh came to the dressing table with a small round box and a brush. "Your uncle sent you this." The lid opened to reveal a fine white powder. "Annie said it's rice powder. For your face."

The powder disguised some of the bruising, but it was still obvious that her lip was cut and scabbed over, and the side of her face still swollen.

Oonagh fixed Deanie's hair and chose a gown for her. At the appointed time, Deanie went downstairs to the dining room. Mr. Fletcher pulled out her chair, and he started when he looked at her face.

Like the automaton doll in Mr. Barnum's oddity show, Deanie made polite conversation when addressed and ate dinner without tasting any of it. When the last course was finished, her uncle invited Mr. Fletcher into his study for brandy and cigars.

Her uncle left the dining room. But Mr. Fletcher took the seat next to Deanie and laid a gentle hand over the clenched fingers she held stiffly in her lap.

"Miss Devane. . .whatever has happened? How did you injure yourself?"

She shook her head. "It's nothing."

Gently, he turned her chin and gazed into her eyes. "Have you thought about my proposal?"

Her heart stopped for a moment, and then despair flowed over her. "Yes," she said slowly. "I will marry you, Mr. Fletcher."

"But that's wonderful news!" He jumped up. "I will speak with your uncle at once to set the date." He leaned over, planted a kiss on her forehead, and hurried out of the room.

In a daze, Deanie left the dining room and walked past the door to her uncle's study. Crystal glasses clinked as her uncle congratulated Mr. Fletcher. She slipped quietly through the rooms of the brownstone to the back of the house, where she opened the french doors and went into the courtyard.

The sun had set, and pale stars twinkled on the horizon. Crickets sang in the twilight breeze as she walked down the path to the summerhouse. All about her, life bloomed and pulsed while inside she was as dead and hopeless as the pile of discarded plants on the refuse pile. She parted the hanging curtain of vines and sank onto the bench. She would never see Michael again.

"Father in heaven," she whispered, "have mercy on me." Then she wept.

Chapter 12

The next fortnight passed with agonizing swiftness while she tried to think of a way out of the dire situation her uncle had forced her into. He had forbidden her to leave the house until the wedding, not allowing her even the comfort of going to Mass. Two private guards stood watch, one in front of Beacon Street, the other in the alley behind the house.

Afraid for Oonagh, Deanie had told her only that she had decided to marry Mr. Fletcher instead of Michael. Oonagh had protested at first, but Deanie told her that she'd realized there could be no future with a spalpeen like Michael.

Oonagh had been doubtful, but Deanie had assured her that she was taking Oonagh with her to the new household as soon as the honeymoon was over.

The honeymoon.

The thought of being in another man's arms instead of Michael's made her blood go cold as ice. Her chaotic thoughts darted in an endless circle, around and around and around, without ever landing on a successful plan to escape her uncle's despicable plan for her.

A forced marriage or a madhouse.

☙

June 12, 1847

The dreaded morning arrived, and Deanie was still a prisoner. How dare this terrible day dawn bright and beautiful when everything inside her felt cold and dead?

Numbly, she allowed Oonagh to put her hair up and help her dress in a pale blue silk gown. She walked downstairs in a fog. Oonagh followed, carrying the delphiniums her uncle had sent up.

He waited at the bottom and held out his arm. But she walked past him through the house to the front entrance, opened the door, and stepped outside. The morning sunlight wrapped her in a warm embrace. Birds were singing in the trees on the Common. She took a deep breath of the rose-scented air. If only Michael would pop up from behind a bush or arrive on a horse to take her away.

Her uncle stepped out, and she walked down the front steps to the carriage. Fergal stood waiting, the door open. "I wish you great joy in your marriage, Miss Devane." He assisted her into the carriage. Her uncle got in and sat opposite her. Four months earlier she had ridden in this same carriage, newly arrived in America. Heartbroken over her father's death, but budding with hope for the future.

A future with Michael in it.

The short drive to the Cathedral of the Holy Cross took only a few moments. Before she knew it, she was in the church, at the small side altar to St. Jude. The patron saint of hopeless causes.

The priest who would say the marriage mass waited there, with Mr. Fletcher at his side. His eyes lit up when he saw her, and he bowed.

Then Michael stepped out from behind a pillar. "Deanie!"

Her feet moved before her head connected with what she was seeing. She dropped her bouquet and ran to him before her uncle or Mr. Fletcher could react.

"What is the meaning of this?" Her uncle's face flushed an angry red. "I'll have you arrested."

"I don't think so. Come out, Mr. Loring."

A tall distinguished Negro man in a suit stepped out. He doffed his top hat and bowed. "Good morning."

"This is Mr. Charles Loring." Michael smiled confidently as he faced her uncle. "Mr. Loring is a lawyer. And he's here to inform you that your plan is illegal. Miss Devane is of age. You cannot force her to marry or keep control of her inheritance."

"This is true." Mr. Loring's voice was as smooth and mellow as cream. "Sir, you have no legal grounds on which to continue. The law will not support you in either endeavor. Miss Devane is entitled to have her full inheritance and to marry whom she chooses."

Uncle Sean's body had gone rigid as Mr. Loring spoke. "You impertinent ruffian!" He stepped forward, his face almost purple, and raised his cane. "I'll, I'll—" His face contorted and went into a spasm as the right side of his face drooped. His eyes opened wide as gibberish emerged from his lips. The cane dropped from his fingers, and he crumpled to the floor.

Mr. Fletcher knelt by his side. "He's having an apoplexy. We must get him to a doctor."

"I'll fetch your coachman." Michael touched her cheek and gave her an encouraging smile. "Don't go anywhere," he whispered.

Uncle Sean had gone quiet, moaning. Mr. Fletcher unbuttoned his collar and loosened his shirt. Then he looked up at her, his eyes filled with pain. "Is it true? Your uncle was forcing you to marry me?"

"Yes." She hated to see his sadness, but he had to know the truth. "He took me to the lunatic asylum where he is a trustee and told me he would have me involuntarily committed if I didn't."

Mr. Fletcher winced and shook his head. "My word." He frowned and looked down at her uncle as if he'd never seen him before. "I had no idea he was capable of such a thing."

"Michael and I were sweethearts in Ireland. We had made plans to marry, and my uncle found out. But before that, he took my father's will, which named me as his only heir, and wouldn't return it to me."

Mr. Fletcher's head jerked. "I—I had no idea." Then his eyes narrowed. "And your face, your beautiful face. Did he do that to you?"

"Yes. He has been extremely cruel."

"I'm so sorry."

Deanie shook her head. "You haven't done anything wrong. You've been so kind to me. We might have had a happy marriage if my heart didn't already belong to another."

The church door opened, and Fergal and Michael hurried in. With the priest's help, the men picked up her uncle and carried him to the carriage, with Deanie following.

Mr. Fletcher turned to her. "I was so happy when I woke this morning, thinking it was my wedding day. I am crushed to find it is not." He looked past her at Michael. "I trust you will take good care of her."

Michel stepped forward and offered his hand. "I intend to. Thank you. You've been a gentleman about this."

Mr. Fletcher shook Michael's hand. "You're a lucky man, Michael Quinn."

"Sure, and I know it well."

She smiled at Mr. Fletcher and gently touched his cheek. "I hope we can remain friends."

"We will if I have anything to say about it. Is there anything else I can do?"

Deanie nodded. "If you could locate my father's will and return it to me, I would be most grateful."

"I will."

"And would you tell Oonagh what has happened here today?" She handed her uncle's cane to him. "I want to have her come and live with us when we are settled."

"I would be happy to." He climbed into the carriage and gave her one last smile as the carriage drove away.

Mr. Loring stepped forward. "I'll leave you two," he said. "You have much to discuss." He tipped his hat to Deanie and hailed a passing hansom cab.

The priest excused himself and hurried away.

They were alone. Deanie turned and went into Michael's arms. "Tell me this isn't a dream."

His arms tightened around her. "It's not."

"How did you know? My uncle found me with your letter and burned it. I never saw what was inside. I had no way to find you." The desperation she had felt crept into her voice.

"The banns." He drew her closer. "I read the newspaper each day. I saw the banns posted with your name and Fletcher's, and I knew something had gone wrong. I had already talked with Charles about your situation. He suggested that he come along to confront your uncle."

"It's like a miracle. I thought I'd never see you again, but I prayed you'd find me somehow."

"And I did." Michael took a quick look about, pulled her to him, and kissed her thoroughly. "I'm never letting go of you again. And now we have a marriage to attend, Deanie Devane. Our own."

Renee Yancy is a history and archaeology buff who works as a registered nurse when she isn't writing historical novels. She has visited Ireland, Scotland, and England to stand in the places her ancient historical characters lived. She lives in Kentucky with her husband, two dogs, and her ninety-five-year-old mother-in-law. Check out her website: www.reneeyancy.com.

Let the Romance Continue with. . .

Seven Brides for Seven Texas Rangers Romance Collection

Let the matchmaking begin. When their commanding officer succumbs to marital bliss, seven Texas Rangers find themselves at the matchmaking mercies of his wife, who believes they each would get much more joy out of life if they weren't married to their work. But what woman can refine a Ranger?

Paperback / 978-1-68322-494-5 / $14.99

The Calico and Cowboys Romance Collection

In the American Old West from Texas across the Plains to Montana, love is sneaking into the lives of eight couples who begin their relationships on the wrong foot. Faced with the challenges of taming the land, enduring harsh weather, and outsmarting outlaws, these couples' faith and love will be tested in exciting ways.

Paperback / 978-1-68322-402-0 / $14.99